Maggie Makepeace came to writing late in life, having begun her career as a zoologist. She had a number of jobs in scientific research and Wildlife Trusts, the most rewarding of which was a three year contract on a Scottish estuary studying the social behaviour of shelducks.

For a brief time in the 70s she was a television presenter for Yorkshire TV and London Weekend, and gradually became more interested in the psychology of human behaviour, especially communication, or the lack of it, and in the way that some people attempt to control the lives of others.

When in the 80s she moved back to the west country, she began to write in earnest. Her first novel was published when she was fifty.

Watershed is inspired by the view of the Somerset Levels from her house, the countryside about her and the influence and beauty of water on the landscape.

WATERSHED

Jonathan arrives on the Somerset Levels and shuts himself away in a lonely cottage to write about his obsession — water. He poses an irresistible challenge for Pamela, a forceful pillar of the community. But why is Jonathan so resistant to her blandishments — and so *rude*? Only Vinny, Pamela's long-suffering companion, has the desire and the sensitivity to get to the bottom of Jonathan's strange behaviour. But she herself is trapped by emotional blackmail. Will Jonathan prove to be her saviour, as much as she is his? Vinny is forced to make a difficult decision, and comes to her own personal watershed. Storms, fire and floods suddenly raise the stakes for everyone. As the waters rise, emotions are also set to burst their bounds.

MAGGIE MAKEPEACE

◆

WATERSHED

Complete and Unabridged

CHARNWOOD
Leicester

First published in Great Britain in 2006 by
Transita, Oxford

First Charnwood Edition
published 2007
by arrangement with
Transita, Oxford

The moral right of the author has been asserted

British Library CIP Data

Makepeace, Maggie
  Watershed.—Large print ed.—
  Charnwood library series
  1. Middle-aged women—Fiction 2. Authors—Fiction
  3. Somerset Levels (England)—Fiction
  4. Large type books
  I. Title
  823.9'14 [F]

ISBN 978–1–84617–808–5

Published by
F. A. Thorpe (Publishing)
Anstey, Leicestershire

Set by Words & Graphics Ltd.
Anstey, Leicestershire
Printed and bound in Great Britain by
T. J. International Ltd., Padstow, Cornwall

This book is printed on acid-free paper

ACKNOWLEDGEMENTS

Grateful thanks to the following people who gave generously of their time and expertise. Especially to the men of the Environment Agency — Jim Barlow, Brian Martin and Dennis Elliott, who put up with a lot of questions but entered enthusiastically into the spirit of the thing and were immensely helpful.

To Richard Duckett for his description of the flash flood of July 1968.

To Ian MacGregor of the Met. Office for weather data.

And of course to all my great friends, past and present, of the Glastonbury group: Janet Laurence, Shelley Bovey, Wendy Mewes, Sarah Wiseman, Maria McCann, Anna Knowles and Gabrielle Palmer, who kept me up to the mark with astute criticism and a lot of humour. Thank you.

Any technical or other mistakes are of course entirely mine.

Maggie Makepeace, Somerset

1

'Then there's the corn snake, scientific name *Elaphe guttata*. It's a lovely colour — orange with dark patches,' the pet-shop man was saying on the car radio. 'It's also hardy, attractive, nice-tempered, inexpensive and a good feeder. An ideal beginner's snake, in fact.'

'Sounds more like the ideal wife,' Pamela said to herself, reaching forward to switch it off. 'A bit like Vinny.'

She turned her attention to the business of driving in the dark on the narrow single-track road ahead of her. In her headlights she could see a row of individual horse turds right down the centre of it, deposited on the hoof, as neat and regular as highway markings. She was just smiling at this, when the engine checked, choked and stopped.

The four by four was still rolling forwards under its own momentum and Pamela just managed to steer it into a passing place before bringing it to a halt. Bloody hell! She sat there in the sudden silence, then she switched the ignition off and tried the starter again several times before she saw that the needle on the fuel gauge was resting at the bottom of the red bit.

'Shit!'

She peered about her, trying to see beyond the range of the lights. There was nothing visible down here on these low lying peatlands but the

1

water-filled ditches on either side of the road, and the flat greenish fields devoid of any features, even trees. Pamela had been so taken up with listening to the radio, that she hadn't been paying attention to the infrequent landmarks on this customary shortcut of hers across the Somerset Levels, or 'the moor' as it was always known. She tried the starter again and then again. No joy.

'Oh God, now what?'

She glanced at her watch. It was a cold March night, and after midnight. Vinny would be fast asleep by now. Tough. She'd have to wake up and come and rescue her in the mini. Pamela opened her handbag, extracted her mobile and stabbed in the number with an irritable forefinger. The numbers on the dial lit up, faded and then vanished. The battery was flat. Vinny always charged it up for her, except now of course, when it really mattered.

She was in for a long slog. There were very few houses in this area because it tended to flood every winter. Pamela turned off the lights to get her eyes accustomed to the dark. At least it had stopped raining and there was half a moon. Ah, but what about Vinny's torch? She felt for the glove compartment and groped about inside. It wasn't there.

It really is too bad of her, Pamela thought. She's the practical one. She could at least have *reminded* me to fill Gertie up yesterday.

She would have to start walking, but in which direction? Pamela put her mind to trying to work out exactly where she was. That pump building which drained the water off this part of the moor should be fairly close. She was pretty sure she hadn't already passed it, so it must be ahead. Maybe there would be somebody on duty there, or a passing vehicle that might give her a lift. But who would be out here at this time of night? She might get attacked, abducted . . . What, at her age? Pamela stretched her mouth in a wry smile. Then she opened the car door and got out, zapping it locked. She buttoned her coat right up under her chin, shouldered her bag, stuck both hands into her pockets and set off along the road.

★   ★   ★

Jonathan was asleep in bed when he was awoken by someone hammering on his front door. He switched on the light and listened. More banging. So he got up, dragged on an overcoat over his pyjamas, and wandered downstairs. He found a short grey-haired woman in a fur coat, standing outside.

'I'm so sorry,' she said. 'My name's Pamela Wood. I broke down miles from here and I've had to walk all this way in the dark.'

'Oh?' She looked in perfectly normal working order to him.

'And when I crossed your little plank bridge thing outside, I very nearly fell into the rhyne!'

'Reen?' Jonathan didn't know the word, but was always receptive to new information.

'You know, the drainage ditch. You're not a local then?'

3

'No.' He glanced up to find her frowning at him. What did she want?

'So, can I please use your telephone?' The woman was advancing bossily into his house as she spoke.

'What telephone?' He was at a loss.

'You mean you haven't got one? You can't exist in this god-forsaken place without one, surely? Not even a mobile to call for help?'

'No,' Jonathan said politely. 'I don't need any help. I live here.'

She had got as far as the threshold of his sitting room, but now to his relief she began edging backwards towards his front door again.

'Right,' she said. 'Er . . . well never mind . . . Sorry to have troubled you . . . I don't suppose you've got a gallon of diesel either, have you?'

She's quite mad! Jonathan thought, but it's OK, I'm bigger than her. 'No,' he said mildly. 'I don't use it. I'm on mains electricity here.'

'What *are* you talking about?' She was holding onto the frame of the door with both hands.

'I haven't got a generator, so I don't need any diesel. It's not as though I'm in Africa now.' He felt he was being extraordinarily patient; doing his best to remember what he had been taught by the Special Needs woman on that communications course all those years ago.

'I-need-diesel-for-my-car.' She said the words slowly and with equal stress. 'I told you. It broke down. I've got to get home to Hembrow. Can you or can you not help me?'

'Ah.' Now he understood. 'Why didn't you

4

say? George Overy will have some, down at Amber Junction.' She was staring fixedly at him, which made him feel uncomfortable. 'He's at the pumping station, about half a mile that way.' He gestured.

'*Half a mile?*'

'Yes ... well probably more like seven hundred metres.'

★ ★ ★

It was now three am and Pamela was at last being driven home by Vinny.

'God, would you believe it?' she said. 'I walked until my feet virtually dropped off and all I found in that house was this idiot boy.'

'What, a child?'

'Oh no, he's probably in his mid-twenties. Nice looking too, but quite loopy. He had me worried there for a moment.' Pamela shook her head in disbelief. 'He doesn't have a phone. He doesn't own a car. I had to bully him into getting dressed and coming with me to find the man who runs the pumping station, and get some help from him. Luckily for me, he was actually there because the pumps were running, but he was on his own and he couldn't leave until his shift ended, so it was ages before he could drive me back to Gertie in his van. And blow me down, even when we emptied a gallon can of diesel into her tank, the bloody cow still wouldn't start!'

'Air lock,' Vinny agreed, nodding her head.

'How d'you know that?'

5

'Diesel engines are different from petrol,' Vinny began to explain. 'If you run out of fuel and get a bubble of air in the pipe then the whole system has to be bled to get it out. It's because it works on pressure you — '

'I don't want a flaming lecture,' Pamela cut in. 'If you'd only reminded me to go to the garage yesterday, then none of this would have happened.'

'Why keep a dog and bark yourself?' Vinny observed.

'Yes! No . . . Damn it, you know what I mean. It's late and I'm bushed.'

'What a good thing you don't have to go to work tomorrow.'

'Darling Vinny, I am sorry! Still, at least your library job isn't too taxing, is it? Anyway, you haven't asked me about my bridge evening.'

Vinny sighed. 'So, how was it?'

'Brilliant. We wiped the floor with them. They were consoling themselves at the bar for the rest of the evening! Oh, now, while I think of it, have we got a spare bottle of whisky do you know?'

'No idea. Why?'

'Well I suppose I ought to take a little something to the Overy man this weekend, to thank him. He was so sweet and helpful.'

'What about the loony youth?'

'I'm not sure he deserves anything at all, except maybe one of your quiches? He looks half-starved.'

'Thanks,' Vinny said, yawning.

Pamela looked with affection at her friend as she drove them both back towards the higher ground, up onto the ridge of a low narrow hill called Hembrow Island — although it had long since ceased to be insular — and the village of the same name, near where they lived. At this time of night there might have been nobody in the whole world but the two of them. She could just see Vinny's profile; chubby, serious, looking straight ahead. And then unexpectedly on a straight bit of road, a car overtook them, lighting up her wispy brown hair and transforming it into a fleeting halo. Pamela smiled.

'What would I do without you?'

⋆   ⋆   ⋆

Vinny put on her old towelling dressing gown and slippers first thing the next morning and went down to the kitchen as usual to make the tea. Standing close to the warm bulk of the Aga as the kettle boiled, she wondered how long it would be before Pamela remembered that her only form of transport was now stranded miles away. And then how soon it would be before she embarked upon a campaign to commandeer the mini.

She carried the two full mugs upstairs on a little tray, leaving one hand free to open Pamela's bedroom door. She was still dead to the world, lying on her back and snoring gently, the lines around her eyes and mouth magically ironed out by sleep. Like this, she looked almost young. Vinny observed her dispassionately, wondering, not for the first time, why she had ever agreed to this arrangement of theirs in the first place. She

7

was obliged to admit to herself that she had allowed Pamela's greater certainty to override her own caution. It was hardly surprising after all. At the time, financial problems had threatened to overwhelm her, and the first anniversary of her parents' death had been very hard to bear. Who wouldn't have been weakened by an overwhelming need to feel secure? But why, after all these years, am I still here? she thought. Habit? Inertia?

Pamela gave a little snort and opened her eyes. 'Whasser time?'

'Seven o'clock. Time you were up.' Vinny put the tray down on the bedside table and sat on the end of the bed, sipping her tea.

'What's today?' Pamela asked, hauling herself up against her pillows.

'Friday,' Vinny remembered with a sigh, 'and I'm working all day until six o'clock.'

'Oh yes.' Pamela frowned — the first creases of the morning. 'I've got a WI committee meeting, and then lunch with Gordon. I'm going to be busy too.' She drank her tea abstractedly, gathering her thoughts for the day ahead. Vinny knew better than to interrupt her, and when she'd finished her own tea, she stood up. 'I'd better get going.'

'Oh *no!*' Pamela sat bolt upright. 'How am I going to get there? I'll have to take you to Otterbridge in the mini and drop you off. I can't possibly be without a vehicle all day.'

'Sorry,' Vinny was about to go to the blue bathroom on the landing; the one belonging to her own bedroom. 'I'm afraid I've got a

8

lunchtime meeting too. I'll need it myself.'

'Oh but you can't. You'll have to tell them to rearrange it for another day. Please, Vinny?'

'The mini is my car, remember?' She tightened the belt of her dressing gown and left the room.

'Only because I gave it to you in the first place,' Pamela called after her.

'Oh,' Vinny muttered, scowling at her own reflection in the mirror. 'What wouldn't I give for some *unpredictability* in life?'

In the end Pamela agreed, with a bad grace, to telephone her garage as soon as they were open and get them to collect Gertie from the moor, and meanwhile to provide her with a courtesy car until they had got her running again.

'I'll go with you tomorrow to take your thank-you presents, if you like,' Vinny offered in an attempt at compensation.

So when Saturday morning came, Vinny found herself being driven by Pamela in a small hatchback belonging to the garage. It was, she noticed, considerably more luxurious than her mini.

'You get no view at all from these nasty little cars,' Pamela complained. 'They're so low down. I like to be up high so you can see over the hedgerows.'

'There aren't any hedges here.' They were driving back across the levels towards the pumping station. 'What's this George Overy man like?' Vinny asked her. 'I couldn't see him properly the other night when I collected you.'

'Oh, in his fifties I should imagine, very

Zummerzet. You know the type. A bit like Bob in fact.'

'Except that he doesn't cut grass for a living.'

'Well for all I know, he might do that too.'

'I hope he drinks whisky.' Vinny leant forward to wrap the sheet of blue tissue paper more firmly round the bottle in the footwell.

'Every man in his right mind drinks whisky,' Pamela said, 'Don't worry, it isn't a malt.'

Trust Pamela to be concerned about the price of the thing, Vinny thought. That wasn't what I meant at all.

'There are hedges here,' Pamela observed as they came to a higher, less boggy stretch, 'and I can't see over them at all, which is highly dangerous on these narrow byways.'

'Well, you could always go a little slower.'

'Don't start, Vinny! I've been driving in these parts for thirty years remember, which is a good twenty years longer than you have.'

There were scrubby trees on either side of them now as the road ran through a small copse. Vinny could see primroses and celandines in flower on the woodland floor and the first haze of green above them as the hawthorn leaves were beginning to unfurl. It would soon be spring.

New beginnings? Vinny pursed her lips in a gesture of resignation.

'What's up with you?' Pamela asked. She had turned her head and was looking accusingly at her. 'It's not my fault that you're a nervous passenger.'

Vinny opened her mouth to protest that Pamela was the only driver in the entire universe who made her feel in the least apprehensive and that was for entirely rational reasons, which any normal person would readily . . .

The car, swinging round a sudden corner over a small hump-backed bridge, almost knocked a girl off her bicycle. A tote bag, which had been dangling from the handlebars, flew off as she wobbled from side to side scattering its contents all over the road. Vinny had a brief glimpse of the girl's face, which looked blank with shock. '*Stop!*'

Pamela braked sharply. Vinny scrambled out and ran back down the road. The girl by now had regained control of her bike and come to a shaky halt. She reached up to pull the iPod headphones from her ears as Vinny approached, panting.

'You all right?'

'Yes,' she said. 'No thanks to *her*.' She jerked her thumb in Pamela's direction. 'She was driving way too fast.'

She had a soft Somerset voice. Her long fair hair flopped over her shoulders as she laid down the bicycle and began to collect her belongings; make-up, a book, a mobile phone and some sweets. Vinny joined in, and glanced sideways at her several times as they were both bent double, picking things up. She saw that the girl's skin had a peachy bloom. Her fingernails were painted purple and her lips crimson. Her short leather jacket flapped open to reveal a top too skimpy to achieve any sort of sensible union with the waistband of her jeans. And in her baby belly button, winking in the light, there was a large ruby coloured stud. She seemed to Vinny to be a child who was anticipating womanhood but not very accurately. She couldn't surely be much older than thirteen? The nursery characters printed on her tote bag were now partially obscured by road dirt. Vinny dusted it off and handed it to her. She took it without a word.

Pamela was busy backing the car up. Then she too got out. 'Well, that was regrettable,' she said, bending down to retrieve the girl's paperback and proffering it with the title ostentatiously uppermost. *How Far Should You Go?* was displayed in large green letters. 'But no harm done then?'

'I can manage,' the girl said, snatching it from her.

'Look, I have apologised . . . ' Pamela began in reasonable tones.

'I never heard no sorry.' She stuffed a handful of lipsticks into the dirty bag.

'Well I don't suppose you could hear much at all,' Pamela said with some asperity, 'with all that rubbishy pop music pounding away in your ears. And in my opinion that makes you an unnecessary hazard on the road. It's you who should be apologising to me.'

The girl picked up her bicycle, hung her bag back on the handlebars and put one foot on the pedal. Her blue eyes looked challengingly at Pamela.

'Fuck you,' she said. 'If anyone's unnecessary round here it's snobby old gits like you.' She took the last toffee from Vinny's outstretched hand, turned her back on them both and cycled off down the road in front of them. Vinny got back into the car without comment.

'Well *really!*' Pamela exclaimed, settling herself into the driver's seat and reaching for a box of wipes to clean her hands. 'I blame the modern education system. There's no respect these days. None.' She rattled her hand around the pocket in the door.

'Just as well you didn't actually crash into her,' Vinny observed.

'Cycling along with those things blocking up your ears,' Pamela pronounced, 'is like driving with your eyes shut.'

Or whilst looking sideways at your passenger. But Vinny didn't actually say that; what would be the point?

'There aren't any wipes,' Pamela accused her.

'Well don't blame me. It's not my car.'

Pamela exhaled sharply in a cross between a curse and a sigh, started up the engine again and let out the unfamiliar clutch rather too sharply. They lurched forwards kangaroo-style. 'Stupid bloody thing!'

As they drew level with the girl on the bike, Pamela slowed down with exaggerated care to little more than walking pace. Vinny, nearest to her, tried a sympathetic smile through the window, but was rebuffed by one finger strategically held at eye level.

'I'm glad I never had a girl,' Pamela said, speeding up again. 'They're far more trouble than boys.'

Vinny was surprised to hear this, schooled as she had been over the years in tales of the struggle Pamela had endured in bringing up Peter, her only child. They focused upon her abandonment by that wastrel of a husband, and the unkindness of the fates in blessing her with a brilliant but hyperactive son who'd run her ragged, and then grown up to be a loser, just like his father.

'Boys are far more straightforward,' Pamela said. 'Girls can be so spiteful.'

They drove on. There were no hedges again here. The fields looked sodden after the recent rain, the grass only just starting to look properly green again after the winter. The ditches were full of peaty black water and there was a great deal of sky. It might look like a nothing landscape to the uninitiated, Vinny thought, but to me it's special for that very reason. It doesn't shout its wares at you. It waits quietly to be discovered, and when you really look, you see sudden jewels like a kingfisher flashing turquoise down a rhyne. Or a redshank perched on a fence-post and revealed as the mist lifts. Or gossamer spiders' webs covered in droplets of dew in the early mornings. Or bright yellow-flag irises reflected in the water . . .

'There's the weird boy's house,' Pamela said.

Vinny was startled out of her thoughts. 'What, that one up on the bank all by itself? It looks derelict.'

'That's about right. You'll see for yourself on the way back.'

Soon afterwards she pulled the car off the road onto a muddy lay-by between two bridges, and they got out. On their right the great wide

14

Kingspill Drain full of grey water stretched into the far flat distance. On their left was the Amber Junction pumping station, an ugly redbrick box of a building with metal windows. Behind it there were yet more waterways. A notice on the gate into its yard said: Employees Only. There was no sign of life. In fact the only sound in the still air was that of a wren, singing.

'But will he actually be here?' Vinny asked. 'He could be at home. I mean, the pumps don't appear to be working at the moment.'

'It's certainly quieter than it was on Thursday night.'

'Did you go inside then?' Vinny was intrigued.

'Only into the office. The rest was far too noisy and smelly.'

'There's no reason to suppose he's here now though, is there?'

'Well his van's parked over there.' Pamela indicated a small white Ford with the Environment Agency logo on its side. She pushed through the gate. 'Come on. And don't forget the whisky.'

Vinny hesitated. 'Which door?' There was a choice of three.

Pamela made for the tall double doors in the centre, which had to be all of twenty feet high. There was no bell so she hammered on one with her fist and after a moment or so it opened. A stocky balding man in green overalls emerged, wiping his hands on a rag.

'Hello George,' Pamela said. 'Remember me from the other night?'

'Oh yes.' He smiled a shade mockingly. 'You

15

got home OK then?' He looked enquiringly at Vinny.

'Oh and this is the friend I rang; Vinny Henderson.'

'Pleased to meet you.'

Vinny was about to hold out her hand, but then noticed that his were covered in oil, so she smiled instead.

'Just doing a spot of maintenance,' George said, displaying them. ' 'Tis dirty old work.'

'We called to thank you,' Vinny said.

'That's all right. Want to come in and see the place now's you'm here?' He opened the door wider to admit them and they followed him in. The building seemed much bigger on the inside, with a vast high ceiling and masses of light coming in through the tall barred windows on either side. It was like a great secular cathedral, Vinny thought.

'My goodness,' Pamela exclaimed, 'What huge machines!'

'Four diesel pumps put in in nineteen forty-two,' George said. 'There's three of 'em runs on diesel still, and that one up the end's been modified for the electric.' He stood next to the nearest one, patting its shiny metallic surface proudly, and then polishing the spot with his rag.

Each enormous green pump took up the entire width of the building and was festooned with dials, wheels, taps and pipes. There were red metal cages over some parts, one of which was open, exposing its innards and a pile of nuts and other components on the floor where George had clearly been working. Hanging on the wall

16

behind them were eight giant sized spanners.

'Nineteen forty-two? That makes them pretty much obsolete, surely?' Pamela said. 'Modern technology would be much smaller and more efficient, wouldn't it?'

'Can't beat these beauties,' George said defensively. 'They knew about engineering in them days.'

'They must be able to pump an awful lot of water.' Vinny was awed.

'Certainly do. They — ' There was a clattering noise outside as someone dumped a bike against the wall.

'Dad?'

'Mandy? Excuse me a moment.' George went back to the door. 'Hello love.'

'Dad, that car outside nearly ran . . . Oh . . . ' Vinny caught sight of the face for a moment, before it retreated hurriedly. 'Never mind,' they heard her say. 'Doesn't matter. See you dinnertime, eh?' And she was off again.

'Teenagers,' George said, coming back again. He was shaking his head but amused.

'Your daughter?' Vinny said.

'That's her. My only one, bless her.'

'We passed her on the road just now,' Vinny began.

'Yes, well anyway,' Pamela said hurriedly, 'we came to thank you so much for all your help, and to give you this.' She proffered the bottle.

'Oh you didn't have to do that.' He looked uncomfortable for the first time.

'Nonsense! It was the least we could do.'

'Well, best put it in here then.' He led the way

17

into a small side office where there was a table and chairs and a drinks machine. 'Can I get you anything? Coffee or tea?'

Vinny opened her mouth to accept. There were maps on the walls of the local waterways and drainage systems, and she would have been interested to hear about them and about George's job in particular. He seemed to her, even on this brief acquaintance, to be a dedicated sort of a man, solid and entirely admirable.

'Oh no,' Pamela said. 'We don't want to hold you up. But there was just one thing I wanted to ask you. You know the young man who brought me here that night?'

'Reckon I do.'

'So is he . . . all right? In the head, I mean.'

'Don't know him that well. He's only been around here a couple of months. Writing a book, so he says. Seems harmless enough.'

'A book?' Vinny said. 'How exciting. What's it about?'

'He didn't say, but he'm always down here asking questions.'

'Is he someone one's heard of?' Pamela asked. 'What's his name?'

'Crankshaw, Jonathan Crankshaw. I remember it particular 'cos it sounds like crankshaft.' He grinned self-consciously.

'I wonder if he's any relation to Adrian Crankshaw the architect?' Vinny said.

'Oh, you mean him off the telly?' George said. 'Could be. He do talk like that, long words and all.'

18

'Well,' Pamela said, 'This won't do. I'm sure you have a lot of work to be getting on with, but thanks so much again. It was very good of you.'

'That's all right.' He motioned them towards a standard-sized door at the other end of the room and ushered them out into the yard again. ' 'Fore you go,' he said, pointing up to a small plaque on the wall at the top of the large doors, 'I shows this to all the visitors. It marks where high tide do get to in the Bristol Channel. Makes you think, eh?'

'Certainly does,' Vinny said. 'I'd no idea this area was so far below sea level. It's really interesting. Thanks for showing us round.'

'You'm welcome.' He raised a hand in farewell as they reached the gate, and then disappeared, closing the door behind him.

'Well, well,' Pamela said, 'so that dreadful girl is his daughter, then? I expect she'll tell him tales about us once we've gone.'

'Very likely.'

'But more to the point, what if this Jonathan really is Adrian Crankshaw's son?' She opened her eyes wide for extra emphasis.

'You mean if he's middle class, educated and of a 'good' family then he's charmingly eccentric, whereas if he'd been merely ordinary working class, then he'd just be mad, and likely to be dangerous?'

'Honestly Vin, you're such an inverted snob!' Pamela opened the doors of the car and they both got in. 'Well I hope he appreciates quiche more than Overy likes whisky,' she said. 'I'm afraid in his case that wasn't money well spent.

We should have taken him beer, or maybe even cider?'

'He was just embarrassed, that's all.' Vinny felt cross.

Jonathan's isolated house, now that they had finally stopped outside it, looked even more unkempt to Vinny. It too was redbrick and built on the north bank of the Kingspill, presumably once the property of the old River Authority. It was accessible only over a pair of planks plus a rail, which bridged a smaller drainage channel between it and the road. The paint on the front door and on all the windows was peeling off, and there were no curtains that she could see. But high up on the gable end there was an oblong stone with the name of the house carved into it: THE PROSPECT.

'Nice irony, that,' Vinny said, pointing to it.

'It's pretty grim inside too, from what I could see last time,' Pamela said. 'Hardly any furniture and a muddy bicycle in the sitting room!' She knocked on the door.

Though every prospect pleases and only man is vile . . . Vinny was thinking. I don't know where that comes from. Must look it up. Then the door opened and a young man was standing there. Not vile at all, Vinny thought; in fact he reminds me of Nathaniel . . . Her heart beat faster at the memory. This man was of similar build and beauty. Vinny was instantly taken back to the time years ago when she and Nat had been together. Not a long time as it had turned out, but one of never-to-be-repeated intensity.

The young man didn't appear to recognise

20

Pamela. 'Yes?' he said.

'Hello Jonathan,' she said. 'Pamela Wood. Remember me? My car broke down the other night and you helped me.'

'Oh . . . yes,' he said. 'But you're wearing different colour clothes.'

'Ye-es. Um, this is my friend Lavinia.'

'Vinny,' Vinny put in quickly. 'How d'you do?'

'Is this going to take long?' Jonathan enquired, 'because I'm right in the middle of something.'

'Oh, I'm sorry,' Pamela said. 'I do realise how important it is not to be interrupted when you're *writing*. No, we just wanted to give you this as a small token of thanks for your kind help.' She handed him a package wrapped in foil. 'I think it might still be frozen, but I expect it will soon thaw out.'

'What is it?'

'It's a quiche.' Then, because she could detect no sign of comprehension in his expression, she added, 'A pie, for you to eat.'

'Oh, right.' He took it from her and waited with a will-that-be-all? expression on his face.

'One last thing,' Pamela held out a hand as if to detain him. 'Do tell me, are you related to the famous Adrian Crankshaw?'

'Yes, I am.'

'Is he your father?'

'Yes.'

'Oh, how exciting! I suppose he'll be visiting you here from time to time?'

'No,' Jonathan said, 'Goodbye,' and he shut the door.

Vinny expected Pamela to be outraged by his

21

rudeness, but when she turned to look at her as they walked back across the plank bridge, Pamela gave her a little grin of complicity.

'Watch yourself,' she warned, putting a steadying hand on Vinny's arm. 'We don't want you falling in now, do we?' She looked suspiciously cheerful. Vinny frowned.

They got back into the car but Pamela made no move to start the engine. Instead she sat there drumming her fingers on the steering wheel with a half smile on her face.

'It seems to me,' she said, 'that young Jonathan must be estranged from his family. Why else would he be living in comparative squalor in the middle of nowhere? Something tells me that he needs help.'

Vinny snorted. 'I'd have thought that's the last thing he wants!'

'Oh no, you can't go by appearances. I've met these clever types before and they can be painfully shy. We'll have to draw him out gradually — find out about this book of his.'

We? 'Why?'

'Because he's interesting, Vinny! Surely even you can appreciate that? And I suspect that he could do with some backing.'

'What d'you mean, backing?'

'I think he needs a patron; some form of assistance to enable him to achieve his full potential.'

'What, you mean sponsorship as in Adopt a Whale?'

Pamela started up the engine irritably. 'Really Vinny, you can be remarkably childish at times.'

22

Vinny was torn between wanting to giggle and to protest. She was beginning to recognise with a sinking heart another of Pamela's projects in embryo. Pamela didn't have hobbies, she had all engulfing obsessions which flared up, flowered — sometimes all too briefly — and burnt themselves out, usually with recriminations on all sides.

Vinny took a deep breath and let it out slowly.

'Cheer up,' Pamela said, patting her knee encouragingly. 'I have a premonition of good times ahead and you have to admit, don't you, that my gut feelings are never wrong?'

2

'Where's my best flan dish?' Vinny asked Pamela two evenings later, as she cooked their supper. Pamela had perched herself on a high stool nearby, sipping a gin and tonic and was attempting to get Vinny's backing in her current dispute with the Parish Council. Vinny had recently opened the oven door to check on the meat, and the aroma of roast lamb hung promisingly in the air.

'Which dish?'

'You know, the flat blue one with the crinkled edges. The one I always use.'

'Oh that one. I think I took the quiche for Jonathan in it.'

'But it was already in a tinfoil dish from the freezer.' Vinny kneaded the pastry into a ball and put it into the fridge to cool off.

'Yes well, I put it into the blue dish as well, to stop it getting crushed on the journey. I had planned to bring it straight back.'

Vinny rinsed her hands under the hot tap. 'Oh Pamela, now we'll have to go all the way down there again to fetch it!'

Pamela raised an eyebrow. 'Oh dear. How sad. Never mind.'

'You left it there on purpose,' Vinny accused her, taking a sharp knife and beginning to peel cooking apples, 'so you'd have an excuse to go back again!'

'And now I can,' Pamela agreed modestly.

'And you wrapped the whole thing in foil so I wouldn't see it.'

Pamela ignored this. 'I thought I'd go and get it tomorrow night.'

'And then what?' Vinny felt exasperated.

'Well I don't know. I might invite him to dinner.'

'Why on earth would he want to come to dinner with us? You're old enough to be his mother.' This, Vinny knew, was below the belt. Pamela was always wounded by any reference to the age gap between them.

'There's no need for that,' Pamela said. She looked suddenly pathetic. 'No need at all.'

Vinny sighed. 'I'm sorry.' She knew perfectly well that as soon as she apologised, Pamela's confident expression would instantly reassert itself. And it did.

'Look at it from my point of view,' Pamela said earnestly. 'I've got all this inheritance from my Aunt Kate, and I don't really need it. We're very comfortable here, aren't we? But no one actually chooses to live like Jonathan, so he clearly isn't well off. Don't you see this is a chance for me to do something useful — to make a *difference*? And you've got to admit it's a good cause.' She drained her gin and poured herself another one.

'But you don't know anything about him,' Vinny protested.

'Exactly. So I need to go and visit him to find out more. Hence the subterfuge with the dish.'

'But why do it behind my back?'

'Ah . . . ' Pamela gave her a knowing look.

25

'Now we're getting to the whole point of this, aren't we? Be assured, Vin, I have absolutely no designs upon the poor young man, truly I haven't.'

The idea was both laughable and grotesque. Vinny turned from the sink to face her. 'Pamela, this is me you're talking to.'

'Of course it is, and I'm just trying to explain that this is a humanitarian project, not a personal one.'

Vinny snorted. 'And what if Jonathan doesn't want to be the object of your charity? Have you considered that?'

'Oh dear,' Pamela said, going back to her stool and settling herself onto it with a sigh. 'Of course I see it all now. You fancy him, don't you? You poor thing.' She shook her head. 'He must be a good twenty years younger than you. Never mind me, *you* could be his mother! You'd make yourself a laughing stock.'

A few years ago Vinny would have laughed this off, but now she was so goaded by irritation that she snapped at her angrily. 'Meat's due out in half an hour. If you want apple tart for pudding, then you can damn well finish it yourself!' And she stalked out.

She went into the garden and wandered about. The sun was setting redly behind the oak tree and the daffodils glowed in the evening light. Vinny inhaled the scent from the half dozen blue hyacinths in the rockery and felt calmer, but also more unhappy. She bent down to pull the head off a precocious dandelion. The weeding season would be starting any minute, and the grass cutting. Bob would be back once a week, deferring to Pamela whilst raising his eyebrows at Vinny in mock irony, as he tramped up and down with the mower for six pounds an hour and a cup of tea. The magnolia would be out soon and the cherry blossom. Pamela would be trading in her bridge evenings for afternoons of golf and aspirational lunch parties in their conservatory. They would each shed layers of clothing as the weather got warmer, and Pamela would once again spoil her delight in the summer strawberries by reminding her that caster sugar and cream were fattening.

Vinny thought, This isn't the way I want to live.

★   ★   ★

Jonathan was glad to be living at The Prospect in spite of its rather spartan accommodation. When he had first arrived there in rain-soaked January, the view from the house hadn't moved him one way or the other. It was inescapable that the land all around was flat, but scenery had never been of any consequence to him. However, he did spend a lot of time staring out abstractedly through the windows. When he stood in his sitting room at the back, he could see the Kingspill Drain flowing past him to the west and disappearing under the first of several bridges, on its unhurried way to a final muddy outfall. To the east, half a mile away was Amber Junction, straddling the great drain and effectively blocking any further view, save on clear days

27

when he could see the top of Glastonbury Tor above it. And if he looked out straight ahead, there was just the wide strip of the drain, a line of electricity pylons from the nuclear power station, some fields and nothing much else. It was a good undemanding outlook.

Jonathan's focus was always on data, collecting it with a passion and sorting it into components in the overall scheme of things. So it seemed to him appropriate that he, a civil engineer, should be living in this house, built as it had been in the nineteen forties on the spoil-bank of this sixty metre wide entirely man-made river. He had by now ascertained that the Kingspill's purpose was to collect and store water from five rivers and some thirty thousand acres of surrounding floodplain. It was designed to serve the dual function of a flood relief channel in the winter, and a reservoir for irrigating the local farmland in summer.

It was, however, the pumping station which intrigued him most. This was one of several which powered what was said to be the largest and most complicated land drainage system in the South West. It lifted water up above sea level into the Kingspill from where it could flow out safely at low tide into the Bristol Channel, just over five miles away, through a large 'clyse'. This sluice gate, he had recently discovered, was one of the great one-way doors at the mouths of some of the Somerset rivers, which prevent the sea from flooding inland at high tide. Jonathan took great satisfaction in finding out as much about all this as he could. He felt it was imperative when living in a watershed of such fascinating hydrological dynamics, that one should understand in every detail exactly how it worked.

Back in January, on only his second evening here, he'd seen from his house that pumping must be in progress, because the Amber Junction building was all lit up. He heard the noise of the machinery getting ever louder as he approached on his bike along the dark road. Once there, he found that the two main doors were wide open and in the bright interior a man was visible, walking about. He felt a buzz of excitement.

He left his bike by the fence, let himself in through a side gate, and began to walk across the yard towards the light.

'Can't 'ee read the notice?' a man's voice said from behind him. 'Employees only.'

Jonathan turned to see a middle-aged man standing beside one of the two white vans parked there. He strained to see him in the gloom.

'Sorry,' he said. 'I didn't see it. I just heard the pumps and I'd really like to see them in action.' The man had by now walked up to him and was looking at him. Jonathan made a big effort to maintain eye contact. 'Are you in charge?'

'Certainly am.'

'Oh good. My name's Jonathan Crankshaw. I live over there,' he pointed.

'You'm never living in The Prospect?'

'Yes.'

'Well, rather you than I!'

Jonathan found his accent difficult to understand, but was encouraged nevertheless by the conversation so far. 'So, can I look inside?'

'Oh well, go on then. Not for long, mind. We'm busy after all the rain us've had.'

And that was how he had met George Overy. Inside the pump-house the electric pump and two of the diesels were running non-stop. George told him that he and two relief mates were doing alternate twelve-hour shifts to keep the huge engines going, patrolling constantly with oil cans ('not self-oiling, see?') and changing filters. Jonathan felt intoxicated by the rhythmic *thump thump thump!* of the great green engines with their red safety cages covering the moving parts, and the miasma of oil fumes everywhere.

'What's the maximum station output?' he shouted above the din.

'Eighteen cubic metres per second.'

'Mmmm.' That was a thousand and eighty metric tonnes every minute, Jonathan calculated. One hell of a lot of water! 'Enough to fill this entire building in just over two minutes?'

'Two and a half, yes. You in the business then?'

Jonathan nodded, and ever since that night, George had been friendly towards him; quizzing him with artless nosiness each time he appeared, on his life, his job and the book. In his turn Jonathan asked George searching technical questions about his experience of local water control and management. He had no difficulty in memorising scientific data, in fact he derived great satisfaction from doing so. He was thus able to write large chunks of his book directly from his head. He started to call in at Amber Junction regularly and even began to feel as though he belonged. It was an unaccustomed and most welcome sensation.

Now and again of course he needed to look something up. The internet would have been invaluable but he had no telephone line. Instead, every so often, he would ride his bicycle to Otterbridge and use the computer and other reference sources in the library there. But it was a long way and took up far too much of his time. The Prospect certainly had its disadvantages but the benefits, at least for the moment, outweighed them. It was cheap and it would do for now.

Today he was getting on well. It was eight fifteen in the morning and he was deep in a description of the Aral Sea bordering on Kazakhstan, and how it had in recent years lost seventy-five percent of its water through the diversion of its feeder rivers for irrigating new cotton fields in the desert.

In some places the depth of water has fallen from 54 metres to 28 metres and the retreat has left hulks of ships marooned on a salty wasteland.

His printer hummed and zonked out sheet after sheet of closely spaced text and figures. But then a Toner Low message popped up on his screen and he remembered that he had forgotten to buy any spare cartridges. If he needed the encouragement of a growing pile of typescript — and he very much did — then he would soon have to waste hours in cycling into town; just when the writing was going so well too.

Someone was knocking at his door. It was probably George, or more likely his wife Gwen, who had got into the habit of bringing him cakes and telling him he was far too thin. He only hoped it wouldn't be their daughter Amanda. He got up from his computer and looked out of the first floor window. Below in the lay-by there was an unknown red mini, but no sign of its owner, who was presumably standing under his porch. At least whoever it was hadn't interrupted him in the middle of a crucial bit. He went downstairs. The woman who was waiting there looked vaguely familiar. He frowned with the effort of working out who she was.

'It's OK,' she said, 'I haven't come to hold you up for long. I'm Vinny, remember, Pamela's friend?'

'Oh yes, you're the dark blue one.'

She smiled. 'I nearly always wear navy, yes.'

'I wish everyone would choose one colour and stick to it,' he said. 'Life's complicated enough without swapping about all the time. I've only changed once. I liked red when I was young, but now all my clothes are brown. It's a kind of grown-up red.'

'I see.' She smiled again.

Jonathan was encouraged to confide in her. 'My toner cartridge is about to run out,' he said, 'and I haven't a spare. It's very inconvenient as I'm right in the middle of the destruction of the Aral Sea.'

'Oh dear,' Vinny said. 'I can see that must be awkward. Can I help at all?'

'Only if you've got a cartridge in your pocket.' How absurd — he'd actually made a joke! He laughed aloud.

'Well no . . . ' Vinny said, 'but I could fetch

you one from Otterbridge if you like. I'm just off to work there, but I've got a half day today so I could drop it back here at lunchtime?'

'You're going to Otterbridge? Wait here.' Jonathan ran upstairs to collect his coat from the mattress on the floor of his bedroom where it did service overnight as an extra blanket. He thrust his arms into it, picked up his chequebook from the chair and ran downstairs again two at a time. 'OK,' he said, 'let's go.'

'You want to come with me?' Vinny said.

'Yes of course! I don't get a free ride very often.'

'And you don't mind staying there all morning?'

'No. I can do with going to the library anyway.'

'Well that's handy.'

'What is?'

'The library,' Vinny told him, 'is where I work.'

* * *

When Vinny drove off with Jonathan in her passenger seat she discovered that her mood was surprisingly buoyant, probably because she had outmanoeuvred Pamela. After work today she would put the blue dish down casually on Pamela's polished granite work-surface in the kitchen, and wait for her to notice it. Then, after her expected exclamations of surprise and annoyance, Vinny would say something like, 'Oh, I thought I'd save you the trouble. It's not a huge detour for me on my way to work, after all.'

33

Then Vinny remembered that she hadn't actually mentioned to Jonathan the reason for her visit and she hadn't collected her dish either. She would have to do so when she dropped him off again at lunchtime. It occurred to her to wonder why Jonathan hadn't questioned why she had come to his house in the first place, but she concluded that he was so caught up in his work that nothing else registered.

She wanted to look at him properly, particularly at his eyes that seemed to her to be an unusual golden-brown colour — tawny — that was it. But she was obliged to watch the road instead. He was sitting beside her but looking out of his window and appeared not at all uncomfortable in the silence.

'What's your book about?' she eventually asked him.

'Water.' He didn't elaborate.

'Oh I see.' Why say that, when she meant the opposite? 'What aspect of water exactly? Drinking water, floodwater, sea water?'

'Oh it's all the same stuff.' Jonathan turned to look at her. 'You do realise, don't you, that there is a finite amount of water on planet Earth?'

'Well presumably there's more when it rains,' Vinny said flippantly.

'No! Why does no one ever understand that? It's so fundamental.' He took a breath. 'I'll give you the simplified version to begin with, OK?' He didn't look at her for confirmation. 'There's the same amount of water that there always was. It isn't created or destroyed, it simply migrates in a great circle.' He gestured with both hands.

'Down in the rain and snowfall; onto the land; into the aquifers or down the rivers, and out to sea. Then up into the clouds again by evaporation from warm tropical oceans. Round and round!'

'Oh yes,' Vinny said. 'Well, I understand the basics, of course. I just hadn't put it all together quite like that.'

'Good!' Jonathan clapped his hands together.

'What's good?'

'What you said. That's why I'm writing my book; to put it all together just like that. You have just showed me that there definitely is a market for such a book.'

'Right.' She glanced at him quickly. He looked triumphant. What could she say that wouldn't be crushing? 'Have you always been interested in water?' she tried.

'Oh yes. When I was five years old I used to stand on the seashore for hours watching the waves. Everyone is different, you know?'

He's clearly intelligent, Vinny thought, and I don't believe he's mad, but he does seem to me to have something crucial missing, and I'm not sure what it is. She didn't feel in any way threatened by him. She even found him endearing, especially when he had laughed so uproariously at his strange non-joke. Vinny smiled at the recollection. He had relaxed so much, that he looked almost childlike; a choirboy with curly dark hair framing his face and those extraordinary leonine eyes all crinkled up in merriment. She wondered if he ever got lonely being by himself.

'Are you just renting The Prospect?' she asked him.

'Yes. It belongs to the Environment Agency. It's the old Amber Junction supervisor's house but George says that when he got the job, Gwen refused to live there. So they had to build them a nice new bungalow right next to the pumping station, with double glazing and central heating.' It sounded as though he was quoting George verbatim.

'Yes, well modern comforts are difficult to do without, once you've got used to them,' Vinny said. 'Pamela insisted on getting our house double-glazed too, soon after I moved in with her. Ages ago now.'

'You and Pamela live together,' Jonathan suddenly said, 'so you must be lesbians?'

'Oh . . . well . . . ' Vinny flushed, 'I suppose it might look —'

'I read about them once,' Jonathan said conversationally, 'but I haven't met one before.'

Vinny was saved from having to reply to this by the happy coincidence of arriving at that moment at a set of traffic lights in the centre of town, right outside a computer shop. Jonathan opened the door and began to get out.

'Careful!' Vinny cautioned. 'I'll see you later on then, at the — ' but he was already on the pavement and walking briskly towards his objective. The lights were changing. Vinny put the mini into gear and moved off.

It was a slow morning at work. She had plenty of time to think, and to ask herself why she hadn't simply answered 'certainly not!' to

Jonathan's question. Why was it that celibacy seemed to her to be even more shameful to confess to than lesbianism? Pamela and I are like an old married couple now, Vinny thought; all exasperation and silences and, of course, separate bedrooms. It had begun so positively too, all those years ago. How did we get here from there? When was it that Pamela began to move the goalposts? Vinny began, regretfully, to think about the past.

★　★　★

It had been the middle of winter and Vinny had only been working in the Otterbridge library for a week, when a woman had come in wanting her to do a subject search on *Ethics in Local Government*.

'I'm doing an evening class, you see,' she explained, 'and I need to do some in-depth reading around the subject.'

'I'll see what I can find for you,' Vinny said, tapping the words into the computer.

The woman leant over the counter to look at the resulting list. She exuded a subtle aura of expensive scent. She pointed. 'That one,' she said, 'and those too, perhaps.'

'OK, I'll see what we can get hold of. What's your name?'

'Mrs Pamela Wood.'

But some of the books proved difficult to trace, and Vinny grew accustomed to the Pamela woman popping in regularly to enquire about them and keep her up to the mark. She would

37

look up from her work to be confronted by a pair of hands planted firmly on her Enquiries desk; hands adorned with assortment of antique rings. And her eyes would travel in resigned slow motion up the well-tailored arms of the coat, to the face above, whilst she formulated the excuse of the day. The woman's wiry brown hair was going grey at her temples and always looked as buoyant and firm as its owner's determination. The red painted mouth smiled at her. 'Well?'

When the last of the books eventually arrived, it felt to Vinny like the end of a quest; one in which she had finally triumphed. But maybe now it was also one that she might conceivably miss? This woman was different from the library's usual range of customers. She had such an air of energy, and such confidence in her inalienable right to demand from the service exactly what she wanted, when she wanted it. Vinny had begun their acquaintance reluctantly but at the end, could only admire her spirit.

'Fantastic!' Pamela said. 'I was sure you'd get them all for me in the end. How about coming for a coffee with me to celebrate?' She glanced at her watch, 'Or even a bite to eat. What time's your lunch hour?' The candid pale eyes regarded Vinny steadily. She was smiling.

'Do come,' she said, 'I've been making your life hell for weeks, and you've been so patient and lovely about it. You must let me make it up to you now!'

So then it all started; this transformation from the unchosen single life to one of easy belonging and mutual support. Vinny relaxed into it gratefully. It never occurred to her to think of herself or Pamela in terms of the 'L' word. Pamela had once been married and Vinny herself had had half a dozen boyfriends. Some, like Nathaniel, had been good and some, like the last one — who at the end had treated her with contempt and cheated her out of all her savings — had been very bad indeed. And now this new friendship had arrived, and seemed to be the answer to so many of her problems.

There was no doubt that Pamela was compelling. When she concentrated her gaze upon you, she made you feel as though you were the centre of the universe. She was impulsive and generous too, taking Vinny into one of the best shops in town and insisting upon buying her an expensive cashmere jacket, when they had only been together for two weeks.

'No,' Vinny protested. 'Really, I couldn't accept — '

'Please, Vinny,' Pamela said. 'Do let me do this for you. You look so wonderful in it. Doesn't she?' This last to the assistant, who was hovering helpfully nearby.

'Very flattering to the figure, yes. We do have it in two other colourways, if . . . '

'No,' Pamela said. 'This beautiful greeny-blue is just right. It matches her eyes.' She smiled at Vinny confidently and muttered under her breath, 'The money is nothing to me. I've got loads, honestly.' Then she said aloud, 'We'll take it,' and whipped out her credit card. Vinny laughed, and it was a done deal. And for almost the first time in her life, Vinny felt cherished and important.

But theirs had always been an entirely platonic relationship, founded upon companionship and trust and mutual need, plus a well-founded distrust of men. Pamela was the house owner and all-round benefactor. Vinny went to work and shared the bills, did the cooking and gardening and everything of a practical nature that needed doing, in order to repay her debt of gratitude. And at the beginning, Vinny didn't notice, let alone feel resentful of this inequality. She was intoxicated by attention; enthralled by approbation. But that was then.

★   ★   ★

Vinny caught herself wondering how much sexual experience Jonathan had had, and was then uncomfortable at having the thought in the first place. She was also concerned as to whether he would arrive at the library at the right time. Had he got a watch? It would be most awkward if he didn't turn up. She could hardly leave without him and strand him here.

She need not have worried. Soon after ten o'clock she saw him coming in through the main door and making his way directly to the reference room. He climbed the stairs gracefully two at a time and watching him, Vinny thought, He looks so lovely you'd never know there was anything wrong with him. She hoped he would get the information he needed; that he would be able to communicate what this was to the member of staff on duty up there, and that the Deputy Librarian — if it was indeed her — would not be brusque or unhelpful to him.

At twelve forty-five after a busy morning, Vinny was ready to go home. She tidied her papers away, put a pile of books onto the Returns shelf and collected her coat and bag from the staffroom. She found Jonathan upstairs using one of the microfiche readers and peering at it intently. A new notebook was open in front of him and he had covered most of the first page with notes in tiny, close-packed writing.

Vinny touched him lightly on the shoulder. 'Time to go.' Jonathan recoiled violently and she jumped too. 'Sorry,' she said. 'I didn't mean to startle you. It's just that I'm going home now, if you want a lift.'

'I'll be finished in ten minutes,' Jonathan said without taking his eyes off the screen.

'Oh.' Vinny felt like asking him exactly who he thought was doing whom a favour? 'Well all right then, I'll be at the Enquiries Desk, but don't be any longer, will you?'

A quarter of an hour later she saw him coming down the stairs and looking vaguely about him as if unsure where to go. She waved, and he came towards her. 'All done?' she asked.

'For now, yes.'

'Right then, let's go.'

'I'm hungry,' Jonathan announced.

'Oh,' Vinny hadn't considered this. 'I usually have a sandwich when I get home.'

'Fish and chips is nice.' He looked expectantly at her.

41

Vinny laughed. 'OK, we'll buy some to take with us.' Another minor rebellion against Pamela.

There was a chip shop on their route out of Otterbridge and even a space to park. Jonathan wanted a pickled egg and a battered sausage as well, and stood there patiently as Vinny paid for it all.

'You'll have to nurse these on the way home,' she told him, handing over the two paper-wrapped parcels. 'I don't want grease all over my car.'

But the moment Jonathan was back in his seat, he put one portion down in the footwell, unwrapped the other and began to eat.

'Chip?' he offered, holding one out.

'I can't,' Vinny said. 'I'm driving.'

'Oh right, I'll feed you then,' and he raised it to her mouth and pushed it in.

'Argh . . . Mmm.' The easiest thing to do was to swallow it, so she did.

He was smiling at her. 'I saw a bird do that once,' he said, 'but it was with a worm, not a chip.'

Vinny consented to eat several more but drew the line at bits of fish. 'I'll eat mine when we get back to your house,' she said.

'OK.' There was a silence while he polished off the sausage and the egg as well. Then he licked all his fingers in turn and, before she could stop him he'd screwed the empty paper into a ball, wound down the window and lobbed it out into the passing countryside.

Vinny stood on the brake. This was too much!

'Why are we stopping?'

She got out without speaking and walked briskly down the road to retrieve it from half way up a bush. When she got back to the car again, Jonathan had begun on the second packet. 'What's the matter?'

'You can't chuck rubbish out of the window,' Vinny said, driving off again.

'I just did!'

'No, I mean you mustn't. It not only looks horrible but you can be fined for littering the place up.'

'It's only paper. Biodegradable, good for compost.'

'Nevertheless,' Vinny said firmly, 'you still mustn't do it.' It was like talking to a child. 'And don't eat all those chips, some of them are mine!'

Jonathan looked cross. 'I hope you aren't going to be like everyone else,' he said, 'ordering me about. I came here to get away from all that.'

Vinny felt she'd handled it badly. 'I'm sorry,' she said, 'it's just that I hate litter and it's so unnecessary. Look, there's a bin over there in this lay-by. Would you pop it in?' She handed the ball to him. Jonathan aimed and threw it as she drew in and slowed the car down. Direct hit.

'Yes!' Vinny cried. 'Great shot.'

She stole a glance at him. He was smiling again and eating chips. I shall have to drive faster, she thought, if I'm to get any lunch at all.

Back at The Prospect Vinny remembered her blue dish and retrieved it from the sink where Jonathan had left it under a pile of unwashed plates. His kitchen had a utilitarian feel to it; a table, two chairs, an electric cooker, a sink and nothing much else. There was a sack of potatoes on the floor, some leeks and carrots in a cardboard box, and that was about it. Vinny was worried about him. She ate what fish and chips were left in her portion, and wondered how he managed. 'Can you cook?' she asked him.

'Oh yes.'

'But do you?'

'Sometimes. I'm not very interested in food.'

'You could have fooled me!' Vinny smiled at him but he didn't seem to understand the joke. 'How about that quiche we brought you?' It had been one of her best asparagus ones. 'Was that nice?'

'Yes, it was OK, but I like cheesy ones best.'

Vinny wondered rather crossly if he ever said 'thank you'. If you really want to help this ungrateful man, she told herself, then you'd better do it without being hopeful of a reward of any kind. That's for sure. But who'd said anything about further help anyway? She'd only done this in the first place as a one-off to tease Pamela.

'Do you go to Otterbridge every day?' Jonathan asked.

'Most days, yes. But I'm often there until six in the evening.'

'Oh I don't mind staying for a whole day,' he said. 'It's nice and warm in the library.'

'I see.' She hadn't anticipated this.

'So you'll give me a lift again?' He stared at her. His eyes really were a striking colour.

'Well, I — .'

'How shall I tell you when I need to go again?'

'I suppose you could ring me. Oh no, you aren't on the phone, are you?'

'There's a public telephone box a couple of miles away that I can cycle to. All I need is your home phone number.'

'Ye-es.' Vinny could imagine only too well what Pamela's reaction would be if Jonathan phoned demanding to speak to her, and not to Pamela herself.

'So what is it?'

'Well,' Vinny said, 'I've got a mobile but it's always switched off when I'm working. But hang on.' She opened her handbag and found one of the library cards. 'You could always phone this number and ask for me.'

'For Vinny?'

'No, you'd better say 'Miss Henderson'. She found a pen and wrote her surname and her extension number on the back, and handed it to him.

'That's good,' he said, beaming. 'I really need assistance like this.'

Vinny was unexpectedly charmed by his candour. She couldn't imagine any other man of his age admitting to needing any help at all, especially from a woman so many years his senior. 'It's a pleasure,' she said. Then she thought, but somehow I don't believe Pamela will be as pleased.

★ ★ ★

45

When Vinny finally got home, she found Pamela in the kitchen eating soup. She looked up accusingly. 'You're late! I waited for ages to begin lunch. Where have you been?'

'Sorry,' Vinny began, 'I — '

'Oh well never mind, you're here now. It's mushroom, your favourite. All right?'

'Well, yes.'

'Sit down then,' Pamela said, spooning the soup from a saucepan and plonking a full bowl in front of her. 'Now then, I've been waiting all morning to tell you about my plans for Jonathan.'

How was your morning, Vinny? Are you hungry? Would you like some soup? Was there a problem at work?

Vinny ate her soup and was glad now not to be full of fish and chips. She was suffering from that particular prickly form of irritation that invariably afflicted her when she knew she was in the wrong.

'I thought we wouldn't wait until this evening, but go down there straight away,' Pamela said.

'Down where?'

'To collect your precious blue dish, of course.'

'Oh look, Pamela, um . . . ' Vinny rather sheepishly extracted it from her shopping bag and unwrapped the newspaper from around it.

'It's filthy!' Pamela exclaimed, 'and it stinks of vinegar!' She frowned at her. 'And how come you've got it anyway?'

'Well I was going past The Prospect on my way to work,' Vinny began.

'But it's *miles* out of your way.'

'Yes, well I decided to save you a journey.'

Pamela stared at her. 'Why?' She looked hurt. 'You knew I was looking forward to talking to him again. So why did you do it? That was a dirty trick, Vin.'

'I just think you should leave him alone,' Vinny muttered. 'For all we know he's perfectly happy as he is. It's none of our business how he finances his writing or what he eats. You can't just barge in and take over his life. It's embarrassing.'

Pamela shook her head sadly, 'I don't know what's happened to you lately. You've changed. You used to be so positive and easygoing and supportive to me. I can't believe how petty you've become, how positively bourgeois. If the world were run by people like you, Vinny, no one would ever aspire to perfection in writing, or in art or music. They'd all be too *embarrassed*. Here I am, just trying to use what talents I have to assist a creative soul in an entirely honourable and friendly way, and all you can do — ' She was winding herself up into a fine state of self-righteous outrage. 'For all you know,' Pamela spat, 'with a little help from me, Jonathan could become the best young British novelist of the decade!'

'No,' Vinny said.

'What d'you mean, no? What do you know about it?'

'He's not working on a novel at all.' Vinny said. 'He's a scientist. He's writing a book about water.'

Pamela looked deflated. 'How do you know?'

47

'I asked him this morning.'

'But you can't write a whole book on water. What is there to say? Apart from the fact that it's wet and there's usually too much of it, or too little.'

'Exactly,' Vinny said, seizing an unexpected opportunity. 'So I was trying to stop you from backing a loser.'

'Well, why didn't you tell me all this in the first place?'

'I was having trouble getting a word in edgeways!'

Pamela smiled ruefully and extended a hand across the table to give one of hers a squeeze. 'Well I do admit that's a bit of a setback,' she said.

'I'm sorry,' Vinny said, 'it's disappointing for you.'

'Yes, well,' Pamela rallied herself and got to her feet. 'I think I'll go out anyway,' she said. 'I need to do some shopping. Want to come?'

'I won't, if you don't mind,' Vinny said. 'I've got some weeding to do.'

'Right then. See you later.' She picked up her handbag and her driving glasses. 'Where are my damn keys?'

'Over there, on the dresser.'

'So they are.' Pamela went into the hall to put her coat on. ''Bye.'

Vinny finished her soup slowly. I seem to have painted myself into a corner, she thought. How am I going to tell her about giving Jonathan a lift and buying him lunch? Especially if I'm intending to do it again. I'll just have to keep

48

quiet. With a bit of luck she'll lose interest in him now she knows he isn't a novelist. Let's hope so.

Next morning before Vinny left for the library, the garage phoned Pamela to say that her car was ready, so she drove off at once to collect it. Vinny went to work as usual, aware all day that Jonathan might telephone her. She rather hoped he wouldn't. Then when going-home time eventually arrived and he hadn't, she mostly felt relief, but also a twinge of disappointment. The road to Hembrow was partially flooded in places after the heavy rain they'd had. Vinny drove with extra care and arrived back at their house feeling tired. She went inside to find Pamela sitting at the kitchen table and pregnant with news.

'You'll never guess what?'

'What?' Vinny said.

'I called in at The Prospect this morning and found a FOR SALE notice outside it!'

Vinny frowned. 'Really?'

'Yes, really. And I've decided there's only one possible thing to be done — I'm going to buy the place myself!'

3

Pamela hadn't intended going anywhere near The Prospect when she'd gone out that morning to collect Gertie, but on the way home she decided on the detour just to make absolutely sure that she was now running as smoothly as the garage man had promised.

The sky looked very black and thunder began to rumble overhead as she reached the network of little roads across the levels. Then a vivid flash of lightning was followed immediately by a crack of thunder. The storm was directly overhead and now the rain was beginning in earnest. It slammed down on the roof above her head and streamed down the windscreen in an instant torrent. Pamela had to concentrate hard on where she was driving, not easy even with the wipers on full speed. Huge lakes of water were already gathering in dips where the road had subsided, sending up great bow waves as she cruised through. The visibility had shrunk as the thundercloud closed in, and all around her the lightning discharged itself to earth with searing brilliance.

Pamela thought, I know rubber tyres are supposed to protect you in a car, but it feels bloody dangerous to me! Maybe I should find shelter somewhere?

★ ★ ★

Jonathan read and reread the letter that had arrived in the post from the Environment Agency. It was couched in terms that were so obscure as to be almost unintelligible: *Due to the prevailing economic climate we are obliged to rationalise our property holdings* . . .

The meaning soon become very clear, however, when a man appeared with a large yellow FOR SALE sign and proceeded to erect it in his garden.

He was at first perplexed and then stricken with anxiety at the choice before him. As a tenant he had two unappealing options; to go and live in the alternative accommodation the EA were offering — a bedsit in town — or to use his own initiative and find somewhere else to live. Although it would be convenient for the library if he were to move into Otterbridge, he couldn't bear the claustrophobia of a flat, let alone all that traffic noise and disturbance. And anyway, he now had a regular lift from here all set up, so that wasn't a problem any more. As to finding somewhere entirely new to rent, he wouldn't have the first idea how to go about it. He'd got The Prospect organised through the friend of a colleague at work whilst he was still in Africa, but he had long since lost their address. Anyway he'd got used to it here. He liked the quiet nothingness of his surroundings. He liked the proximity of the pumping station. He liked his regular talks with George. He didn't want all the disruption of moving, especially now that the book was going so well.

He had switched off his computer at the first

distant rumble of thunder and now he stood by his study window watching the storm as it travelled eastwards, allowing his mind to drift, and wondering what would happen if lightning were to strike Amber Junction and start a fire. He speculated about the pumping station failing altogether during a flood, and tried to estimate how many hectares of land would be inundated and to what depth.

A bolt of lightning fizzed down almost audibly and the crack of thunder followed it so closely it made him jump. His desk light flickered and then went out. It came on again briefly and then went out again. Now, in his enforced break from work, he couldn't even make himself a cup of tea!

He walked across to the front window to see whether the back edge of the storm was yet visible. The sky was clearing to the north-west and already the rain was easing off. The yellow sign below was rocking in the wind. Then he saw the lights of an approaching car and watched as a white four by four slowed down and stopped in his lay-by. Someone poked an umbrella out of the door and opened it before emerging under its shelter. Then whoever it was walked rapidly across his bridge and hammered on the door. Oh well, never mind, he thought. I can't work anyway. He went downstairs and opened the door onto the still-dripping porch.

'Jonathan,' the woman said. 'I've just seen the sign! What is going on?'

Short, greying hair, wearing dark green and red in stripes . . .

'It's Pamela,' she said, 'Pamela Wood, surely you remember?'

'Oh yes.'

'Well, can I come in? It's filthy weather out here!'

He stood aside and followed her into his kitchen.

'I just happened to be passing,' she said, sitting down on the chair he always used. 'And I thought to myself, What on earth will happen to Jonathan when the house is sold? Who is your landlord anyway?'

'The Environment Agency.'

'And have they asked you to leave?'

'Yes.'

'So where will you go?'

'I don't know.' He felt helpless and stood there with his elbows close to his body, and his hands drooping.

'Oh you poor dear,' Pamela said, jumping to her feet. 'Look, you sit down here and I'll make us both a nice cup of tea. OK?'

'There's a power cut,' Jonathan said, clicking the light switch to demonstrate, but as he did so the electricity came on again. 'Oh, good.'

'Sit down, then.' He reclaimed his chair and watched her as she located the kettle, put water in it and set it on the electric ring to heat. She picked his two mugs out of the sink, rinsed them under the hot tap and put them upside down to drain. 'Now then, where do you keep your tea?'

'In that cupboard.'

'Oh I see, you use bags.' The kettle boiled and

she made the tea in the two mugs. 'And where's the fridge, for the milk?'

'Haven't got one.'

'Fine,' Pamela said, 'we'll have to have it black then.' She plonked it down in front of him. It looked very dark.

'No, that's too strong,' he said.

Pamela said something like 'Tuhhh!' and snatched it away again to pour it down the sink. Then she got out a new teabag and began again. 'Say when,' she said.

'Stop!'

Pamela moved a pile of papers off the other chair and sat down opposite him, pushing his mug of tea towards him. 'But, getting back to business, this new development must be very difficult for you,' she said. 'Couldn't you simply go home to your parents for a while?'

'No,' he said.

Pamela frowned. 'Now I know it's not really my business,' she said, 'but I do feel concerned about you. How are you managing to live here? Do your family finance you? I mean, you can't be earning money from your writing yet?' Jonathan wondered which question to answer first, but before he could say anything, she spoke again. 'I don't expect you've ever had a proper job, have you?'

'Yes of course I have!' He was indignant. 'I've been working in southern Africa for the past eleven years on the problems of water supply in arid regions. I'm employed by the aid organisation Waterway.'

'Oh I see,' Pamela said. 'And you've saved up

54

enough money to live on while you write this book. Is that it?'

'Yes. I've taken a sabbatical year to do it.'

'So you must be an expert on drought?'

'I'm an expert on water.'

'Right. So, how's the writing going?'

'Very well.'

'I've always thought I should write a book too, you know. I've led such an interesting life!'

Jonathan couldn't think of any possible reply to this, so he said nothing.

Pamela sipped her tea, pulled a face and put it down again. 'Having to move house just now will be very distracting for you?'

'Yes.'

Pamela glanced round the kitchen. 'I can't imagine who is going to buy this place anyway,' she said. 'It would need so much work on it to make it even halfway habitable. I suppose someone might take it on and do it up for use as a holiday cottage — someone interested in nature and that sort of thing?'

Jonathan drained his tea and put the mug down with a thump. Now that the electricity was on again, he was keen to get back to work.

'Hey!' Pamela suddenly burst out, making him jump. 'I've just had a thought. Why don't I buy it?'

'But you've already got a . . . '

'Buy it, do it up and let it to *you*,' Pamela said. She was smiling all over her face.

'You mean, I could stay here?'

'That's what I'm saying, yes. Then you'd be able to finish your book in peace and when you left, I could let it out to people for holidays and get an income from it. I came into some money recently, you see, and these days property really is the only safe place for it. So that would suit both of us, wouldn't it?' She got to her feet again. 'You'd better show me round,' she said, 'so I can see exactly what I'm getting myself into! Is this the sitting room through here?' She went in and walked straight over to the window. Jonathan followed her. 'My goodness,' she said, 'It's very close to the river, isn't it? I see you've been digging the garden. It's a bit long and thin, but I suppose one could make something of it. Oh and we'll need a shed too; somewhere more suitable to keep your bicycle.'

She led him upstairs to the east room: 'You can see Glastonbury Tor from here,' she said, 'how lovely! This is a bedroom of course but I see you're using it as a study. There's no doubt it's a lovely peaceful spot for a writer.'

And the west room. 'So this is where you sleep? Isn't it dreadfully uncomfortable with just a mattress on the floor?'

And back to the bathroom between them. 'Oh dear, that's the trouble with these old enamel suites, they do chip so badly.'

And then downstairs again. 'Well it's small, but I expect it's all you need, living alone?'

'Yes,' he said, edging her towards the front door.

'I do hope the storm is over by now,' she said. 'I have to admit it was rather alarming. I could barely see where I was driving! But from your perspective I suppose you think we should be grateful in this country not to be short of water?'

'Oh yes, absolutely,' Jonathan said, forgetting his need to get rid of the woman in his eagerness to impart some important facts to a willing ear. 'In Europe you've got about four thousand and sixty-six cubic metres per person per year, but of course it varies within the region. Some areas of Spain have far less.'

'Well . . . '

'And did you know that water is the only substance whose solid form is less dense that its liquid one?'

'No, I can't say I . . . '

'This is what makes all aquatic life possible, even at the poles. The ice floats and the creatures live in the free water beneath. If it was the other way around, they'd all freeze to death.' He smiled triumphantly.

'Yes, I see . . . '

'And did you also know that over a billion people in the world have no access to clean drinking water?'

'No, I can't say I did,' Pamela smiled. 'You're a veritable walking encyclopaedia!'

Why did people always say that? he wondered. 'Are you laughing at me?'

'Not at all. I'm just surprised that you can carry so many facts and figures in your head.'

Where else? 'Why?'

'Well I can only speak for myself,' Pamela said, 'but my memory isn't that good.'

'It's probably your age,' Jonathan said. 'I've had to learn not to tell people over fifty more than three facts at a time. It's all they seem able to grasp.'

'Yes, well . . . Moving swiftly on . . . ' She felt about in her handbag and produced a small gold address sticker. 'This is where I am if you need me.' She put her hand on the door latch. 'Now, the first thing for me to do, is to get in touch with the estate agent and find out the asking price. Then if it's reasonable, I'll get back to you. OK?' And she opened the door and went out.

Jonathan relaxed. Most people were unfathomable, and this woman seemed no worse than some. If she was going to be the means whereby he could stay put, then he supposed he might even come to tolerate her.

★   ★   ★

Amanda Overy was determined that if anyone was going to take home-made scones along the road to Jonathan, it should be her and not her mother.

'Don't you stay pestering him, mind,' Gwen warned. 'He'll be busy writing that book of his.'

''*Course* not. Do me a favour!' Mandy arranged the scones inside a biscuit tin and put the lid on.

'And don't forget you've still got that homework to do.'

'I know.' She took the full tin up to her bedroom and left it on the bed while she checked herself in the mirror. The slit she'd made in one knee of her jeans was beginning to fray in a satisfactory manner. Her trainers had a stripe in them the exact pink colour of her crop top, and her stomach looked well flat. She peered more closely at her face and the new mascara. She'd do. She pursed up her mouth and blew a kiss at her reflection. Then she went downstairs again, slipped on her leather jacket, put the tin into her tote bag on the handlebars of her bike, and pedalled off.

It had been a miserable March so far and this afternoon was no exception. The wind whipped back her open jacket, raising instant goose pimples on her midriff, but it would never have occurred to Mandy to do up the buttons. That would be uncool. Instead, she imagined herself living in a hot country with unlimited sun, delicious tropical fruits and leisure unlimited . . . Anything would be better than naff old Somerset where fuck all ever happened.

She swerved the bike so that she could keep kicking a discarded coke can along the road in front of her, imagining that it represented the bullies at school — that's for you . . . and you — and then thinking about Jonathan. When he had moved into The Prospect all by himself nearly three months ago, she'd been fired up at once and determined to make him notice her. It was the first time in living memory that there had been a lad that fit, living this close. But now, suddenly his house was for sale and there was every chance that he'd have to leave. And so far she'd got nowhere with him! Why couldn't he see how much she fancied him? She liked his curly hair and his weird coloured eyes and the way he rode his bike without a helmet, just like her. At first she'd wondered how old he was, but then what did it matter? Age was nothing.

She wished she could leave school *now* and get on with her life. Jonathan was lucky. He'd be flying to Africa, travelling the world, helping people. Mandy wanted to go with him. She gave the can one final hard kick so that it lifted up and fell into the rhyne where it bobbed and floated. Or we could go by boat, Mandy fantasised, and sail round the world together, walking on deck in the moonlight and drinking champagne . . . Then the pedal came round and whacked her trailing foot painfully on the back of the ankle.

But The Prospect, as she approached it, still looked romantic. She could see Jonathan out in his garden bending over, working on something. Her fingers tightened on the grips in nervousness. So far, she had to admit that her conversations with him had been deeply disappointing. Her mother reckoned he was shy and Mandy supposed that must be it. I need to see him more often, she thought, so he can loosen up. But how can I, if he leaves? She went through the ideal scenario in her head as she approached:

I'd go: '*Brought you some scones.*'

And he'd be like: '*Wicked! Thanks.*'

And I'd go: '*I'm really sorry you're being chucked out. Where you going?*'

'*No idea, at the moment.*'

'*You could come and stay with us.*'

'*Oh, no, that'd be well out of order.*'

'*It'd be no trouble. Really.*'

Then he'd smile all over his face, and he'd be like: '*Well, if you're sure? That'd be well good. You've just saved my life!*'

★ ★ ★

In spite of Pamela's promises, Jonathan had felt too frazzled to work. Instead he was digging his vegetable garden, even though he might not be able to stay there long enough to harvest anything. The soil was heavy and he sweated under his thick jersey, but the rhythm and earthy neutrality of the manual labour quietened his mind and soothed his anxieties.

Then he glanced up and there she was, cycling along the straight road towards the house — George's daughter — yet again! She always seemed to be there, hanging about outside his house. She cycled past twice daily anyway, on her way to school, but never straight past. She always seemed to find an excuse to stop and accost him and he had no idea what it was she expected, nor had a clue how to speak to her. He just wished she would leave him alone.

'Hi,' she called, across the rhyne. 'I've got some scones for you.'

'Oh, good.' He liked scones.

'What are you doing?'

'Digging.'

'Well I can see . . . Where shall I put these then?'

'By the front door.' He stuck the fork into the ground and went to meet her as she came over the footbridge. 'D'you want the tin back now?'

'No it's OK. I can collect it any time.'

Bother, he thought. That means she'll have to come again.

'Is it sold yet, the house I mean?'

'Might be. There's some woman interested in it.'

'What's she like?'

Impossible question. 'She made me take her to Amber Junction late on Thursday night to get some diesel from George, for her SUV,' he said. It was the only memorable thing about Pamela that he could think of.

'You're kidding? My dad told me about her and her 'friend'. Couple of old dykes, I reckon. She nearly killed me on the road, you know. Snobby old cow, mutton dressed like lamb.'

Why was she suddenly talking about *livestock*? 'I don't know.'

'So why the fuck does she want to live here?'

'She doesn't. She wants to rent the house to me.'

'Oh, that would be great! But . . . I don't get it. What's in it for her? Don't tell me I've got it all wrong and she fancies you?'

Jonathan shrugged.

'Oh no. You and her aren't . . . you know . . . Are you?'

Jonathan didn't understand the question. 'I've got to finish my digging,' he said, 'before it gets dark.'

His words had an extraordinary effect on Amanda for some reason that he was quite unable to fathom. She slammed down the tin she was carrying onto the doorstep, bawled at him,

'But that is so gross!' and then rushed away across the footbridge. She grabbed her bike and rode it off down the road, pedalling furiously and without a backward glance.

Jonathan watched her progress with some astonishment. Then he shook his head and thought, Well with luck it might discourage her from coming back. And he went over and picked up his fork again.

⋆   ⋆   ⋆

Pamela spent that afternoon and the following morning on the telephone to Mr Booty her solicitor, and to the estate agent. She was on the *qui vive* lest someone else should already have staked a claim to The Prospect. Then, over the next few days once her modest offer had been haggled over and finally accepted, she lived in fear of being gazumped. Not that anyone in their right mind would want to buy the house in its present state, but you never knew. Pamela felt irritable at having to wait for other people to do the job in their own way and at their own pace, and was impatient to be in control again. She had great plans.

The house would have to be gutted of course, an archway made between kitchen and sitting room, and those dreadful metal windows taken out. The roof needed repair, and some under-pinning and damp proofing was also required plus a new white bathroom suite and some form of central heating — presumably oil fired? — before any redecoration could be done.

Then there were various essentials she would have to buy: garden shed, washing machine, fridge-freezer, microwave, television, maybe even a dishwasher? It would be pricey, no doubt of that, but after Jonathan had left to go back to Africa she would be able to rent it out for holiday letting at maybe four hundred pounds a week, or more. It would also be a pleasant little business to run. Pamela could see herself driving down there each Saturday morning with fresh linen and a pint of milk for the new arrivals, perhaps with a small bouquet of flowers from her garden to welcome them in . . . No children or dogs, naturally; professional people only.

She would be obliged to move Jonathan out temporarily of course, whilst the work was in progress. He'd have to come and stay with them for a bit. There was plenty of space in the attic spare room for him and his computer, and it would be an excellent opportunity to get to know him, and perhaps to break through the barrier of his reserve?

Pamela did hope that Vinny wouldn't be difficult about this. She wouldn't have to interact with him much anyway, being away at the library most days. It was hardly an imposition. It'll be fine, she thought. Vinny will see reason, for my sake.

At lunch however, Vinny had other ideas. 'Why on earth do you want to saddle yourself with a second house?' she demanded.

'It'll be an excellent investment,' Pamela said, 'property prices being what they are.'

'But it needs so much doing to it, and how will

you ever get it done with Jonathan there? He needs peace and quiet to get on with his book.'

'I'm sure we can sort something out.' Pamela was adamant.

'I thought you'd given up on his writing, with him not being a novelist after all?'

'On the contrary. Non-fiction is far more prestigious. You only have to look at his father!'

Vinny frowned. 'So, what did you tell Jonathan?'

'Simply that I plan to buy The Prospect and would be delighted if he'd stay on as my tenant.'

'And what did he say?'

'Oh, first of all he gave me a whole catalogue of facts about water. He's certainly a strange young man, but he's relieved of course. I think he was worried about having a new landlord but as he already knows me, that won't be a problem.'

'Mmm,' Vinny said. 'And you'll charge him rent?'

'A modest amount, yes. One that will just about cover my expenses. He certainly couldn't afford the peak-time holiday rate, but I've told him that's OK with me. I don't want to upset him whilst he's in this vulnerable position.'

'What position?'

'Being a writer, what else? He needs support, not exploitation. My reward will be to know that I'm fostering his talents.'

Vinny stared at her with one hand over her mouth.

'There's no need for mockery,' Pamela said sternly. 'I'm also planning to give him some help with his social skills, while he stays with us. After all, if he's going to be a successful author he'll need to be able to express himself more fluently.'

'He's staying *here*? Thanks for consulting me in advance.'

'This is my house, Vin. It won't be a problem, believe me.'

'And what does Jonathan think about it? And how's he going to write if you're in the house all day?'

'I hope, at my age, that I know how to behave.' Pamela was indignant. 'Anyway, I shall be out at my committee meetings a lot of the time. And when I am home, I shall take him up coffee every now and then, but I certainly shan't interfere. Do give me some credit.'

'But why can't you wait until he's finished the book and gone, before you start work on the house?'

Pamela frowned. 'I can't have a tenant of mine living in such squalor,' she said, 'when we're so comfortable. It wouldn't be ethical.' Vinny was silent. Pamela smiled victoriously. 'Come on Vinny, since you've got the afternoon off, let's go out somewhere nice, and maybe take tea with friends on the way home. Yes?'

★ ★ ★

Later in the week, Jonathan rang Vinny at work and asked her to take him to the library again, but this time for the whole day. As they drove towards Otterbridge together, Vinny struggled with conscience versus loyalty. Should she tell

66

Jonathan what was in store for him with Pamela? Should she warn him off; urge him to find somewhere else to rent? It was a ticklish situation. But then again, how could she, without being horribly disloyal? She'd just have to stick to generalities.

'Perhaps I should explain a little bit about Pamela,' she began, staring straight at the road ahead as she drove. 'She's a tremendous enthusiast. Once she gets an idea into her head, she can be very determined; won't take no for an answer. She tends to rush in where angels fear to tread and grab the bull by the horns. But then, once she's burnt her bridges, it can all go dreadfully wrong. I wouldn't want you to be caught up in that sort of upheaval, just when you're in the middle . . . ' She risked a quick glance in his direction. 'If you see what I mean?'

Jonathan was frowning. 'I haven't the least idea what you're talking about,' he said crossly.

Vinny blushed with embarrassment. 'Forget it,' she said quickly. 'It's none of my business anyway. Sorry.'

'People keep talking to me about animals,' Jonathan said. 'You about bulls, and George's daughter about lambs. It makes no sense at all and it's very irritating.'

Vinny seized the opportunity to change the subject. 'Oh, you know Mandy then?'

'She keeps pestering me. That's annoying too.'

Vinny smiled. 'I expect she's got a crush on you.'

'What d'you mean, crush?'

'I mean, she probably thinks you're an

67

attractive man, of course.'

'But she's only a child!'

'I don't believe age is very important in these matters.'

'Oh really? Do you think I'm attractive too, then?'

'Well, yes of course . . . that is . . . ' Vinny felt herself reddening still further. 'That's not the sort of question you're supposed to ask,' she said.

'Why not?'

'Because it puts a person on the spot; makes them feel silly.'

'I can't see why.' She could feel him looking searchingly at her. 'You're not silly,' he said. 'Not silly at all.'

When they arrived at the library, Vinny told Jonathan the time she had to leave at the end of the day. 'You'll be here then, won't you?' she said. 'I don't want to be late home.'

'Yes, that's fine.' And off he went.

It turned out to be a good morning for Vinny. There were no awkward customers, no time wasters, no complainers, no vandals, not even a frown.

'Have you noticed, Cheryl,' she said to a colleague just before lunchtime, 'how pleasant everybody is for a change?'

'It's not them,' Cheryl said, 'it's you. Every time I see you today you're grinning from ear to ear. Now, if I didn't know any better — '

'Vinny,' Jonathan said, appearing unexpectedly at the desk and interrupting her. 'It's my turn to buy you something to eat. Shall we go?'

'Mmm,' Cheryl said with a rising intonation in the middle. 'Say no more!'

'Oh,' Vinny was flustered. 'Well, I — '

'Go on,' Cheryl said. 'You're only five minutes early. I'll cover for you.'

★ ★ ★

'I should like to be friends,' Jonathan said to Vinny, 'if that's all right with you?'

The importance of friendship had been impressed upon him many times by his parents and others. And now he was settled in this new area, he felt that he really ought to make an effort in that direction. Of course George was his real friend, whom he could talk to on a satisfyingly technical level, but Vinny would be very useful too, especially since she was gay. She would pose no threat at all, in a sexual way, so there would be none of the usual misunderstandings and complications, which he invariably encountered where women were concerned. She also seemed willing to interpret the rest of the world for him, which was a very large point in her favour. Except of course for this morning, when her conversation had suddenly degenerated into nonsense. Perhaps she'd been speaking in metaphors? He always had trouble with those.

They were sitting at a table in a café eating their lunchtime sandwiches. Vinny was smiling at him in what he hoped was an encouraging way, so he was emboldened to say it.

'I should like to be friends.'

'Lovely,' Vinny said. 'I'd like to be friends with you too.'

'Oh good! That's settled then. We'll have to see each other regularly.'

'That's fine with me.'

'This morning,' Jonathan said, 'you were talking about angels. You don't really believe in the supernatural?'

Vinny laughed. 'Oh no,' she said, 'that was just a figure of speech.' She took a bite of her sandwich and chewed it.

He was relieved. 'Oh that's good! But next time, would you explain to me what you mean by them? I've learnt quite a few metaphors and similes over the years, but they still catch me out. I've even tried understanding syllepsis and zeugma too, but I find that sort of thing very confusing. It's so much easier when people say exactly what they mean, don't you think?'

All Vinny could recall from her days as an English student, was one example of zeugma: *She left in a Hackney carriage and a flood of tears*. Or was that syllepsis? She couldn't remember. So how did a scientist like Jonathan know anything at all about such obscure grammatical terms? He was extraordinary! She found herself wanting to know more about him, eager to discover the things he could do, as well as those he had trouble with. Perhaps she'd already assumed too much? She took a sip of water, and hoped he hadn't thought she'd been in any way patronising.

'Well, I suppose figures of speech make what we say more colourful, more *fun*,' she said.

70

'But the purpose of language is to communicate, isn't it? Not to have fun.'

'If we're going to be friends,' Vinny said, smiling, 'then I shall expect you at least to make an attempt at wit.'

'You mean humour?' Jonathan pursed his lips. 'I find Mr Bean and Fawlty Towers very funny and I do like some jokes, but others I can't understand at all. If I asked you the definition of the word 'joke', what would you say?'

'Well shall I tell you one that amuses me, first?' Vinny said, 'just as an example. Let me see . . . oh yes, this one's in the form of a Japanese haiku — you know, a short poem that has to be exactly the right length. It goes like this: *To express one's self*
In seventeen syllables
Is very diffic —

Vinny stopped and then raised her eyebrows at him.

Jonathan hesitated. 'Is that it?'

★   ★   ★

Vinny got back to her desk at two pm to be greeted by an alert Cheryl. 'Nice lunch?'

'Yes thanks.'

'So, what's his name then?'

'Jonathan.'

'Jonathan eh? Very nice.' Cheryl looked impressed. 'So, what did you talk about, if it's not a rude question?'

'Oh it's not rude at all.'

71

'What then?'

'He asked me to explain why jokes are funny,' Vinny smiled. 'Hard work, but in fact one of the best conversations I've had for ages.'

'Bloody hell,' Cheryl said. 'Hark at you! Not only is he a looker, but he's clever as well, eh? Will you be seeing him again, then?'

'Oh yes, almost certainly.' Vinny couldn't prevent her expression from betraying her satisfaction. Not only did she have a new friend, but all of a sudden and by no effort of her own, she seemed at last to have acquired a degree of credibility with at least one of her workmates. Life was definitely improving.

4

Jonathan was sitting at his computer and typing:

The river water we use today will be replenished, but used groundwater may be gone forever. Much of the water in huge underground reservoirs, such as the ones beneath the Sahara desert or the American high plains, is tens of thousands of years old. Over-exploitation or 'mining' of resources like these can destroy the aquifers, and this accounts for some of the shortages . . .

when he was disturbed by the arrival of the white four by four and Pamela.

'Yoohoo! Anyone at home?' she called from the bottom of his stairs. 'I'm just going to measure a few things down here. Don't worry about me, I shan't disturb you.'

Hell! Jonathan thought. What was I going to put next? He sat there, growing more and more resentful of the interruption until finally in disgust he went downstairs to make himself a coffee.

'Oh good,' Pamela said, appearing at the door with a clipboard and pen in one hand. 'I hoped I'd catch you in a coffee break. Perfect timing, eh? D'you know, the more I look round this place, the more potential I find.'

Potential for what? It was just a house. It kept the rain off him and his books and ensured him a place to sleep and write. What more did it need to do, or be? Jonathan said nothing.

'I do have your best interests at heart you know. Mind if I — ?' She put the kettle on again and washed up a mug for herself. 'I can quite understand that you need peace and solitude, and I guarantee not to infringe that.' It was his *special* mug! Jonathan, with difficulty, controlled the urge to snatch it out of her hands. Pamela reached for the jar of coffee and took a heaped spoonful. 'Oh, and by the way I've brought you some dried milk stuff. It makes black coffee almost drinkable.' She produced another jar from her bag and spooned out some of the white powder. 'Anyway, all I want in return is a small weekly rent and maybe just a brief mention on the acknowledgements page of your book, when it comes out. Nothing excessive.' She poured on the boiling water, cleared a space for herself, and sat down. 'I've a son a few years older than you,' she said, 'so I do understand what your needs are, and that privacy is paramount.' Then she stopped stirring her coffee and gave him a full-on smile.

Jonathan looked away quickly. He supposed he could do worse. The EA's proposed bed-sitter in Otterbridge would have meant sharing a bathroom with four unknown people. That would have been unendurable.

'You don't say much, do you?' Pamela asked.

'No.'

'I'd have thought that a little gratitude might not go amiss.'

He looked up again to find her staring at him.

Something was clearly expected. He ran through his repertoire of hard-learned phrases, and came up with one that he hoped was appropriate; suitably modified of course, so that it made more sense.

'I can thank you enough,' he said.

Then, without much expectation of success, he tried studying her expression to divine whether that was what she wanted, or not.

'Yes, well,' Pamela said. 'We shall have to work on that one, shan't we? Time I was off.'

The minute she had got up and gone, and before he could sigh with relief, he suffered yet another interruption.

'Just came to collect the cake tin,' Mandy said. 'I saw *her*, leaving.'

'Yes, thank goodness,' Jonathan said.

'Oh, I thought you liked her? Have you fallen out?'

'Out of what?'

'You know, had a row? She's far too old for you, you know.'

'Don't be silly,' he said. 'There's no fixed age for a landlady to be.' Was now the right moment to explain his attitude to her? He decided to do it anyway. 'Look Amanda, you must stop coming to see me. I'm not sexually interested in children in general, and especially not in you. All right?'

'I'm not a child!' To his consternation, she burst into noisy tears. 'And I wouldn't be seen DEAD having sex with you anyway, so there!'

He held out the tin, which he had been keeping just inside the front door in order to get rid of her as quickly as possible, but she smashed it out of his hands with a force that surprised him. Then she rushed out, and he could still hear her crying as she cycled away.

Jonathan took a deep breath and closed his eyes. Then he went upstairs and turned the taps on until the bath was three-quarters full, took all his clothes off and immersed himself in the healing hot water. And only then did his heart rate begin to slow down.

I think I need help, he thought, as his face broke the surface and he began to breathe again. I'd better phone Vinny.

★ ★ ★

George's shift was just ending when Mandy rushed into the pumping station, red in the face and tear-stained. 'Hey, come on love, what's the matter?' He held out his arms and gave her a cuddle. 'Tell your old dad, eh?'

'It's nothing,' but she went on crying into his overalls.

'Well it must be something. Someone upset you, is that it?'

' . . . Yes.'

'Who then?'

'That Jon-a-than . . . '

'Jonathan? What's he done then?'

'N-nothing.'

George held her a little away from him so that he could see her face. But he read nothing from it. 'Come on, love, you can tell me.'

'No . . . can't say.'

'Tell 'ee what, you go home directly, Mand. I'll

76

go and have a word.'

'No dad, there's no need . . . '

'We'll see about that. Off you go, now. Go on.'

George jumped into his van, reversed it at speed and drove the short distance to The Prospect. He didn't bother parking in the lay-by, but stopped in the middle of the road and began hooting. Then he jumped out and shouted, '*Jonathan!*' several times as loudly as he could manage.

One of the upstairs windows opened and Jonathan himself leant out.

'Hello George. Is something the matter?'

He wasn't wearing anything! As far as George could see, which wasn't anything below the waist, Jonathan was stark naked. George's concern turned instantly to disgust and fear. He felt sick. He couldn't believe the evidence in front of him. But he knew straight away that a good belting wasn't going to solve this one. There were important things to be done and no time to lose.

'You just wait . . . ' he managed to shout. 'I'll get you. You see if I don't.' Then he jumped back into his van, did a bungled four-point turn and sped off homewards again.

★   ★   ★

Pamela had spent the morning doing voluntary work at Elm Lea House, her local old people's home, and was now driving home feeling rather smug. She had assisted in marking the clothes of those individuals who had no family to do it for them, and she had exhausted two whole marker pens, but she had made a *difference*. Maybe that was all one could hope for in this life?

As she drove, she was thinking about Jonathan and the possible ways in which she could transform his life as well. She was beginning to wonder whether there might be more to his reticence than mere shyness; a form of social phobia perhaps? He was a very attractive young man, no doubt of that; good bone structure, a neat nose and striking coloured eyes. A little on the thin side, and not as tall as some, but there was potential there and a decent haircut would help.

She wondered whether he had any other trousers than the khaki combats he had been wearing every time she had seen him so far. Come to that, he seemed to have very few possessions at all. Pamela had never really considered minimalism until now, but if it meant that a person had the freedom to up sticks and live anywhere in the world at a moment's notice, then perhaps there was something to be said for it?

I have so many 'things' she thought, that I suppose I've always taken for granted. But what would it be like to need so little? Maybe I could get through to Jonathan better if I made some effort to meet him half way? Perhaps I should sell Gertie and get a more modest car? I could also wear my clothes for two years instead of one. And only buy black or beige shoes so that they would go with everything.

She drove up the hill towards her house. But

first, she thought, before I go completely minimalist, I shall have to do up The Prospect and kit it out.

★   ★   ★

Vinny was working in the garden. It was sunny and still for a change, with barely a cloud in the sky. Above her a pair of buzzards were soaring on a thermal and mewing as they circled higher and higher. She had just seen the first Brimstone butterfly of the year. It was a perfect spring day. Vinny moved her kneeler further along the edge of the flowerbed and lowered herself onto it again, daisy-grubber in one hand and wheelbarrow close by.

'Ha!' Pamela said, coming down the path. 'What are you up to, then?'

'Weeding,' Vinny said, and managed not to add, Isn't it obvious?

'Well, I've done an excellent morning's work. It was just like getting Peter ready for boarding school — although of course in those days we had name-tapes to sew on — but P WOOD would have been a great deal quicker to write than some of the ones I've had to do today. Would you believe it, the woman with the most clothes at Elm Lea House is called Scholastica Rodney-Stoke! So I had to compromise and write S R-STOKE. Just hope the poor old girl won't notice. She's a lot less gaga than most.'

'Oh, well done,' Vinny said, hoping that a little genuine enthusiasm would cancel out some of the irritation with Pamela which niggled at her a

79

great deal too often these days. The outside telephone bell began to ring. 'I'll go,' she said, getting to her feet and running indoors. 'Hello?'

'Vinny?' It was Jonathan.

Vinny looked quickly over her shoulder to check that Pamela wasn't right behind her. 'How did you get this number?'

'I rang the library and a woman called Cheryl gave it to me.'

'She did?'

'Yes. She said she wasn't supposed to, but she reckoned it was about time you had some happiness in your life. What did she mean by that?'

'No idea,' Vinny said hastily.

'Well anyway, it's handy you've got the afternoon off, because I need to talk to you about something.'

'About what?'

Pamela appeared at the door. Vinny shook her head, to indicate the call was not for her.

'George's daughter. She's acting very strangely and I don't know what to do. Will you come over to see me?' Pamela was still within earshot.

'Well, I could come in I suppose, yes.'

'What d'you mean, 'in'?'

'Don't worry,' Vinny said. 'I'll be there.' And she put the phone down.

'You're not going back to the library, surely?' Pamela asked.

'Sorry,' Vinny said. 'There seems to be a problem of some sort.'

'They take you far too much for granted,' Pamela said. 'It's really not fair. Perhaps you should consider working somewhere else?'

Vinny was busy washing her hands and cleaning soil from under her nails. 'Mmm.'

'So, when will you be back?'

'Not sure, but it won't take very long, I shouldn't think.' Vinny dried her hands and collected up her shoulder bag, her coat and her car keys. 'See you soon.'

Do I feel guilty about deceiving Pamela? Vinny asked herself as she drove away down the hill. No, I don't. It just feels necessary. Then she thought, I must have words with Cheryl!

It was warm enough to drive with the car window half-open. Vinny savoured the breeze round the back of her head as she drove, and wondered what Mandy had been saying to Jonathan this time. Poor girl, Vinny thought. I wouldn't be at all surprised if she fancies him. I'm just pleased that it's me he's turned to for advice. She looked out at the passing countryside as she went. The blackthorn was now out, coating the hedges thickly with white blossom. We'll be due for a cold spell again, any minute, Vinny thought; the usual blackthorn winter. I wonder if Jonathan knows anything about the natural world, or whether he's just fixated on water? I wonder if he ever gets bored? It must be a lonely life.

But when the mini turned the corner onto the straight road that ran past The Prospect, Vinny saw that this time he was not alone. Parked in the lay-by outside his house was a white vehicle and as she got nearer, she saw that it was a police car. She stopped the mini behind it and was just getting out, when the front door opened and Jonathan was led out struggling to throw off two policemen, one on either side of him, who were holding him by his forearms. He looked pale and frightened. The policemen side-stepped awkwardly over the bridge and then marched him briskly across the road.

'What's happening?' Vinny called. 'Jonathan?'

'I don't know.' He looked ready to weep.

Vinny appealed to the nearest policeman. 'But, what's he supposed to have done?'

'Sorry, can't divulge that.'

'So where are you taking him?'

'Otterbridge nick. In you go.' He put a flat hand onto the top of Jonathan's head and propelled him into the back of the panda car, slamming the door behind him.

'But I must come too,' Vinny began, starting forwards. 'I'm his friend, and he'll need help. You see, he's — '

'Sorry.' The other policeman cut her short.

'But can I drive myself there and wait?' Vinny felt desperate.

'Well we can't stop you, but it may be a long one.' Then they both got in, and drove off.

Vinny felt winded with shock. She looked helplessly around for several seconds. Then she got back into her car and made for Otterbridge.

There was nowhere to park outside the police station so she was obliged to go to the nearest multi-storey three streets away, and walk back. When she got inside, there was no sign of Jonathan, but Vinny did see a man she recognised. George Overy was sitting in the waiting area looking anxious.

Something must have happened to Mandy, Vinny thought. But Jonathan can't be responsible, surely? But then again, why did he ring me? She approached George diffidently, not knowing quite what to say. 'Hello.'

'Who're you?'

'Vinny Henderson, remember? We have met, but I expect . . . um . . . could you tell me what's been going on? D'you know why Jonathan's been brought in?'

'Course I do.' George glared at her. 'And it don't bear repeating. If you knows what's good for you, you'll keep well away from he from now on.'

'But what's he supposed to have done?'

'There's no 'supposed' about it. Ask them.' He gestured towards the open hatchway where the Duty Sergeant was standing.

Vinny went across. 'I'm a friend of Jonathan Crankshaw's,' she said. 'Can you tell me why he's been brought in here?'

'Suspected assault on a minor,' the man said.

'What kind of assault?'

'That's all I can tell you at present.'

'But will he need a solicitor? Can I phone someone?'

'He'll be given the option if he's charged.'

'But, can I still phone?' She got out her mobile.

He shrugged. 'It's a free country.'

Vinny went back to the front door and stood just outside, pressing buttons automatically. 'Pamela? It's me. I'm at the police station in Otterbridge.'

'I thought you were at the library?'

'Yes, well I . . . oh never mind all that. I'll tell you later.'

'Is something wrong, Vin?'

'They've arrested Jonathan, and they won't tell me what for, except that he's supposed to have assaulted someone.'

'*Jonathan?* Are you sure?'

'Well of course I'm sure!'

'But . . . hang on a minute. What's this got to do with you?'

Vinny sighed. 'He rang this morning while we were in the garden.'

'But you told me that was the library!'

'No, actually I didn't. You just assumed it.'

'Well you certainly didn't say that it wasn't!'

'Look Pamela, can we do this later? I'm really worried about Jonathan.'

'And I'm worried about you, Vin. This really is no way to behave.'

'Oh look, forget it. I shouldn't have phoned.' Vinny was about to switch off her mobile.

'No, wait! Who's Jonathan assaulted then?'

'I think it must be Mandy Overy, because her father's here. But I don't know for sure. I can't believe — '

'But she's only a child!' Pamela interrupted her. 'That would be paedophilia!'

'Don't be ridiculous. Jonathan wouldn't hurt anybody!'

'I'm not talking about *hurting* anyone, Vin, but isn't it just possible that he might have tried it on with her? He is a man, after all.'

'How can you even think such things?' Vinny

hissed furiously, looking around to make sure she wasn't being overheard.

'Come on,' Pamela said, calmly. 'The police don't arrest people without any reason, you know. My friend Keith, the Chief Constable, always says . . . '

'*Please* Pamela, not now!'

'All right, Vin. Calm down. And don't worry. I'm sure it will all sort itself out. And on reflection, you're probably right. Now I think about it, Jonathan strikes me as the sort of man who has very few carnal urges. Wouldn't you agree?'

'No,' Vinny said shortly.

'Well make your mind up. You can't have it both ways. Are you OK? D'you want me to do anything?'

'No . . . It's all right, Goodbye.'

Vinny went back in and chose a chair on the other side of the room from George, who didn't look up. And there she sat, trying to take her mind off her annoyance, firstly with herself for automatically turning straight to Pamela, and secondly with her, simply for being *Pamela-ish*. What did she expect?

Vinny needed to clear her mind and concentrate her energies on Jonathan. What if he didn't know what was going on? What if he didn't understand the charge they were making against him? What if *they* thought the replies he made to questions were self-incriminating, when they weren't? He needs help, she thought, but I don't have enough information to be able to do anything. I can hardly go up to the man at the desk and say, 'treat him gently, won't you, because he's rather vulnerable, and different from most people.' That would immediately make them think that he was mad, and therefore bound to be guilty. And I'm sure he can't have assaulted Mandy although he's undeniably strange, and there was some sort of a problem between them . . . I wish I knew what it was that makes him behave as he does. I need a definite medical diagnosis. If only I could say something like, 'He's got Down's syndrome, so he'll need professional help.' Then they'd understand, but he hasn't. I don't even know if there is something officially wrong with him. I don't know what to *do*.

After what seemed a long time, a policewoman led George away down a corridor and they disappeared through a door, but then nothing further happened. Vinny watched the hour hand of the clock on the wall, progressing between the numbers in a series of tiny jerks.

★   ★   ★

Vinny seemed to have been here for hours, and had already glanced through the magazines and looked at all the notices on the walls. People came in and went out without speaking. The air smelt stale. The ceiling could do with a fresh coat of paint. How could anyone work in a place like this, with no windows?

Eventually when she had nearly given up hope of ever moving from this sticky plastic chair, two things happened one after the other. Doors

86

opened and then George, a woman — presumably his wife — and their daughter were walking towards her along the corridor. Mrs Overy came first with her mouth tightly pinched, looking straight ahead, and followed by George and Mandy. Mandy's face was red with crying and she walked along with her eyes cast down, supported by George's arm round her shoulders.

'It was a mistake,' she was saying. 'I just want to go home. I shouldn't of . . . I didn't mean it. I'm sorry.'

'That's as maybe,' George frowned. 'Can't trust them loners though; not normal are they? No, there's more to it, bound to be.'

Vinny had started to rise as they approached, but they went past without looking at her, and out through the main doors. She bounded over to the desk. 'What's happening?' she called. The Duty Sergeant had his back to her, drinking a mug of tea.

'Eh?'

'Jonathan Crankshaw. Is he being charged?'

'I'll see if I can find out for you.' He picked up the phone.

Vinny could feel her heart beating much too fast. The palms of her hands were sweating.

'You're in luck,' the policeman said, smiling at her at last. 'Released without charge.'

'Ooohh . . . ' Vinny held onto the counter with both hands and as she did so, Jonathan came into view, walking towards her. Vinny ran up the corridor and threw both arms around him in a hug. 'I knew you hadn't done it,' she said. He felt stiff and awkward in her arms so she let him go, and stood back to study his face. 'Are you all right?'

He was frowning. 'They said I had sexually assaulted Amanda,' he said. 'And they went on saying it, even though I *told* them I hadn't. I don't think they can be very intelligent.' Vinny found herself laughing immoderately. It must be the relief of it all. 'It wasn't funny,' Jonathan reproved her.

'I'm sorry. I'm just so glad it's turned out all right. Let's get you home now.'

Once they were in the car and out of Otterbridge, she said to him, 'So what was it that you wanted to talk to me about, when you rang earlier? That was something about Mandy, wasn't it?'

'Yes, it was. She keeps on pestering me; turning up at my house when I'm trying to work. She did it again this morning, and I thought I would explain to her why I didn't want to see her. So I did.'

'What did you say?'

'That I don't have sex with children, and certainly not her.'

'Oh I see,' Vinny said. 'You softened the blow then?'

'What?'

'Never mind. I was attempting irony.'

'Better not do that,' Jonathan said. 'It only causes confusion.'

'Yes, well, seriously, it sounds to me as though the only real mistake you made, was to put the idea into her head in the first place. Then what happened?'

'Well I said that, and then she suddenly started howling and crashing the cake tin about, for no reason at all. So I wanted to ask you why she would do such things?'

'I don't know. Maybe she felt very hurt and rejected and seized upon the idea to get her own back on you.' Jonathan frowned. 'She wanted you to find her attractive,' Vinny explained gently, 'so she was very upset when you said what you did. It was too blunt, too hurtful.'

'So what should I have said?'

'Oh, I don't know. Um . . . maybe that you're flattered by her attention, but you're afraid you can't reciprocate because . . . '

'But I'm not flattered at all! That would be a lie.'

'Yes, but sometimes you have to pretend things in order to spare another person's feelings. For example . . . you can't feel the way she does, because you've already got a girlfriend, say.'

'But I haven't.'

'No, but she doesn't know that, does she? And it's the kindest reason you could have for spurning her, because it doesn't mean that you find her unattractive.'

'But I do! And who could I say was my girlfriend, anyway?'

'How about me?' Vinny smiled at him.

'Well that's no good, is it?' Jonathan said at once, 'because you're *gay*.'

Vinny tried to stop herself from recoiling from this. She felt wounded, and far too awkward even to begin to explain that he'd got it all wrong. She gripped the steering wheel harder and tried to speak reasonably. 'Even if I was,' she said, and had to pause to clear her throat, 'it would be irrelevant because Mandy wouldn't know that either, would she?'

'She told me that you and Pamela are dykes,' Jonathan said. 'I looked it up in the dictionary, but it said a dyke (spelt with either an i or a y) is a trench or ditch. So she can't have meant that.'

Vinny was silent. She felt ready to burst into tears. It's the tension, she told herself. It's been a bloody awful afternoon, and I'm simply stressed-out. I'll just get him home, and that'll be the end of it.

'The police kept asking me about having a bath,' Jonathan suddenly said. They tried to tell me that it was an abnormal thing to do in the afternoon. Why would they say that?'

'When did you have this bath?'

'After George's daughter left.'

'You immediately had a bath? Why?'

'Well it's obvious. It's the best way to relax. I always do it if someone upsets me. It's comforting. I like water, especially when it's warm.'

'So, how exactly did Mandy upset you?'

'She said she wouldn't be seen dead having sex with me. That's called necrophilia isn't it? It's a disgusting idea, so naturally I felt bad.'

'And this is what you told the police?'

'Well of course. It's the truth.'

'Yes I see.' The innocence of the man touched Vinny's heart. She felt sudden concern for him; a worry about how he could possibly cope alone, everyday and without guile, in this impatient and unsympathetic world. She patted his knee soothingly.

'Why did you do that?'

Vinny glanced at him for a moment and then back again to the road ahead. 'I don't know. I suppose it's a gesture of friendship and solidarity.'

'Well, would you please not do it? I don't like being touched.'

'Oh.' Vinny took a breath. 'I'm sorry. I'll try to remember that in future.'

'Good,' Jonathan said.

They drove the rest of the way in silence and when they arrived at The Prospect, Vinny decided not to go inside.

'I am so glad to be back here,' Jonathan said, getting out of the car. 'I'm right in the middle of a really important bit of the book. I'll probably need to go to the library again next week.'

'Well you'd better ring me nearer the time,' Vinny said. 'But not at home, OK?'

'Why not?'

'Because Pamela will be cross if you do.' She looked up at him. Jonathan was smiling, but not at her.

'Yes, she is a bit bossy, isn't she?' Then he pushed the car door shut and walked away across the bridge to his house.

Vinny turned the mini round. I have a choice, she thought. I can give up on Jonathan now, simply because he's a self-centred, graceless, emotional and social cripple. Or I could decide to weather all his put-downs and go on doing my best to help him; perhaps do some research to discover what it is that makes him behave as he does. But have I got the stamina for that? Do I even want to try?

The sun was low in the west and shining into her eyes, despite the visor. Vinny was pleased to get to the end of the straight road and be able to turn away from its glare. Maybe I'll emulate Jonathan and have a good hot soak, she thought. But first, what am I going to say to Pamela?

★　★　★

Pamela had spent most of the rest of the afternoon telephoning people to solicit or offer information. Her Chief Constable friend, Keith, had been amiable as always but was disappointingly non-committal about Jonathan's case.

Next, she tried Directory Enquiries for Jonathan's father's number, but as she had no idea where he lived, apart from a generalised guess at London, this was unproductive. She telephoned the TV company, which made his popular series about buildings, but met with an adamant refusal. So then she rang a friend whom she knew was interested in architecture, to get the name and address of the company which published his books. Furnished with this, she phoned them and asked for Adrian Crankshaw's home number.

'No, I'm sorry. I can't give you that.'

'But I have important news about his son Jonathan, that I'm sure he'll want to hear. He's in trouble, you see. I must speak to him!'

'No, we don't divulge our authors' personal details, but if you wish, you can leave your name and number. Then it will be up to Mr Crankshaw whether or not he contacts you.'

Pamela grudgingly supposed that this was better than nothing. But then she felt obliged to wait within earshot of the telephone for as long as it took, however long that might be. And he still hadn't got back to her. It is surprising, she thought, how ungrateful people can be. It never ceases to amaze me. She went into the kitchen. Vinny had been a long time in coming home too. When she does, Pamela thought, she's got some explaining to do.

There was a scrunch of gravel outside as the mini drew up. 'Oh good,' Pamela said to herself, putting the kettle on. 'About time too.' Vinny came in, plonked her bag down on the dresser, and flopped onto a chair. She looked exhausted.

'Well?' Pamela said, 'what's happened?'

Vinny leant forwards with her head almost touching the kitchen table. 'They didn't charge him in the end. It seems Mandy made the whole thing up to spite him, because he wasn't romantically interested in her.'

'Well!' Pamela exclaimed. 'Fancy that! But on reflection I'm not a bit surprised. That child is quite out of control. I blame the parents. That Overy man is clearly far too soft with her.' She frowned. 'But now I want to know why it was that you got involved in all this, when it was clearly *me* that he was trying to contact in the first place?'

'Tell you about it later. I'm going for a bath,' Vinny said.

'Tell me now.'

'No!'

'Well there's no need to snap my head off!'

'I'm sorry. I'm worn out. OK?'

The kettle boiled, and Pamela went to take it off the hob. She felt aggrieved. So, when the telephone rang, she answered it rather crossly. 'Pamela Wood.'

'Ah, hello. My name's Tancred Burden. I'm Adrian Crankshaw's agent. I believe you have a message for him?'

'Oh!' Pamela perked up at once. 'Well of course I was hoping to talk to him personally, because what I have to say is very confidential.'

'Well he's asked me to speak to you on his behalf. I gather it's about his son Jonathan?'

'Yes it is. Of course I couldn't divulge to you the exact nature of the offence he was arrested for, except to say that it was very serious. But I'm happy to be able to tell you that it's now all been resolved, and the police have released Jonathan without charge.'

'So he's all right?'

'Well he's fine *now*, but considerably upset of course. But luckily we were here to help him. We're great supporters of his, you see. We have faith in him and in his book. As it happens, I'm in the process of buying the house he's currently living in and I have great plans for it, which will guarantee Jonathan a very comfortable standard of living. In fact we're great friends. So if Adrian would like to hear news of him at any time, would you tell him just to give us a call? We'd be delighted to help in any way we can.'

'All right. I'll tell him.' And he put the phone down.

A bit abrupt! Pamela thought, but I suppose that's what one should expect. He must have to fend off so many gormless fans. But I think I may have penetrated the armour. I believe there's a pretty good chance that next time someone phones it might well be the famous Adrian himself.

5

'So, why didn't you tell me at the time that it was Jonathan on the phone?' Pamela demanded next morning, 'And more to the point why didn't you let me talk to him?' She was not going to let it drop.

Vinny took a breath. 'I thought he wanted to ask me about something else,' she said.

'Like what?'

'A lift to the library.'

'Why should he?'

'Because I've given him one before.' Vinny looked uncomfortably red.

'You never said!'

'No, well I thought you'd . . . '

'You wanted to keep him all to yourself. That's it, isn't it?'

'Not at all. He's just got no transport and it seemed the logical — '

'Don't you trust me any more? Well, don't you?'

'Yes of course I do. Honestly Pamela, it was no big deal.'

'But he could have asked you over the phone. You didn't have to go rushing down to his house. Come on Vinny, let's have the whole story.'

'He said he needed some advice about Mandy, if you must know.'

'What, and I couldn't help with that?'

'I just thought that two of us might be rather overpowering.'

'You mean you thought I'd be.'

'Well, yes, actually.' Vinny raised her chin defiantly.

'I'm disappointed in you,' Pamela said. 'I can't tell you how much. We've always had such trust and honesty in our friendship. How can you jeopardise something so precious?'

'I'm sorry,' Vinny began. 'I didn't mean — '

The telephone rang and Pamela turned her back to answer it. 'Pamela Wood? Oh, hello Mr Booty . . . Yes . . . On Thursday, good. Thank you so much for the recommendation.' 'Bye.'

She turned back to Vinny. 'The survey's booked for The Prospect,' she said.

'That's good.'

'It certainly is. So now I'm going down there to tell Jonathan, and normally I'd ask you to come too since it's your day off, but under the circumstances . . . '

Pamela set off, still upset by Vinny's deceit. She's changed, she thought, become harder and a lot more bloody minded. I wonder why?

It had been foggy earlier but only a low layer of it remained, down on the moor below. At her house up at Hembrow, a thin March sun was shining and, looking down, Pamela could see the tops of the trees as they emerged soggily through the grey blanket of cloud. Pamela steered Gertie down the steep hill and turned on her lights as they descended into the murk. I'm glad I don't live down here, she thought, with all this lying damp, and of course it's even worse in the autumn. But as she progressed along the back roads towards Jonathan's house, the mist lifted

97

and with it, Pamela's mood. It should be about six weeks until we exchange contracts, she thought, and then a week or so until completion and then I can actually start transforming the place. She savoured the prospect of spending a tranche of Aunt Kate's legacy; creating something really stylish out of a wreck, with a view eventually to having a nice little earner, to say nothing of saving Jonathan and putting him firmly onto the right track at the same time.

Pamela began to sing, '*If I cain't take it with me when I go, I jest ain't gonna go . . .*'

But The Prospect when she arrived was all locked up. Pamela peered through the downstairs windows but saw no sign of his bicycle. Damn, she thought, how dare he be out when I need to see him? If only I could just telephone him when I need to. I really can't traipse down here all the time on the off chance he'll be in. I must investigate the cost of getting a proper BT line put in, but in the meantime, I suppose I'll have to buy him a mobile. It'll have to be the cheapest kind, pay as you go. I just hope and trust he's going to be suitably grateful for all the trouble I'm taking over him. She looked up and down the road again.

'Oh good, here he comes now.'

Jonathan was cycling towards her. Pamela waved, and then waited by his front door until he'd walked the bike over the bridge and leant it against the porch.

'Jonathan,' she began, 'Hello. I came to tell you that my surveyor will be coming here on Thursday to give the house the once over. You will be here . . . ?' Then she noticed that he was looking very upset indeed. 'What's the matter?'

He put his key in the lock and opened the front door without replying. Pamela followed him into the kitchen. 'What's wrong?'

He slumped down on his chair and rested his elbows on the table. 'George doesn't want to see me ever again,' he said. 'I don't understand why. I went down to Amber Junction as usual and he said I'd got a nerve and then something silly about no fire without smoke. What does that mean?' He wasn't looking at her.

'Oh dear,' Pamela said, 'but I'm afraid it's to be expected, you know. These peasants are simple creatures and mud does tend to stick.'

'What mud?' He now looked exasperated. 'George is my friend. You mustn't speak of him like that.'

'Oh pardon me!' Pamela said. 'And far be it from me to try to tell you who your real friends are, but I think you'll find that George Overy won't be one of them from now on.'

'But he's my *best* friend.' Jonathan sniffed fiercely.

'Coffee or tea?' Pamela asked. 'A cup of something will make you feel better.'

'No it won't.' He covered his face with his hands.

It was like talking to a child. 'Look, I'm sorry about George,' she said more kindly. 'I can see that it's upsetting for you, but I expect it will all blow over eventually. That little madam, his daughter, will forget about it soon enough, don't you worry.'

'But I didn't do anything to her.'

'No, of course you didn't.'

Jonathan raised his head. 'I always tell the truth,' he said. 'Why are you and Vinny the only ones who believe me?'

'Well of course I can't speak for her,' Pamela said rather crossly, 'but in my case I put it down to experience.' She smiled. 'I rather pride myself on my understanding of human nature, as a matter of fact.' She pulled a tissue from her pocket and handed it to him before going across and putting the kettle on. 'Well I'm going to have a coffee anyway, so I'll make you one too.' Then she had a sudden thought. 'Did George threaten you at all?'

'He called me a pervert and said I ought to be thrashed. And he said he's not the only one around here who thinks like this.'

Pamela made a snap decision. 'Right, well drink this up as quickly as you can. I don't think we should take any chances. We don't want you lynched after all, do we?'

'What d'you mean?'

'I think you should come over to Hembrow and stay with us for a while — bringing all your computer stuff of course. It needn't be for long; just until we're quite sure that there won't be any repercussions.'

'But, why should there be?' Now he just looked confused.

'Well, local people can get quite angry about this sort of thing.'

'Even though nothing happened?'

'Well you can't be too careful.'

Jonathan leapt to his feet and began pacing up and down the kitchen. '*You can't be too careful,*' he repeated. 'What the bloody hell does that mean? Of course you can be too careful. For example, I could build an impenetrable fortress to keep angry people away from me. That would be 'being too careful', but everyone knows that's ridiculous. So what's the point of you saying it? It doesn't make any sense, and it certainly doesn't help.'

Pamela put her mug down and backed away a little towards the door. 'Well you're not meant to take it literally,' she said. 'It's just an expression people use. It means that it's sensible to take precautions, that's all. Look Jonathan, you'll have to come and stay with us anyway, once I've bought the house and the building work begins. So why don't you just think of it as a trial period.'

★   ★   ★

Vinny relaxed gratefully onto the sofa after Pamela had gone. She wondered how Jonathan was now, and felt concerned that he might be suffering from some form of delayed shock after the events of the day before.

Perhaps Pamela will sort him out, she thought. Maybe I should leave him to her? I'm sure he'll tell her where to go, if he wants to.

The telephone rang, and she reached for it. 'Hello?'

'Oh, hello. My name's Crankshaw. I'm Jonathan's father. I believe you rang my agent?'

The imperious voice was familiar from *Skyline Design* on ITV.

'Oh!' Vinny tried to collect herself. 'Well . . . actually . . . um . . . '

'So what was it you wanted to say to me?'

'Well . . . I think it must have been Pamela who rang you, but I'm afraid she's out at the moment,' Vinny pulled herself together. 'It was me though who was with Jonathan when he was arrested, so can I help at all?'

'Thank you, yes. My wife and I were a little concerned about him, you see. Is he all right? But more to the point, what was he being accused of?'

'Assault,' Vinny said, 'He's fine now, although I think he was very alarmed and confused at the time. It was a local girl — well more like a child really — who claimed he'd assaulted her.'

'What, sexually?'

'Yes, I'm afraid so. It wasn't true of course, but I think she felt slighted by him.'

'Oh dear, not again,' he sighed.

'It's happened before?'

'He's got himself into quite unpleasant misunderstandings with women before, yes. Poor old Jon; he's never been the most intuitive of boys, but he really hasn't an ounce of malice or lechery in him, believe me.'

'Oh I do!' Vinny said at once. 'I'm . . . we're, very fond of him. But don't worry, he's quite all right now. The police aren't going to take it any further and, as for Jonathan himself, I believe he's gone straight back to writing his book.'

'His book? Well, I'll believe that when I see it.'

He sounded amused.

'No honestly, he's written a lot,' Vinny protested. 'He comes to the library with me and does loads of research.'

'I suppose it's about water?'

'Yes, it is.'

'Well, if it keeps him out of mischief, so much the better. Look, Mrs — er — '

'Miss Henderson. Vinny Henderson.'

'Mrs Henderson. Thank you so much for taking an interest. His mother was rather concerned naturally, but now I shall be able to reassure her. I should be grateful though, if you were not to mention this call to my son. He's very keen to be independent these days, you see.'

'Oh, but what if there's another problem in future?' Vinny put in quickly, fearful that he was about to hang up. 'Could you give me your phone number?'

'Best get in touch with Tancred,' he said, 'like you did before. Thanks so much. Goodbye.'

''Bye.' Vinny put the phone down. '*Keeps him out of mischief!*' she said aloud in disgust. Then thought, Oh hell and damnation! I should have asked him what's actually wrong with Jonathan, whilst I had the chance. Not that he seems unduly concerned; it's almost as though he's ashamed of having a son with some kind of disability, so he tries to make light of it. The patronising bastard!

She got up to make herself a cup of coffee and while she was waiting for the kettle to boil, another thought came to her, which made her smile. So, now we know. Pamela secretly phoned the great Adrian Crankshaw but didn't get to speak to him. How very remiss of her not to have told me anything about it.

After she'd drunk her coffee, Vinny busied herself in the kitchen making lentil soup for their lunch. As she chopped onions, carrots and celery into neat cubes, she wondered about Jonathan's relationship with his father, and wondered if he'd always been a disappointment to him. Poor Jonathan, she thought. No wonder he's screwed up.

She tipped the cubes into a heavy-bottomed saucepan with some oil, and stirred them absently as they sizzled. He seems to need someone to interpret the world for him, she thought; someone who is both sensitive and intuitive. She added a dash of curry powder and a touch of dried coriander. A voice in her head mocked her: 'And you're leaving him to Pamela?'

'No of course I'm not,' Vinny said aloud. 'It clearly has to be me.'

★ ★ ★

'Ha!' Pamela said, coming into the kitchen. 'Lovely smell. Is there enough for another one?'

'Yes, I'm sure there is,' Vinny said. 'Oh, it's you, Jonathan, how nice to see you.'

'I probably won't be here very long,' Jonathan said.

'Long enough to eat a bowl of soup, I hope?'

'He's come to stay for a while,' Pamela explained. 'Just in case of any unpleasantness down at his place.'

'Oh?' Vinny frowned.

'Tell you about it later,' Pamela said. 'Now then, Jonathan, will you have bread with your soup, or toast?'

'Toast,' he said, 'and butter.'

'*Please*,' Pamela said firmly.

'Eh?'

'Toast and butter, please.'

'Do sit down,' Vinny interrupted as she placed two slices of bread under the lid of the Aga. 'I hope you're hungry?'

'Yes, I am.'

They sat opposite him as he wolfed down two large bowls of soup and four pieces of buttered toast.

After lunch, Pamela left Vinny with the washing-up, while she showed Jonathan to the fourth bedroom in the attic, and supervised him as he carried up a bag of his things, plus the various components of his computer.

'There's a double power-point here,' she showed him. 'And another one there, and I thought this table and chair would do as a desk. What d'you think?'

'It's all right,' Jonathan said.

Pamela decided to begin on his re-education in earnest. There was no time like the present. 'If you'd put yourself out for someone,' she said, 'and they said that what you'd done was 'all right', what would you think?'

'That it was all right.'

'You wouldn't be disappointed that they weren't more appreciative?'

'No.'

'Well, I'm afraid that's not good enough.'

Jonathan sighed. 'Go on then, if you must,' he said. 'Tell me what I've said wrong.'

'Ah, so you do realise that it wasn't entirely appropriate, then?'

'Not really, no,' Jonathan said.

Pamela persisted. 'Well, it would have been better to say that the table is very nice and that you're grateful to me for taking the trouble to help you.'

'It's a bit low, actually.'

'It's *Georgian*.' The ingratitude of some people! 'You'd better get yourself sorted out, and we'll see you downstairs later on. OK?'

'OK.'

Pamela went down to the kitchen. 'Can I help?'

'Well timed,' Vinny said, emptying the bowl of greasy water down the sink. 'All done.'

★　★　★

Vinny decided to wait to tell Pamela about Adrian Crankshaw's phone-call until after Jonathan had gone to bed and was safely out of earshot. But Pamela knew her too well and soon sensed she was holding something back.

'What is it Vin?' she asked.

'There is something I've got to tell you in private,' Vinny admitted, 'but not here.'

'What?'

'Later,' Vinny said.

'Tell me now.'

Jonathan appeared in the doorway. 'We should

have brought my bike,' he said. 'How am I going to be able to go where I want to?'

'Don't worry,' Pamela said. 'We'll cross that bridge when we come to it.'

'What?'

'Don't *worry*.'

Jonathan went upstairs again, looking annoyed. Vinny collected a cloth and a spray-can of Pledge and followed him out. She went into the sitting room, and she was busy dusting, when Pamela slipped in, closing the door firmly behind her.

'Well?' she demanded.

'Oh, Pamela, it's nothing dramatic.'

'So tell me.'

'It's just that Adrian Crankshaw rang while you were out.'

'Shit!' Pamela was red in the face with resentment. 'That really is sod's law. So, when can I ring him back? You did get his number of course?'

'He wouldn't give it to me. Said I could phone someone called — um Tristram — I think it was — his agent — if necessary.'

'*You*? And it's Tancred, not Tristram.'

'Ssshh! I'm sorry, Pamela. I did tell him you were out, but he didn't seem bothered who he talked to.'

'But, he did ask for me by name?'

'No, I'm afraid not.'

'Well!' Pamela exclaimed in disgust.

'So, don't you want to know what he said?'

'Go on, then.'

'He wanted to know what had happened; said

he and his wife were 'a little' concerned, and then told me not to mention that he'd phoned to Jonathan, because he 'wants to be independent'.'

'Adrian does?'

'No, Jonathan of course. So you mustn't tell him, Pamela. I promised not to.'

'Can't think why not.'

'Because it's between them; none of our business.'

Pamela sniffed. 'So, what else did he say? Was he interested in what we're doing for Jonathan?'

'Not at all, and he thinks his book is a waste of time. He came across as a rather unpleasant person, to be honest.' One thing I'm definitely not going to tell her, Vinny thought, is that Jonathan has been in trouble before. She really doesn't need to know that.

'Did you talk to him for long?'

'No, hardly any time at all.'

'Well, that explains it,' Pamela said. 'What a pity I wasn't here. I'm sure I would have been able to draw him out. Such a fascinating man. It really is too bad.' She began to hunt about for her keys. 'But I mustn't hang around. I've got a committee meeting about the Farmers' Market in half an hour.'

'Haven't you forgotten something?' Vinny asked, 'apart from telling me what the trouble was, down at The Prospect, that is.'

'No, I don't think so.'

'You didn't for instance think to mention that you'd got in touch with this Tancred person in the first place.'

'Slipped my mind,' Pamela said carelessly.

Vinny fixed her with a look. 'What?'

'Nothing. I just hoped the words 'trust' and 'honesty' might spring to mind.'

★ ★ ★

A week later over breakfast, Vinny watched from the sidelines as Pamela told Jonathan how to write his book.

'You want to achieve maximum sales,' she said, 'so you'll have to aim for the popular approach. It needs to be readily accessible to the general public. Now, we were watching this documentary on TV last night when you were working, weren't we Vin?' she said, glancing in her direction. 'And it mentioned some river in China which has actually started running dry before it gets to the sea.'

'The Yellow River,' Vinny said.

'Yes, and about the nations that control the um — '

'The headwaters.'

'Stop it, Vinny! — The headwaters, being able to hold the lives of all the people downstream to ransom, by stealing all their water. It was fascinating.'

'You said you were bored rigid by all the over-hyped predictions of imminent eco-doom,' Vinny put in crossly.

'I did not! Anyway, it gave me a wonderful idea for a title for your book; one that you probably won't have thought of.'

'It's called *Water*,' Jonathan said.

'Oh that won't do at all; far too bland. It's so

vitally important you see. But I do believe that *Water Wars* says it all. It's nice and arresting — short but punchy — the sort of thing that would draw your eye in a packed bookshop.'

'Or library,' Vinny murmured.

'It's not that kind of book,' Jonathan said, buttering toast. 'I'm a scientist, not a journalist.'

'But popular science books are very *in*,' Pamela said, 'as I'm sure you realise. And they can attain cult status if you play your cards right. Just look at the success your father's had! Now, would it be any help if I read through your manuscript so far?'

'No,' Jonathan said. He helped himself to marmalade. 'It wouldn't.'

Vinny smiled inwardly. Pamela wasn't accustomed to people saying exactly what they thought without apology or explanation. It would put her on her mettle. Jonathan's directness was not something she could wilfully misunderstand.

'As a proofreader, of course,' Pamela said. 'I wouldn't presume to correct the science, naturally.'

'No,' he said. 'I'm going to finish it first.'

'And will you, soon?' Vinny put in.

'Not as soon as I'd planned.' He sighed. 'At the rate I'm going, I'll have to take more than a year off from work.'

'Will your boss mind?' Vinny asked.

'That's not the worry; money is. I've only estimated for twelve months, and I doubt my funds will last for much longer.'

'No problem,' Pamela said at once. 'I'm sure

we can help you there.'

We? Thought Vinny.

'I could let you have The Prospect rent free, if you like?' Pamela suggested. 'That's if the sale goes through as expected, of course. You can pay me back later, out of the royalties you get for your book.'

'There may not be any royalties,' Jonathan said.

'Of course there will,' Pamela said archly, 'when you're the second famous Crankshaw! Of course we'll have to keep financial records, but that's straightforward enough. So, what do you say?'

'I'm not sure.'

'Well, you think it over,' Pamela said, pouring herself another coffee. 'And when you have, I'm sure you'll see that I'm right.'

Why is she being so hasty? Vinny wondered. It's as though having been thwarted over Jonathan's book, she's determined to get her own way somehow. And why help him to this extent, anyway? She barely knows him . . . unless of course she sees him as a kind of substitute son, to fill Peter's absent place. I do hope not.

★ ★ ★

'Coffee!' called Pamela cheerfully next day, as she opened the door of Jonathan's room and interrupted him in the middle of a complex argument.

He held up his hand as if to protect himself. 'Wait.' Then he swiftly typed half a dozen crucial

111

words on screen, to capture its essence. Pamela never just brought coffee. Her very presence was enough to delete, at a stroke, an entire subdirectory of memory files from his brain.

'Those trousers are almost out at the knee,' she observed. 'Why don't we cut them off and make them into shorts for the summer?'

Jonathan took the mug of coffee from her. 'If you did that, I'd be cold now.'

'But, you've surely got more than one pair of trousers?'

'No.'

'But how do you *wash* them? I can't imagine . . . ' she stopped. 'I think we should go into Otterbridge this afternoon and buy you a couple more pairs. You must have one on, and one in the wash at the very least!'

'Can't,' Jonathan said, turning back to his keyboard. 'I've got to write.'

'Well I'll get you some then. What's your waist size and leg length?'

'Dunno.'

'Back in a minute.' Pamela left, and then reappeared with a tape measure in half that time. 'Stand up. Right.' She put both arms round his waist and drew the tape round to the front. He recoiled involuntarily and had to grab at the chair for support. It was true; he did need more clothes. He held his breath and stood there stiffly. 'I knew you were too thin,' she said. 'Now for the leg. You'd better hold it there,' she pressed one end of the tape into his hand at his groin, and got down on her knees on the carpet. 'And I'll measure it here, just

112

above your shoes. Right, let go. That's done.' She coiled it up again and stood up. 'Now, do you have any preference as to what sort of trousers you'd like? Jeans? Cords? Combats again?'

'Yes, I want them just like these ones.'

'Well I'll see what I can do. Anything else; shirts, underpants, socks?'

'No.' He just wanted her to go.

He waited until she was out of the room before sitting down again. Despite the prompts on the screen, he'd completely lost his train of thought. He was desperate to be back at The Prospect where he could live his own life. He'd never intended to stay here for so long. Eight days! But whenever he mentioned going home, Pamela would alarm him with stories of mobs breaking the windows or painting anti-paedophile slogans on the door, or even actual physical attacks.

Of course it wasn't all bad here. It was very pleasant to have meals cooked and washing done, and a decent sized table to work on, but he fretted about not being able to keep to his essential routine. He liked to get up at seven o'clock exactly, to begin writing at eight, to stop and work in his garden at four in the afternoon and to go to bed promptly at ten-thirty. He had always been accustomed to sleeping effortlessly, but these days . . . He thought, I'm drinking too much coffee.

★ ★ ★

'It's time we had a dinner party,' Pamela said to Vinny. 'Who shall we invite? I thought, our usual five. What d'you think?'

'How about Cheryl as well?'

'From the library? No, I really don't think so, Vin. I'm planning this evening very carefully; call it Jonathan's introduction to society, if you like. I think Cheryl's a little too down-market.'

'Oh,' Vinny said. 'Now I see it all. You want Sue to psychoanalyse him, Polly to give you a medical diagnosis, Ron to draw up a legal document, Arthur to stretch his poetic horizons, and Gordon . . . well, to be truthful, I can't see any actual function for Gordon.'

'Stop it, Vinny! They're our friends. You're fond of them; you know you are.'

'But you do admit you want some moral support with Jonathan?'

'Well yes, I suppose I do. You have to agree that he's rather hard work. Anyway, are you coming with me to buy him some trousers?'

'Yes, OK.'

They set off together in Gertie in bright sunshine, but were soon running through brief but heavy rain.

'April showers,' Vinny said. 'Isn't the cherry blossom wonderful at this time of year?'

'Ours is the best,' Pamela said. 'I'm going to cut some sprays of it for the big vase, and have it as a centrepiece on the dinner table. And maybe some in the sitting room too.'

In the big store in Otterbridge, Pamela led the way to the men's department and began to hold up various trousers for Vinny's agreement.

114

'He says he wants them to be the same as the ones he's already got,' she said, 'but that's rather unadventurous, isn't it? These jeans look good, or what about these?'

'No, they've got to be brown,' Vinny said.

'Why?'

'Because that's the only colour he wears. You must have noticed?'

'Oh, that's nonsense, surely? Look, these are exactly the right size.'

'Well, just as long as you keep the receipts safely. And don't say I didn't warn you.'

They emerged with three pairs in a bag, one of them brown, and on the journey home, Pamela began to confide in Vinny about her concerns for Jonathan.

'Do you find him difficult?'

'In what way?'

'Well, try as I might, I can't seem to get through to him. Have you noticed, he never says 'please' or 'thank you' or laughs at jokes. And he'd rather lecture you than converse in a normal manner. And he can be astonishingly tactless . . . '

'I think he's just honest to a fault.'

' . . . And he's obsessive about routine. He just doesn't seem to inhabit the same planet as the rest of us.'

'He does seem to be missing a whole chunk of normal human emotions,' Vinny agreed. 'I wish we had a name for his condition; something to get to grips with.'

'He's not mentally handicapped,' Pamela felt adamant. 'I'm quite sure of that. He just needs help. After all, sociability is something we can all learn.'

'Not if we have no theory of mind,' Vinny said.

She's showing off her book knowledge as usual, Pamela thought.

'So, what's that when it's at home?'

'It's the ability to understand that another person can think differently from yourself; to be able to imagine being in someone else's shoes. Having the capacity for empathy, in other words.'

'Oh, but everyone has that.' Pamela brushed the idea aside. 'It's surely the essence of being human? It's what distinguishes us from the animals.'

'Mmm,' was all Vinny said. I do wish sometimes that she'd have the courage of her convictions, Pamela thought, and disagree with me properly. It's so *feeble*.

'I don't think it will do any good, you demanding that he say 'please' every time,' Vinny said. 'He doesn't seem able to learn from it.'

'Well he's going to have to try. I'm schooling him in certain phrases to use when they all come for dinner. You'll see.'

★　★　★

The following Saturday evening Vinny, (pink from the Aga) and Pamela, (perfumed and elegant from her dressing table) were waiting for their guests to arrive. Jonathan was still working upstairs.

'Perhaps I should have bought him some smarter trousers to wear, when we went back to

116

change those other two for the brown ones,' Pamela said, 'and a nice white shirt and a tie?'

'Pointless,' Vinny said. 'Don't worry, he'll be fine.'

'I do hope he won't be rude to anyone. Gordon tends to be a bit intolerant of the young.'

'Gordon's intolerant, full stop.' Vinny said.

'Well, if you'd lost your seat in parliament after thirty years, and your wife to cancer, both within a couple of years, so would you be,' Pamela said. 'Poor man, he needs our indulgence.'

'And cheering up.'

'Yes, well you're good at that, Vinny dear. Jonathan is my problem. I've been encouraging him to ask questions, draw people out — have you noticed he never does that — and getting him to take an interest in other people's lives; appreciate how they look, and notice how they're reacting to what's being said. In other words, to give and take gracefully. I really do believe that no one's helped him in this way before. Oh, there's someone at the door.'

★ ★ ★

'Jonathan?' Vinny called up the stairs. 'Everyone's here. Are you coming down?'

He rose to his feet with great reluctance. The only reason I'm joining this dinner party, he told himself, is because it's past suppertime and Vinny's cooking is very good.

She was waiting for him at the foot of the stairs. 'Don't worry,' she reassured him. 'All of

117

them are great talkers. There won't be any awkward pauses.' That wasn't what concerned him at all. He liked silence. It was the bits in between that were difficult.

'Ah, here he is,' Pamela said, rising from the sofa in the sitting room. Five strangers also got to their feet, all baring their teeth at him in what he had to assume were friendly smiles. 'Jonathan, this is Ron and Sue Foster. Ron's a solicitor and Sue's a psychotherapist.' They reached forward to shake his hand, but he kept both of them firmly behind his back. Pamela hesitated a moment. 'Then . . . this is Polly Wyatt our GP and her husband Arthur Truelove, who's a poet. And finally Gordon Topliss who used to be our Tory MP, and is now writing a book, just like you.' Pamela turned back to face him. 'Now, what will you have to drink, sherry, g&t, whisky?'

'I'll have a beer.' He turned and went out to the kitchen to get one. He was never going to remember all those names, but he could pin them down to their professions: lawyer and therapist-woman, doctor-woman and poet, and ex-MP with no partner — provided that they went on sitting in the same places relative to each other.

'All right?' Vinny asked him. She was pouring boiling water into a saucepan.

'Yes.' When he got back into the sitting room, beer in hand, Pamela had put on a CD as background music. He recognised it as the one she played all the time, and went to sit as far away from the speakers as possible. All this talk

118

was bad enough without that, let alone the smelly flowers in the vase. He wondered how the others didn't notice this appalling amount of sensory overload.

'Jonathan's not keen on music,' Pamela said.

'Really?' said the MP. 'How strange. Now, if it was Shostakovich I'd understand it, but Mozart?'

'I hear you're renting a house down on the moor?' doctor-woman said to him. 'The one Pamela is in the process of buying?'

'Yes,' Jonathan said.

'But he'll be staying with us for a while,' Pamela put in, 'particularly when the building work starts.'

'Is it going to take long?' the solicitor asked.

'Oh, about four weeks, max.'

A whole month! Jonathan thought, horrified.

'It must be very stimulating to live down there,' the poet said to him. 'On the *sumor saete* of the Anglo Saxons: that rich summer grazing — the land of the summer man. And in the autumn too of course, in the realms of mists and silver water meadows.'

'No, it's nice and quiet,' Jonathan said.

'Haven't we had a lot of rain?' the doctor-woman said. 'I do hope we get a good summer this year.'

Jonathan remembered Pamela's instructions about contributing. 'One inch of rain equals a hundred tons of water per acre,' he volunteered.

'Good gracious!' therapist-woman said. 'How astonishing.'

'And the total capacity of all the pumping

stations in Somerset is seventy thousand litres per second.'

'Oh dear,' the poet said. 'I do so hate the metric system, it means absolutely nothing to me.'

'Me n — ' began the ex-MP

'Just multiply by nought point two two,' Jonathan interrupted impatiently, 'to get gallons per second. So, that equals fifteen thousand, four hundred. It's easy.'

'Did you do that in your head?' doctor-woman asked.

'Naturally. And of course Amber Junction is a large component of that total. Each pump down there has a capacity of seventy-one thousand gallons a minute.'

'You don't say!' therapist-woman said.

'I just did.' Right, Jonathan thought. I've contributed. That'll do for tonight. Pamela was frowning at him, or maybe she was concentrating on something? There was a blessed silence. Everyone sipped their drinks.

'Supper's ready,' Vinny announced, putting her head round the door. 'Jonathan, can you give me a hand carrying things?'

He went to help her, ferrying bowls of hot vegetables to the table in the dining room. When he had finished, they were all seated round it exclaiming about the food and all the hard work it must have been for Vinny. And of course they were sitting in the wrong places, all muddled up . . .

'Would you pass the apple sauce to Sue?' Vinny asked him as he sat down in the empty chair. He picked the bowl up and looked from one to the other of the two strange women, in indecision.

'Over here, thanks,' said the one on the right.

'So, Gordon,' Pamela said, as they began to eat. 'How are you these days? It must have been so difficult for you.' She turned to explain to Jonathan. 'Poor Gordon lost his wife recently.'

Jonathan was surprised. 'And he didn't find her again?'

'No,' Vinny said. 'She died. How's the book coming on, Gordon?'

'Slowly.' The ex-MP had gone a funny shade of red in the face, Jonathan noticed. 'Writing is a dreadful business — hugely stressful — but it is coming on slowly at last.'

'Is it a political memoir?' the other woman asked.

'Yes, part that, part autobiography. A lot about my family in fact.'

'Do you have a family, Jonathan?' Sue asked. Therapist-woman?

'Yes, my parents and six younger brothers.'

'And do you see them often?'

'No.'

'So, how do you feel about that?'

'How do I feel?' Jonathan was at a loss.

'Yes.'

'Well rather hot actually.' He sat back in his chair and stripped off his jersey.

'*More roast pork?*' Pamela offered the company at large.

After that, everyone seemed to talk at once. Jonathan got on with his food and spoke as little

121

as possible. He had two helpings of pudding, looked at his watch and saw that it was ten thirty five, got to his feet, recited, 'Nice to have met you,' (which was not the case, and troubled him rather), left the table and went to bed.

★   ★   ★

'Oh dear,' Pamela said, once Jonathan had left the room. 'I'm so sorry. I'm afraid he's rather a strange young man.'

'Extraordinary behaviour!' expostulated Gordon.

'Refreshingly honest,' Arthur said.

'Well, I'll just go and make the coffee,' Pamela said, getting up, 'after Vinny did the food so marvellously.'

'Tremendously good,' agreed Ron, as she went out.

Sue leant over to Vinny. 'So, what's going on?' she asked.

'Yes,' Polly said. 'What's the set-up with Pamela and this Jonathan?'

'Oh you know Pamela,' Vinny said flippantly. 'She's never happier than when she's ordering somebody else's destiny . . . no, that's unkind. She's just doing her Lady Bountiful bit, but Jonathan doesn't seem to have grasped his side of the bargain.' She began to giggle. She must have drunk too much, or maybe it was the relief at having got the cooking successfully over with.

'But honestly Vin, there's something definitely wrong with him,' Polly said. 'Wouldn't you say so, Sue?'

'Wrong with Jonathan?' Pamela said, bringing

in the coffee. 'Nothing at all. He's just socially naïve.'

'No,' Vinny said. 'I think there's more to it than that.'

'What's the diagnosis then, Doctor?' Arthur jovially asked his wife.

'Not my field.' Polly looked across at Sue. 'What d'you think?'

'Well . . . ' Sue paused. 'Totally unprofessional of course, without a proper consultation, but . . . how about high-functioning autism?'

* ★ *

'Where's Pamela?' Jonathan asked the next day, at breakfast.

'Visiting her elderlies,' Vinny said automatically and then felt she should explain. 'She cheers up the inmates of an old people's home on Sundays sometimes.'

He looked doubtful. 'Why?'

'Because it's a good, kind, generous thing to do.'

'Will you take me home?' he asked suddenly.

'Oh Jonathan,' Vinny said, putting down a cup of tea in front of him. 'I'm sorry. You really aren't comfortable here, are you?'

'Too much coffee,' he said.

Vinny smiled at him. 'I do understand,' she said. 'Tell you what, we'll go down to The Prospect and make sure everything's all right, and if it is, then of course you can go back there.'

'Great!' He leapt to his feet and ran upstairs. Vinny cleared up the breakfast things, and by the time she had finished, she discovered that Jonathan had already dismantled the components of his computer and packed them into the back seat of her mini, wedged securely by the new trousers Pamela had bought him, now all crumpled into padding shapes.

'Oh dear,' she said. 'Have you been dying to leave us for ages?'

'Yes,' Jonathan said simply. 'It's easier to write at home.'

'You and I have the same problem,' Vinny said, and when he looked blank, she added, 'We both need to stand up to Pamela more.'

They set off soon afterwards, driving down from Hembrow and across the moor.

'Sorry about last night,' she said. 'Did you hate every minute?'

'Yes,' he said. 'That cherry blossom in vases everywhere was horrible. It smelt like tom cats.'

Vinny laughed. 'You're right,' she said. 'It did.'

'I said, 'Nice to have met you', even though it wasn't,' he offered.

'Yes, that was good.' She glanced sideways at him as she drove. He was looking extra serious.

'I do try to learn things,' he insisted. 'I know I don't say what people expect, but most of the time, I can't remember what it is I'm supposed to say, so I pretend I don't care.'

'That must be very difficult for you.' Vinny suppressed an urge to pat his knee in sympathy.

'It's mostly in this country that I have trouble. I didn't have it in Africa.'

Yes, Vinny thought, I can imagine that. People don't use nuances of speech to foreigners. They

124

usually say exactly what they mean, and in the simplest of terms. 'Will you go back there again?' she asked.

'Oh *yes*. There's lots of work to be done.'

Vinny wanted to ask him what it was like, working there, but thought she'd be likely to get either a one-word answer — 'hot' — or a long scientific exposition.

Conversation with Jonathan was difficult; it didn't flow. Any normal form of communication requires people to take turns, she thought, while expressing an interest in the other's point of view. But he doesn't seem to understand this. She'd noticed that he mostly did maintain eye contact whilst he was speaking to you, presumably to check that you were still paying attention to him, but then he looked away as soon as he had finished, and didn't watch you reply. She supposed that it might be different if she was someone like George, with a lot of technical knowledge. Maybe if she could discuss horsepower or revolutions-per-minute, it would be easier?

There was a silence. Vinny noticed that the field ditches were full to overflowing.

'Were you always fascinated by water?' she asked, 'even as a child?'

'Always, yes.'

'So, you like swimming too?'

'No, I can't swim.'

There was another silence. Then Vinny said, 'I'm sorry about George. I expect he'll get over it in the end, but it must feel very hurtful to you.'

'Yes, it does. What can I do about it?'

Vinny looked at him again and saw that he was genuinely asking for her help. She felt flattered, and at the same time, acutely sorry for him. 'I should just carry on as usual and hope for the best. I don't believe he'd do anything against you. He's a nice man really; just misguided.'

When they arrived at The Prospect everything looked entirely normal. No graffiti, no vandalism, nothing out of the ordinary. Just Pamela over-reacting as usual, Vinny thought. She helped him carry his things over the footbridge to the front door. He turned to her, smiling.

'I'm glad to be back,' he said. Then he leant towards her, quite unexpectedly, and brushed his lips very delicately against her cheek.

'Oh!' she said, astonished.

'It's all right,' Jonathan said. 'That wasn't a sexual advance. I only do this with very special people. It's one of the things I did manage to learn as a child. You don't mind, do you?'

'No!' Vinny said, 'I'm delighted. Can I do it too?'

Jonathan stood to attention as she delivered her kiss. His cheek felt very slightly sandpapery, and completely masculine. He smelt of coal-tar soap. She remembered it all with a flood of recognition.

'There is something that puzzles me though,' he said,

'What's that?'

'I thought you and Pamela would sleep in the same room, in the same bed, but you don't?'

'No,' Vinny agreed. 'We never have done.'

'So, you're not lesbians at all?'

'No.' It felt like a public declaration.

Jonathan looked anxious. Vinny smiled reassuringly at him. 'Don't worry,' she said. 'You're quite safe with me.'

6

At last! Jonathan thought, it's Monday morning and I've got a clear week ahead of me for getting on with my writing. He typed:

24 million cubic kilometres of the earth's fresh water are unavailable for use, as they are immobilised in ice caps and permanent snow cover. 16 million cubic kilometres are too far underground . . .

He got to his feet and began to pace the room, getting his brain in gear. There was a heavy shower going on outside. He noticed that low grey clouds had obscured the top of Glastonbury Tor. He could also see a bright red umbrella bobbing along the road towards his house. Surely not?

It was. As Mandy got closer, she looked up at the window and waved. What the hell did she want now? I'll give her back her damn cake tin, he thought, and that'll be an end to it.

'Hello,' she said as he opened the door. 'Where've you been? I was afraid you'd gone for good, and I'd never be able to apologise. I got hold of the wrong end of the stick the other day, see. I'm ever so sorry.'

The rain was dripping off her umbrella onto his feet. 'Here's your tin,' he said, holding it out. What stick?

'Oh, right. It's all dented innit? I suppose that's down to me too? Where've you been then?'

'Hembrow.' He began to shut the door, but she put out a hand to hold it.

'Oh, where all the snobs live. You haven't been with — ?'

'Got to go,' he said, pushing at the door.

'Look,' she said, pushing back, 'I don't blame you for feeling pissed off about what happened. I was upset. I didn't know what I was doing, but I'm fine now.'

'Good, well in that case you can go away and leave me alone. I've a book to write and no time to waste with children. OK?'

'But I'm not a child. I'm *sixteen*. We could be friends, yeah? We've got a lot in common. I like water too; I'm the best swimmer in my year . . . ' Jonathan leant against the door until it closed, and then pushed up the snib on its Yale lock. She banged on it a few times, yelling, 'You can't treat me like this. I hate you! My dad says you're a loser and a wanker and a . . . poofter, *so there!*'

Jonathan walked slowly back upstairs, shaking his head. Surely George wouldn't speak of him like that? The mere mention of his name made him feel sad. When he got to his study, he stood well back and looked cautiously out of the window. She was walking down the road away from him, going slowly with dragging feet. As he watched, she suddenly chucked the red umbrella into the rhyne and stood there as it floated upside-down on the water, its handle in the air. He saw her bend down and pick up a stone from a pile beside the road and throw it. Then another and another. She was dancing about now, and yelling like a madwoman. He watched, perplexed until finally the umbrella lurched under the weight of stones and sank. Mandy, apparently wet through, slouched off homewards.

'So, what now?' he said aloud. 'Am I supposed to go on writing as though nothing's happened? Why can't people just leave me alone?'

Then he thought, I need a coffee. This reminded him of Pamela, and then of her telling him the builders would be starting the day after completion of the sale. 'Seven weeks from the acceptance of my offer to the exchange of contracts, all being well', she'd said, 'and then another week to completion, hopefully on the twenty-fourth of May'.

Hopefully was not the word he would have used. He only had a few weeks grace until the onslaught began, and the thought of it was enough to put him off writing altogether.

★   ★   ★

Vinny came home from the library in the rain feeling thoroughly fed up and more than a little anxious. She'd felt entirely justified in her unilateral decision to take Jonathan back to The Prospect the day before, but had still expected a furious reaction from Pamela. People like her, who were not afraid of anger, were invariably the winners in any verbal contest as Vinny had found to her cost. I wish I was more confident, she thought, and could think quickly on my feet. She had waited in trepidation for Pamela's return, but when it came it wasn't at all as she had expected.

'Ha!' Pamela had said, bustling indoors. 'Well that's a good morning's work done for the poor old dears. I do hope I die before I'm ninety. You'll have to shoot me, Vin, if I don't.'

'Glad you've had a useful time,' Vinny said.

'Maybe I should take Jonathan there for an educational visit? It would certainly make him aware of how lucky he is.'

'I'm sure he knows already.'

'Upstairs working, is he? Didn't see him at the window.'

Vinny took a gulp of coffee. 'No. He's down at The Prospect.'

Pamela looked up sharply. 'Is he indeed, and how did he get there?'

'I drove him.'

Pamela put her keys down on the dresser and sat down opposite Vinny. 'Probably right,' she said.

'Eh?'

'Well of course it wasn't overt, but I was getting subtle hints that he was wanting to get back to his own space. I suppose it's hardly surprising. A couple of oldies like us are unlikely to be company for a young man.'

Speak for yourself! Vinny almost said. 'I thought you'd be cross.'

'Good heavens, no. It'll do him no harm to have a bit of a break from us. He'll be back again soon enough when the building work starts.'

But that was yesterday, and Pamela was nothing if not changeable. She'd had plenty of time to work up a head of steam today.

Vinny had endured a hard day at work. She drove wearily up Hembrow Hill and turned off to their house. There was no sign of Gertie in the drive. Instead a dinky little Ford Ka was parked outside their house. She frowned, put her key into the lock and went inside. Pamela was in the kitchen, singing, 'Summer time, and the living is easy . . . '

'Hello-o,' Vinny called, dumping her bag in the hall and hanging up her mac.

'Vin, is that you?' Pamela appeared in the doorway, beaming from ear to ear. 'So, what d'you think?'

'About what?'

'My new car of course. Gertie was far too hard on fuel and unnecessarily large, so I've traded her in.'

'What, just like that?'

'Why not? We've all been consuming far too much. I was going to delay until I'd bought everything for The Prospect, before I began on the minimalism thing, but then I thought, why wait? The Ka's second hand you see. It came up, and I didn't want to lose it. I don't believe I've ever bought a used car before; my first effort at living in harmony with my environment!'

'I take it this is Jonathan's influence?' Vinny went past her into the kitchen to make a cup of tea, grateful for the reprieve, but still tired.

'But, don't you want to see inside it?'

'Why? Is it different from any other car?'

'What's the matter? Bad day amongst the bloody books?'

'You could say so.' Vinny sat down at their kitchen table and put her chin on one palm with a sigh.

'Tell me about it.'

'Oh it's just the usual staff problems. Nothing new.'

'But?'

'Well, the last straw was when some yob threw up right in the entrance, and when I went to clear away the sick, there were two pigeons actually *eating* it!' Vinny screwed up her face in disgust.

'Vegetable soup for supper then?' Pamela teased her.

'Shut up. I'm not in the mood.'

'Poor old Vin.' Pamela sat down opposite her. 'It seems to me that you're stagnating in that potty little library. So maybe this is the right time to put a proposition to you, one that I've been thinking about recently. How about this for an idea — why don't you give up your job and come and work for me, as my agent?' She looked triumphant.

Oh, not again, Vinny thought. Not another ridiculous scheme in which Pamela 'rescues' me, and then I'm supposed to spend the rest of my life being abjectly grateful . . . 'I don't think so.'

'Well at least hear me out,' Pamela said huffily.

'Go on, then.'

'Thinking of The Prospect, it occurred to me that this could be a major business opportunity if we did it on a larger scale. I mean, buying and doing up grotty places and then renting them out to summer visitors, or even longer term tenants. It could be a real moneyspinner. Obviously we'd have to do repairs on all the properties and clean them up after each lot of guests, but the returns would be good and it's an excellent way of maximising Aunt Kate's legacy. I'm sure she would've approved.'

'But you wouldn't get any income for almost half the year,' Vinny pointed out.

'No, but it'll be enough, and the bonus is the free time. In the winter we could jet off somewhere hot — South Africa perhaps — see the world, and take in some of the parks and wildlife reserves you've always fancied. Wouldn't that be marvellous?' Pamela leant across the table and took both of her hands. 'What about it, Vin?'

Vinny sighed. 'You're too late,' she said. 'The buy-to-let market has peaked now, and there aren't any cheap grotty places left to buy.'

'What about The Prospect?' Pamela raised her eyebrows.

'That was a one-off. And anyway, I don't want to spend my life ironing sheets and sorting out domestic disasters.'

'Oh you're always so *negative*,' Pamela retorted crossly, 'and so selfish! Here I am, presenting you with an unequalled opportunity to change direction in a truly life-enhancing way, and all you can think of is petty domestic trivia! Rise above all that, Vinny. It's time to relax and open yourself up to a wider canvas. Life's too short. You've got to seize the day, not sit about carping.'

Easy for you to say that, Vinny thought. *Carpe diem* was most likely the motto of the rich. The poor were too busy trying to seize their next meal. She sipped her tea and said nothing.

'So, am I to take it that you refuse to resign?'

'Yes.'

'Then the whole idea is a non-starter,' Pamela said. 'It would be far too much work for me on my own. I'd be ill. This is very uncaring of you, Vinny — not like the real you at all.'

'It's not me,' Vinny protested, stung. 'It's you who's selfish; always wanting your own way!'

'How can you say that?' Pamela challenged her. 'When have I ever asked you for anything? Go on, tell me!'

'Well . . . I can't . . . off the top of my head . . . but that doesn't mean . . . ' Vinny was furious at her own inadequacy.

'Anyway, how can you even *think* that?' Pamela demanded, 'after all I've done for you?' Her eyes were wide with outrage.

It was the last straw at the end of a tiring day. Tears dripped down Vinny's cheeks. She put her face in both hands and sat there. Now that she had cracked, Pamela would be kindness itself.

'Come on, Vin,' Pamela said sympathetically, getting up. 'Don't be upset. We'll sort something out, you'll see.' She stood behind her, putting both hands on Vinny's shoulders and squeezing them gently.

Vinny stood up abruptly. 'I'm all right,' she said.

* * *

It was a warm green day at the very end of May, but relations between Pamela and Vinny had remained cool. Pamela felt betrayed. She was tempted to insist that if Vinny was determined to be stand-offish; more like a lodger than the friend she'd always been, then she was morally obliged to pay rent or look for somewhere else to live. But maybe not yet. She'd keep that threat in reserve, to use as a last resort.

At least things were progressing, as far as The Prospect was concerned. Pamela had finally got completion of the sale. The money had gone through, and the keys were in her hand. Of course it was a week later than she'd expected, and now the builders had said they wouldn't be able to begin until the second Monday in June but it was, at last, a firm date.

So, the Sunday before B-Day — as she thought of it — Pamela picked up the telephone to tell Jonathan she'd be down to collect him and his things in an hour or so, and to be sure to be ready. But the mobile she'd bought him was switched off. She left him a terse message and hung up.

'I don't know what that young man's thinking of,' she complained to Vinny, who was reading the *Observer* on the kitchen table.

'Mmm?'

'Why does he imagine I went to all the trouble of buying him a phone in the first place, if it wasn't so I could talk to him whenever I need to? What *is* the point, if he can't be bothered to switch the bloody thing on?'

'I doubt that he imagines anything at all as far as we're concerned,' Vinny said, looking up. 'If he really is autistic, then it just won't occur to him to see things from your point of view. So, if he doesn't want to phone anyone, he'll save the battery and keep it switched off. It's quite logical, if you think about it.'

'Logical, my arse,' Pamela spat. 'And anyway, I don't believe for one moment that he is autistic. He's far too clever for that.' She went over to the Aga and slid the kettle onto the hotplate. 'That's given me an idea, though,' she said. 'I think we should get him diagnosed. That would make life so much easier for us.'

'Like neutering a tom-cat, you mean?' Vinny enquired, 'Or is he going to have a say in the matter?'

'I shall ask Sue,' Pamela went on firmly. 'She's bound to know the best man for the job. Then I'll set up a consultation with him and invite Jonathan to go along with me.'

'And if he refuses?'

'It's entirely in his best interest. Surely you see that? But if in the unlikely event that he can't, well then I'll remind him of his obligations to us and tell him it's the least he can do.'

'Emotional blackmail.' Vinny turned over a page of the newspaper and went on reading.

Pamela ignored this too. 'Well, I'd best be off then,' she said, 'I shall just have to hope the wretched boy's in. Lunch at one o'clock as usual?'

'Mmm. Fish pie.'

'Good. See you then.'

'Kettle's boiling,' Vinny called after her, but she'd gone.

★　★　★

On the Monday, the builders arrived at eight o'clock and began to carry timber, plasterboard, ladders, bags of cement and insulation material into The Prospect, followed by a long steel girder, a portable orange concrete mixer, a wheelbarrow, an assortment of power tools and a ghetto-blaster tuned to Radio 1. Pamela tackled the last item first.

'I'd be grateful if you'd turn that thing off while I'm here,' she said. 'Can't hear myself think! Now then, what are you going to begin with, Mr . . . er?'

'Dave,' said the foreman. 'That's me, an' that's Jack over there, and Charlie by the van. So, what do us call you then, my love?'

'Well, certainly not *that*,' Pamela said crisply. 'Mrs Wood is my name.'

'Right you are, Mrs Wood. Well, today it's the demolition between the kitchen and the lounge — ' Pamela shuddered at the word. ' — for the archway. Course we'll need to put in that there RSJ to hold things up, since he's a supporting wall. There's likely going to be a considerable amount of dust, so if you'd care to remove a few more things, like that bike f'rinstance?'

'Oh dear,' Pamela said. In all the kerfuffle of extracting Jonathan that morning and taking as many of his possessions as they could cram into the Ka, she'd had to over-rule his demand to include his bicycle too. It simply wasn't possible, but he'd still sulked. 'I'd like to, of course, but my car's far too small.'

'You'm up at Hembrow, right?'

'Yes.'

'Well that's handy. Charlie do live over that way an' all. I'll get him to pop it in his van and drop it off when he goes home.'

'Thank you — Dave,' Pamela said. 'That would be most kind. Now then, what about the new windows?'

'We'll be measuring up for they today, and the order will go in tomorrow. All right?'

'You've got my number if you need anything?' Pamela asked.

'Oh yes, my l — Don't you worry. Us'll just get on, then.'

Pamela found herself politely dismissed, and since there really was nothing she could usefully do at this stage, she got into her Ka and went home.

Jonathan was at the high window in his room under the roof again, working away as usual. You certainly couldn't fault him on that score, at least, Pamela thought. And while he was in her mind, she decided to telephone Sue there and then to get the ball rolling. Sue, however, wasn't available so Pamela, thwarted in her desire to do something at once, made two coffees and went up the stairs to sort it out with Jonathan himself.

'No coffee,' he said, holding up a hand like a policeman on traffic duty.

'Oh well, I've made it now,' Pamela said, locating the coaster and putting his mug down on it. Then she sat down on the bed and took a sip at hers.

'I'm really busy,' he said.

'That's very good,' Pamela said. 'Who'd have

thought that there would be this much to write about water!'

'I would.'

'Well yes, evidently. Look, Jonathan, there's something important I want to suggest to you. Do you remember Sue Foster?'

'No.'

'Yes, you do. She came to dinner. She was the psychotherapist, remember? I told you at the time.'

'So?'

'So how about you having a few sessions with a colleague of hers, to assist you with your communication problems. I'm sure it would be an enormous help. What d'you say?'

'No,' Jonathan said shortly.

Pamela got rather ungraciously to her feet and moved towards the door. 'Well I can see you're preoccupied with work at the moment,' she said. 'I'll drink my coffee downstairs. And you'll think about what I've said, yes?'

★　★　★

When Vinny came home from the library, she found Pamela in the kitchen and on the phone to a friend of a friend-with-whom-she-played-bridge, who happened to be a builder.

' . . . Well, they say they've found an unacceptable amount of rising damp downstairs, and they suggest injecting the walls and digging out all the floors to put in a dpm, whatever that is? Oh, I see . . . would that cure it? Oh good. Well, thanks so much for your advice. 'Bye.' She turned to Vinny. 'I should have got Fred's firm to do this work for me,' she said. 'He's far and away the best builder around here, but of course he's booked solid until Christmas.'

'Problems with damp?' Vinny asked, going over to put the kettle on.

'Yes. That flash harry surveyor should have discovered it in the first place,' Pamela complained. 'He charged me enough. No wonder he can afford to drive a Mercedes!'

'Well, to be fair, he did mention it,' Vinny said. 'Don't you remember? He advised seagrass matting rather than carpets downstairs.'

'The Prospect isn't going to be some tatty hippy squat,' Pamela said. 'After Jonathan's gone, I shall have a much better class of person . . . Oh, hello Jonathan. Finished work, then?'

'Just making some tea,' Vinny said, as he came in.

'Good.' He sat down at the kitchen table and ran a hand through his hair, straightening out the curls momentarily.

He looks tired, Vinny thought. I do hope all this effort of his is going to be worth it. Although I fear it may not be, and then what?

'Now then, Jonathan, have you considered my offer of a course of psychotherapy?'

'Yes,' Jonathan said.

'Oh, excellent. I'll give Sue a ring at once.'

'No,' Jonathan said. 'You misunderstand me. I've given it all the thought it needs and the answer is still no.'

'But why?'

'Because — if you must know — I've done all

141

that, over many years, beginning when I was twelve. My parents put me through every possible diagnostic test and treatment, and I know exactly what's 'wrong' with me. So I have to tell you that no amount of therapy, psycho or otherwise, is going to make any difference at all. I have a form of autism called Asperger's Syndrome. OK?' He turned on his heel and took his mug of tea upstairs.

Vinny and Pamela looked at each other.

'Don't,' Pamela warned her. 'Don't you dare say, 'I told you so'.'

★ ★ ★

Jonathan sat at his computer with glazed eyes, unable to work. He hadn't meant to tell Pamela anything about his personal life, and was angry with himself for having done so. It was none of her business! All he wanted was to be left alone to write. That was surely not too much to ask?

'Jonathan?' Vinny was tapping at his bedroom door. She opened it a crack. 'Supper in ten minutes. Are you all right?'

'No.'

She came in. 'Are you upset, or cross?'

'Both.'

'I'm sorry. Pamela does mean well, you know?'

'So you always say, but does she?' He shook his head. 'She appears to be trying to take over my life, in order to run it *her* way. And then there's all this coaching in 'social behaviour' that she keeps going on about. I've *had* all that. I've had it a million times! I've studied every 'polite

142

phrase' and metaphor in the English language. They don't make any sense to me, so it's hardly surprising I don't remember them. In fact they annoy me so much that I *don't want* to remember them! And as for body language: bodies do not speak to me — except with their vocal cords of course. The things that people do with their faces or their hands or whatever, do not 'say' anything to me. So, you see *I am already doing the best I can.*'

'So, why not explain it to Pamela, the way you've just told me?'

'Because I don't want to discuss it with her. It's private.'

'Well, she knows now. So perhaps you could tell her a few things about it, to help her understand you better?'

'Why should I?'

'Because she's doing her best for you, and you're really not helping her. That's not very fair, is it?'

Jonathan felt stricken. The one thing he could not bear to be accused of was not being fair.

'I could help you,' Vinny said.

'What sort of things?'

'Oh, I don't know . . . how it feels from your point of view? Although, come to think of it, I suppose it would be difficult to describe those things which are impossible for you . . . '

'One of my doctors told me to explain it like this,' he offered tentatively. 'If you're blind, no amount of talking by a sighted person will create the colour blue for you. Or any other colour, of course.'

'That's it, exactly!' Vinny said. 'If you say that to her, she would understand, because she really does want to help.' She smiled at him. 'Pamela tries to run my life as well, you know. She's a control freak. It's a deep form of insecurity, apparently.'

He was surprised. 'But I don't like to be 'owned',' he said.

'Neither do I.'

'So why do you stay here?'

'I've been asking myself that question recently, as well. I think I'm too scared to make the move.'

'You? Scared?'

Vinny came nearer to him. 'I'm human too,' she said. 'I can feel vulnerable, like anybody else. Would you give me a hug to make me feel better?'

'Now?'

'Yes.'

He stood up, uncertainly and let her approach him. His instinct as always was to pull away from her, but now because it was Vinny and he had begun to trust her, he made himself stand still.

He tried to analyse the sensations, and once he'd got over his initial panic, he found he could cope. Better than that. She felt solid and dependable as she put her arms around him. He smelt a pleasant warm scent. Her hair tickled softly under his chin. She was actually comforting, entirely unthreatening.

'That's lovely,' she said. 'Thank you.'

'Vinny?' Pamela said, as she popped her head round the door. 'The spuds were boiling over, so I've . . . oh!'

144

7

Bloody builders! Pamela thought, as she drove down to The Prospect. What a good thing I went down yesterday to check. That work surface in the kitchen sticks out a whole inch more than we agreed, and two of the doors on the wall cupboards don't meet properly, and they haven't tiled the whole area as I told them to. Honestly, you can't leave workmen for one minute these days, without them cocking something up.

Everything seemed to her to be stressful these days. She was worried about Jonathan and about Vinny, to say nothing of the nagging anxiety about her son, Peter, which was always there, niggling away in the back of her mind. She'd tried to look up the definition of Jonathan's condition in her dictionary, but there was nothing between 'asperge' to sprinkle and 'asperse' to slander. If he's suffering from some incurable mental condition, she thought, then how best can I play it? Is there any point in my trying to help him? She felt discouraged and not a little annoyed with him. This was a fine time to be telling her! Why hadn't he been honest with her at the very beginning, three whole months ago? Pamela thought, I really cannot be expected to cope with someone who isn't right in the head! She realised that her attitude towards him had changed irrevocably.

And then there was Vinny. What was Pamela supposed to think about the scene she'd all unknowingly stumbled upon three weeks earlier, and had still not been given a satisfactory explanation for? 'I was just giving Jonathan a hug because he was upset,' Vinny had said. 'Don't be ridiculous. It's no big deal!'

Do I believe her? Pamela wondered. Is there something going on there? He's young enough to be her son for heaven's sake! She pursed her mouth, sniffed, and then deliberately thought about her own son instead. He'd been living abroad for the best part of nine years now, with less than half a dozen visits to Hembrow in all that time, and fleeting ones at that. She wondered where he was at that moment, whether he was earning enough money to finance his footloose lifestyle. Better not to speculate . . . but she did hope she wouldn't have to bail him out financially, yet again. Above all, she wished he were someone she could be proud of. It certainly wasn't for want of trying.

Down on the one-track roads across the moor, she either held her ground or pulled in ostentatiously at passing places to allow other motorists through. She couldn't bear ditherers. Today, however, there seemed to be more of them than usual, and all without a brain between them. She was obliged to mouth angrily at them through the windscreen.

'Oh please don't bother to acknowledge me, will you? You ungrateful bastard!' And, 'Well, come on then, you stupid little man. I'm not just here for my health!' And 'Don't you bloody well flash your lights at me, you miserable sod. It was *my* right of way!'

By the time she arrived at The Prospect with her clipboard of notes at the ready, she was all set to do battle. Two of the builders were outside the house; red-haired Dave, the boss and Charlie with that ridiculous ponytail, but no sign of the other one.

'No Jack again today, then?' she asked, crossing the foot-bridge.

'Mornin',' Dave said. 'And what can us do you for today, then?'

'Well a finished job would be nice,' Pamela said, 'and a full complement of workers too.'

'Jack's missus have just passed on,' Dave said, 'so he've mebbe got other priorities, wouldn't you think?'

'You never told me!' Pamela was furious. 'How was I to know? Well of course the poor man can't come to work under those circumstances. You'd both better take time off for the funeral.'

'Oh we will, believe you me,' Dave said, and Pamela could have sworn that Charlie sniggered. Well really! She thought. Some people have no *idea* how to behave. She went indoors and walked from room to room, checking on jobs still outstanding. It was still a long way from being finished, but Pamela had to admit that it was beginning to look more encouraging.

What a blessing I've got imagination, she thought. So few people have their inner eye developed to the degree that mine is. An idea came to her: perhaps she and Vinny could do the final decorating themselves? It was a long time since they had worked as a team on anything. It would be healing, as well as fun. Vinny was due a summer holiday, so she'd be free for a couple of weeks. She was also very good at painting. Yes! Pamela thought, feeling instantly more cheerful. Vinny will be home at lunchtime today, but I think I'll wait a bit for exactly the right moment before I put it to her.

★ ★ ★

Vinny had escaped from Hembrow without telling Pamela she had the morning off. She'd done some food shopping in Otterbridge and, since she was passing, had collected two books she'd ordered from the library. Now she was driving idly across the moor for some space in which to think. It was getting towards the end of June and, apart from one brief thunderstorm, it hadn't rained for nearly three weeks. The grass by the roadside was growing yellow and brittle. The fields looked parched too. The mini bumped over the ridge, which had once carried the old *Slow & Dirty* Somerset and Dorset Railway line, and she negotiated a little humpbacked bridge on a corner over a rhyne, before pulling off the road and getting out into the sunshine.

Vinny sat on the bank close to the water with her arms round her knees and tried to measure its slow flow, almost imperceptible above the black peaty bottom. She threw a grass stalk in and watched it drift sluggishly seawards. She began to breathe slowly and more deeply, feeling comfortable as ever under these wide-open skies, caught up once again in the spirit of the place. When she'd been here in late May, the yellow-flags were blooming at the margins of the ditches, and there were water lilies in flower on the quiet backwaters. Fishermen and herons often came here too, waiting for hours, staking their opposing claims. Today there were little electric blue damselflies with dark patches on their wings, zipping about just above the water, like fairies in lycra.

She glanced up as a cormorant flew overhead, and when it had gone she looked down along the rhyne again and saw a ring of ripples. The rounded tip of something that could have been a tail was just disappearing. Was it an otter? Vinny could not be sure. The only sounds were from the dozen or so black and white cows, as they gathered in a line along the opposite bank and stared at her across the water, munching grass and burping gently.

She let go of her knees and stretched her legs out, leaning backwards on her arms and squinting up at the blueness above. I'm forty five, she thought. The age when people begin to ask, 'Is this all there is?' Am I really too scared to leave Pamela and be on my own again? It wouldn't be that hard; no divorce to negotiate, no house to sell. Just a few trips in my car from Hembrow to some rented flat or other, and it would be done.

But, her conscience chided her, what about Pamela? She relies on you. Who will cook for her, or weed the garden, or put up shelves, or change plugs, or tell her where she's left her keys, or dig her car out of the snow . . .

'What rubbish!' she said aloud. 'We hardly ever have snow, these days!' Then she quickly looked round to make sure there weren't any humans within earshot. Just the cows.

Vinny got to her feet and turned the car round, heading for home. The elder bushes in the hedges were in full bloom now, and on this lovely hot day the big creamy-white heads would be bursting with nectar and bathed in that mildly unpleasant scent of theirs. It was the time of the year to make elderflower cordial.

When she got back to Hembrow, Pamela was in the kitchen, on the telephone.

' . . . No, there's no mains gas down there. That's why I want to know the cost of a tank and regular supply of LPG . . . Oh well, all right, but I must have a price list. Right? Fine. Goodbye.' She turned to Vinny. 'I'm sure bottled gas will turn out to be far too expensive,' she said, 'but I have to explore every possibility. D'you know, If I'd known at the beginning that there'd be this much to do, I really don't believe I'd have started it at all.'

'Be worth it when it's done,' Vinny encouraged her. 'It'll be great.'

'It had better be! I've just had a bright idea about the decorating, but I'll tell you nearer the time.' She bent her head and lowered her voice, pointing, to indicate that Jonathan was upstairs. 'There is one thing that worries me — when it's beautifully finished and spotless, will he mess it all up again? He's not the world's most housetrained young man, after all.'

'Course he won't!' Vinny put her shopping bag on the table and fished the two books out of it. 'I've got this for us to read,' she said, pushing the first one across the table towards her. 'Should help us to understand him more.'

'It says it's for parents of children with AS?'

'Yes well, I suppose we're *in loco parentis*, aren't we?'

'Yes. Well done, Vin. What's the second one?' Vinny showed her. 'But it's called *Water Wars*! Some wretched man's pinched *my* title!' Pamela was outraged.

'There's no copyright on titles,' Vinny pointed out.

'Well we can't use it now, can we?'

'Maybe it doesn't cover the same ground,' Vinny suggested, without much conviction. 'There must be hundreds of books about water. It doesn't mean that Jonathan's won't be — '

'And worse than that, he's got there first! I *told* Jonathan he should get on with his book more quickly, or someone would steal a march on him, and I was right, wasn't I?'

'And not for the first time,' Vinny said.

'What? Oh . . . . yes. Look Vin, we'll have to tell him, but I'm afraid it will be a dreadful blow. After all that hard work too, and all for nothing!' She turned to her friend, smiling ruefully. 'But maybe now, at least, he'll let me read his manuscript. We may be able to salvage something between us.'

'I doubt — ' Vinny began, as Jonathan himself came down the stairs and into the room. His eyes lighted on the book at once.

151

'Ah!' he said. 'I was hoping to read that. Good.'

Pamela was taken aback. 'You already know about it?'

'Read a review,' Jonathan said, taking it from Vinny and flicking through the pages. 'Yes, this is most helpful.'

'But this is your subject,' Pamela persisted. 'Aren't you upset that someone else has published first?'

'I doubt there will be much overlap,' Jonathan said, absentmindedly. 'Oh this is an important chapter. I'm glad he's covered this. Now I don't have to bother.' He turned, still reading, and wandered back upstairs again.

'I'm very worried about that boy,' Pamela said after a short silence. 'I don't believe he's living in the real world. Doesn't he realise how competitive the market is, these days? I'm even beginning to wonder if he knows the subject well enough to be able to write about it in the first place!'

'Oh, I'm sure he does.'

'And is he even writing a book? We haven't seen much evidence of it, have we? Maybe it's an almighty con trick to take advantage of my kindness and get a free roof over his head.'

'He was writing it before he even met you,' Vinny protested.

'Well he *says* he was. But that's as maybe. It doesn't detract from the fact that you've got to be *first* these days, to get anywhere.' She sighed. 'It's all a big let down. I'm usually so discerning about character, but it seems I was badly misled this time. If only I'd had the full facts . . . But that was certainly not my fault.'

'But Jonathan didn't ask for your help,' Vinny said, reasonably, 'You did it because you wanted to.'

'And that gives him the right to wreck it all?' Pamela shot her a reproachful look. 'I thought you of all people would understand how I feel, especially now, when he's turning out to be such a disappointment. He seemed such a good investment, at first . . . '

'You weren't in it for money, remember? You said you wanted to help Jonathan for his own sake, and you still can. He hasn't changed.'

'Ah, but he has.' Pamela shook her head sorrowfully. 'He wasn't straight with me, and you know how much I hate that. No, I'm afraid I'm going to have to have a radical rethink where he's concerned.'

'What d'you mean?' Vinny felt alarmed.

'You'll see.' Pamela would say no more.

★ ★ ★

'What's fifty grams in English?' Pamela asked, squinting at the print on a small packet of citric acid powder.

'A couple of ounces.' Vinny said, 'enough to go with the amount of flowers we've picked. Shall we sit outside to sort them?'

'Yes,' Pamela said. 'You organise the chairs and I'll bring the rest.'

They sat opposite each other near the cherry tree. Vinny tried counting her blessings, and

153

began to feel a little happier. It was rewarding to be a gatherer of things from the wild, in their season. She felt privileged to be sitting in a garden like this, bathed in afternoon sunlight. She began to snip away with scissors at the saucer-shaped umbels of elderflower heads, which they'd collected by the bucketful that morning, dropping the stalks into a bowl at her feet, and the florets into a large saucepan on the garden table between them. Her fingers were soon covered in yellow pollen and felt greasy to the touch. Her nostrils were assailed by the heady scent. All was well. She had remembered to buy the lemons that Pamela had forgotten to mention, and they had enough sugar in stock. They were all set to make the cordial, which would refresh them both for the rest of the summer. Vinny flexed her bare toes on the lawn, enjoying the feel of the cool grass, but checking also that there weren't any ants. When she got bitten, she swelled up and itched for days. Somehow they never dared to bite Pamela.

Vinny glanced across at her, as she sat there working away. There were more lines at the corners of her eyes and between her brows now, and parallel furrows running from beneath her nose to her upper lip. She looked permanently discontented these days. Vinny felt both sorry for her and out of patience at the same instant.

'You're dropping stalks in the wrong pot,' Pamela accused her.

'Sorry.' Vinny fished them out. 'What's the matter?'

Pamela shook her head. 'Just the builders,

what else? They've been working at The Prospect for weeks now and they're nowhere near finished. So, they're behind schedule, and what do they do? They bugger off altogether! I can't even get them on the phone. It's driving me mad.'

'Mmm.'

'Well, I won't pay them! They can whistle for it.'

'Builders do tend to do this, though,' Vinny said hesitantly. 'All your work is interior now, so I suppose it is logical from their point of view to get on with other people's outside stuff when the weather's fine.'

'Whose side are you on?' Pamela demanded. 'They promised me a month. One month and I naturally assumed that meant twenty-eight consecutive days! Wouldn't you? It's just not good enough.'

'But it is almost finished, isn't it?'

'Upstairs, yes, but the kitchen still isn't. Well, it's too bad. I can't wait any longer. I'm taking Jonathan back down there tomorrow.'

'What, for good?'

'Yep.'

'But why?' Vinny frowned. 'You said you couldn't have a tenant of yours living in squalor; that it would be unethical?'

'There's nothing remotely squalid about it,' Pamela retorted. 'It will be a little inconvenient for a while, that's all. I don't see why he shouldn't suffer for his art!'

'So, what's brought on this sudden *volte-face*?'

Pamela looked round carefully to check that Jonathan hadn't suddenly appeared within earshot. 'The thing is,' she said in hushed tones, 'I'm afraid mental illness isn't something I'm very comfortable with.'

'He is *not* mentally ill!' Vinny hissed. 'I can't believe you're so *prejudiced*.'

'Well, he's not normal, is he? What if his condition changes? What if he gets violent? You hear such terrible stories . . . '

'Oh, come off it, Pamela! Jonathan's not dangerous. He's not some raving nutter, is he? He's autistic. There's simply been an abnormality in the development of his brain which sets him apart from the rest of us.'

'I expect his parents were cold and undemonstrative to him,' Pamela agreed. 'That sort of thing can scar a person for life.'

'No!' Vinny cried, exasperated. 'You're not listening to me. It's not caused by family inadequacy or abuse or neglect. It's a neurobiological condition, maybe genetic, maybe caused by damage to the brain. They don't know for sure.'

'How come you're suddenly such an expert?'

'I spoke to Jonathan. He really does know what he's talking about. Why don't you ask him yourself? He understands all about it, and you've absolutely nothing to fear from him. With Jonathan, what you see is what you get.'

'Who said anything about fear?' Pamela looked affronted. 'Anyway, I've made up my mind. He's going back down tomorrow.'

'Well fine,' Vinny said. 'He'll be delighted.'

'And you won't?'

Vinny sighed. 'I have no feelings one way or the other.'

Pamela raised an eyebrow. 'There, that's done,' she said, dropping the last flower into the saucepan and stretching her arms in front of her. 'Now, shall I make the syrup, or will you?'

'I will, if you like.' Vinny shuffled her feet into sandals and stood up. And when she was in the kitchen again, weighing out the sugar, she reflected with reluctant admiration on Pamela's capacity for ordering her about without actually seeming to do so.

★   ★   ★

The next day, Vinny got on with her job as well as she could. She smiled at people and answered their questions. She did some photocopying for an old man. She attended to the computer, scanned bar codes, handed novels over the counter, pacified an irate colleague, and, during occasional lulls, read bits of a book she'd come across on assertiveness training.

It was a long day and she was worn out by the time she got home. She drove round the large chestnut tree at the entrance to their drive and there, in front of her, was a brand-new 4 by 4, gleaming black, doors open, standing where Pamela always parked her car. As she squeezed the mini in beside it, Pamela herself appeared, struggling with Jonathan under the weight of a chest minus its drawers. Vinny could see now that these were already stacked on top of each

157

other in the back of the 4 by 4. She got out of her car with difficulty. 'What on earth — ?' she began.

'Mind out!' Pamela warned, 'this is heavy. OK Jonathan, both together, *lift*!'

'What are you doing?' Vinny asked her.

'Sorting out the furniture,' Pamela said. 'There's too much up here and too little down at The Prospect, so the solution would seem to be obvious. Oh, and while I think of it, I shall need you to take some photographs of each room down there, when it's finished, for insurance purposes.'

Vinny was barely listening. 'But . . . whose vehicle is this?'

'Mine. Its name is Bertie.'

'I thought you'd decided you only needed a small car?'

'Changed my mind,' Pamela said crisply.

'What about the Ka?'

'I traded it in. No problem.'

'So much for minimalism then.'

'You could lend a hand,' Pamela said. 'If you're not too busy sneering, that is?'

'I could,' Vinny said, 'but I need a cuppa first.' She went indoors and looked about her anxiously, half expecting to find an empty house. Nothing important seemed to have gone, but the place did look less cluttered. She put the kettle on, and reached for the caddy and teapot.

'We could do with some too,' Pamela said, coming in. 'Isn't that right, Jonathan?'

'No,' he said, 'I need to work.' He went upstairs at the first opportunity, looking thoroughly browned off. Vinny wondered if Pamela had had him moving furniture all day. The kettle boiled and she made a pot of tea.

'You might have warned me that I couldn't possibly manage with less than the capacity of your average four by four,' Pamela said to her. 'The Ka was clearly far too small for my day-to-day needs. I thought you were supposed to be the practical one?'

Vinny recognised this tactic of old, and played along for the sake of peace. 'Of course,' she said. 'Silly me.'

Pamela patted her arm and then sat down with a sigh. 'I'm gasping for tea,' she said. 'How are you, love? Good day?'

'So so,' Vinny said.

'That's the last load, thank goodness. I've taken that big orange rug and the ugly standard lamp to go in the sitting room down there. Never liked either of them much. And now all Jonathan's got to do is to collect his stuff, and then we'll be away.'

'And you'll leave him down there? Has he even got a bed?'

'One for him and one for the spare-room, delivered this morning from MFI,' Pamela said, 'And a wardrobe for his clothes too. All mod cons.'

'The carpets aren't in yet, are they?'

'No, but he won't mind that. He's accustomed to bare boards.'

'But won't it be difficult to get them laid, if there's furniture in the rooms already?'

'Oh, I shall wait until after Jonathan's left. I'll

159

have to reorganise everything then anyway; maybe even get some better quality stuff in. Don't worry, Vin, I've thought it all through. And this way, I shan't have to waste my time worrying about Jonathan soiling all my lovely new carpets, shall I? Where are you going?'

Vinny had got to her feet to prevent herself from exploding. 'To see if he needs a hand.' She went out of the front door, and was just in time to help Jonathan lift his bicycle onto the roof-rack, and find some baler twine with which to tie it on.

'Won't be long now,' she encouraged him.

'Thank goodness!' He smiled at her.

Then Pamela came out. 'All aboard,' she said. 'We won't need any help at the other end, Vinny. There's not a lot in this last load, and anyway you'll be busy getting supper, won't you? Right, off we go!'

Vinny watched them leave, and then went indoors to check on exactly what Pamela had removed. Vinny had few possessions anyway, mostly in her bedroom and all, to her relief, still there. The rest of the house would need a little reorganising to fill the gaps, and a lot of cleaning in the newly exposed places. 'But, supper first,' she said to herself and went downstairs again to prepare it.

Pamela was back within the hour and spent most of the time while they were eating their risotto enthusing about Bertie.

' . . . Leather upholstery, and a CD player of course, and it's so good to be high up again. It feels so much safer, especially when you meet those huge new lorries on narrow roads.'

'How many miles to the gallon?' Vinny asked.

'Well, I don't know yet, do I?' Pamela put her fork down and wiped her mouth on a napkin. 'Now Vinny, when we were moving furniture this morning, I came across something that I want to show you.'

'What?'

'Come and see.' Vinny followed her into the sitting room. Pamela went over to a pile of photo albums on the floor, and lifted up the top one, turning the pages and then showing one to Vinny. 'See how gorgeous you used to be,' she said.

Great! Vinny thought. So what am I now?

It was the year she and Pamela had first met. There she was, magically younger, laughing and looking straight at the camera. She'd had longer hair then, looked thinner, and so utterly trusting.

'I haven't opened these for years,' Pamela said, beaming at her. 'Come and sit with me on the sofa.'

Vinny went over reluctantly and sat down beside her. And there was Pamela in a bright orange survival suit, canoeing down the river rapids in Wales, Pamela striking a pose beside a cairn on top of a Scottish Munro, and Pamela languorous in the long grass of a Devonshire hay meadow. Those who actually *take* photographs are the most unrecorded people of all! Vinny thought sourly.

'Here's another one of you,' Pamela said, laughing. 'D'you remember? You'd just fallen in the water and you were so cross because you'd

161

got your hair all wet!' She picked up another album. 'And look at this one. Here's our group climbing up that mountain. D'you remember how upset you were when you couldn't get right to the top? It was that final precipice that did for you, wasn't it? Dreadful vertigo you had. I'll never forget the look on your poor little face when the rest of us came down again from the summit. It was such a shame.' She put her hand on Vinny's arm in a sweet gesture of sympathy and solidarity. Vinny stood up. 'We've had some good times together, *great* times, haven't we?' Pamela said, smiling up at her. 'And no one can take those away from us.'

'No, I suppose — '

'What about that spring when we went riding in the New Forest? Do you remember how beautiful it was?'

Vinny did. She also remembered that Pamela had somehow ended up with the most biddable horse and the undivided attention of their guide. At the time, it had seemed no more than her due.

'And those lovely canals in France with endless sun and wine and wonderful food . . . '

Yes, Vinny thought, that was good.

' . . . and that stupid cushion that wouldn't sink!'

A little moan escaped Vinny as it all unfolded again in her mind's eye, its clarity undimmed by all her previous attempts to block it out forever. She remembered how heavy her period had been; how it had seeped through her summer clothes onto the pale blue cloth beneath

. . . How they had smuggled the cushion into their cabin and tried to wash it off, and just made it worse . . . How Pamela had finally, surreptitiously, slipped the soggy ruined thing overboard at the sharp end . . . And how it had floated past, bloody side up, the entire length of the riverboat in full view of the elegantly attired passengers, assembling on deck for an evening string quartet recital . . . Vinny turned abruptly and rushed out of the room.

'Come back!' Pamela called. 'I need your help . . .'

Vinny slammed the door behind her and ran to her car. Anywhere but here, she thought. I don't care. I've had enough. She drove down the hill and across the moor, trying to shut out the images.

This is a new strategy of Pamela's to keep me miserable and under her control, she thought. How can I put it? Yes — *loving humiliation* — that's it absolutely. And I haven't a clue how to fight it.

She could imagine the scene all too easily; Pamela's hurt rejoinder to the charge. 'But Vinny, I'm on your side! I couldn't sympathise more.'

She drove until she found a wide passing place. Then she stopped the car and wondered what to do next. She didn't want to go home, but she couldn't face inquisitive friends either. She wanted to be somewhere calm and neutral where she wouldn't be badgered by questions. Of course! Jonathan's house.

★ ★ ★

163

'Is this a bad moment?' Vinny asked him as he opened his front door.

'For what?'

'For coming to see you.'

'No. I'm eating my supper.'

'Oh, sorry. Maybe I should come back another time?'

'No, I meant, It's a good moment because I'm not working.'

'Oh, I see.' Vinny went in. Jonathan sat down at the kitchen table and picked up his spoon. Beside his bowl was a piece of bread and cheese. Vinny sat down opposite him. 'Tomato soup?'

'Yes, it's my favourite.'

Vinny felt the need to explain herself. 'I just felt like escaping from Pamela for a short while.'

'I see.'

Vinny relaxed. No questions, no need to justify herself, no pressure. She'd done the right thing in coming here. She'd had supper, so she wasn't hungry. She felt content to wait for a cup of something until he was ready for one too. The fact that he hadn't offered her anything to eat did not worry her. She understood now that if she were to ask him for food, he would willingly share what he had with her. It's just a question of knowing what to do, she thought, and it filled her with a warm sense of progress achieved.

'I'd like a cup of coffee,' she said, 'if you're having one, when you've finished that?'

'OK.' He took her at her word, finishing his soup unhurriedly and eating his bread and his cheese down to the last crumb. Then he got to his feet, washed out a mug for her and put the kettle on.

Vinny watched him as he did so. He is beautiful, she thought. It's really the only word to describe him. 'Handsome' is too ordinary — or just too masculine? No, she thought, he is absolutely male, but he also has an aura of innocence about him. It's an almost angelic quality; one that I've never found in anyone else. I find it completely beguiling. I'd never tell him, of course.

'What is it that you actually do in Africa?' she asked him. 'Tell me in human terms rather than in statistics.'

'We find low technology solutions to local problems,' Jonathan said, sitting down again. 'We go and live with the people and see for ourselves what they need. Then we talk to them to find out if they agree with us. And then together we devise a solution, if we can.'

'What kind of problems?'

He thought for a moment. 'Well, when it rains in a hot country the soil is baked hard and the precious water just runs away down the slopes without penetrating the soil, and eighty percent of it just evaporates in the sun without doing any good to the food plants. So we teach them about tied ridges on slopes, where you hoe the ground into vertical ridges with cross bits between them to catch the water. And on flatter land we do subsurface irrigation where we sink lines of clay pipes under the ground, with a bent one at one end of each course, which sticks up, and with the far ends blocked by stones. Then you pour water into the visible ones, and it seeps out at the joints between the pipes all along under the soil in the root zone, where the roots of the crops are. And that way the water goes straight to where it's needed and isn't wasted, and it's really easy to do too. You should see the difference it makes!' He was animated just by the thought of it.

'Where do the clay pipes come from?' Vinny asked.

'Oh we make them. I teach them how to do it. All you need is some heavy clay soil, some water, a wooden frame, a sheet of plastic, a wooden rolling pin, a knife and a short length of PVC pipe, cut along one side. And five minutes later you have your first clay pipe!' He looked triumphant. 'It's easy for me. I used to make things out of mud all the time, when I was a child. But then of course you have to dry the pipes slowly in the sun, before you fire them in a pit. And as soon as they're cooled down, you can use them. They change people's lives.'

'Yes I'm sure. And the people, what are they like?'

Jonathan considered this before answering. 'It's the women mostly who grow the crops and fetch the water,' he said. 'Did you know that the average African family uses about five gallons a day, as opposed to the average American one which uses more than a hundred gallons?' He stopped. 'Oh, sorry, that's a statistic.'

Vinny laughed. 'And the African women have to go on foot and carry it all by themselves?'

'Yes. In the last village I was in, the women

166

had to walk for half an hour to draw water from a well, and then all that way back again, and they had to do this journey at least four times a day, carrying the water in a *debe* on their heads. It was a tremendous labour.' Jonathan shook his head. 'But we managed to help them too.' His eyes glowed at the recollection. Vinny could see that this was a true vocation for him. 'We thought if the men would carry water as well, this would ease the burden, but a man with a headload would be ridiculed. They simply couldn't do it. But we discovered that if we give them a plastic jerry can to take on a bicycle or cart, then that is masculine enough for them and they *will* do it.' He smiled at the recollection. 'It's so important to discover the local customs before you try to help people,' he said.

That sounds almost like empathy, Vinny thought. How is it possible? 'That must be so satisfying,' she said. 'You must really feel you are doing something worthwhile. Do you make friends with the local people too?'

'Well, not really,' Jonathan said. 'It's work, so it has to be very businesslike. There's so much to do.' The kettle boiled and he got up to attend to it.

Oh, I see, Vinny thought. He treats it more like anthropology than a proper human relationship, but actually that doesn't at all detract from the achievement. He's found something he's really good at, and he does it with a passion. That's so admirable. 'You must be very happy out there,' she said.

'I am, yes.' He placed a mug of coffee in front of her.

'Thank you.' But what about now? Vinny thought. 'How's the book coming on?'

'It's good.'

'Have you found a publisher for it yet?'

'No, I'm going to finish it first.'

'Did you read the water wars one?'

'Yes.'

'And were there any bad overlaps with yours?'

'No. I was never writing that sort of book anyway.'

'Is that why you won't show the manuscript to Pamela?' He gave her a what-d'you-think kind of look, without speaking. 'I'm sure that was a wise move,' she said. 'I don't suppose you'd let me see it either, would you?'

'Do you want to?'

'I'd love to. In fact, would you like me to proofread it for spellings and typos?'

'Typos?'

'Typing errors. We all make them.'

'Are you any good at proofreading?

'Yes, I am, as it happens.'

'Can you start now?'

'Well,' she laughed. 'I don't know. I suppose I could . . . Yes, why not? It would have to be our secret though, OK?'

He showed her upstairs to his study and indicated a pile of papers on the floor. 'There it is.'

'You've only got one copy?'

'Yes.'

'That's a shame. It'd be a lot easier if I could

take one with me — to the library of course. Not home. Have you thought of running off another copy?'

'No. It would take far too long and be too expensive. I try to save myself trouble.' Then he brightened. 'But there's a photocopier in the library. You could photocopy it for me?'

★   ★   ★

At one fifteen pm the next day, the post arrived. Really! Pamela thought crossly, seeing the red van outside and looking at her watch. It's too bad. The wretched man must have been gossiping over cups of tea again. Why else would he be so late? She went to pick up the letters from the mat, and carried them into the kitchen. It was high time for lunch but Vinny was still in bed. This wasn't like her at all. Pamela would normally have gone up to see if she was all right, but Vinny had been so sulky when she got home late the night before, that Pamela didn't see why she should.

She decided to eat without her. She got out the bread and butter, some mushroom paté and an apple, and put the kettle on for instant soup in a mug. Then she sorted the proper post from the junk mail and found a crumpled, rather dirty envelope bearing an Australian stamp. It was from Peter!

She tore it open in haste, and read:

Dear Ma,
Surprise, surprise a letter from your son!

Remember me? I'm here in Oz working as a motorcycle courier. I've managed to pick up an old 500cc Matchless — great bike. Not sure how long the job's going to last since I haven't got a work permit, but hey, who needs one. My main news — I'm thinking of getting hitched. Don't rush to book an airline ticket though — we're not having that kind of a wedding. We plan to grab a couple of witnesses off the street and then take off into the bush for our honeymoon — no fuss, You'd like Kelly. She's tough and direct, just like you — keeps me in order! Don't get us a present. There's no point until we have a home to put it in — way down the line in the future. How's life in little old Somerset? Hope you and Vinny are not too comfortable — that way lies the death of the soul. Maybe see you sometime.
Love, Peter.

Unaccustomed tears sprang to Pamela's eyes and dripped onto the unsalted butter. She lowered her head into her hands and began to sob. The wetness squeezed between her fingers and ran down inside the sleeves of her blouse.

Her own boy! Would she ever see him again? Would he live, marry, have children, even die, and all without reference to her? It was too cruel.

8

After a few minutes Pamela sat up and caught sight of herself in the mirror over the mantelpiece. Her eyes and nose were red, and her face was creased with self-pity.

This isn't like me, she admonished herself. I don't lose control like some fluffy fool of a female. But more tears welled up and overflowed. She reached for a tissue and blew her nose loudly. It isn't so much cruel, she thought, as *ungrateful*. A spurt of anger stopped the flow. She dried her eyes with the soggy tissue and rested her chin on one palm, thinking.

She remembered Peter as a child, exhausting and difficult, but so intelligent, so challenging. She'd had such high hopes for him. He could have been anything, a surgeon, a professor, a QC but he'd ended up as — a bum. She couldn't hide that fact from herself any longer. How had any son of hers turned out to be so feckless?

Pamela breathed out heavily. It was obvious. He got it from his father. And now this. He clearly didn't want her at his wedding. She turned to the front of the air letter. The date stamp was unreadable, and he hadn't even given her an address to reply to.

She became aware that the kettle was boiling its head off, filling the kitchen with steam. She got up and moved it off the hotplate, putting the lid down. She didn't feel like soup any more. She went instead into the dining room and poured herself a generous tot of whisky, filling the glass up with green ginger wine. Medicine for the heart, she told herself, took a good swig and went back into the kitchen.

The only other letter was a bill from the builders. It was for far more than she had anticipated, and she remembered with annoyance that Vinny had warned her of this eventuality. 'If you keep on adding while-you're-here jobs, it'll cost a fortune,' she'd said. Blast her for being right! And where the hell was she anyway?

Pamela sat down again at the kitchen table with her glass half-empty, and began making herself a sandwich. She wondered what was up with Vinny, and then it came to her. She's probably realised just how badly she's been treating me lately, she thought, and is too embarrassed to face me. The best thing I can do is to be magnanimous. It's probably just a phase, maybe even an early menopause? Perhaps she should take HRT like me? She took a hefty bite of her sandwich and felt better. That was one problem solved, but what of the builders' bill? There's only one thing for it, she thought, I shall have to reassess the whole situation where Jonathan is concerned, especially now there aren't likely to be any royalties from his so-called book.

* * *

Vinny finally got out of bed at two o'clock in the afternoon, feeling guilty but refreshed, and determined to hold her own with Pamela. I shan't apologise, she thought, and I won't explain. That's the first rule when dealing with control freaks. I won't tell her I've got Jonathan's manuscript either. I'll take it to work with me on Monday and take a copy, and then I'll proofread it during my lunch hours.

As she went down the stairs, she smiled to herself at the thought of Jonathan. Photocopying his book was far too much work and expense for him, and yet he quite expected her to do it for him! It was a curious thing, this inability of his to empathise, but she knew that when she pointed this out, and asked him to pay her the cost of it, he would do so. He was always scrupulously fair. I don't mind, she thought. I want to help him.

'So there you are!' Pamela said as she came in. 'Are you ill?'

'No,' Vinny said. Pamela surely hadn't been crying?

'Tell me, have you been having hot flushes?'

'Certainly not!'

'They'll come.' Pamela put on a martyred expression. 'It's just that you seem so irritable lately, and that's one of the symptoms.'

'I'm *fine*,' Vinny said.

'Well lucky old you,' Pamela snapped. 'I, on the other hand, am anything but.'

Here we go, Vinny thought. I have no choice but to ask why. 'Why?'

'Read this.' Pamela pushed a letter towards her, over the table.

173

Vinny scanned it swiftly. 'Good lord!'

'Is that all you've got to say?'

'Well . . . no . . . '

'He doesn't tell me anything about her. No photograph, nothing. And he says *you'd* like her, not *you'll*. Doesn't that sound to you as though he's no intention of my ever meeting her?'

'Oh, I don't suppose he's weighed up every word that carefully,' Vinny ventured.

'Why not? It's only his third letter in as many years!'

'Well, I suppose . . . '

'And he's working without a permit. What if he gets caught and imprisoned?'

'Oh, I doubt whether . . . '

'And he says maybe see you sometime. *Maybe?* My own son!'

'Yes, that is hard. I'm so sorry.' Vinny sat down opposite her and prepared to be sympathetic.

'But he's got something right.' Pamela stared at her challengingly.

'What's that then?' Vinny looked down at the table.

'I wouldn't describe us as *too comfortable*, would you?'

'No,' Vinny agreed. 'We're not comfortable at all.'

'And whose fault is that?'

'You think it's mine?'

'Well, you've definitely changed, Vinny, and it's not for the better.'

Vinny looked out of the window and saw a spotted flycatcher on a bush outside. One summer they'd made a nest in the front porch and the three youngsters had seemed, by a trick of plumage, to be frowning down at her each time she'd passed by underneath.

'*Vinny?* Are you listening to me at all?'

'Sorry. Yes, I am.'

'Do you admit it's all your fault?'

Vinny remembered a page in the assertiveness book on the strategy of nondefensive communication when under attack: Don't argue or try to defend yourself. Don't attempt to understand what's in the other person's mind. And don't try to buy their approval with grovelling apologies. Just change the script. Easier said than done.

Vinny took a brave breath and produced the first stock phrase. 'I'm sorry you're upset.' She said.

'Too right I am! Everything's falling apart between us and you're *sorry I'm upset!*' She mimicked Vinny's voice uncomfortably accurately.

'Let's talk when you're feeling calmer,' Vinny suggested. Phrase number two.

'What *are* you on about? I'm perfectly calm. It's you that's wrecking everything, and you know it!'

Oh hell, Vinny thought. I've only got one more shot in my locker. What if it doesn't work? I don't suppose the author of that book has ever met anyone quite like Pamela.

'Well?' demanded Pamela dangerously.

'You're absolutely right,' Vinny said, fingers crossed behind her back.

'Oh!' Pamela appeared nonplussed. 'Well . . . good.' There was a short silence, and then she said, 'Would you like some lunch?'

Jonathan sat in his newly refurbished study a week later, relaxed and happy for the first time in ages. It was true that he missed his old concrete-block and plank desk because it had been exactly the right height and this new one was not, but he wasn't going to complain. He was free! Free at last from intrusive questions, mind-dislocating interruptions and endless bloody coffee. And maybe in time he would get peace and quiet too. The builders were back again downstairs and at the moment it sounded as though they were beating something with a couple of sledgehammers. He didn't care what they were doing. It wasn't his problem, and perhaps with practice he could learn to shut his ears to the noise.

The men themselves were no bother, apart from their radio. The senior one, a large man with ginger hair, said very little, and kept the younger one with the blond ponytail in order most of the time. The third man didn't seem to be coming any more. Jonathan had no wish to know their names, and restricted himself to 'Morning,' and 'Hello,' when he met them, and 'fine,' and 'yes,' in reply to their greetings. It was an ideal form of communication; friendly, undemanding and entirely adequate.

Jonathan typed:

At the Amber Junction pumping station on the English Somerset Levels, three quarters of the machinery is obsolete. An experienced senior operator runs and maintains 4 Sultzer horizontal pumps, 3 of which are powered by 2-cylinder horizontal Crossley diesel engines, which were made in 1931 and for which there are no spare parts.

He sat back and looked out of the window. It still hadn't rained, and the level of the water in the Kingspill was going down as it was used up for irrigation purposes. He wondered what George was doing, now there was no need for so much pumping. He felt sad at the loss of his friendship. Had it been all his fault? He didn't believe so, but then none of his social solecisms had seemed so to him, until the error of his ways was pointed out by busybodies like Pamela.

He shrugged, shuffled himself upright in the unfamiliar chair and typed:

One of the 3 diesel engines is already non-functional with a damaged cylinder lining, and will probably have to be broken up for spares to service the other 2. The cost of replacement (in today's figures) for new engines would probably be in excess of £100,000 but in an Agency habitually starved of funds, this is not an option. In parts of Africa . . .

The hammering had stopped. Jonathan lifted his head and listened. He could hear a woman's voice but it wasn't Pamela's. Mildly curious, he went to the top of the stairs and listened

' . . . so my mum thought you could maybe use some fruit buns?'

'Ta very much,' Ponytail said. He had a much lighter voice than Big Ginger. ' 'Bout time I knew your name innit?'

'It's Amanda Overy, but you can call me Mandy.'

'Mandy, eh? Very nice!'

'What, cakes is it?' Big Ginger's voice sounded further away. Jonathan was about to beat a retreat, hoping Mandy wouldn't realise he was there, when Ginger spoke again. 'You got some for computer man upstairs? His need is greater than what ours is, I shouldn't wonder.'

'Oh, he's back is he? Nah, he don't deserve them like you do. I could tell you a thing or two about him . . . ' She lowered her voice. Jonathan could hear them laughing together. He thought, What could she tell them? I don't care. He went back to his desk.

★   ★   ★

'George?' Gwen called to her husband. 'Have you been at them buns again? A good half dozen's gone since yesterday and it can't be our Mand, not with her on that daft diet!'

' 'T'aint me neither,' George said, coming into their kitchen. 'She's never been up The Prospect again, have 'er?'

'Surely 'er wouldn't dare? Not after all us've said on that subject! Anyway there's them two builders up there most the time, 'cept when the big bloke's off getting' supplies. You seen 'em?'

'Can't say as I've noticed.'

'And that Jonathan, he's got no interest in a child of her age!'

'Well I still says there's no smoke . . . '

'Fact is, us can't trust her these days!' Gwen clutched both her hands together. 'And she was always such a truthful little girl.' Tears came into her eyes.

'Don't you fret yourself. I'll keep an eye out for her,' George promised.

The following Saturday the drought broke and it rained hard all day. By chance George was driving past The Prospect on his way to open some sluices, when he caught sight of Mandy disappearing through the open front door.

'Well, I'll be — ' he exclaimed, braking hard and stopping in the lay-by. He sat there for a moment, blowing out his cheeks in indecision. Then he got out, marched across the footbridge and went in at the door.

A sexy female giggle followed by a male voice murmuring something softly, precipitated him into action. He tiptoed across the hall to the kitchen door, and there she was, his Mandy, all wrapped around some bloke he'd never seen before. He had blond hair like a bloody girl's and was so busy sticking his tongue down *his* daughter's throat, that he didn't hear George's furious approach and only stopped when he was physically hauled off her and slammed back against the kitchen wall.

'*Dad!*' Mandy shrieked, tottering and almost falling.

'What the fuck?' Ponytail blurted out.

'You take your filthy hands off her,' George shouted. 'She's only *thirteen!*' He made as if to hit the youth, who cowered away from him.

'How was I to know that?' he protested. 'She come on to me that strong. How the fuck should I — '

George took a deliberate step forwards. 'That's assault, that is! Your boss'll be hearing from me, don't you worry.' Then he grabbed Mandy by the wrist. 'And as for you, you little slag . . . ' He dragged her out of the house and over the bridge before throwing her into the front seat of his van. 'What you bloody playing at?' he demanded, once they were sitting side by side. 'Haven't us told you over and over, *not* to come up here?'

'You hurt my arm,' she sobbed, rubbing it.

'I'll hurt a lot more'n that if you goes on like this. You'm acting no better'n a common tart! You'll break your mother's heart, you know?'

'I was only snogging him.' Her face took on the defiant expression he knew so well, and it was all he could do not to slap her.

'And you're telling me you don't know where that leads?' George looked away from her in disgust, shaking his head. His eye was caught by the sight of a figure upstairs, peering out. It was Jonathan. George suffered a twinge of conscience. 'Don't you move from there!' he ordered Mandy. Then, getting out of the van, he walked over and stood beneath the window.

Jonathan opened it and leaned out. 'Hello George.'

'Seems I owe you an apology,' George called up.

'Oh?'

'I blamed you, when t'wasn't your fault.'

'Does that mean we can be friends again?' Jonathan looked childishly hopeful.

George felt embarrassed, but kindly. 'I reckon so.'

Jonathan's face was transformed into one huge smile. '*Good*,' he said.

Poor simple soul, George thought. I've made a bad mistake. I did ought to make it up to him. 'Come down Amber Junction,' he said. 'Any time. You'm more'n welcome.'

★   ★   ★

Vinny had begun to proofread Jonathan's book with high hopes. She wanted so much to be able to praise it, but then found herself in the difficult position of wishing to encourage him without, honestly, being able to. It was just a list of facts. She supposed that to an aficionado, the superabundance of information might be profoundly satisfying. To Vinny, however, who took water pretty much for granted, it was interesting enough to begin with, but there was a limit to the number of times one could exclaim 'Good gracious!' or 'Who'd have thought it?' Jonathan had been right about one thing — it was not at all like the water wars book. It had no emotional appeal in it, no humour, no structure. It was a book written by a scrupulously accurate automaton — erudite, meticulous and — dry.

Vinny used the dictionary of Science and Technology from the library and checked all the scientific terms for spelling, and the text for general intelligibility, but was in a quandary as to what she should do next. Should she tell him what she thought? He'd probably defend it by saying that it wasn't written for a layman like her. So who was it written for? It was more like a manual for the obsessive collector of data, the nerdy anorak type . . .

That's it! Vinny thought. I've got the perfect title — although I can hardly tell Jonathan — *The Train-spotter's Guide to Water.*

★ ★ ★

It was mid August before the builders left The Prospect. The work had been completed — to Pamela's exacting satisfaction — by ginger Dave and the third man, Jack, swiftly called back to replace ponytail Charlie on the job. Pamela went over with her clipboard and was finally unable to find fault with anything. All that remained to be done was the decorating.

Perhaps Pamela will give us some peace now, Vinny thought, especially poor Jonathan. She had the next two weeks off from the library, but had kept quiet about it, hoping against hope that Pamela wouldn't suggest they took a holiday together. She really couldn't bear another one. At least while she was at Hembrow she could escape whenever she wanted to.

'Vinny?' Pamela called.

'I'm in the kitchen.'

'I've got a proposition for you,' Pamela said, coming in.

Oh God! Vinny thought. Here we go. 'What?'

'How do you fancy a spot of painting? At The Prospect?'

'Oh . . . ' Relief made Vinny generous. 'Yes, why not?'

Pamela came over and hugged her. 'I knew

182

you'd agree,' she said. 'It'll be fun, and it'll cost a lot less too.'

She surely didn't mean — decorate the whole house? Why is it, Vinny thought sourly, that my main function these days seems to be to save other people money? 'I thought you were getting the painter Gordon recommended to do most of it?' she said.

'Well, I did consider it, but then I thought you and I could work at it together, during your holiday.'

'You're going to do it as well?' Pamela was rubbish at painting.

'Yes, I thought I'd give it a go. I mean, how hard can it be?'

Too hard for you! 'You mean the whole house?'

'Naturally.'

'It'll take some time,' Vinny pointed out. 'Longer than a fortnight.'

'Yes, well we can break the back of it in the first two weeks and then perhaps get Gordon's man to finish it off. Oh Vinny!' Pamela looked as delighted as she always used to in the old days. 'It'll be such fun. It's so long since we did anything together, isn't it? Now, we'll need to get the paint of course and choose the colours. Nothing too personal, I think — pastel shades — you really can't go wrong with magnolia.'

Vinny couldn't help being touched by Pamela's enthusiasm for spending time with her, but wondered how long it would last. They took Bertie to B&Q and filled his boot with tins of paint, brushes, white spirit, a paint-kettle and hook, packets of latex gloves, an expensive double-jointed step ladder and two sets of paper overalls. Then next day they wore their oldest shoes and took their bath hats (just in case of drips) and arrived at The Prospect, raring to go.

Jonathan was less than welcoming. 'I didn't know you were coming to paint today.'

'I did try to phone you,' Pamela said, with exaggerated patience, 'but of course your mobile was switched off, and I don't suppose you've bothered to listen to your messages?'

'I never get any.'

'Well, there you are then. Complete waste of time. Now then, Vinny, I think we'll begin upstairs. It's probably best to do Jonathan's study first, to be sure it'll be finished as quickly as possible.'

'But I'm in the middle . . . ' he protested.

'Don't worry. You can move all your computer stuff down to the sitting room. We'll be much less disruptive than the builders were — no blaring radio to drive you mad! You won't know we're here.' She gave him a dazzling smile.

'But I will!'

'I'm sorry, Jonathan,' Vinny said soothingly. 'I know it's inconvenient, but once the painting is done then you really will be left alone.' He looked unmollified. 'And,' Vinny added to encourage him, 'whilst we're here, I'll cook for you too.'

'Oh well, that's better.' He went upstairs at once to collect his things.

'Well done Vin. Good bribe!' Pamela said *sotto-voce*.

184

No, Vinny thought. Actually I'm on *his* side, not yours.

★ ★ ★

The rest of August passed, and with it most of Vinny's free fortnight. In the garden at Hembrow the apples ripened in the sun, Michaelmas daisies were coming into bloom, and the bird droppings on the terrace were stained purple with blackberries. It was still hot at noon but the days were shorter, and the nights crisper. The beginning of September signalled the inevitability of autumn. It's backendish now, Vinny thought. Bob will soon stop coming to cut the grass every week, and the year will begin to shut down. Another one gone by and what have I got to show for it? A few rooms bright with fresh colour, and a lot more still to do.

The joint painting enterprise had gone much as Vinny had imagined it would; Pamela on the first day all kitted out and enthusiastic, slapping it on with verve and abandon. Vinny herself, painting more slowly and methodically, stopping every so often to wipe up Pamela's splodges on the floor and elsewhere.

'Never mind that,' she'd say. 'It'll all be covered up by the carpet eventually.'

'Yes, but it can get on the soles of our shoes now,' Vinny said. 'And we don't want it all over the brand-new ceramic tiles in the kitchen, do we?'

'Lovely Vinny,' Pamela said. 'Such a perfectionist! What would I do without you?'

After a couple of days of course, Pamela got bored. She began to complain of arthritis in her wrist and neck, and then discovered more than the usual number of committee meetings that required her presence.

'I'm sorry, Vin,' she said. 'The fact is, they really *need* my input. Gordon says they're lost without me, bless him!'

'You go,' Vinny said. 'I'll struggle on here.'

And 'struggle' she did, savouring the mess-free quietness with no one else to get in the way. She felt not only a sense of achievement, but also very much enjoyed Jonathan's friendly company over lunch.

'I like having you here,' he said. More than just for the food? Vinny hoped so.

'I like it too,' she said.

'And your proofreading is very accurate too. That's so useful.'

'D'you know what would mean a lot to me?' Vinny asked, greatly daring. 'It would be so good to know that I was appreciated, not just because I'm useful or can cook well, but because you're genuinely fond of me and enjoy having me around.'

'But of course I do.' He looked surprised.

'The thing is,' she explained, 'I won't know it unless I actually hear it from you. So I really want you to tell me exactly what it is about me that you like. I'm not a very confident person, you see. I need to be told.'

'Oh, right.' He considered for a moment and then counted things out on his fingers. 'Well . . . I like your generosity and your patience with me and your friendship and intelligence and your ability to say the right thing at the right time' He stopped to look searchingly at her. 'And I like your hair, and your wide smiling mouth . . . Will that do?'

'Yes, very well. Thank you.' Vinny felt warm inside.

A week or so later, when she had made him an especially good lunch, she ventured further. 'Jonathan?'

'Yes?'

'Did you enjoy eating that?'

'I certainly did. It was delicious.'

'So, I wonder if you could begin to make a habit of saying 'thank you' to me? Then I'd know you were pleased with what I'd done for you, and that would please me very much. And then we'd both be happy.'

'Ye-es,' Jonathan considered. 'Yes, I see what you mean. I've never thought about it like that before. They always seemed to me to be two rather meaningless words that you were supposed to keep using. And the more people nagged me about them, the less I wanted to say them. But they do make more sense now,' and he smiled at her.

Vinny thought, At last! I'm getting through to him. We're really communicating! She felt triumphant.

But every so often this tentative intimacy of theirs was interrupted when Pamela came back to do another half-hour's painting, and to keep an eye upon Vinny's work in progress.

'It looks good,' she'd said towards the end of

the fortnight, 'but you're back at the library on Monday, aren't you? And there's still a hell of a lot to be done. So I suppose we will have to get a professional in, after all, to finish it off.'

'No,' Vinny said at once. 'It's OK. I'd like to go on with it. I can do evenings and days off, no sweat.'

'You've started, so you'll finish, eh?'

'Something like that.'

'Good for you!' Pamela stroked her arm. 'It's such a delight that you're doing something for me again, so unselfishly, just as you always used to. I've really got the old Vinny back. Come here.' Pamela enveloped her in a bear hug.

Vinny felt like Judas.

★   ★   ★

By early October, Vinny was still painting but the end was in sight. What shall I do, she thought, when I can no longer escape to The Prospect and spend time with Jonathan? Today's Saturday, so I've got all day. Perhaps I'll go for a little walk this morning. I can't unravel my painting every night to make it last longer, but I could do it more slowly!

'Just going to post a letter,' she called to Pamela, and then left quickly so that she couldn't come with her. Once out of sight she walked slowly out of their drive and along the lane towards the post-box.

She looked about her. The night had brought the first frost and the leaves were already turning colour; the field maples and hazels to yellow and the brambles to red. Ropes of scarlet-black bryony berries decorated the hedgerows, competing with the rosehips and the occasional marvellously clashing pink and orange spindle-berries — nature's best invalidation of colour co-ordinated correctness. Vinny looked up at the sky, which was blue and perfect. It was empty. The swallows must have gone, she thought. I should like to go to Africa too.

She reached the post-box in the wall, posted her letter and set off again homewards, turning her mind to practicalities. The Aga needed its six monthly service. She must phone their man. The bramley apples could do with picking before the autumn gales blew them down, bruised them and prevented them from keeping. And she really must buy some flyspray. Every year at this time, dozens of bluebottles crept in around the edge of their window casements to hibernate. Then, when anyone innocently opened one, they would all fall out on their backs, dozy and disgusting, recovering briefly to crash witlessly about from pane to pane before eventually expiring. Pamela would try to usher them out into the frosty air to perish slowly. Vinny, though usually against chemicals, thought a quick death preferable.

Why on earth am I wasting my time on *flies*, she thought. I should be making plans for the future. But this is what people like me, do. They can't cope with the big picture, so instead they concentrate on trivia. I have got to change.

★ ★ ★

189

It's now October, Pamela thought, and when did Jonathan begin that book of his? January, wasn't it? Surely he must almost have finished it by now? Whenever she saw him — which was not often these days — she would ask him how it was going, but he seemed to get more and more cagey about it and wouldn't let her see so much as half a page of his precious manuscript. Perhaps it's no good? Pamela wondered. I mean, we only have his word for it that he can actually *write*. His father clearly doesn't think much of his efforts, after all and he should know. What if it's total rubbish and here I am, subsidising him? *I have a right to know.*

By the time Vinny came home from work, Pamela's mind was made up. 'I've been trying to get Jonathan on his mobile all day,' she said, 'but of course it isn't on and he hasn't replied to any of my messages. I shall just have to go down there tonight and speak to him in person. Damn!'

'What's the rush?' Vinny asked, hanging up her coat in the hall.

'Finance,' Pamela said crisply.

'Sorry?'

'It's high time he paid his way,' Pamela said, frowning at Vinny's slowness. 'It's not good for him to be sponging off me the way he has been. It won't do him any favours in the long run.'

'You mean you're going to charge him rent, now? You said he didn't have to pay anything!'

'Changed my mind.'

'But that's not fair! How much rent?'

'I'm not sure yet, but I shall be guided by the

fact that I could get up to five hundred pounds a week for The Prospect if I rented it out to summer visitors.'

'Surely not that much?' Vinny objected.

'Oh yes, absolutely. I made a point of getting comparable figures from the Tourist Office in Otterbridge. I know what I'm talking about.'

'No. I meant, you won't charge Jonathan such a huge amount?'

'Why not?'

'He couldn't afford it, for a start.'

'Well, that's his lookout. Let's face it. I'm not running a charity here.'

'Look Pamela, you simply can't treat people like this.' Vinny's face was red with indignation. 'You can't take them on one minute, and then price them out of existence the moment you lose interest. This is someone's life you're playing with!'

'You are getting into a state, aren't you?' Pamela observed with satisfaction. 'Relax, for goodness sake. It's not the summer season now, is it? I shall charge him a reasonable winter rate but warn him that it will have to go up next summer, if he's still here. So then he can please himself what he does about it.'

'You mean that you'll turf him out then?'

'Well, he'll have finished his wretched book by January anyway, won't he?'

'And if he hasn't?'

'Oh, I've no patience with people who can't stick to deadlines — shows a complete lack of forethought and discipline.'

'Weren't you supposed to have looked out some information on planning law for the WI

191

committee for last week?' Vinny looked unpleasantly triumphant.

'Totally different!' Pamela retorted at once. 'That's *voluntary* work.'

I feared it was too good to be true, she thought, Vinny being so sweet about the painting. I might have known that she'd turn out not to have changed at all. She seems to be turning into a thoroughly snide and sarcastic person. She never used to be so critical or so quick to sneer. Doesn't matter what I say — she attacks me. It's almost as though she doesn't even *like* me any more. The thought made her feel quite wobbly inside. She had to steel herself against the unwonted emotion.

'You know,' she said. 'I'd been so much looking forward to it being just US again. Just you and me together, as it used to be in the good old days. Remember? We were so happy then. But Jonathan's been back at The Prospect for months now and, as for you, you seem hell-bent on spoiling everything!'

★   ★   ★

Jonathan couldn't understand why Pamela suddenly wanted to charge him rent, after all she'd previously said to him. How was he going to find the money anyway? One minute she was being friendly and praising his literary efforts and the next, she was threatening to evict him! It was this last thought that finally provoked him into retaliation, as she stood there, facing him in his kitchen.

'You can't throw me out anyway,' he said. 'I'm a sitting tenant.'

'I think you'll find,' Pamela said, 'that tenants pay rent. Legally you're a squatter and therefore have no rights.'

'But you invited me to live here!'

'I let you stay out of the kindness of my heart,' Pamela said.

'But — ' Jonathan tried to marshal a coherent argument fast. ' — if you're right — and I don't necessarily acknowledge that you are — if I now begin to pay rent, then I *will* become a tenant, and then you really won't be able to get rid of me.'

'Look here,' Pamela said irritably, 'No one said anything about evicting you.'

'Yes you did. You said people who refuse to pay their rent get thrown out.'

'I was just trying to *explain* how the system works. There's no need to get so heated about it, is there? You're living in my property and now it's all been done up so nicely, it's worth a lot more and I'm entitled to expect an income from it.'

'But you don't need the money.'

'That is neither here nor there!'

'*What on earth does that mean?*'

'Look Jonathan . . . ' Pamela was sitting on one of the four new chairs at his kitchen table.

He'd been standing opposite her, leaning back against the sink, but he straightened up and leant towards her as he said, 'No, you look. I want some answers. Why have you changed your mind? Have I said or done something wrong? If so, you should tell me.'

Pamela sat back in the chair and with both hands, drew her coat closed at the throat. 'There's no need to be quite so aggressive.'

What did she mean? 'But I'm not. This is stupid.'

'Yes it is. So, why don't you make us a coffee and we'll talk it through rationally.'

'Don't want coffee.'

'Well I do.'

Jonathan put the kettle on with a bad grace and then sat down opposite her. What was going on? In the beginning she was a stranger who had offered him something he'd needed, and he'd been grateful. She'd said 'Don't mention it', so he hadn't. What else was he supposed to do? He couldn't afford to be homeless at this juncture, especially when the writing was going so well . . .

'So, when do you expect to finish the book?' Pamela asked him.

'Two months, maybe three. I'm not sure.'

'And have you approached any publishers?'

'No, not yet.'

'Well, isn't it about time you did? It's hardly going to be a bestseller at this rate, is it?'

'What d'you mean? It won't be anyway. I keep telling you, it's not that sort of book.'

'Well if something as boring as longitude or cod can make it, I don't see why yours shouldn't too,' Pamela said. 'It's very disappointing. I had high hopes of you.'

Jonathan frowned. Why should she have hopes of any sort? What was it to do with her? 'Why?' he asked.

'I should have thought that was self-evident. Why do you think I've been helping you all this time?'

Jonathan tried to work it out logically. 'Because bestsellers make an author famous, and you want to claim some of the credit?'

'The very idea!' She laughed loudly.

Had he said something funny? 'Well anyway,' he said. 'You'll be appearing in the acknowledgements at the front. Both you and Vinny.'

Pamela's face changed. 'Vinny, why?'

'For the proofreading of course.'

'*Vinny* is proofreading your manuscript?' She had gone very red. Then, without any warning she suddenly leant forward with her face only inches from his own. 'Now, see here young man . . . '

Jonathan turned away instinctively, putting an arm up to ward off this intolerable intrusion into his space, and his elbow somehow caught her cheekbone a glancing blow.

'Ohh!' Her chair skidded backwards as she scrambled to get away from him. She was holding the side of her face with one hand, and her eyes were wide open. 'You *struck* me!'

'No,' he said, standing up uncertainly. 'You got too close to me. I was just — '

'You haven't heard the last of this, believe me.' Pamela got to her feet, picked up her handbag and walked very strangely backwards to the kitchen door, before she turned. He heard her running to the front door and leaving.

Jonathan sat down with a thump, feeling winded by this alarming and unexpected outcome, and totally at a loss as to what he should have done. Would she go to the police? Would he be in trouble again? The unfairness of the whole thing was staggering. Time passed in a daze, and it was only when he noticed that the kitchen windows were steaming up, that he took the kettle off the stove and carried it upstairs to add the boiling water to a bath.

★　★　★

The front door slammed and Pamela rushed into the house, her whole body electric with indignation.

'How *dare* you?' she shouted to Vinny as she came in.

'Uh?'

'You know very well!'

'No.'

'How dare you be so devious! *I* was going to proofread Jonathan's book, not you. And now you've brainwashed him into giving it to *you*.'

Oh Lord, Vinny thought. He must have told her. Why did he do that?

'You used to be so ethical, Vin,' Pamela said. 'I just don't know you any more.' She flopped down onto a chair and the light over the kitchen table illuminated her face. One cheekbone was red and swollen and the flesh around that eye was darkening.

'Whatever's happened?' Vinny asked. 'You're all bruised!'

'Your precious Jonathan hit me.' She leant forward and supported her head on both hands.

'Never!' Vinny said. 'I don't believe you. He wouldn't do that.'

'Well, is this a black eye or not?' Pamela thrust her face forwards.

'Yes, but . . . '

'I've a good mind to report him. Ohh . . . I feel faint.' She had gone a dirty grey colour.

Vinny jumped to her feet and went round to help her. 'Put your head down low,' she said, guiding her, 'to let the blood back into it.'

'Aaahh,' Pamela breathed after a while. 'Brandy.' She sat up again, pinker but still shaky.

'I'll get you one.' Vinny went to the dining room and came back with a glass half full of the neat spirit.

'Just look what you've done to me, Vinny. This is all your fault.' Pamela looked up at her pathetically and took a long gulp.

For once, Vinny felt entitled to lie. 'I didn't volunteer to do the bloody proofreading,' she said. 'Jonathan asked me to, all by himself.'

'So why not be honest and open about it? Why the mean-spirited secrecy? You knew I wanted to do it. You know that I'm good at that sort of thing. Is that the action of a true friend?'

'But he didn't want you to see it,' Vinny insisted. 'He was afraid you'd try to interfere and make him write it your way.' She waited for the explosion.

'That can't be true. You don't know that!'

'Yes, I do.'

'So you've been talking about me, behind my back?'

'No, I — '

'How could you, Vin? After all the years we've known each other? It's nothing short of a betrayal!'

'Oh don't be so melodramatic,' Vinny snapped. 'You know I'm far better qualified than you, to proof . . . '

'I'm talking about your deceit,' Pamela interrupted. 'Your underhandedness, hypocrisy, *furtiveness*. How will I ever be able to trust you again?'

Vinny began to go. 'I've had enough of this. I'm going to bed.'

'That's it, run away! I'm injured and you're just going to desert me?'

'You'll live.'

Pamela managed one more barb. 'So what's this wonderful book like, then? You owe me that much at least.'

Vinny turned her back without a word. What could she say?

'Oh, I get it,' Pamela crowed. 'It's rubbish, isn't it? Well I'm sorry to have to say this, but *I told you so!*'

★   ★   ★

Pamela was woken in what seemed to her to be the middle of the night, by bumping noises on the stairs. The outside light was on too. She could see its brightness through the crack between her curtains. When she went to investigate, she found Vinny pulling a heavy suitcase down after her — the large one they always used on foreign trips — the one which held everything.

'What are you doing?' Pamela asked, rubbing her eyes.

'What's it look like?'

'But . . . where are you going, and for how long?'

'Don't know yet.'

'But Vin . . . ' Pamela leant over the banisters helplessly.

Vinny looked up at her from the front hall. 'Look, Pamela, it's clearly not working at the moment, is it? We need a break from each other. Don't worry, I'll keep in touch.'

A righteous anger erupted from Pamela without warning and spewed forth, laden with spit. 'Don't bloody bother! *Just piss off then.*'

She watched in disbelief as Vinny lifted the bag with difficulty and dragged it to the front door. Then she slipped into her bedroom and peered out from behind the curtain as Vinny lugged it into the back of the mini, got in herself, and drove off.

'And don't come back!' Pamela screamed after her.

She was full of rage — far too angry to be shattered by Vinny's defection, and she was still looking out of the window in this frame of mind, when she saw the lights of another vehicle turning into her drive and stopping outside the porch. It was a taxi.

For one wonderful moment she thought it might be Peter, but no. It was an unknown young woman who had got out, and was now standing with just her head inside the cab, as though talking to someone.

Hell! Pamela thought. Who's this, for Christ's sake? Whoever it is, I can do without them just at this moment. She withdrew behind the curtain and breathed hard. If she stayed there long enough, whoever it was might go away again. The taxi was still there. She could hear its engine ticking over.

The doorbell rang stridently, cutting the quietness in half. She stayed where she was. It rang again, for longer this time. This is silly, she told herself. I'm not going to achieve anything by hiding, am I? I'll go down and get rid of her, and then I'll decide what I'm going to do about Vinny.

She took a determined breath, put her shoulders back and swept downstairs to the front door. The bell rang again, deafeningly, just as she was opening it. She jumped, '*Oh!*'

'G'day. Did I wake you?' A freckled red-haired girl in her twenties was standing there, with two holdalls at her feet and a baby in her arms.

Pamela was brought up short. 'Yes?' she said crisply, as though to a door-to-door salesman.

'Do me a favour and pay the driver, would you?' the girl said, hitching the baby onto her hip. 'I'm totally skint.'

'What . . . ?' Pamela frowned uncomprehendingly.

'You haven't figured out who we are yet, have you?' The girl broke into a wide grin. Her teeth were beautifully white and even. The hazel eyes smiled confidently into Pamela's own. 'I'm Kelly, and this is Chloë, your grand-daughter.'

9

Vinny drove away from Hembrow that morning after a sleepless night, feeling oddly disconnected from herself. It was still dark, but she'd been unable to wait any longer before making her escape. Pamela and I have lived together for over ten years, she thought, and now it's come to this. Have I wasted the best years of my life for nothing?

Tears oozed down her cheeks. She felt about in the door pocket with one hand, and wiped them away with the little leather-covered sponge she used for the windscreen. She kept driving. Where was she going? What about work?

I need to make sure that Jonathan is all right, she thought. Once I know, then I'll think about work. I've never phoned in sick when I wasn't, but maybe today will be different.

Where was she going to live? Ron and Sue, Polly and Arthur, and Gordon were more Pamela's friends than hers. I suppose I could stay with Cheryl for a while, she thought, but she'd drive me mad in no time. She's one of those people who mean well. But how long will it take me to rent somewhere? Will I be able to afford it?

What am I playing at? I never do things on impulse, like this! I always plan in advance. It's the only way to feel safe. I've cast myself adrift . . . I'm frightened. Vinny clutched the steering wheel tightly and breathed as deeply as she could, so that when she arrived at The Prospect, she'd be able to deal with whatever it was that had happened. She parked in the lay-by. One window upstairs was lit up. She switched on the interior light and looked at her watch. I'm much too early, she thought. I'd no idea. How stupid I am! Shall I sit here and wait? No, he must be awake.

She got out of the car and walked across the footbridge with care. The sky was lightening and there was just enough daylight to see by. She knocked on his front door. No answer. She tried again, louder.

'Who's there?' His voice came from above her.

She backed out of the porch and looked up. 'It's me, Vinny.'

He closed the window without saying anything, and a few moments later opened his front door. He was dressed in beige stripy pyjamas and he just stood there. His body language betrayed his anxiety.

'Oh, Jonathan!' Vinny stepped over the threshold, closed the door behind her, and gathered him into her arms. She hugged him close to her. 'It's all right. Everything's fine.'

He rested his chin on the top of her head, and allowed himself to be held. 'I was afraid you were the police,' he said.

'No,' Vinny said, 'just me.' She reached up to kiss his cheek. 'Are you all right?'

'I am now, yes.' Then he put his arms round her as well, and they stood there together in his hall for what seemed a long time.

Vinny closed her eyes and inhaled the warm scent of him. I was trying to reassure him, she thought, but actually now it's him who's comforting me . . .

'Damn!' Jonathan said, releasing her suddenly. 'Sorry . . . er . . . I'd better get dressed,' He turned and ran upstairs, holding the front of his pyjama trousers as he went.

A broad smile crept over Vinny's face. She went into his kitchen and put the kettle on, washing up a couple of mugs and looking in his cupboard for teabags. She hoped he wouldn't be embarrassed when he came down again.

After ten minutes or so, Jonathan reappeared. He was wearing his usual combats and a thick brown jersey. 'Oh good, tea,' he said, and sat down opposite her. 'Vinny?'

'Yes?'

'If a man gets an erection when he's very close to a woman, does that mean he's in love with her?'

'Well, yes, sometimes . . . but not always,' Vinny felt bound to tell him the truth. Then she thought, For God's sake! Why didn't I just say 'Yes'?

'That's all right then.'

There was no way Vinny could continue with this theme. 'So,' she said. 'What happened between you and Pamela last night?'

'She said, 'Now see here young man' and suddenly put her face this close to mine,' Jonathan said, showing the distance with finger and thumb. 'And I put my arm up, like this,' he demonstrated, 'because she was far too close and

203

I couldn't bear it, and then she hit her own face on my elbow. I've got a bruise on it, look!' He pulled up his sleeve and showed her. It was purple, and totally convincing.

Vinny sighed with relief. 'I knew it wasn't your fault,' she told him.

'Is she going to tell the police?'

'I doubt that very much.' Vinny smiled at him. 'What had you just said, before she did it?'

'I told her both your names would be on the acknowledgements page of my book.'

'You told her I was proofreading for you?'

'Yes.'

'Well, that's why she was angry.'

'But she must have known that anyway?'

'No.' Vinny understood now what had happened. She strove to make it easy for him. 'She didn't know,' she explained, 'because no one told her. People only know what they see, or what they're told. Just because *you* know something, it doesn't mean that everyone else does too.'

'Oh.' He thought about it. 'And you didn't tell her?'

'No, I deliberately didn't. I knew she'd be horribly jealous and upset.'

'And she was!' He rubbed his elbow. 'But how did you know that?'

'Because I can usually predict what she's likely to do. I know how her mind works.'

'Oh, so that's why you said it had to be a secret?' He looked crestfallen.

'Yes, but don't worry. I'm sure you'll manage it better next time.' She waited for him to ask what had happened to her when Pamela had got home the night before, but he didn't. Did he have no imagination at all? 'So, do you want to know why I'm here, then?' she said.

'OK.'

'It's because Pamela and I had a quarrel.' She was consciously simplifying everything she said. 'We can't agree about things like we used to, so I'm not going to go on living with her any more.' The night without sleep was beginning to catch up with her. She felt suddenly tearful and anxious.

'That sounds logical,' he said.

He has no idea how I'm feeling, Vinny thought. He can't read the expression on my face, and hasn't even the faintest chance of seeing things from my point of view. I shall have to spell it out.

'So, I've got nowhere to live,' she said, 'and that's making me feel very unhappy.'

'You can live here!' he said at once. He looked delighted.

'I can?' She felt a wave of relief.

'Of course. You can help me pay the rent too! But . . . ' He stopped to consider.

'But what?'

'If we're going to live together, will we sleep in the same bed?'

Vinny couldn't look at him. 'No.'

'That's good. It'd be far too narrow!' He smiled at her. 'I'm glad we've got the ground rules established. It's just as well, because otherwise things can develop into a dreadful muddle.'

Sometimes, Vinny thought, he sounds just like someone from the 1950s! 'So,' she said, 'I can have one of the rooms upstairs, then? Would you like to keep your bedroom, and let me sleep in the new bed in your study?'

'No,' Jonathan said. 'I sometimes have an idea in the night, and have to get up to put it on my computer.'

'Well, all right. Shall I sleep in your bedroom then, and move your bedding to the study?'

'What, you mean I'd have to work and sleep in the same room?'

'Yes.'

'But that's not supposed to be good for a person.'

'Years ago,' Vinny said, 'before I went to live with Pamela, I lived in a bed-sitter. I lived, slept, ate, everything in the one room, and it didn't do me any harm at all.'

'Oh, OK, that's all right then.'

Vinny relaxed. 'That's wonderful.' And then without meaning it literally, she said, 'You've no idea how this makes me feel.' The tears overflowed, and she made no attempt to stem them.

'So tell me.'

'Relieved, grateful, *happy*.' She smiled at him. 'Thank you.'

'It's a pleasure,' Jonathan said.

★   ★   ★

'Why aren't you breastfeeding?' Pamela asked, the following morning as Kelly sterilised bottles

206

and made up some feeds for Chloë.

'Can't.'

'But why not? It's so important for a child's health.'

'Never had enough milk,' Kelly said shortly.

'Oh what a shame! What bad luck. It saves so much time too.' Pamela frowned and appeared to collect her thoughts. 'Now then, I think we should go to Otterbridge at once, and buy a few essentials for Chloë.'

'Sounds good, Pam,' Kelly said.

'*Pamela*,' Pamela said.

'Excuse me?'

'My name is Pamela, *never* Pam!'

'Oh . . . right.' Who's rocked her boat? Kelly thought. 'I get called all sorts,' she said. 'Doesn't bother me.'

'That's as maybe,' Pamela said. 'Now, let's go and do the shopping.'

Peter had been right about one thing at least. His mother might be tough but she was also generous, and her reaction to Chloë — after the first shock — had been beaut. Pamela seemed to have bonded with the baby from the outset. Horses for courses, Kelly thought.

'We'd better get a pram or some sort of a buggy first,' Pamela said as they drove off. 'Then you won't have to keep carrying her about.'

'Yeah. She gets heavier every day.' Kelly gave the baby on her knee a squeeze, and Chloë gurgled contentedly.

'What a poppet you are, aren't you?' Pamela cooed, taking her eyes off the road for longer than Kelly herself would have done. She decided to talk less, so that Pamela could concentrate more. 'And of course she'll need a cot for the night, or maybe I could hire one? It all depends upon your plans. I mean, are you intending to stay for some time?'

'Oh yes, definitely,' Kelly said quickly.

'Better to buy one then. And of course nappies, or do you call them diapers?'

'Whatever,' Kelly said. 'And we'll need some more baby formula.'

'Yes . . . and what about a changing mat? Heavens! It's so long since I did this for Peter, that I've quite forgotten what's required.'

'Was Peter a good baby?' Kelly asked.

'Well, no,' Pamela admitted. 'I don't think in all honesty I could say he was. He was very demanding and needy.'

That figures! Kelly thought.

'You say he's not coming back to England for a while?'

'Nah. He's busy in Oz right now, finishing a job.' The lie came to her easily. No sweat, she thought.

'But, what I can't understand, is why Peter didn't mention your pregnancy in his letter,' Pamela said, frowning. 'Since she's three months old now, he would've had to write it over a year ago, if it wasn't a deliberate omission. It's very puzzling.'

'He wrote you?' Kelly was alarmed. 'What'd he say?'

'Very little. Just that you and he were getting married and having a honeymoon in the bush.'

'Was the letter dated?'

'No, it wasn't.'

Kelly relaxed a little. 'It's just that . . . Sounds to me like it *was* written about a year ago. Maybe it got lost in the mail, and then found again?'

'Possible, I suppose,' Pamela said. 'The envelope was certainly very crumpled up and dirty.' She shook her head. 'So, what was the wedding like?'

'Very quiet.' Kelly looked out of the window to prevent Pamela from reading her thoughts.

'And what was the date?'

'Uh?'

'So I can write it on my calendar.' Pamela was looking at her expectantly. The 4 by 4 swerved, and she looked back at the road again

Kelly's mind was a blank. 'Oh . . . October ten.'

'But that's today's date! What a shame you can't be together on your first anniversary.'

And the rest, Kelly thought. 'Yeah.'

'But Peter will telephone you?'

'Doubt it. He'll be too busy working. Probably forget anyway.'

'Surely not! That isn't the sort of behaviour I expect from my son.'

No wonder he skipped to the other side of the world, Kelly thought. It's definitely not going to be a breeze, crashing here with Pamela, but it'll be worth it if I can hang in there. Good on you, she said to herself, you're doing a great job.

'And whilst we're on the subject of manners,' Pamela went on, 'I do think you might write first next time, or telephone or *something* before you arrive out of the blue. It could have been most inconvenient.'

'But it isn't, is it?'

'You were lucky this time, but don't make a habit of it.'

'I won't. No worries,' Kelly said, and changed the subject. 'I was hoping to meet Vinny?' That Vinny's gotta be one tough Sheila, she thought, to give someone like Pamela a black eye!

'She's away at the moment,' Pamela said.

'And when's she coming back?'

'Oh, fairly soon. Now, here we are . . . I'm pretty sure there's a good Mothercare in the arcade, so we'll park in this multi-storey here . . . '

From then on, Kelly began to enjoy her day. Pamela went mad in the baby shop, scrabbling through racks of little dresses, dungarees and babygro sleepsuits.

'Not pink, I think — too wishy-washy,' she said. 'Blue would suit her colouring much better, and yellow's so cheerful. What d'you think?'

'Whatever you like.' Kelly was astonished as the purchases stacked up.

Pamela bought toys too, and a mobile to hang above the shiny white cot, and a baby duvet with two covers and, for when Chloë was older, a pair of neat little red and orange padded bootees. She even bought a special car seat, and phoned her garage to check that they'd be able to put it in for her. She only stopped when Chloë — laid back luxuriously in her brand new state-of-the-art buggy — got hungry and began to grizzle.

Then they repaired to a corner of the poshest

café in Otterbridge for coffee and cream cakes, and got them to heat up Chloë's bottle (which Pamela had had the forethought to bring along). Then Kelly hitched the baby onto her knee and stuck the teat into her complaining mouth until she too was content.

★ ★ ★

In the middle of October it began to rain in earnest, day after day. Ground water levels rose, the roadside ditches burbled constantly and the limestone caverns inside the Mendip hills filled beyond their usual levels. In all the old Somerset cottages built on the clay, the walls did their annual adjustment to the swelling of their foundations and the windows started to stick as their frames warped, becoming difficult to open.

Down on the peatlands flood plain the rivers and rhynes were swollen and unable to get rid of their burden of water fast enough, despite the all-out efforts of the pumping stations. At high tide in the Bristol Channel when tide-lock closed their clyses, they overflowed their banks and covered the meadows in sheets of silver.

Jonathan watched with pleasure as the waters rose. He enjoyed riding his bike along roads which had become causeways through the inundated featureless flood-scape, identified only by avenues of pollarded willows. There seemed to be more sentinel grey herons than usual but still solitary, in contrast to the ever increasing herds of so-called mute swans, which now swam, grunting, over the fields.

This is so much better than drought, Jonathan thought. He remembered the dust and aridity and ever-present threat of famine in Africa. It was less than a year since he had left, but it may as well have been another lifetime. He hoped to go back there very soon, but even the idea of it seemed unreal. Then suddenly, although he couldn't put it into words, he found himself pining for the place, craving the fierce sunlight which narrowed his eyes and bleached out all the colours; that potent intensity which waned so fast at every sun-down, fading to black insect-loud night.

These thoughts spurred him on with his writing and now, undisturbed by builders and supported by Vinny's undemanding presence, he made even better progress. He noted with satisfaction the thickness of his manuscript, growing ever fatter. He began to allow himself regular time off, especially when he knew it to be the end of George's shift; a good time to watch those wonderful pumps working and to ask him some questions before he went home.

'George has stopped cutting the grass now,' Jonathan said to Vinny, when the subject of lawn mowing came up for some reason.

'Oh? I didn't know he did it anyway.'

'Oh yes, throughout the summer. There's quite a bit of grass all round Amber Junction.'

'Have you spoken to George lately, then? I thought he was ignoring you?'

'Oh no, I speak to him all the time!'

'I didn't know that?'

'You should have asked.' He smiled at her.

'There's a logical error in that suggestion,' Vinny pointed out. 'If a person doesn't know something has changed or happened, then they don't know to ask about it either, do they?'

'Suppose not, no. Well anyway, he apologised to me, said he'd made a bad mistake. Then he said I could go down there whenever I liked, so I do. He's my best friend.'

'Oh,' Vinny said. 'Good.'

The next time he went to Amber Junction, Jonathan questioned George avidly about the recent history of the levels within his lifetime, and the part that water had played in the scheme of things. He discovered that George was a good talker, and that all he himself had to do was to get him started and steered in the direction of his own preferred topic and George would do the rest. Jonathan had never known communication to be so uncomplicated. There were no awkwardnesses, no more misunderstandings and best of all no unfulfilled expectations.

'You should've been here in nineteen sixty eight,' George said one evening, 'if it's floods you'm after.'

'Why?'

'I 'ent seen nothing like it, before nor since.' He shook his head. 'Winter floods is in the nature of things, but this 'un was in July! Flash flood they called it.'

'Were you here then?'

'No. I wasn't much more'n eighteen. My father had a farm in them days, up on Hembrow. Water three bales high there was, pouring down

213

the sides of the hill. Ground was summer-baked as hard as rock, so it all just runned off, see? We had thunder and lightning from two o'clock that afternoon till midnight, and the rain! That was tropical. In't no other word for it. Then it stopped like a tap being turned off. Just like that!' George snapped his fingers.

'And that was the end of it?'

'That was just the start of it! All the tarmac was stripped off Hembrow Hill road, and Cheddar Gorge too; rolled up just like one of them swiss rolls, it were. And then there was fallen trees, potatoes, garden ornaments, soil, you name it, all finished up down on the moor below. Only you couldn't see 'em at first 'cos the water was up top of the gateposts! Mess was dreadful. You wouldn't believe it if you 'ent seen it.'

'So what did you do?'

'Father and me, we went out and swam the cattle to safety on the hill, but there was hundreds of sheep lost. We rescued a dozen or more wild hares an' all, but there was ever so many drowned. And t'wasn't just the animals neither. One old man was washed clean out of his house, bed an' all! Stone dead he were, when they found him.'

'Amazing,' Jonathan said.

'Course the hay crop was ruined — over a hundred thousand pounds worth of damage that'd be in today's money, and that's just the one farm.' George sighed. 'Then, when the water went down, all the fish an' that from the rhynes was left dying and stinking on the fields. Took

years to get the ground back to what it was
. . . years . . . '

'Good thing your father had some land on the
hill,' Jonathan observed

'Well course 'ee did,' George said. 'Can't farm
round these parts without some high ground.
Stands to reason.'

'I see.'

'Then of course there was the great storm of
December eighty one. I could tell 'ee a thing or
two — ' He was interrupted by a shout from
outside.

'Yoohoo!'

'Sounds like a woman,' George said. Jonathan
followed him through the workshop to the side
door and stood under the light, peering out into
the darkness of the yard.

'Ah, Jonathan!' Pamela's voice called from
beyond the gate. 'I had a feeling you might be
down here. Could I have a word please?'

Jonathan turned to George. George looked
back at him with a half smile. 'You'd best be off,'
he said, not bothering to lower his voice. 'Looks
like playtime's over.'

★ ★ ★

Pamela had been so busy and so tired ever since
Kelly had arrived that she didn't have the time or
energy to make enquiries as to where Vinny
might be staying. But after a couple of weeks she
wanted to tell Jonathan what she had decided
was a fair winter rent, and make sure he was
prepared to pay it.

215

She slipped down to The Prospect on an evening when Chloë was safely tucked up in bed and Kelly was absorbed in some rubbish on television. There was a light on downstairs and in the porch, so he was clearly in. Pamela banged on The Prospect's front door, but it was not Jonathan who answered it. It was Vinny!

'What are *you* doing here?' Pamela demanded.

'And a good evening to you too,' Vinny said. 'I'm staying here.'

'Not in my house, you're not!'

'Oh I think I am. I'm Jonathan's guest.'

'Huh! Is that what you call it!'

'Was there something you wanted?'

'Well obviously! A word with Jonathan.'

'He's down at the pumping station.'

'Right. I'll go there then.' She turned to leave.

'Just one thing,' Vinny said. 'If you were by any chance thinking of trying to turf me out, or even put Jonathan's rent up higher because I'm here, do remember, won't you, that we're keeping your little house warm and safe over the winter. It would be a great mistake to leave it empty and at the mercy of vandals.'

'It's none of your business what I do!' Pamela walked as briskly as she could back over the footbridge, and drove down to Amber Junction.

Later that evening, after she had spoken to Jonathan and come to a tentative agreement about his rent, she drove Bertie home with some relief. Although she wouldn't have admitted it, she was glad to know where Vinny was. Pamela might have guessed. But just wait until she finds out about my beautiful Chloë, she thought.

When she sees the two of us together, she'll be so jealous!

When she got back to Hembrow, Kelly seemed to have gone to bed already. She was constantly complaining about how 'totally wiped out' she was after her journey from Australia. In fact she'd been spending a lot of daytime in bed asleep, leaving grandma to look after Chloë. Pamela, who wasn't good at co-operative endeavours anyway, moved the cot into Peter's old room and greatly enjoyed being in charge of her grand-daughter.

Usually Pamela had no difficulty in dropping off. Tonight though, she lay awake for some time. She was thinking about Vinny — missing her — wondering how to mend the rift between them. Vinny has admitted it's all her fault, Pamela thought. It really is up to her to make the first move. So, do I mind that she's living at The Prospect? Yes I do. It's a bloody cheek! But then again, if she contributes to the rent, it would be a great help. And if she looks after the house over the winter, that is undeniably a bonus. And maybe, pretty soon, she'll find Jonathan unliveable-with and want to come home . . .

A wail from the next room distracted her from her thoughts. She pushed back the duvet and went to attend to the baby.

Next morning at breakfast Pamela decided to sound Kelly out on a brilliant idea she'd had at 3am in another period of wakefulness. She put her plans before the girl with certainty, confident of a positive response.

'When Peter gets home,' she said, 'you and he and Chloë can live together in this little house I own, not far from here. It's all been done up recently, just needs some new carpets and it will be the perfect place for you all! I've got a tenant in it at present but he'll soon be gone — the sooner the better as far as I'm concerned. Then we can do up the smaller of the two bedrooms with some lovely nursery wallpaper and you can live your own lives, but I'll be on hand for babysitting.'

'Great,' Kelly said.

It's funny, Pamela thought, how Australians never sound as *enthusiastic* as your average English speaker. I'm sure it's just the idiom, but it can be a little discouraging at times. I'm also surprised she doesn't ask any questions. Pamela, however, was not cast-down by something as nebulous as this. She felt her energy and purpose returning; the way she had been when first on HRT, as she rediscovered her old bounce.

'I'm going down to The Prospect this morning,' she said. 'Would you and Chloë like to come too?'

'Yeah, OK.'

'I'd better warn you that Vinny's there at the moment. She's staying with Jonathan, my tenant, that is.'

'What, permanently?'

'Heavens, no,' Pamela said. 'She's just taking some time out.' She was pleased to have produced an appropriately contemporary phrase.

'So, Vinny and this Jonathan — are they an

item, then?' Kelly looked considerably more alert than usual.

'The very idea!' Pamela laughed, and changed the subject. 'It's most inconvenient, but I have to go all the way down there each time I need to speak to him. Because although I went to the trouble of buying him a mobile phone, the wretched boy never turns it on!'

'Good oh,' Kelly said.

★ ★ ★

As Pamela drove her down Hembrow Hill in Bertie, with Chloë safely strapped into the new baby seat, Kelly looked about the interior of the 4 by 4 with interest. Could do with one of these, she thought. Make life a lot easier.

'So, what's this tenant of yours like?' she asked Pamela.

'Jonathan? Well, he's quite a complex person I think. Rather strange and difficult in many ways, but very clever. He's writing a book and I'm his patron.'

'Say again?'

'I'm supporting him until the book's finished.'

'Really?'

'Yes. He comes from a very distinguished family, you know. His father is a famous architect.'

'Rich?'

'Undoubtedly. He's the star of the popular TV programme *Skyline Design*, but of course you won't get that in Australia.'

'Oh but we do!' Kelly felt a surge of interest.

'They did Sydney waterfront. It was awesome. What's his name . . . Adrian something?'

'Crankshaw, yes.'

'And this Jonathan, not married then?'

'Oh no. He's far too busy writing.'

'Cool,' Kelly said.

She was busy with her thoughts as they drove, and happy not to talk. Then finally they arrived at this really isolated house in the middle of nothing.

'Here we are,' Pamela said proudly. 'This is The Prospect.'

I'd die rather than live here! Kelly thought. She extracted Chloë and carried her across a couple of rickety planks to the door. Pamela knocked.

The door was opened by a woman in her mid-forties, wearing a navy polo-necked jersey under a denim pinafore dress and a long red cardigan. On her feet were a battered pair of red clogs.

'This is Vinny,' Pamela said to Kelly.

$$\star \quad \star \quad \star$$

Vinny had seen Pamela parking in the lay-by and opened the front door reluctantly, prepared to have to stand her ground. But Pamela was not alone. With her was an attractive young woman, carrying a baby.

'And this,' Pamela said proudly to Vinny, 'is my daughter-in-law Kelly, and my grand-daughter Chloë.'

'Good gracious!' Vinny said. She stepped

backwards to let them in, and led them into the sitting room.

'You can hold Chloë,' Pamela offered. 'Just sit down on the sofa there.' The baby was handed over. Vinny held her gingerly.

'Isn't she wonderful!' Pamela said.

'Well . . . yes.' She looked like a standard infant to Vinny. Quite sweet, though. She glanced round. The young woman seemed to have gone. 'Where's what's-her-name?'

'Kelly?' Pamela followed her gaze. 'Oh, she's probably popped upstairs to see Jonathan. I thought it'd be nice for her to meet someone more her own age.'

'But he's working!' Vinny said.

'Come on Vin, it's Sunday. He can't work all the time. It's not healthy.'

'He doesn't like being disturbed.'

'He'll be pleasantly disturbed when he sees Kelly,' Pamela cackled. 'Do him good!'

Vinny frowned. 'But, how — '

'Turned up on my doorstep,' Pamela said, sitting down next to her. 'Completely out of the blue. I couldn't be more delighted. We're very happy together, aren't we darling?' She stroked the baby's cheek with her forefinger.

Thank God! Vinny thought. She doesn't miss me.

'So, how are you getting on?' Pamela asked her.

'Fine,' Vinny said.

'I'd like to let bygones be bygones,' Pamela said, 'but it's a little soon for that.'

'Yes of course,' Vinny said.

221

'But if living here becomes intolerable,' Pamela said, 'you know where to find me.'

'Yes,' Vinny said.

★   ★   ★

Kelly peered into the kitchen as she passed and then went up the stairs, looking about her. It was all very fresh and clean and, apart from the bare floorboards, nicely kitted out. But that didn't make it any less godforsaken. Now then, she thought. About this man — British, unattached, rich family . . . Could be just what I'm after. She put her head round one of the bedroom doors. He was sitting at a computer with his back to her, but he turned as she appeared.

'Who are you?'

'My name's Kelly. I'm from Australia, a friend of Pamela's son Peter.'

'Is she here too?' He got to his feet.

'Yeah. She's downstairs, talking to Vinny.'

His clothes are crap, but otherwise he looks well fit, Kelly thought. Long curly hair. Amazing eyes. Good wide shoulders. Neat butt.

'I like your hair,' Jonathan said.

'Likewise! Maybe we could get together sometime. Go out?'

'Out where?'

'Anywhere. The cinema?'

'Yes,' Jonathan said. 'I like films.'

'Cool. Well I'll give you a call sometime, OK?'

'Right.' Jonathan sat down at his desk again and turned back to his screen.

'See you,' Kelly said, and made her way

downstairs again. So far so good.

As she went back into the sitting room, Vinny was kneeling at the coffee table writing a cheque. Pamela and Chloë were having a cuddle on the sofa, and Chloë was smiling enough to break your heart.

'Thanks Vin,' Pamela said. 'Now, don't forget what I said, yes?'

'Yes,' Vinny said.

'Well, best be off then.' Pamela held Chloë up for Kelly to take, and got to her feet. Give my regards to Jonathan, won't you?'

'I will,' Vinny said. She saw them to the door and they walked away across the bridge.

'Hold tight,' Pamela said, taking Kelly's arm as they went. 'You've got precious cargo.'

Once they were all three back in Bertie and on their way home, Pamela quizzed Kelly about The Prospect. 'So, what d'you think? Isn't it a lovely little house?'

'Certainly is.'

'And could you see you and Peter and the baby living there?'

'No sweat,' Kelly said. 'Fair dos!'

A tinkle of laughter escaped from Pamela. 'D'you know,' she said, 'for a moment there, I thought you were going to say 'fair dinkum'!'

Oh, very funny, Kelly thought.

* * *

After supper that evening Vinny thought she would edge Jonathan a little further into proper communication by trying him with a little

223

poetry, and attempting to share with him the evocative use of metaphor. She felt encouraged by the progress they had made together already and was keen to take it further.

'How about one of Shakespeare's sonnets? *Shall I compare thee to a summer's day, thou art more lovely and more temperate,*' she suggested. 'I think it's such a beautiful way to praise someone.'

'But how can a person be anything like a day?'

'Well . . . what do you like best about summer?'

Jonathan thought about it. 'The heat. The way it stays light until late in the evening. The salad crops I can grow in my garden.'

'Well yes, but he's saying she's lovelier than all that.'

'What, better than heat, light and lettuce?'

Vinny sighed with exasperation. 'Don't be so *literal*,' she said. 'You have to let your imagination range freely. Haven't you ever pretended you could fly, or seen castles in the clouds?'

'No,' Jonathan said flatly. 'I wish you wouldn't go on like this. Why does everyone I meet, think they have the right to try and change me?' He looked angry and bewildered. 'I like myself the way I am.'

'I'm sorry,' Vinny bit her lip. 'I'm really sorry.' *I'm as bad as Pamela!* 'It was very thoughtless of me. I just assumed that appreciating poetry would enhance your life, the way it does mine.'

'Well it doesn't. It just makes me feel like an alien.'

★ ★ ★

'Can I borrow the 4 by 4?' Kelly asked Pamela a couple of days later.

'Why? Where d'you want to go?'

'Oh, just about. Nowhere special. I get kinda hemmed in, being indoors all day.'

'I'm afraid the answer has to be no,' Pamela said. 'It's illegal, you see, driving without insurance. Look, I've got to go to a meeting for an hour or two this morning, but I can take you anywhere you want after that.' She had a thought. 'Or you could use Peter's old pushbike. I know it's in working order because Vinny often goes out on it. It's in the shed.'

'Yeah. I might do that.'

Kelly contemplated leaving Chloë in her cot there and then, and just riding off, but common sense made her pause. If Pamela came back and found the baby unattended, then her cover would be well and truly blown.

The minute Pamela returned from her meeting, Kelly said, 'Hi. I'm just off on the bike. OK?'

'Will you be long? Don't forget it gets dark early.'

'Sure. 'Bye.'

'Oh, goodbye, then.'

It was a cold crisp day with pale sunshine. Kelly rode down Hembrow Hill, hoping the brakes would function and then, encouraged by success, pedalled even harder. Once down on the levels it was easier, although it was a long way and finding the right turns on these tiny back roads was tricky. Now for a bit of fun, she thought. Anything to liven things up a bit. I am so fucking *bored*.

By the time she arrived at The Prospect, she was hot and sticky, which suited her plans perfectly. She banged on the door, hoping that the Vinny woman would be safely at work, miles away.

A window upstairs opened. 'Who is it?' Jonathan said.

'It's me, Kelly.'

'Who?'

'The one with the nice hair.' She went round and looked up at him. 'Are you going to let me in?'

'Yes.' Jonathan came down and opened the door.

'Sorry to bother you,' Kelly said, 'in the middle of your work and all that. I was wondering if I could possibly take a shower?'

'Take a shower?'

'Yeah. I've cycled God knows how many miles from Hembrow and I'm all hot and sweaty. I need to feel clean.'

'I haven't got a shower.'

'No? That's weird! But you do have a bath?'

'Oh yes.' He led her upstairs. 'It's in there.'

'That's real kind. Thanks.' Kelly went into the bathroom and left the door ajar as she turned the taps on, added some of Vinny's 'aromatic foaming bath' stuff, and then removed all her clothes.

She lay in the hot water with the white foam covering most of her body. The smile on her face grew ever wider.

'Jonathan?' she called.

'What?'

'Could you come here a minute?'

'What?' His voice sounded nearer.

'Would you mind washing my back for me? I can't reach.'

'You mean . . . come in?'

'Well yes — unless your arms are three metres long!' Jonathan pushed open the door and came in. 'Great,' Kelly said, 'Thanks. Here's the sponge and there's the soap. OK?' She sat up with a swirl of water and bent over. Her hair fell forwards, shielding her face. Her nose was almost touching the foam. She waited for him to touch her.

There was a pause, then the first tentative feel of the sponge on her back. He rubbed it up and down a few times.

'Harder,' she said. The more soap he used, the faster the bubbles disappeared. 'Then rinse it off without the sponge. OK?'

At last, he had his hands on her! She sat back abruptly, pushing her hair out of the way so that she could see him. 'My front needs rinsing too.'

His hand wavered. 'There?'

'There.'

He was kneeling by the bath. He dipped into the water and poured some of it over her, his hand following it, smoothing her skin, over the hard nipples and down as far as the bright ginger patch of her pubic hair. Then he stopped and stared at her. He didn't speak.

'That's good,' she said. 'Do it more.' She parted her legs just a little and smiled at him.

He suddenly got to his feet in apparent panic and towered above her, turning clumsily to leave.

'Don't go,' she said. 'We haven't finished yet. Looks to me like you could do with a fuck. Yeah?'

10

'Can I borrow your mobile?' Kelly asked Jonathan, as they drank coffee together in his kitchen.

'Yes.' He went to find it. 'Here.'

'Thanks. What time does Vinny get back from work?'

'About six thirty.'

'Right, well I gotta go, then. I'll get Pamela to come and fetch me.' She keyed in Pamela's number and waited. 'Pam? It's me. I've had a puncture, but I've managed to walk to Jonathan's place. Can you come and get me? Right. See ya.' Kelly slipped the phone into her pocket and turned to Jonathan. 'Keep shtum, eh? And one more thing — d'you have anything sharp? A skewer or a pin, or anything?' Jonathan opened a drawer and produced a kitchen knife. 'Yeah, that'll do.'

She took it from him and went outside. The bike was where she'd left it, beside the front porch, now all wet with rain. Kelly took aim and stabbed the front tyre, which went down with a satisfying hiss.

'What are you doing?' Jonathan said, behind her.

'What'd you think? I said I had a puncture, and now I have!' He looked perplexed. 'Hey, lighten up!' Kelly said. She went closer to him and, unzipping his flies, slipped her hand inside his trousers. 'Did we, or did we not have some fun just now?'

'We did!' He looked pink in the face and as randy as a dog all over again.

'Woah there, tiger!' Kelly said, zipping him up smartly and giving his crotch a friendly pat. 'There's plenty more where that came from, but not right now. Once I've figured out some more reliable transport I'll be back, OK? You'd like that? You wanna do it again?'

'Oh yes, indeed I do!' Jonathan said.

Weird bloke, Kelly thought. And no bloody good long-term, but nice dick. Reckon I could teach him what to do with it too, if I could be bothered.

Pamela took a while, but eventually turned up outside looking concerned. They went to the door to meet her.

'I've left Chloë in the car,' she said to Kelly, 'so we must be quick. Are you all right?'

'Yeah,' Kelly said, 'pretty much.'

'Hello Jonathan,' Pamela said. 'I hope you've been looking after Kelly?'

'Well actually,' Jonathan said, 'she's been teaching me about sexual intercourse.'

'*I beg your pardon?*' Pamela stood up very straight. 'Whatever do you mean?'

'*Nothing!* Nothing at all,' Kelly said rapidly, pushing herself between him and Pamela. 'He's just having a kinda fantasy about me. Good thing you arrived when you did, Pam. C'mon, let's go.' She ushered Pamela swiftly out of the door and across the bridge, wheeling the useless bicycle with her as they went. Then, while

Pamela was busy putting part of Bertie's back seat down to make room for the bike inside, Kelly glanced back at the front door. Jonathan was still standing there. What in God's name did he have to say that for? She thought. Well, that settles it. It's gonna have to be sooner rather than later.

★ ★ ★

'Now then!' Pamela said as they drove home. 'Why did you cycle so far? And what on earth has been going on? What *did* Jonathan mean?'

'Relax,' Kelly said. 'It's nothing, believe me. I turned up like I said and maybe he got the wrong idea, who knows? But I can take care of myself, no worries.'

'Did he touch you?'

'Nah,' Kelly said. 'He just got horny. What d'you expect? He's a man.'

Pamela had a sudden worry. 'I shall have to warn Vinny!' she said.

'Don't bother. Jonathan told me he doesn't do it with her. They're just good friends.' Kelly smirked.

'Oh . . . ' Pamela felt a frisson of relief. 'But I shall certainly warn her nevertheless. I mean, who knows what he'll do next? The sooner he leaves, and you all move in there, the happier I shall be.' She smoothed the hair off her forehead with one hand. Bertie wobbled, and she put the hand back more firmly. 'Now, the next thing I really must do, is to get in touch with Peter,' Pamela said. 'It's high time he shouldered his responsibilities. I shall ring the British Embassy in Australia tonight, as soon as the working day begins over there.'

'Is that really necessary?' Kelly asked.

'Why?' Pamela glanced sharply at her. 'Don't you want me to find him?'

'Yeah, yeah, course I do.'

'Kelly?' she said, 'is there something you're not telling me? Something I ought to know?'

'Like what?' Kelly stared at her, wide-eyed.

'Is there?' Pamela held her gaze.

'Watch the road!' Kelly shouted. Pamela wrenched at the steering wheel just in time to prevent Bertie from sliding into a rhyne. 'You trying to kill us all?'

'You still haven't answered my question.'

Kelly looked away. 'Nah, what could there be? Life's a breeze.'

Pamela frowned. Something's definitely not right, she thought, and the sooner I talk to Peter, the better. But at least my darling Chloë is safe and well. That's the main thing.

As they got back to Hembrow, Pamela remembered with annoyance that she'd forgotten to think about supper. 'Damn!' she said. 'We've got nothing to eat tonight.'

'Phone for a takeaway?' Kelly suggested.

'Oh, I don't know where . . . '

'There'll be one in the phone book. I'll do it, if you take Chloë. Indian or Chinese or what?'

'Whatever you like,' Pamela held out her arms.

She was such a lovely baby. Pamela would never tire of stroking her soft blonde hair and gazing into her innocent grey-blue eyes. She had already become proficient in changing her nappies, bathing and feeding her, and took a delight in ironing her little outfits and keeping her spotlessly clean. 'How's my baby then?' she would croon, waiting for the reward of a gummy smile and maybe a gurgle of appreciation.

Kelly had caught her at it one afternoon, and Pamela jumped back rather guiltily, afraid she might be jealous or proprietorial. But Kelly just smiled and said something like 'Good to see you're both hitting it off so well,' in that rather coarse accent of hers.

If the boot was on the other foot, Pamela thought, *I'd* mind! She couldn't make Kelly out. She'd got this deliciously cuddly responsive little person with perfect toes and plump bendy legs, who belonged to her, and yet she seemed remarkably casual. In the night if Chloë cried, it was invariably Pamela who woke to attend to her. At first the baby had rejected her overtures of love and affection and had screamed loudly for her mother, but after a few days she began to take her bottle well and would often consent to lie happily in Pamela's arms without crying.

Pamela could see a definite resemblance to Peter as an infant. After they had eaten their curry that evening, she got out all the old photographs and sat Kelly down on the sofa to go through each one with her. 'See this one? Look how alike they are!'

'Mmm,' Kelly said. Was she stifling a yawn?

'But Chloë is so *good*, isn't she? You don't know how lucky you are! Peter kept me awake every night for months on end. I'd get quite desperate sometimes, trying to stop him bawling.'

'Musta been tough.' Now she certainly was yawning!

'You can't still be tired?' Pamela asked, 'Surely?'

'I'm fine,' Kelly said. 'No worries.'

'Perhaps I should take you to see our doctor? You may be anaemic.'

'*Absolutely not!*' Kelly said. And that seemed to be the end of that.

Ideally Pamela would have liked Vinny to take a series of photographic portraits of Chloë. (Trust her to be absent, just when she's really needed.) Instead, she rushed out herself and bought an expensively simple point-and-shoot digital camera and popped off shot after shot of the baby.

'They change so quickly,' she said, 'and once babyhood has gone, you can never re-capture it.' She thought Kelly looked a little upset as she said this, and was glad to discover that she did have some feelings for her daughter after all. She must be one of those people who don't show their emotions, Pamela decided.

'Now, how about one of you both together?' she called, levelling the camera. 'Smile!'

'*No!*' Kelly said forcibly, putting her arm over her face just as the camera clicked.

'Oh . . . ' Pamela was dismayed. 'Why did you do that?'

'Hate being photographed. OK?' Kelly said from behind her arm.

'But don't you want some of you and Chloë together?'

'No.'

'Oh well, fair enough.' Pamela would never understand this girl. The sooner she got Peter home, the better. Then she would be able to enjoy all the delights of Chloë without having to put up with — let alone financially support — her unpredictable daughter-in-law. Can't be soon enough, she thought. But I do *wish* he'd get in touch off his own bat. It does seem odd that Kelly hasn't heard from him once in all the time she's been here. Pamela pressed her once more.

'You're quite sure you don't even have a contact phone number?' she asked.

'Not at present, no.'

Pamela felt distinctly uncomfortable. 'But why not?'

'Well he's on the move a lot, and what with the time difference . . . ' Kelly's voice tailed off.

'There's nothing wrong between you, is there?' Pamela looked searchingly at her.

The hazel eyes met hers steadily. 'Course not.'

Pamela went to bed that night and lay awake again, worrying. Was Peter as feckless as his own father had been where paternity was concerned? She did hope not. She really could not face having to take over his duties herself, at this late stage in her life. That would be too much . . .

She finally slept, but was awoken twice in the night by Chloë. By six o'clock in the morning she was worn out and sleeping heavily. By seven thirty she was still asleep. She heard Chloë crying and came to from the depths, then remembered that it was certainly Kelly's turn to cope this time, and turned over to resume her dream. In it, she was walking the baby in a huge black pram, and she was wearing a grey suit and felt hat, like a nanny. The baby, who was Chloë — in spite of having thick black hair — was smiling and smiling. But suddenly she wasn't smiling at all, but howling . . .

Pamela woke with a start to find that it was indeed so. It was eight o'clock. She slid her feet out from under the duvet and sat up, rubbing her eyes. Where was Kelly? She walked a little unsteadily to the door, and called her name. No answer. Wretched girl! Pamela thought crossly. Why should I do all the work? It really isn't fair!

Chloë was crying so hard that her face was scarlet and her little pudgy hands were clenched into fists. 'There, there,' Pamela said, lifting her out of her cot and rubbing her back, gently. She kissed the top of the soft downy head and rocked her back and forth. The volume of crying abated a little. Pamela carried her to the spare room door and knocked on it loudly.

'Kelly?' No reply. Pamela opened it, went inside and saw immediately that it was empty. The two holdalls had gone. So had the clothes and shoes that were usually spread all over the floor. With one hand Pamela managed to open the wardrobe, and found it bare. In a panic she searched the room with her eyes for some clue as to where Kelly might be.

On the dressing table was a small blue envelope. It had *Pam* written on it.

'*Sorry*,' Kelly had written on a piece of Pamela's own headed notepaper, '*just trying to be honest here. I can't do the mother thing.*

236

Chloë's better off with you. I just needed to make sure you'd love her and it's really obvious you do. Don't try to find me. I REALLY MEAN THIS. Thanks for everything. Kelly'.

Pamela sank down onto the unmade bed in a kind of trance. Chloë was crying, in a normal grumbly way, not with Oh-my-God-I've-been-abandoned histrionics. But indeed it seemed that she had been.

'This can't be true,' Pamela whispered to their reflection in the dressing-table mirror. It looked back at her, grey and insubstantial. 'I don't believe it. I've literally been left holding the baby . . . '

★ ★ ★

After Kelly and Pamela had left the evening before, Jonathan went up to his study and looked up the word shtum in his dictionary. *Stum — unfermented grape juice: a mixture used to impart artificial strength to weak beer or wine.* No, that clearly wasn't what Kelly had meant. He'd got something wrong, yet again.

He wandered downstairs to the sitting room, picked up Vinny's *Guardian* and looked idly through it, ignoring the human-interest story of a snatched child on the front page, and going straight to an article on global warming. He was still there when Vinny got home from work.

'Hello,' she said as she came in. 'Had a productive day?'

'Yes, very.'

'Lucky you. I've had a really dreary one. I hate

the bloody library sometimes!'

'You should get a new job,' Jonathan suggested.

'Doing what?'

'Well . . . you could join a mobile camel library and supply books to Africans.'

'I could *what*?'

'There's a picture of the camel train here,' he said, indicating the newspaper. 'And an article. It says every camel carries two trunks on its back, each full of textbooks and stories destined for schools in remote nomadic settlements. It's part of the National Library Service in the semi-desert of north-east Kenya.'

'But I couldn't do a job like that!'

'Why not?' Jonathan demanded. 'You're a qualified librarian.'

'That's all I am,' Vinny sighed. 'I'm also fed up. D'you fancy going out somewhere, to see a film or something?'

'And get fish and chips?'

'Yes, if you wish.'

'Good!' He was delighted.

'There's a film on at the Odeon that's had really good reviews,' Vinny suggested, as she drove them into Otterbridge.

'OK.'

They parked in the multi-storey, walked along the street to the cinema and went in.

'Two for screen three,' Vinny said to the woman at the desk.

'Wait a minute,' Jonathan interrupted. 'There's a choice of four films.'

'Sorry,' Vinny said, 'back in a mo.' She turned

to Jonathan. 'So, what do you want to see?'

'That one.' Jonathan pointed to a poster, which displayed large amounts of naked female flesh.

'Oh no, it had dreadful reviews,' Vinny said, 'and anyway I really want to see that one.'

'That's all right,' he said very reasonably. 'You see yours, I'll see mine and we'll meet afterwards.'

'But *sharing* is the whole point of going to the pictures . . . ' Vinny said, 'Oh never mind. You do whatever you want. But you will wait for me here afterwards, won't you?'

'Course I will.'

Jonathan's film was confusing and very much too long. He didn't learn as much from it as he'd hoped, either. He met Vinny in the entrance lobby afterwards, glad to be away from the darkness and the heavy breathing.

'Fish and chips?' he said.

'Come on then.' Vinny led him back to the mini, went to get their supper, put it in the boot to stop him eating it all en route, and drove them home.

'My film was really good,' Vinny said, as they tucked into it later. 'How was yours?'

'Not much use.' Jonathan banged the end of the tomato sauce bottle vigorously. A large amount splurted out onto his plate.

Vinny frowned. 'But, did you really expect it to be useful?'

'Well yes. I need to learn some new techniques, you see.'

'Why?'

Jonathan smiled delightedly. 'Because I'm in love, and I need to be able to do it better.'

Vinny put her knife and fork down and stared at him rather disconcertingly. 'In love? Who with?'

'Well, with Kelly of course. We had sex today.'

Vinny's mouth opened into a perfect O. Then she pushed her plate of fish and chips away from her and went on staring.

'You went to bed with *Kelly*?'

'The second time, yes. The first time was in the bathroo — '

'*Stop it!*' Vinny shouted. 'I don't want to know all the gory details. All right?'

'But you asked.' Jonathan felt distinctly rattled at the sudden turn of events.

Vinny began to cry. She put her head on her hands and her elbows on the table and sobbed. The wet dripped through her fingers and landed on the pine surface.

Jonathan went on eating his fish because he didn't like cold batter, and anyway he wasn't sure what else he should do.

After a while, Vinny sniffed loudly and sat up. She got some tissues out of her pocket and blew her nose several times.

'Why did you do it?' she said.

'Because Kelly asked me to.'

'What, just like that?'

'No, she'd been cycling and she was sweaty, so she came here for a bath, and then she wanted me to wash her back.' He smiled at Vinny. 'I was as surprised as you are.'

Vinny looked across at Jonathan with red-rimmed eyes, shaking her head from side to side.

'The bitch! The bloody bitch.' There was a silence.

'So, how are you feeling?' Jonathan finally ventured.

'How d'you *think* I'm feeling?'

'Well,' he said, considering it. 'Tears are not a good guide, because I've noticed that you cry when you're happy as well as when you're sad. But I've never seen your lips disappear inside, like they are now, when you're happy. So I assume you're unhappy now. Is that right?'

'Yes,' Vinny said. 'And I'm not just unhappy. I'm bloody *furious*. OK?'

'And is it my fault?'

Vinny sighed deeply and got to her feet. 'I'm going to bed.'

She left the room, and Jonathan could hear her going up the stairs. He looked at the plate she had left behind. It was still three-quarters full. It would be a shame to waste all that food. He stuck out his fork, speared a chip, dipped it in the ketchup and put it in his mouth.

After he had finished all Vinny's fish and chips, he began to feel anxious. He didn't like it when Vinny was unhappy or furious. He needed her to be the same calm and friendly person that she always was. If it was his fault that she was like this, then he must try to do something about it.

He went upstairs and looked round her bedroom door. She still had all her clothes on, but was lying face down on the bed.

'Vinny?' He went across and knelt down next to her. She didn't respond. Jonathan remembered a scene from the film. He put out his hand

241

and very gently, stroked her hair. Vinny gave out a little moaning noise and turned over. 'I'm sorry,' he said. 'I'm very sorry.' Vinny did that disappearing thing with her lips again.

'It's not your fault,' she said. 'I can see how it happened.' She reached out and touched his cheek. 'But I'm afraid for you.'

'Why?'

'Come and lie down next to me, and I'll tell you.'

They lay side by side on their backs, on the narrow bed, looking up at the ceiling. Vinny gave a great sigh. 'Women like Kelly are predatory,' she said. 'She doesn't love you. She just wants to use you for her own pleasure.' She turned her head to face him. 'Was she kind, or did she laugh at you?'

'She said I wasn't doing it right,' Jonathan said, 'and she did laugh, yes. I thought it was because she was happy.'

'I doubt that very much,' Vinny said. 'I don't know for certain of course, but I think it's much more likely that she was jeering at you.'

Jonathan thought about this without speaking, for a while.

'I thought you hated being touched?' Vinny said.

'Well I do, usually, especially when I'm not prepared for it, but this was different. It felt good.' There was another silence. Then he turned to her. 'Vinny?'

'Yes?'

'I can see why you were cross with Kelly, but not why you're so sad.'

She smiled, but her eyes didn't crinkle up as they usually did. 'Because it's me, not Kelly,' she said. 'I do so wish you could see that.'

'See what?'

'That it's *me* who really loves you.'

*   *   *

Vinny's mobile phone suddenly rang, making them both jump. She got off the bed, found her handbag on the floor and extracted it.

'Hello?'

'Vinny? I've been trying to phone you all evening!' It was Gordon.

'Oh?' Vinny frowned, confused that he should be trying at all. 'Why? What's — '

'Pamela's in great trouble. She really needs you to come home at once!'

'Whatever's happened?'

'You might well ask. That wretched girl, Kelly, went and ran away last night in Pamela's brand new four by four,' he said. 'Left little Chloë behind! Can you believe such wickedness? And there's Pamela stranded at Hembrow. She's completely distraught of course, almost incoherent when she rang me. I've done my humble best to comfort her, of course, but it's you she wants, Vinny. And where have you *been?* I would have phoned you at the library first thing, but Pamela made me wait until after business hours. She said she couldn't disturb you at work. Typical of the woman — totally selfless!'

'But that's awful,' Vinny said, as soon as she could get a word in. 'Let me speak to her.'

'I'll see if she's able to.' There was a short silence.

Then, 'Vinny?' Pamela said in a world-weary voice.

'Are you OK?' Vinny asked, sorry for her in spite of herself.

'I think the phrase is, as well as can be expected under the circumstances,' Pamela said.

'Is there anything I can do to help?' She felt she had to ask.

'Oh, it's all in hand now,' Pamela said. The police are searching for Bertie, and for Kelly I suppose, although she can go to hell for all I care. They asked me for photographs to identify her, but she wouldn't let me take a single one of her face. I can see why now!' She sighed heavily. 'I've also phoned Australia House to try to get them to trace Peter, so we shall just have to wait and see.'

'What a good thing you've got Gordon there,' Vinny said, crossing two fingers.

'Yes,' Pamela said faintly. 'He's a real friend.'

There was another silence and then Gordon came back on again. 'You see?'

'Yes,' Vinny said. 'Poor Pamela.'

'You might have thought of that before you left her all on her own,' Gordon said sternly. 'She's devoted to you, you know. Can't do without you. Anyone else would be proud ... ' His voice cracked. Vinny listened in amazement. 'Wonderful woman,' he said and cleared his throat. 'Harrumph!' Good Lord! Vinny thought. Silly fool's in love with her!

'Well thanks for ringing,' she said. 'Do keep in

244

touch, won't you?' Then she switched off her phone and felt only a faint tinge of guilt, obliterated at once by an unaccustomed surge of power.

⋆   ⋆   ⋆

The next afternoon, her half day off, was unexpectedly sunny and mild with a brisk southerly wind, which nudged Vinny into activity.

'Why don't we take the car to the coast and go for a walk?' she suggested to Jonathan, 'and talk at the same time.'

'What about?'

'Us? Anything you like.' Vinny spread the Ordnance Survey map out on the table. 'Is there anywhere you'd especially like to go?'

'Kingspill Clyse,' he said, without hesitation.

'Which is where?'

'Here.' Jonathan pointed.

'And what exactly is a clyse?'

'It's a very large set of sea doors at the end of a river. I'll show you.'

'Have you been there before?'

'Yes. George monitors the water levels and operates the sluice gates. He took me.'

'But, you want to go there again?'

'Yes.'

Oh well, Vinny thought. At least it will be a walk.

She drove them along small roads through the village of East Zoyle, over the bridge above the M5, and into West Zoyle.

245

'Left here,' Jonathan instructed.

'Can't,' Vinny said, slowing down. 'That notice says *Kingspill Depot — No unauthorised Entry.*'

'But that's the way in,' he insisted.

Vinny stopped the car, and backed up into the lay-by. She got out the map again. 'Look, if we park by the church, we can take this footpath. George is allowed to go that way because he is authorised, but we aren't.' She could see that he didn't agree with her. He looked mutinous. 'Trust me,' she said lightly, 'we'll still get there.'

'No!' Jonathan looked agitated. 'We have to go in this way.'

Predictability and set routines, Vinny remembered from reading about Asperger's. They're clearly much more important to him than my conformist reluctance to trespass.

'OK,' she said.

They drove in over a cattle-grid and soon came to a long straight road, which ran parallel with the Kingspill Drain on their left. It was a lot narrower here than at The Prospect, more like a canal. Vinny could already see the big concrete sluice at its far end. It had a one-storey control room above it, and was double arched like a bridge.

'There are three doors in each of the two sections,' Jonathan began to explain as they approached it, 'Two tidal flaps on the outside, which open at low tide and are closed by the rising high tide — that's called tide-lock and lasts for about four hours. Then there are two vertical inner sluices which go up and down like guillotines — but don't cut anything, obviously

— and on this side you can see the two penning gates which are also vertical. They regulate the discharge and are also used to pen up the water for irrigation in the summer.'

'Oh.' I only wanted a walk, Vinny thought, not a flaming lecture tour!

'I'm afraid it will be all locked up,' he said, 'so we won't be able to see inside.'

'Never mind.'

'It's extra well protected,' Jonathan went on eagerly, 'with a huge padlock inside a steel cage, to prevent anyone from breaking in.'

'But why should anyone want to?' Vinny asked. It was hardly the kind of place one might seek out for an amusing spot of vandalism.

'Elver fishermen used to,' he said. 'The men who catch baby eels. George told me about them.'

'But why would they?' Vinny said automatically. She was thinking, OK so far, no gates, locked or otherwise and no one around to tell us off. Good.

'So they could wind up the sluice gates by hand.'

'Why on earth would they want to do that?' They had arrived at the end of the road and she was concentrating on parking the car.

'To create a big seaward rush of fresh water, of course,' he said.

'Oh,' Vinny yawned in spite of herself.

'Then at night time in spring when the moon is full and the elvers are running, they swarm up the estuary over there because they're attracted by the smell of fresh water. And the fishermen wait in the channel outside the clyse, with lanterns and scoopnets on poles, and catch them in enormous numbers to sell for a huge price to the Germans!' He looked jubilant.

'Oh, I see.' Vinny was amused by his enthusiasm.

'George says there was one time when the fishermen broke in, using gas cutting equipment on the gate. Then they stuck the cut ends together with putty and painted them silver so that no one would notice the damage, and they could come and go as they pleased!'

'Really?' Vinny perked up. 'Now that is interesting. Why don't you put some good stories like that into your book?'

'Serious scientific books don't have *stories* in them,' he said sternly.

He still hasn't asked me what I think of his book, Vinny thought. Is it because he assumes I'm thinking the same as he is? Or doesn't he credit me with having any worthwhile opinions? Or does the question simply not arise in his mind? I just can't get my head around what it must be like, to be him.

⋆　⋆　⋆

They walked up to the entry gate of the clyse and stood on the earth embankment that formed the sea wall, looking both ways across it. To the east, the Kingspill River cut through the land as straight as a ruler, and disappeared under the first of the road bridges. To the west, a meandering muddy exit channel joined up with

248

the sluggish brown estuary of the river Pawlett. Beyond that, the opposite river bank appeared as a low-lying spit of land, empty of features, just a sliver of matter between water and air. A brownish bird with long orange legs was picking over the mud below them.

'There's a redshank,' Vinny said.

'Mmm.' He wasn't interested in birds.

The southerly wind was much stronger here. They had to brace themselves against it as they walked along the sea wall.

'This wind's making my eyes water,' Vinny said. 'Are you warm enough without a coat?'

'Yes.' He was impervious to cold.

Overhead, half a dozen grey geese suddenly whooshed northwards with the gale up their tails, letting out a warning cackle as they sighted the two humans below.

'Geese!' Vinny said. He didn't look up. 'Jonathan?'

'What?'

'Have you thought at all about what I said yesterday?'

'About Kelly?'

'Well . . . partly that, yes. You do realise that she tells lies? Didn't she tell you that she's Pamela's daughter-in-law; Peter's wife?'

'She said she was a friend of his.'

'She didn't mention their baby?'

'No.'

'Well, there you are then. You can see she's not to be trusted.'

Jonathan was more concerned about the consequence of such lies. 'That means I've

249

committed adultery then? If you don't know, does it still count?'

'Well, I suppose so,' Vinny said, 'but what's more important at this moment is something else altogether. Would you be upset if you didn't see Kelly again?'

'Oh but I will. She said so.' He was striding ahead of her along the wall, thinking about sea defences.

Vinny caught up with him and put her hand on his arm. He jumped.

'Sorry! Look, Jonathan, I'm afraid I've got some bad news for you. Kelly has run away. She's taken Pamela's car and disappeared.'

'Oh.' He was surprised for a moment. Then a phrase of his mother's came to mind. 'Probably just as well, under the circumstances,' he said. 'Did you know that this embankment was constructed to the one-in-a-hundred-year defence standard?'

'No.'

'That means it's likely to be over-topped by the sea only once in that time.'

'Huh!' Vinny said. 'What about global warming?' She had both her arms wrapped around her and her teeth were banging together.

Jonathan pointed inland to the low farmland behind the wall. 'If it did, then all this would be inundated. And if it went as far as that ridge of hills over there, then Hembrow would become an island again, like it was in prehistoric times.'

'I'm cold,' Vinny said. 'Let's go back.'

They got back to the car and set off again. Jonathan was quiet. He didn't mention Vinny's declaration of love. Perhaps he had already forgotten it?

Vinny, prompted by a road sign and trying to make the best of things, said, 'I suppose there must once have been otters at Otterbridge.'

'Saw one today,' Jonathan said.

'Where?'

'Outside the house.'

'Outside The Prospect? Today?'

'Yes. While you were washing up, after lunch. It was sitting on the bank for about ten minutes.'

'But why didn't you tell me? I'd have given anything to see it.'

'Oh. I didn't think of that.' He said it pleasantly, but with no suggestion of culpability.

She glanced at him. He looked perfectly at ease. Now I think about it, Vinny thought, he never does point things out for others to marvel at. He has no capacity for sharing experiences. He has no idea that it might be expected of him, let alone rewarding. She sighed deeply. If anyone's an island, it's Jonathan.

They drove on in silence. I'm not needed, Vinny thought, overcome with wretchedness. I'm just useful sometimes. I'd be better on my own. Being with someone who has no concept of warmth or togetherness is much worse than being alone.

By the time they got back to The Prospect, Vinny had decided she needed some time on her

251

own, to think. Her conscience had also begun to prick her about Pamela and the baby. Driving over there might give her the necessary breathing space. 'I think I'd better pop over to Hembrow this evening,' she said, 'Just for half an hour or so, to make sure everything's OK.'

'Vinny?' Jonathan said.

'What?'

'Will you have sex with me now, instead of Kelly?'

She stared at him. 'You *are joking*?'

★ ★ ★

When Vinny arrived at Pamela's house, it was obvious that something was wrong. A hired car was in her usual place outside, but there were no lights on. Vinny was puzzled. She fumbled in the dark and eventually let herself in with her own key and switched them on.

'Pamela?' she called. 'Are you there?' She went upstairs and looked into every room, but found neither her, nor the baby. I expect Gordon's taken them out somewhere, she thought. She went back into the kitchen, took her coat off, and slid the kettle over onto the hotplate to boil.

She was just sitting at the table, sipping a mug of tea, when she saw the headlights of another car coming up the drive. That's OK then, she thought. She stood up, took a deep breath, reminding herself to keep strong, and went to the front door to help with Chloë. But she was almost knocked over as an utterly distraught figure rushed into her arms.

'Pamela! Whatever is it? What's happened?'

'Oh Vinny, thank god you're here. They've taken the baby away. The police and Social Services — ' She burst into tears. 'They think I *stole* her!'

11

In all the years she had known her, Vinny had never witnessed Pamela in such a state.

'Please, Vinny,' she sobbed, 'you *must* stay here with me. I really can't cope with this on my own.'

Vinny hugged her. What could she say? Pamela's hot tears dripped down her neck and made her shiver. Then she held her away a little, so that she could look at her properly. She had no make-up on, and her hair was wild and uncombed. Her face was all creased up with emotion and her eyes were bloodshot with weeping. She looked truly pitiful.

'Come into the kitchen,' Vinny said gently, 'where we can sit down, and you can tell me about it. They went and sat at the table. 'Tea?' Vinny offered.

'Whisky,' Pamela said, wiping her eyes with a tissue.

Vinny went to get her one from the dining room. The day before she had glanced at a story in the newspaper about the latest child abduction. There had been a fuzzy photograph of a little blonde baby and her smiling teenage mother. Vinny hadn't paid much attention to it at the time, beyond feeling a detached kind of dismay. But now it felt all too real. One thing was certain; Pamela hadn't taken the child. But Kelly could have done so? Then again, to what end? Vinny went back into the kitchen and sat down opposite Pamela.

'So, what happened?'

'It was this morning when I got Chloë up — Pamela hiccuped, took a long breath and waited a moment to calm herself, ' — She was all red in the face, feverish! And she wasn't behaving normally either, she seemed really apathetic. So of course I was worried to death . . . '

'Yes, of course,' Vinny said.

'Well, I rushed out to the car the garage lent me, to take her to the surgery to see Polly, but of course — no baby seat — so then I had to ring for a taxi, and we finally got there, but by this time I was frantic . . . '

'I can imagine.'

'And it was that new, rather snotty female in reception, you know, the one with the bun?'

'Yes.'

'So I told her Chloë was really ill and *must* see Polly at once! But she said Polly wasn't on duty that day; that we'd have to see another doctor. I *explained* that she was my grand-daughter from Australia, and that her mother had run off, but she looked as though she didn't believe me!'

Pamela spread out her hands on the table between them. They were visibly trembling. Vinny reached across and took them in hers for a moment to give them a sympathetic squeeze. 'So what happened?'

'Well she made us go and sit down. And I could see her through the glass, on the phone, and I thought she was trying to find a space with

255

one of the doctors. Well she must have done that too, because eventually after we'd waited what seemed like *hours*, we got to see a young female locum.'

'No one you knew?' Vinny asked.

Pamela sighed. 'Not at all, no, but she could've had two heads for all I cared. I was so worried . . .'

'Of course you were.'

'So she examined her really carefully, I'll say that much for her. She took a long time over it. And then she said she thought we ought to get a second opinion, so I was in a total panic by then. I was sure it must be meningitis. I was terrified Chloë was going to *die!*'

'Dreadful,' Vinny said, nodding.

'So then the senior doctor, whatsisname, Clark, came in and examined her all over again, and then they asked me to go back to reception on my own to fill in some forms, and that took time too, because I didn't know most of the answers. She's got no documentation, you see,' Pamela went on, 'no NHS number, no record of vaccinations. I didn't even know her date or place of birth! Only that she's called Chloë Wood and she's *ill* and needs *help!*' Pamela covered her mouth with her hands. Tears came into her eyes at the thought of it all, and she wiped them away. 'Of course I see now that they were just playing for time.'

'And then?'

'And then I looked round, and the police were coming in at the door and making straight for me!' Pamela blew her nose fiercely. 'Mrs Pamela

Muriel Wood?' they said. Then they got hold of both my arms and marched me outside to their car. I was beside myself!'

'I can imagine,' Vinny said.

Pamela shook her head. 'And all this time there was no sign of Chloë. I didn't know *what* was happening to her or how she was, and I hadn't the least idea why they were carting me off to the police station.'

'You hadn't seen the bit about the snatched baby on the TV news?'

'No. I hardly have time to watch television at all these days. It was a nightmare, Vin, a total bloody nightmare!' She looked up at Vinny with wild eyes and downed her whisky in a couple of greedy gulps.

'Another one?' Pamela nodded. Vinny went next door to get it, and came back. 'So, what then?'

'Well, then they arrested me on a charge of child abduction! I told them if I'd been wicked enough to snatch someone else's child, I would at least have had the wit to *invent* its birthday and NHS number and all the rest of that crap, well, wouldn't I? Aaaah . . . ' Pamela folded her arms on the table and lowered her head onto them.

'Did they tell you if Chloë was all right?' Vinny asked.

'Not for hours! It was sheer bloody torture. I *told* them I was a friend of their Chief Constable, but they just looked at each other as though I was some sort of lunatic, and shoved me into a cell.'

'So, where's Chloë, now?'

'The Social-fucking-Services eventually turned up and took her away for 'safe keeping'. They said she had a feverish cold, nothing more, thank God. I pleaded with them; told them that if I'd snatched a baby, I'd hardly be likely to take it straight to the sodding *doctor's*, would I? But they wouldn't listen. A bunch of hard-faced, fat-arsed bloody little Hitlers, the lot of them!' Pamela sat up and began on her second drink.

'So, then they let you go?'

'They drove me back here in a police car and told me not to leave the country.' Pamela grimaced. 'It'd be funny, if it wasn't so dreadful.'

'So, what next?'

'Well, I suppose they'll show Chloë to the mother who's lost her own baby. They'll get all her hopes up, only to have them dashed again when she sees it isn't hers, the poor unfortunate woman.'

'But, Pamela — ' Vinny hesitated. 'What if Chloë isn't Peter's child, after all?'

'Oh, but she *is*. I just know she is. She looks exactly like he used to.'

'But Kelly could have snatched her from her real mother?'

'What for? To dump her on me? What would be the point?' Pamela said. 'Kelly's a devious little shit, I'll give you that, but why go to all that trouble?' She downed the last of her whisky and closed her eyes.

'You should go to bed,' Vinny said. 'There's nothing more you can do tonight, and Chloë will be well taken care of, I'm sure.'

'I shan't sleep,' Pamela said, 'but I will go up. Vinny?'

'Yes?'

'You won't leave me on my own, will you?'

Vinny hesitated. 'Of course not.'

★　★　★

At seven thirty the following morning, which was Saturday, another police car arrived at Hembrow. Vinny opened the door to them and looked for Chloë, but she wasn't with them.

'Mrs Pamela Wood?'

'No, she's upstairs. Is everything all right?'

'We've got some good news for her, yes.'

'Pamela!' Vinny shouted up the stairs. 'It's the police. Good news!'

Pamela rushed out of her bedroom and down the stairs with her dressing gown flapping and no slippers on.

'*Chloë?* You've got my Chloë?'

'Er, no.' The young policeman stepped backwards a fraction. 'We've come to tell you that your black SUV has been recovered undamaged at Heathrow Airport.'

'Aaaah!' Pamela sank down onto the stairs and put her head in her hands.

'It's been checked over and is ready for you to collect. There will be no parking charges.'

'I should think not!' Vinny said.

'So, if you could just check this and sign here?' he proffered a clipboard.

'You do it, Vinny.'

Vinny verified the registration number. 'Is the

child seat still in it?' she asked.

'I believe so, yes.'

'But no sign of the driver?'

'No. Looks like she's left the country. So, if you could just sign, Mrs Wood?'

Pamela got to her feet and signed. 'So perhaps now you people will *believe* me?' she spat.

'Er,' the young man looked baffled. 'Thank you. We'll be off then.' And they drove away.

'He'll be from a different department — traffic or transport or whatever,' Vinny said. 'He probably didn't have a clue what you were talking about.'

'None of them do!' Pamela said. 'They're all as thick as shit. How dare they get my hopes up like that? I could have had a heart attack!'

'Let's go and get some breakfast,' Vinny said, soothingly. 'Shall I make you some porridge?'

It was still dark outside. 'It's far too early,' Pamela said, but when it was put in front of her, she did eat it.

'You'll have to go and get Bertie,' Pamela said as she put her spoon down. 'Thank goodness it's Saturday! I'll phone Gordon at once and get him to give you a lift there.'

'Oh,' Vinny said. 'Won't *you* go with him?'

'I can't, can I? I need to be here when they bring Chloë home.' She went over to the phone and began keying-in numbers.

Oh no! Vinny thought. It's at least a two-hour drive. I've never driven Bertie. He's much bigger than anything I'm used to. I don't know my way around Heathrow, and Pamela is so much more intrepid in these matters than I am . . .

260

'Gordon?' Pamela was saying on the phone. 'Could I ask you to do me a huge favour?'

* * *

Gordon was feeling pleased with himself as he drove Pamela towards Heathrow to collect Bertie — damn silly name for an SUV, but quite endearing too. At first he had been presented with a *fait accompli*; Vinny was to go with him. Of course he had nothing against the woman. You couldn't dislike someone like Vinny, but he did have the distinct impression that she disapproved of him.

Anyway, he'd eventually managed to get his own way by being ever so reasonable, and by pointing out that Chloë was unlikely to be brought back without warning, and that Vinny would be there anyway to see to her. More importantly he'd pressed the point that he, Gordon, would *so* much appreciate having Pamela with him.

And finally Pamela had given in. She'd even blushed like a girl at his protestations. He took this to be a good sign. Vinny had looked very relieved too. I'm right, Gordon thought. She doesn't like me.

'Have you got the spare set of keys?' he asked Pamela.

'Yes. Vinny found them for me.'

'You do depend on her a great deal, don't you?'

'Well, she's the practical one,' Pamela said.

'I believe I have that reputation too,' he ventured.

'Really?' She had turned her head away from him, but he could see her reflection in the wing mirror and she was smiling. I'm sure I'm right, he thought. I can't believe they sleep together. All a strong woman like her needs is the love of a good man. He gave the steering wheel a little victory squeeze. *Softly softly catchee monkey . . .*

The traffic on the M4 was heavy and Gordon was obliged to pay a lot of attention to his driving, especially when they arrived at the rabbit warren of Heathrow and had to navigate their way to the correct car park.

'There he is!' Pamela called out excitedly. 'Over there behind those three red cars. 'Oh, I do hope he isn't damaged.'

Bertie was fine. The baby seat was still in position and there were no obvious bumps or scratches on his paintwork. There was no note from Kelly either. Pamela turned the key and he started first time.

'Better check the fuel gauge,' Gordon said. 'Don't want to run out on the way home.'

'Yes, it's very low,' Pamela said. 'Little bitch!'

'Right,' Gordon said. 'We'll go in convoy, yes? I'll take you to a petrol station first, before we head off towards home. OK?'

'Thank you Gordon,' Pamela said. 'I don't know what I'd do without you.'

They set off. Gordon kept tabs on Bertie all the way in his mirror, slowing down if he lagged behind and not going through traffic lights if there was a chance they might change to red. Sometimes other vehicles came in between them, and then he would slow down to such a pace that they'd be obliged to pass him. Let them hoot. He was on a roll. He was a general, leading from the front!

When they arrived back at Hembrow, Pamela rushed straight indoors. He heard her calling, 'Vinny? We're home! Any news?' but as he got into the kitchen it was clear that Chloë had not been returned.

'Don't worry,' he said, patting Pamela comfortingly on the shoulder. 'It'll only be a matter of time.'

'Oh I do hope so.' She looked up at him so sweetly, and then turned to Vinny. 'Gordon was quite right to insist I went with him,' she said. 'A few hours in his company has really cheered me up.'

'That's nice,' Vinny said. Gordon gave her a smile.

'Well, best be off now,' he said. 'I was a little distracted when you rang this morning, and I forgot to feed my cats. Do let me know if I can be of any further help, won't you?' he squeezed Pamela's hand warmly, nodded to Vinny and took his leave.

★ ★ ★

Vinny was released at last to go down to The Prospect, to collect some overnight things.

'I'm glad you're back,' Jonathan said. 'I don't like it here without you, now.'

'Do you get lonely?' Vinny asked him. They were sitting on his sofa in front of an open fire, watching the logs spit and the flames leap up the

263

fireback. The whole room was warm.

'I'm not sure what that means,' Jonathan said.

'Do you feel unhappy when you're on your own?'

'No. I'm usually too busy. But I do like it when you get back.' He smiled at her so openly, so entirely without artifice, that Vinny was ready to forgive him anything, except maybe . . .

'What about love?'

'What about it?' A small frown gathered his brows.

'Do you know what it is?'

'Never having to say you're sorry!' He trotted this out pat, and added, 'which is fine, because I hardly ever do.'

'No,' Vinny said. 'That's just a stupid phrase from an old film. It couldn't be more wrong. Seriously though, have you ever been in love?'

Jonathan made a face. 'Dunno. Probably not. How would I know if I had?'

'You'd think about that special person most of the time, especially when she wasn't with you.'

He turned to face her. 'What would be the point of that?'

'Well,' Vinny said, 'Um . . . for example you might be in a shop and see something, and think to yourself, that's just the sort of thing she'd like. And then you might buy it as a present for her.'

'Even if it wasn't Christmas?' He bent forward and put another log on the fire.

'Yes, but — ' Vinny struggled to explain. 'It's not really about buying things. It's about thinking of the person, and imagining what she might be doing, because that makes you feel close to her even if you aren't physically so.' She looked at him. He showed no obvious signs of comprehension. 'It's about doing things that you know she'd appreciate, but without being asked to. You care about how she's feeling and you do your best to make her as happy as possible. You try to get to know her, and the way she thinks; even better than you know yourself. You try to anticipate her every wish. You feel that she is more important to you than anyone or anything else.'

'Even water?'

'Especially water.' Vinny sighed. 'You're never likely to feel any of these things, are you?'

Jonathan's beautiful eyes met hers for a moment and then he looked away. 'Probably not,' he said.

I won't give up, Vinny thought. I won't! He isn't a hopeless case. Some people with AS *do* form loving relationships. I shall just have to be more understanding, less demanding; give him some space.

'It's OK,' she said. 'It doesn't matter.'

'Do you think about me a lot?'

'Yes, I do.' Vinny smiled at him apologetically.

'And have you bought me a present?'

A lump came into Vinny's throat. She swallowed hard. 'Not yet,' she said, 'but I'm sure I will one day.' She looked vaguely round the room, trying to find something less painful to talk about. 'I promised to spend just one more night at Hembrow to keep Pamela company,' she said. 'Is there anything I can do for you, before I go?'

'There's some ironing.'

'Yes, all right,' Vinny said. Jonathan stood up and made for the door. 'Where are you going?'

'Upstairs,' he said. 'I've got work to do.'

★ ★ ★

That Saturday afternoon, Mandy was bored. As bored as a sheep chewing the cud, she thought, looking out of the dormer window of her attic room in the bungalow, but at least they're all lying down together being sociable. Life was as boring as being a leaf gradually changing from green to brown, or the water passing slowly down the Kingspill . . . or as bloody boring as trying to think of something equally boring! For fuck's sake, get a life.

When she set out along the road, she hadn't consciously decided to call in at The Prospect. There wasn't any point any more. That builder had gone and she'd heard nothing from him — not even a phone call. He was only after one thing, she realised, and I thought he really liked me.

It was grey. It had begun like so many autumn days on the moor with a thick mist lying on the cold ground, so low that sometimes the odd tall poplar might emerge through it with its crown in the sunshine. Today there was no sun and the fog had been slow to clear. Mandy idled along the road, kicking things with her old Doc Martens, which weren't cool any more. She reckoned she should be paid for doing the washing up and hoovering her room, so's she could buy new

266

proper fashion boots.

As she approached The Prospect she saw the red mini parked outside again and wondered whose it was. Jonathan never had visitors. He didn't have any friends. He might have been bullied at school, just like her. They had lots of things in common. Mandy sighed. She hadn't been able to get him out of her head, even though it was months — way back in April — since she'd last spoken to him. She remembered with shame that she'd totally lost it then, and called him rude names. No wonder he'd turned his back on her! But Jonathan had real class (not like that lame builder) and he was dead fit too. Maybe she could have one last try . . .

She looked up at the house as she passed. There were now curtains in all the windows. The old cow with the big SUV, the one who now owned this place; she must have bought them. Perhaps she was in there now? Maybe this Mini belonged to her too; like having a little dinghy when you also owned a big yacht? Mandy was pleased with this flight of fancy. I'm not totally stupid, she thought. I've got imagination. I could make up a reason for turning up.

She turned back, crossed the footbridge and hammered on the door. She heard footsteps and prepared herself to talk to Jonathan. She would put her foot in the door so he couldn't shut it on her. She'd say, '*It's OK. I haven't come to bother you. My Dad just wondered if you could help him out sometime. He's been trying to make this spare part in the workshop — dunno what it is exactly . . . '*

But it was a middle-aged woman who answered the door. Mandy recognised her as the one who had helped her pick up her stuff off the road, on the day the old cow had almost knocked her off her bike. What was she doing here?

'Hello?' the woman said.

'Oh — is Jonathan in?'

'Well he's working at the moment. Can I help?'

'I've seen you before.' It just came out like that.

'Yes. You're Mandy, George's daughter, aren't you?'

'Mandy Overy, yeah.'

'Would you like to come in?'

'Yeah, I would.' She stepped over the threshold with alacrity and looked about her. The Prospect looked even better than it had on her last visit. This time it was all finished and now there was a bowl of fruit on the kitchen table and a pot-plant on the windowsill. It looked welcoming and cared for.

'I'm Vinny,' the woman said. 'I've been staying here for a while. D'you fancy a cup of tea or coffee? We've got some milk for a change.'

'Tea'd be OK. No sugar,' Mandy said, and sat down while Vinny put the kettle on. She saw that the cooker and the working surfaces were clean and uncluttered, like her mum's. There was an ironing board set up in one corner with a half-finished man's shirt on it. *She's doing his bloody ironing!* Mandy thought. They must be *at it.* But what the bloody hell does he see in *her*?

'So, you and Jonathan are friends?' she asked.

Vinny gave her an old fashioned look. 'Just friends, yes,' she said. 'Nothing more, nothing less.'

Mandy turned the words over in her mind whilst Vinny made the tea in two mugs. 'Why did you say that?' she eventually asked, 'nothing more, nothing less?'

'I though it was what you wanted to know.'

'Why should I?'

'Look Mandy, I know the story. You know I'm a friend of Pamela's.'

'Pamela?'

'The woman who owns this house.'

'Oh . . . her.'

'Can I try to explain something?' Vinny asked.

'What?'

'Something about Jonathan.'

'Don't tell me he's gay?'

'No, I don't believe so. What I do know for sure is that he's not interested in having a relationship with anyone just at present. He's totally focused on getting his book finished, and he really can't cope with distractions.'

'Oh I get it. You're saying *fuck off*. Is that it?'

'Not in so many words.' At least she didn't protest at the f-word. 'What I am saying is that there's no point in you trying to see him. It'll only upset you.'

'But you're here. *You* see him.'

'Yes, but I'm only here temporarily, and the difference is,' she smiled ruefully, 'that I don't expect to get anything in return.'

'You're saying I would?'

'No, Mandy. I'm just trying to tell it as it is.'

'Well I still want to see him. Where is he, upstairs?' Mandy jumped to her feet and nipped to the foot of the stairs. 'Jonathan!' she shouted. 'You up there?' Vinny tried to take her arm, but she shrugged her off, crossly. '*Jonathan?*' She could hear the sound of a door opening, but he didn't come into view.

He just called, 'Go away. I'm busy,' and shut the door again.

'He does mean it,' Vinny said.

'How d'you know?'

Vinny appeared to be coming to a decision. 'OK,' she said, 'I'll tell you why, but in confidence, yes? It's not the sort of thing you tell just anybody.'

'You mean my dad's right? He's a nutter?'

'Ssshh! No, not at all. Come back into the kitchen.' Vinny shut the door behind them and they sat down again. Mandy looked across the table at her as she began to explain, and interrupted when she didn't understand. And by the end of it, her whole feelings about Jonathan felt as though they'd been stood on their head. She actually felt sorry for him!

'So, he can't help it?' she asked Vinny.

'No, he was born that way. It's very hard for him. Imagine how you'd feel yourself.'

'Yeah.' Mandy was thoughtful.

'And now try to imagine what it would be like if you couldn't even do that!'

Mandy frowned. 'Yeah.' Then she felt stupid and disappointed and cheated and angry with herself, all at once. It was too much. 'I just

— just wanted him to *notice* me, like I existed,' she said, breaking down. 'Wanted him to *do* something, Oh I dunno . . . ' She wiped her eyes angrily with the back of one hand.

'Yes,' Vinny said. 'It must have been horrible for you.'

'He just ignored me, like I was *nothing!*' Mandy wept.

'He didn't mean to. He just doesn't understand about those sort of feelings,' Vinny said. 'I'm sorry, it's really hard to take. I do understand.'

'Going home,' Mandy muttered with her hands over her face.

'Come on,' Vinny said, offering her a tissue. 'Blow your nose, eh? And then I'll run you down there in my car.'

★ ★ ★

After Vinny had finally left to go back to Hembrow, Jonathan was able to concentrate upon taking security copies of his computer discs. She had suggested that he should make a set for her as well, so that she could help him in selling the book. She said it was part of her plan to help him any time he needed it. I must discuss it with her, he thought, and get her to find me an agent. Then he remembered that she had gone; that there would be no one to talk things over with and no effortless supper on the table that evening.

I wish she were here, he thought, and was surprised at himself. He realised he had got used to her unobtrusive presence. He liked the way she kept the house tidy and made sure there was always enough food in the fridge. He supposed he might have to go on his bike and do some shopping soon, but not today. If there wasn't anything for supper, he would do without.

He stood in front of the sink and ran the taps to fill it, recollecting how as a child he would let the water run and run, watching it with fascination as it splashed and gurgled, often forming itself into a clockwise vortex as it disappeared down the drain. He thought of how he had been desperate to go to the southern hemisphere to witness it going down the other way round . . . and his confusion when finally as an adult he'd discovered that it didn't always go down anticlockwise, as he assumed it would.

He liked everything about water — the feel of it, the look of it, the unexpected weight of it — one cubic metre of water weighing a ton — the nothingness and at the same time the ubiquity of it. The way it flowed on command from these taps in a never-ending stream . . . The way it steamed when it was hot and condensed on cold windows, and ran into runnels down the panes of glass. The circularity of it . . . the eternal indestructibility of it . . . The way it rose into the air with the sun on misty mornings and formed clouds which sailed overhead. The way it dropped back as rain, which swelled into rivers, which flowed into cold seas, which merged into warm seas and evaporated into the air all over again, and . . .

Jonathan put his hand under the hot tap. The

water had gone stone cold. He must have run off all the hot without realising it. He closed the taps again and shrugged his shoulders. The day's washing up could wait.

* * *

Vinny had packed only a few of her things into a bag, determined to spend no longer than one more night at Hembrow. She wondered what Pamela would do if she did get Chloë back. How would she cope with a baby, at her age? Surely it was up to Peter now to take over the care of his daughter — if indeed she was Peter's child? But if Chloë was not returned, what then? Pamela would be inconsolable. She might demand her help even more. Vinny would have to be on her guard lest she should be imprisoned once again by feelings of duty.

She drove up Hembrow Hill with reluctance. Bertie was parked outside the house as usual. Vinny opened the front door.

'Pamela?'

'In here.' She was in the sitting room. Vinny went in all prepared to administer a hug, some reassurance, help with phoning the social services, anything. But Pamela was sitting on the sofa by the fire with a blissful smile on her face and in her arms, sucking lustily on a bottle of milk, was Chloë! Vinny stopped in her tracks.

'I told them,' Pamela crowed, 'but they wouldn't listen. Oh no! Officiousness gone mad. But I suppose one should expect that. They're fairly low grade these days, aren't they?'

'Who?'

'The police and social services, of course. Time was when they would have seen at a glance that I couldn't possibly be implicated in child abduction. But these days . . . ' She sighed. 'Two social workers brought her home about twenty minutes ago. Of course they did their best to justify themselves. Told me that they'd been concerned by the absence of Chloë's mother; that Immigration had been unable to trace any Australian woman by the name of Kelly Wood either entering or leaving the country in the last month. And they were surprised that I didn't have even one photograph of my supposed daughter-in-law.' Pamela snorted. 'It wasn't for want of trying!' She looked down at the sucking baby. 'All right, my precious?'

'Is she all right? Not ill, I mean?'

'She's fine. Don't just hover in the doorway. Come and sit down with us.' Vinny did as she was told. 'All I can think of now,' Pamela said, 'is the appalling disappointment of that poor girl, the mother.'

'So she wasn't — ?'

'Well naturally not.' Pamela beamed. 'As I told them all along, this is my beautiful Chloë.'

Vinny looked at the baby. She took in the small pink fists, opening and closing in a contented rhythm, the little toes, and the unblinking blue eyes. 'So, what now?' she said.

'We'll manage, won't we, Chloë?' Pamela said to the baby. She looked up at Vinny. 'I wasn't confident before, but I am now. I shall make sure the Australian authorities keep their word and track Peter down, and then I shall extract the whole story from him. We'll come to a proper arrangement; with or without Kelly, it makes no difference to me. And in the meantime we'll be fine. Hold her for a moment, would you, Vin? I'm bursting to go to the loo.' She put Chloë into Vinny's unready arms. 'Lay her back a bit . . . there,' Pamela instructed. 'And the bottle . . . Right, there you are. You'll be an expert in no time!' And she jumped to her feet and whisked out of the room.

Vinny looked down at the baby in alarm. This is not me, she thought. I don't belong here. I don't want . . .

Chloë spluttered and began to cough and cry at the same time. Vinny snatched the bottle away and waved it about vaguely before standing it upright on the carpet. Chloë started yelling, going dangerously red in the face. Vinny hesitated but then, thinking it might be wind, put both hands under the well-padded armpits and hitched her awkwardly upright. She held her against her own chest and patted her back experimentally. Chloë roared louder, right in her ear.

'What is it my darling?' Pamela crooned, nipping back in again. 'Has nasty auntie Vinny taken um's bottle away then?'

'Here,' Vinny said hastily, 'you have her.' Her neck felt uncomfortably damp. She put up a hand to investigate and discovered on her collar a small patch of warm vomit.

'Never mind,' Pamela said cheerfully, expertly quietening the baby with the bottle again, whilst at the same time registering Vinny's dismay. 'You'll soon get used to minor inconveniences like that. We'll have you fully trained in no time.' She cradled the baby cosily. 'Won't we, Chloë-bee?'

Oh God! Vinny thought. *Why* did I come back? 'Look, Pamela,' she began. 'I'm only here for one more night . . . '

'Come on Vin,' Pamela said, giving her the sweetest of smiles. 'You can't mean that, surely? After all the years we've lived together. I admit I may have taken you rather for granted lately, what with all the fuss about Chloë. If so, I'm truly sorry. But from now on I promise things will be much more like they used to be. We need each other. We live well together. I'd be lost without you; you know that. Come back for a couple of weeks anyway, just until I get Chloë settled in again. What d'you say?'

'Well . . . ' Vinny could feel herself weakening.

'Two weeks,' Pamela said. 'It's all I ask.'

*   *   *

Two days later as Vinny, Pamela and Chloë sat together watching the six o'clock news on BBC1, the top story was the happy recovery of the missing baby.

'I know just how that mother feels,' Pamela said, as though claiming membership of an exclusive club. 'But hers isn't as pretty as ours, is she?'

Ours? 'No,' Vinny agreed. She looked at the child in Pamela's arms and wondered how she would react, once grown into a teenager, to being 'managed' by her. She thought, much better if I don't stay to find out . . .

'Oh Vin,' Pamela said, leaning forward over Chloë to pat her knee. 'It is lovely to have you home again. I missed you so much. Did you miss me?'

'Yes,' Vinny said. 'Of course I did.'

'But now,' Pamela said, shuffling herself upright, 'our lives are going to have to change a lot, aren't they? I shall have to drop most of my committees for a start. I'll just be too busy looking after Chloë. And in the not too distant future it would probably make sense if we moved to a bigger village or even a small country town, where there's a thriving playgroup and some good schools. What d'you think?'

'Goodness!' Vinny exclaimed. 'That's a bit long-termist, isn't it?'

'Well why not? If Chloë's mother really doesn't want her, and if — God forbid — the authorities are finally unable to trace Peter, then it's up to me to bring her up.'

'But you don't know. It's too soon to — '

'Face facts Vinny. This is likely to be our job for the next twenty years — you and me and Chloë. It's the answer to a prayer! If anything can make things good between us again, it's this. I feel it in my bones. Don't you?'

12

By the end of November Jonathan had finished the first draft of his book and was busy going over it for mistakes. He had become accustomed once more to being on his own at The Prospect, although he didn't understand why Vinny was now living with Pamela again, when she'd originally told him she was only staying for one night, and then for a couple of weeks. She'd also said she hated it there.

'Pamela can't manage without me,' Vinny had told him, 'She begged me to stay longer, and I just feel I can't let her down.'

In fact he and Vinny still saw each other on most weekdays, when he travelled with her to the library to search the internet for elusive facts and send emails to contacts in Waterway to check on crucial points. Now he really needed a telephone at home, and it was also now that he discovered that his mobile phone was missing. Kelly had it last, he remembered. She must have stolen it!

Otherwise, everything was coming on well. Jonathan felt confident and hopeful. He had no doubt that some publisher somewhere would buy his book, but he still had to find an agent to punt it about. Vinny was trying to help him, but she was a provincial librarian with no experience and she'd been unsuccessful so far. Jonathan realised that he would have to make an effort too.

The prospect of actually finishing his task and then being able to return to Africa filled him with energy and enthusiasm. His stay in Somerset hadn't turned out at all as he'd expected, but it had been a good choice from the water point of view. He would miss his talks with George. That would be his main regret.

He looked at his watch. It was a quarter past four. I'll go along and see him now, he thought — if he's on duty, that is. I'll tell him that I'll probably be going back to Botswana in just over a month's time.

He got his bike, walked it across the footbridge and cycled towards Amber Junction. When he arrived there he saw the lefthand entrance, the one to the workshop, was open. He propped his bike against the fence, went quietly across the yard and in at the door. He had to be careful when he first arrived, in case George wasn't there. His younger workmates, Jim, Steve and Tom were not only rather unhelpful about his enquiries, but were quite likely to tell him to 'sling his hook'. This had turned out to be a slang expression for 'Go away!'

Jonathan could hear voices beyond the workshop in the main pumping hall. One wasn't George's and the other, much nearer to him, was Mandy's. He certainly did not want to see her! He went in as far as he could and peered through another half open door at the far end. The first thing he saw was a young trainee, up a tall ladder painting the inside of the window frames. Then Mandy crossed his narrow field of view, walking towards the ladder, with her back to Jonathan, looking up and chatting to the boy as she approached the foot of it. He saw her foot knock over a plastic container with brushes sticking out of it. Most of the liquid that had been inside gushed out over the metal floor and disappeared through the cracks between the panels. Jonathan saw Mandy and the boy staring at one another.

He heard Mandy hiss, 'Don't tell Dad?'

And the boy said, 'Not fucking likely. I'm not getting in trouble.'

'Mand?' That was George's voice coming from the direction of the office. Mandy looked up at the boy and put one finger to her lips.

'Hi Dad,' she called, and walked away out of sight, towards him.

'What you up to, then?' he heard George say to her.

'There's something I haven't told you. Known it for a bit. S'posed to be a secret.'

'What's that, then?'

'That Jonathan, up the Prospect.'

Jonathan stiffened, straining to hear.

'Oh now, come on Mand. Don't be starting that nonsense all over — '

'No Dad! Just listen. I know what's wrong with him, now.'

'What's that, then?'

'He's got a sort of symptom — *syndrome* beginning with A. A kind of ortolan — no that's not right. Anyway, it means he don't relate to other people like normal.'

'Oh well,' George said, 'that's no great surprise then, be it? We all knows he's not right in the

280

head, don't us? But he'm a nice enough boy and I've been doin' my best; going out of my way to put up with he, when 'im do come down here a' pestering.'

Not right in the head? Pestering? Put up with? How could George say such things of him? Jonathan felt as if the ground was sliding out from under him. He wanted to roar out a rebuttal to those stupid, insensitive, complacent, so-called normal people, but he couldn't bear to listen to any more. He left the workshop and ran blindly, stumbling in his distress, towards the gate, his bike, and the safe solitude of The Prospect.

By the time he got there, he was entirely spent. He banged the front door behind him and locked it. Then he dragged himself upstairs and collapsed, prone, onto his bed. It was clear to him once again that he had got it all wrong. George and he were not, and never had been, friends. He was quite alone.

★　★　★

Pamela was exhausted. She was simply not getting enough sleep. People in their fifties cannot survive endless broken nights, she thought. Vinny is younger. She really ought to do more. In truth Vinny's reaction to the baby had been puzzling. She gave every appearance of being *afraid* of her! Pamela couldn't understand it. She had naturally assumed that Vinny would find it all a little strange at first, but would soon get the hang of it as they went along. We all have

281

to learn to cope, she said to herself. Look at me! I'm not in this situation by choice, but by golly, am I rising to the occasion!

She felt disappointed in Vinny and — yes — hurt. She'd been no help at all in the struggles Pamela was having towards getting Chloë properly registered, and her inoculations begun. In fact she seemed to be using her library job as an escape route to get out of doing her bit. She'd taken to leaving for work earlier than usual, and returning home later. And when Pamela thankfully unloaded Chloë onto her at the end of the day as she came in, she didn't appear to understand that she — Pamela — was absolutely whacked. Looking after a child is a ceaseless job and totally draining, she thought. I can't be a single mother at my age. It's not reasonable. Vinny needs to appreciate that.

She changed Chloë's nappy and stood at the window, holding her in her arms. Outside on a hawthorn bush there was a large bird eating the berries. One of her neighbours had already lit a bonfire and wreaths of smoke were drifting casually across her lawn.

Well really! Pamela thought. Some people have no *consideration*. 'Look at all that nasty dirty stuff,' she said to the baby. 'Just as well we're indoors. Eh?'

'What?' Vinny asked, coming in.

'Just talking to Chloë.'

'Right. Have you seen my green scarf? I can't — oh here it is. Good.'

'You're not going to work *this* early, surely?'

'Have to, I'm afraid. Got a lot on.'

'But what about breakfast? Chloë's on solids now, you know. So I need more support from you, and there'll be all the mess to clean up too!'

'Sorry,' Vinny said. 'I'll watch you tonight, OK?'

'No, I need your help now . . .' But Vinny had gone. Pamela heard the front door bang, and watched her through the window as she got into the Mini and drove off.

A surge of righteous indignation, flooded Pamela's very being.

'*Well!*' she said to the baby. 'How selfish can you get?'

★　★　★

As Vinny left the house, she noticed the fallen leaves of the cherry tree glowing a frosty orange in the morning sun. The aromatic smell of bonfire smoke pricked her nostrils pleasantly, and she began to feel calmed by the normality of things. She saw that the winter-flowering viburnum was now in bloom. Downwind of it, the scent would already be forming a plume of sweetness in the cold autumnal air.

She drove down Hembrow Hill with a lifting of spirits with every yard as the distance between herself and Pamela increased. She yawned, and rubbed her eyes with one hand. She'd been up twice in the night with Chloë and she was tired. Thank God for the respite of the working day, she thought. Although if anyone had foretold, a few weeks ago, that this would be my attitude, I'd have laughed at them.

The weekends were the worst. Then there was no excuse to be absent. Even walks were circumscribed. They had to be taken on roads suitable for Chloë's buggy. My life has been taken over without my permission, Vinny thought. My loyalty is being strained to breaking point.

At least she was seeing Jonathan regularly, doing a detour to pick him up and take him to the library. But she felt concerned about him. None of her efforts on his behalf had so far borne fruit. Doing the proofreading had given her a proprietory interest. She wondered how he would react when the book failed to be taken up by any publishers at all. She felt worried, and responsible for helping. He hasn't anyone else to depend upon, she thought. And no one but me understands him.

As she went into the library, Vinny's attention was drawn to the stack of daily papers by a large headline:

WATER SHOCK!

She scanned the page quickly.

For the first time in human history, more water is being taken out across the globe than nature is putting in . . .

Between 1990 and 1995 global consumption of fresh water rose six-fold — a rate twice that of population growth . . .

This problem will dwarf any oil crisis we have known . . .

Water is no respecter of national boundaries. Great rivers like the Nile, the Tigris, the Mekong, the Brahmaputra and the Indus, flow through many countries, all of whom want to extract as much water as possible . . .

Hostile countries upstream can — and do — hold their downstream neighbours to ransom . . .

Control of sub-aquifer water resources is as contentious an item on the Israeli/Palestinian agenda as the question of statehood . . .

The wars of the next century will be over water . . .

'Miss Henderson?' someone called. 'There's Mrs Wood on the phone for you.'

'Coming,' Vinny said, but her mind was still on water. It's the right time, she thought. It's *topical*. I do wish Jonathan's book could be published. It's so full of information, but has so little in the way of human interest; more of a list of facts, really. It's a great shame but publication doesn't seem at all likely. She picked up the phone.

'Pamela?'

'Ah, Vinny. Sorry to disturb you at work. I've been thinking, and it just seems to me that things haven't been working so well between us lately. I feel we need to have at least some quality time on our own. What d'you think?'

'Oh,' Vinny said. 'Well I — '

'So I've booked us into our favourite restaurant for dinner. Polly's daughter says she'll bring her own toddler and babysit for us. Isn't that kind?'

'Yes, it — '

'Better go,' Pamela said. 'I'm sure you must be busy. See you this evening.'

'Yes, 'bye.' Vinny put the phone down with a wry smile.

★ ★ ★

Pamela was at her most winning as they took their seats in the restaurant. She beamed at Vinny across the table. 'This is on me,' she said. 'No expense spared!'

'This is nice,' Vinny said dutifully, accepting the menu from a waiter. It was certainly a treat not to have to cook.

'So,' Pamela studied the menu. 'What's it to be? I fancy the steak myself and . . . the moules marinière to begin with. How about you?'

'Um . . . chicken I think, with prawns as a starter.'

'King prawns are not at all pc, you know,' Pamela warned. 'Farming them causes a lot of environmental damage. You of all people should know that!'

'I *like* prawns,' Vinny retorted.

'And the sauce that comes with the chicken looks far too rich to me. Wouldn't you be better off with something less fattening — the sole for example?'

'So in fact *I'm* not actually here to enjoy myself, but you are. Right?'

'What?' Pamela looked hurt. 'I'm only encouraging you towards healthy eating, Vin. If I didn't care about you, I wouldn't bother, would I?'

'You'd better choose the wine,' Vinny said abruptly. 'I won't have much because I'm driving.'

'And maybe you should have the salad instead of those delicious buttery potatoes . . . ' Pamela went on undeterred. 'And we'd both better steer clear of their sticky toffee pudding, however tempting it might be!'

What *is* the point of this? Vinny wondered. It's like being a dog on a lead — Look! There's a lovely wide green field to play on. But, oh no, your paws mustn't actually touch the grass . . . Is this how it will be for poor Chloë too? It's no good. I can't stand it for much longer.

★   ★   ★

Pamela smiled at her across the small table. Vinny looks very sweet by candlelight, she thought, but she's still a tad too grumpy. What more could I do to make her relax, than to bring her out and treat her to a lovely meal in this beautiful old pub? She took in the genuine log fire burning on the hearth, and the horse-brasses gleaming in the subdued light. There was only one thing wrong. She lifted her hand and summoned the waiter again.

'Yes madam?'

'Turn off that awful muzak, would you? It really does lower the tone.'

'Well, I'm sorry madam, but the other customers do appreciate it.'

'Do they? Have you ever asked them? Perhaps we should take a straw poll here and now?' Pamela began to rise to her feet.

'No,' the waiter said hurriedly. 'That won't be necessary.' And he scuttled off.

'Just like a beetle!' Pamela observed delightedly. She smiled across at Vinny, who looked pink and flustered.

'I do wish you wouldn't do that,' she muttered.

'Don't be so bloody British,' Pamela teased her. 'I want everything to be perfect, especially for you.'

In the background, Frank Sinatra stopped abruptly in the middle of *'My way'* and a muted Beethoven sonata trickled in.

A man at the next table leant over. 'Great improvement,' he said. 'Thank you.'

A woman on the other side said, 'Thank goodness! I wanted to do that too, but hadn't the nerve. Thank you so much.'

Pamela acknowledged them both graciously. She was about to turn to Vinny with a *'See?'* but thought better of it. Instead she said, 'How are your prawns?'

'Delicious,' Vinny said defiantly.

'That dress really suits you, you know,' Pamela said. She was doing her utmost to cheer Vinny up but it was hard going.

'Thank you.'

'I'm sure I was right to buy that colour for you, although I could have got it in green.' Vinny was actually scowling now. 'What's up with you?'

'I was just wondering if there was any other part of my life that you'd like to take over?' she said. 'Any tiny aspect which, up to now, you've managed to overlook?'

'What *are* you talking about?' Pamela raised her voice.

'Nothing,' Vinny said, looking round nervously. 'Never mind.'

'No, come on,' Pamela persisted. 'You can't say something as insulting as that and expect to get away with it!'

The waiter hovered at her elbow. 'Everything all right?' he enquired.

'*Yes!*' Pamela hissed. 'Go away!' He withdrew.

'I don't like being manipulated,' Vinny said sullenly.

'Who's manipulating anybody? You're eating your prawns, aren't you?' She put out both hands across the table, but Vinny took hers away and wouldn't meet her eyes. 'Look Vin,' she said, summoning up all the understanding and good will she could manage. 'I do know what this is all about. Really.'

'You do?'

'Yes, and I want to reassure you that I'm just as fond of you as I always was. Chloë's arrival hasn't changed anything. You're still absolutely essential to me.'

Vinny looked at her over the top of her wine glass, but said nothing.

Pamela sensed victory. 'So, let's not quarrel,' she said, 'let's just eat some good food and talk about happy things, like we used to?' She smiled sympathetically at Vinny. 'That reminds me,' she said, 'how about us giving a dinner party before Christmas? It's ages since we did one and I know how much you enjoy cooking special meals.'

★ ★ ★

Vinny discovered that Pamela had invited the guests to the dinner party without any further consultation with her. I ought to have made a fuss at the time, she thought, but I was trying to avoid a scene in the restaurant. And now it's a *fait accompli*!

It was true that she did enjoy cooking, but only when *she* felt like it.

Nevertheless, in spite of growing resentment, Vinny began in good time on the Sunday afternoon of the following week, dutifully going through the preliminaries, cutting up the meat for a stew, making pastry for a fruit tart and chopping onions.

As she worked, she tried unsuccessfully to talk to Pamela who was also in the kitchen, with the baby.

'What time did you tell everyone to come?' she asked.

'Eight o'clock.'

'That's later than usual.'

'Yes, well your poor old granny has to put you to bed first, doesn't she, my little sweetypie?' Pamela crooned to the baby.

'And shall we have the potatoes mashed, or what? — Pamela?'

'Uh-oh!' Pamela said, sniffing the air. 'Something tells me someone's done a pooh pooh!'

'Are you listening to me?' Vinny asked irritably. She turned her head to see Pamela upending the baby on the table, and investigating her nappy. 'Not while I'm *cooking*!' she protested. This distraction caused her to lose her grip on the slippery inner skin of one of the onions. Her favourite extra sharp knife slid abruptly sideways, slicing off the very tip of her little finger. '*Ow!*'

Vinny dropped the knife on the floor and stared at the blood dripping all over the pine surface.

'What have you done now?' Pamela barely glanced up.

Vinny ran water from the cold tap over her left hand. Her eyes were smarting from the onion fumes anyway. She pulled off a sheet of kitchen towel and wrapped it round her bleeding finger. Then she sat down rather suddenly. She felt sick.

'Vinny?' Pamela was still busy with the baby.

'Cut myself,' Vinny managed to say.

Pamela sighed ostentatiously and put Chloë down in her high chair. 'OK, let me see.' She unwrapped the bloody paper. 'What on earth? Why did you do this?'

'*What?*'

'You did it on purpose, didn't you?'

'Of course not! Why would I?' Vinny was outraged.

'To get attention, of course. It's so silly of you, Vin. I don't know why you can't see it yourself, an intelligent person like you. You'd better go up to the bathroom and I'll bandage it for you. But I shall have to change Chloë first.' Pamela looked long-suffering but heroically patient.

'Forget it!' Vinny snapped. 'I'll do it myself.' She ran upstairs in a rage. How *dare* Pamela suggest such a thing? She wouldn't dream of injuring herself on purpose. How could Pamela even think she would? She leant against the bathroom basin, feeling wobbly. In the mirror her face looked back, unusually pale. She put the lid of the lavatory down and sat on it with her head between her knees until the swimming sensation wore off. Then she got some lint from the medicine cupboard and some plaster tape, and bound the wound up as neatly as she could.

That's it! She thought, sitting down again. Pamela can stuff her precious dinner party!

Pamela came up the stairs carrying Chloë. 'What was all that about?' she asked. 'Isn't one baby in the family enough?'

Vinny stared straight at her. Pamela looked so sure of herself, so unequivocally, unbearably *right*, that she was finally spurred into outright rebellion.

'The meat for the stew is in the fridge,' she said. 'It wants some garlic, some chopped carrots, some blood-free onions and half a pint of red wine. Then two to three hours in the bottom right oven. Right?'

'What d'you mean?' For the first time Pamela looked flustered. 'Where will you be?'

'Out,' Vinny said.

'But, what shall I tell the others — Gordon and Sue and Polly..?'

'I don't care,' Vinny said. 'You'll think of something. *I have had enough*. OK?'

She got to her feet, ran downstairs, grabbed her handbag, coat and scarf, and let herself out of the front door. Her little finger throbbed as she drove, but so far there was no blood seeping through the dressing. It'll be fine, Vinny thought.

So, where was she going? Her aim was to be

well away from the house until all expectations of her doing the cooking became academic. She looked at her watch. It was half past three. It'll be dark in half an hour, she thought, but there's still time to go for a walk as the sun goes down. I need some air.

She made for the local nature reserve down on the moor, turning into a small side road and parking on a rough drove, pitted with potholes. She walked along towards the main reserve area where there was a wooden hide for birdwatching. The sun was sinking on the western horizon, reflected in a stretch of open water, dotted with coots and the odd duck in silhouette. Vinny drew in deep breaths of cold dusky air and began to recover herself. A moorhen squawked loudly close by making her jump, and then the first of the starlings began to pour in around her.

They came from all directions, in small groups at first, but rapidly amalgamating into one vast flock until there were hundreds of thousands of the birds all swooping together in perfectly co-ordinated formation flying. Vinny watched in awe as they went over her with a terrific *whirr!* of wings and spattering of droppings before spiralling upwards over the reedbed as one; a single shape-shifting organism, creating fantastic evolving patterns high in the sky. Then all at once the birds dropped down and alighted amongst the reeds to roost, gossiping together noisily.

'A murmuration of starlings,' Vinny said aloud.

She saw with amusement that other birds — crows, blackbirds, pigeons, ducks, were all scooting off in the opposite direction, displaced by this vast invading army. A few times the starlings fell suddenly silent, prior to taking off again in huge numbers with a *whoosh!* and snaking over the tops of the reeds in the gathering dusk, before settling again finally in their chosen position for the night. Then as suddenly as it had begun, and in less than ten minutes, it was all over.

It was almost dark. Vinny left the chattering hordes and picked her way carefully back to her car. She was on a high; elated to have been there at just the right moment. It felt like a gift — an unlooked-for privilege. It gave her unexpected self-confidence.

Her hands were freezing. She let herself in and sat in the mini hugging herself, rubbing her arms to get warm again. Ten years as one half of a couple seems to have brainwashed me, she thought, but now I've finally seen the light. I shall wait until Christmas is over and then I'm bloody well going to get the hell out!

* * *

Under the circumstances Pamela hadn't seen why Vinny should get any credit at all for having contributed to this dinner party. So she'd ignored her partly prepared ingredients, and telephoned everyone to ask them to come early and bring food.

'Vinny's let me down,' she'd said, 'and what with the baby and everything, I can't — '

'No, of course you can't.' They'd all been very understanding.

Polly and Arthur promised to defrost some chicken pieces and cook them when they arrived. Sue and Ron had a gooseberry fool and several small chocolate mousses in their freezer, and a large packet of assorted salad in their fridge. Gordon could lay his hands on a couple of lamb chops, a tin of pilchards and a bottle of redcurrant jelly. They all said, 'Don't worry about it. The food really doesn't matter. It's *you* we're coming to see.' So she'd scrubbed and pricked seven large potatoes and had put them in the top oven to bake. Then she busied herself with bathing Chloë and putting her to bed.

Pamela had decided not to say anything about Vinny's disappearance. That subject should stay between the two of them, and be sorted out in private. She was pretty sure that Vinny would slink back in sometime during the evening, anyway. She's acting like a spoilt child! Pamela thought, and felt agreeably superior.

Ron and Sue arrived first, bearing baskets of goodies and unloading them onto the kitchen table. 'Oh, is that your little Chloë?' Sue said at once, picking up a framed photograph. 'Isn't she divine?'

'Come up and see her,' Pamela offered. 'She looks even more angelic when she's asleep.'

Ron stayed downstairs to let in the other guests as they arrived. Pamela and Sue faced each other over the sleeping baby's cot. 'Are you all right?' Sue asked in a whisper.

'Just about.' Pamela managed a brave smile.

'You're doing a marvellous job, you know?' Sue said. 'We all admire you so much, but it

295

must be very exhausting?'

'Especially at our age!' They both smiled ruefully.

When they got back down to the kitchen, they found everyone there and a buzz of activity. Pamela observed her friends with a benevolent eye. Polly, brisk and efficient as ever, had laid out the chicken and the chops in an ovenproof dish and was about to put them into the Aga. She was wearing a simple red dress, which had clearly cost a lot of money.

'Which door?' Polly asked.

'Top right, below the spuds.'

Arthur was arranging the salad artistically in a large bowl. He was in his usual baggy striped jersey and faded cords. His hair flopped in his eyes and tangled at his neck. How did they ever get together in the first place? Pamela wondered, not for the first time, and why doesn't Polly make him have a haircut?

Gordon, short and portly in his habitual dark suit with a pristine white handkerchief folded expertly in the top pocket, was uncorking several bottles of good red wine with grunts and flourishes. Dear Gordon!

And finally there was Ron, in smart casuals and spotless suede shoes, collecting up the cutlery and glasses to lay the table in the dining room. Even out of a suit he looked like a solicitor.

'What would I do without the kindness of my friends?' Pamela said.

'It's a pleasure,' Gordon said cheerfully. 'Haven't had a good midnight feast since I was at school!'

'Oh, but you need condensed milk for that,' Polly put in.

'And cold baked beans!' Arthur said.

When supper was announced, there seemed to be plenty to eat. Pamela was pleased that her decision not to take over Vinny's cooking had paid off. The meal was more like a picnic than a dinner party and seemed to go all the better for that. Even Gordon relaxed and appeared to relish the informality. He picked up a drumstick and ate it in his fingers, waving it about to illustrate a point.

' . . . And that was that,' he finished his story. 'Frozen!'

'Bloody cold out tonight,' Arthur said, making a salad sandwich with two slices of bread and butter. 'Wind's coming straight from Siberia and bringing the snow with it. I wish I'd listened to the forecast, now.'

'Oh it won't be a problem,' Ron said. 'We've lived here over twenty years, and I could count on the fingers of one hand the number of times when we've actually had the stuff in inches on the ground.'

'It lies regularly on the Mendip hills,' Gordon argued.

'But not on the magic Isle of Hembrow.' Pamela said.

'Are we going to go on like this?' Polly suddenly demanded, 'talking about the boring old weather, or shall we discuss the things we're all pussyfooting round?'

'Which are what?' Gordon asked.

'Which are — how is Pamela managing with

an unexpected baby, and where is Vinny?' There was an awkward silence.

'The fact is,' Pamela began, 'I think poor old Vin is having some sort of mid-life crisis. I'm afraid she's very jealous of the baby.'

'Ron was the same, weren't you, love?' Sue said to him. 'But it all worked out perfectly well in the end.'

'Well, I certainly hope she'll come round,' Pamela said, 'because I definitely can't manage Chloë on my own.'

'Nor should you,' Polly said.

'Certainly not!' Gordon agreed. 'Vinny has a duty to stand by you.'

'She hasn't *walked out*, has she?' Arthur asked.

'Oh no,' Pamela assured him. 'She'd never do that. She's just having a bit of a sulk.'

'That's not like Vinny,' Sue said.

'Well she's definitely not herself, these days.' Pamela smiled round at her friends. 'But never mind, eh? You're all here and I feel wonderfully supported. She began telling them stories of Parish Council shenanigans, whilst they supped their wine and laughed.

In the midst of it all, the baby started to cry. Pamela rose unsteadily and went upstairs to see to her. The telephone rang.

'I'll answer it,' Arthur offered.

Pamela found that Chloë was hungry and decided to feed her downstairs to show her off. When they went back through the hall, Arthur was on the phone, saying, 'Oh the starling spectacular? Yes, know it well. Wrote a poem on it once.'

'Who is it?'

'It's Vinny.' He passed her the receiver.

'Vinny love? Where are you?' Pamela asked, conscious of the audience in the next room.

'I'm at Jonathan's. I don't think I'll be able to get back tonight.' She sounded distant and formal.

Pamela suppressed her instinctive response, with difficulty. 'Oh? And why's that?'

'You obviously haven't looked outside lately,' Vinny said. 'Are you all right?'

Did she care? 'You're missing an excellent party,' Pamela said.

'Good. Well, probably see you tomorrow then.'

'Vin?' But she had switched off her mobile. Pamela went straight to the back door and opened it. There was snow, a foot deep and still falling in thick muffling flakes! The world outside was bitingly cold and unnaturally silent. Pamela withdrew speedily.

* * *

When Vinny had left the nature reserve she wasn't sure what to do next. She had no wish to arrive at the dinner party half way through and be obliged to justify herself. She decided to visit Jonathan instead.

As she drove over the moor the first flakes of snow began to fall, compacting into two lines of ice on either side of her windscreen wipers. Snow! She thought, childishly delighted. How lovely. Perhaps we'll be cut off for a week and I won't be able to go to work! But then she remembered her present situation and stopped smiling. It won't amount to anything anyway, she thought. It never does.

Jonathan seemed pleased to see her when she arrived at his house. 'How are you?' she asked him.

'Not good.'

'Oh dear, why's that?'

'All the agents say their lists are full. I've sent sample chapters to ten publishers too, and none have replied.'

'Well it will probably take two or three months,' Vinny said, worried by his naïveté.

'What, to read one chapter?' He was incredulous.

'No, before they even get around to reading it.'

'Well, I can't wait that long,' he said. 'I've got to get back to Africa.'

'Oh dear,' Vinny said again. She felt sorry for him. He clearly had no idea of the difficulties involved in selling a book, or of the fact that he would almost certainly have to write a second draft, and maybe another . . .

'But,' he said, brightening, 'you can sort it out for me once I've gone, if nothing's happened by then.' He looked at her more closely. 'What's that white stuff on your shoulders?'

'Probably snow,' she said.

She expected him to react with pleasure but he just said, 'No, it isn't.'

Vinny took off her coat and looked at the shoulders. 'Oh, it must be starling droppings,' she said. 'I saw thousands of them going to roost just now. It was an amazing sight!'

'Did you bring any food with you?' was all he said.

'No. Haven't you been eating properly?' she asked him.

'Not really, no.'

'Why not?'

'Can't be bothered.' He looked depressed.

'Shall I cook us both something now?' Vinny looked in the fridge and found some eggs and a piece of furry cheddar. 'How about a cheese omelette?' Jonathan nodded. 'And I'll do some food shopping after work tomorrow and bring you enough to keep you going for a while. How would that be?'

'And cook it?'

'Well, some of it, maybe.'

'That would be good.'

A little later, as they sat down together to eat, Vinny said gently, 'What's the matter?'

Jonathan shrugged.

'Come on, I can see you're upset about something. Do tell me. It might help.'

He looked at her. 'D'you think so?'

'Well, you never know.'

He put his knife and fork down and rested his forehead on his hands.

'I heard George saying things about me,' he muttered.

'Nasty things?'

'Yes. He says I'm not right in the head, and that I pester him.'

'Oh dear.' Vinny wanted to stroke his hair. 'I am sorry.'

'I thought he was my friend,' Jonathan said.

'He knows so much about water.'

'There's more to being a friend than just sharing an interest,' Vinny said.

'What more?'

'Well, a friend has to care about you, accept you for what you are and never say cruel things behind your back.'

'Like you, you mean?'

'Like me, yes. Eat up, or it'll get cold.'

Jonathan did so. Then, when he had finished everything on his plate he breathed a sigh and said, 'Thank you, Vinny. That was delicious.'

Vinny broke into delighted laughter, leant across the table and kissed his forehead.

'What was that for?' He was smiling too.

'For being a lovely appreciative man,' Vinny said. 'Let's have our coffee in the sitting room. Is the fire alight?

'Yes, I was sitting by it when you arrived.' They got to their feet and went into the next room. Jonathan threw the last of the scrap wood left by the builders onto the fire, plus a couple of logs. Then they settled themselves comfortably before it, on the sofa.

'I am feeling better,' he said.

'You sound surprised.'

'Yes, well I didn't expect to.'

'I'm glad.'

They sat in a companionable silence for a while, watching the fire. One of the bits of scrap was burning with a spurt of greenish flame from one end.

'Copper,' Jonathan said.

'Eh?'

'The presence of the element copper shows up green in a flame test. Calcium is red and sodium is yellow.'

I was hopeless at chemistry at school,' Vinny said. 'I was good at English and languages, especially Italian. But I wish I'd done psychology at university now. I'd like to have become a clinical psychologist.'

My father wanted me to be an architect,' Jonathan said. 'To follow in his footsteps, he said, but I didn't want to.'

'Was he disappointed?'

'He says I always disappoint him, yes.'

'So, he's not very supportive of you?'

'He's very impatient.'

'And your mother?'

'Oh she's always busy. She lives in France most of the time now.'

'And your brothers? There are six, aren't there?'

'Yes. One's in Australia, one in Singapore, one in Canada and the other three are mostly in London.'

Trying to escape, Vinny thought. 'Do any of them have AS as well?'

'Not as much as I do, no.'

They watched the fire again. Some of the logs were applewood, and the fragrance of it filtered into the room with odd puffs of escaping smoke.

'You mustn't give up on your writing,' Vinny said. 'There's an increasing amount of coverage about water in the papers these days. It's going to be a major issue soon, and your book will appear just at the right moment.'

'I hope so,' Jonathan got up to poke a log further in.

Vinny wished she could stay here in this warmth, unchallenged and content. She had no wish to go back to Hembrow, now or ever.

'This won't do,' she said eventually. 'I'm afraid I'll have to be going. It's getting late.'

She opened the front door and attempted to walk across the footbridge but during the time she had been inside, the east wind had picked up in strength and was now blowing the snow horizontally into great drifts. It was freezing too. She found herself slipping on the icy boards and in danger of falling into the rhyne. It's no good, she thought. I don't want to drive in the dark in this.

'I thought you'd gone,' Jonathan said, when in response to her banging, he'd opened the front door again.

'Weather's too bad. I think I'll have to stay the night.'

'Good,' he said, letting her back inside.

'I'd better phone Pamela to tell her what I'm doing.'

'I haven't got a phone any more,' he said. 'Kelly stole it.'

'Really? I wonder why that doesn't surprise me. Don't worry, I've got my own mobile,' Vinny got it out of her handbag. 'Hello? Who's that? Oh, it's you, Arthur.'

★ ★ ★

304

The following day was cold and grey, but dry. It took Vinny twice as long as usual to struggle into work after first getting Jonathan to dig the mini out of the lay-by, and give her a push to get it started. She drove very carefully along the road, which had been reduced to two ruts of hard-packed snow. She was relieved eventually to reach a wider one that had been salted and snowploughed. Once there, she found the streets of Otterbridge unusually free of people — the pavements banked up with dirty slush and grit — so it was quiet in the library. She wondered why she had bothered coming.

Vinny drove slowly to the supermarket in her lunch break and stocked up with some food for Pamela and herself as well as for Jonathan, including tins and a tin opener; iron rations in case of need. Just as she got back, and was getting out of her car, her phone rang. It was Gordon.

'Look Vinny,' he began, 'apologies for being blunt and all that, but you know me well enough by now not to take offence at what I'm going to say.'

Oh dear, Vinny thought. When people say things like that, it's usually because they're about to be very offensive indeed. 'Go on.'

'Well, not to put too fine a point on it — ' He seemed to be struggling, uncharacteristically, for words. ' — We all think that your place is with Pamela at the moment. She needs all the help you can give her, you know. It can't be at all easy for her, suddenly to be plunged into the situation she's in.'

'I know that,' Vinny said indignantly. 'Of course I do!'

'Yes, well, tell me to mind my own business if you like. I'll bid you good day.' And he rang off.

Bloody cheek! Vinny thought. What the hell does he know about anything, anyway?

Five minutes later Sue phoned her. 'Just wanted to make sure you were all right,' she said.

'Fine thanks,' Vinny said.

'Pamela seems to be bearing up remarkably well.'

'Yes,' Vinny said. 'She's in her element.'

'Oh, well I'm not so sure of that, Vinny. She's got a hard row to hoe for the next how-many years.'

'Yes, I do know that.'

'I can see that it must be difficult for you too,' Sue said.

'In what way?'

'Well, having to share Pamela's affections with a newcomer. That can't be easy.'

'Sue,' Vinny said firmly, 'I am *not* jealous of Chloë. OK?'

'If you say so,' Sue said understandingly, and changed the subject. 'We had a terrible drive home last night. We went in convoy with Polly and Arthur, and it was just as well that we did. Their car got stuck in the snow and we had to tow them out! Gordon had the best of it. He very sensibly volunteered to stay with Pamela.'

'Did he indeed!' He hadn't mentioned this on the phone just now. Was he there still?

'You will be back at home today, won't you Vinny?'

'Look Sue, I'm sorry but it's really none of your business,' Vinny said, resentfully. 'You don't know the whole story.'

'But — '

Vinny interrupted her. 'I'm leaving any minute. There's no point keeping the library open today. I've just got to deliver some food to Jonathan and then I was going back to Hembrow anyway.'

'Go there *first*,' Sue urged. 'Pamela's need is greatest.'

So at two o'clock Vinny began the journey home. The roads were in as bad a condition as they had been that morning, with no sign of a thaw in progress. Snowploughs had pushed back the drifts into banks on either side, but several cars — presumably abandoned the night before — were still causing a hazard. If it's as bad as this tomorrow, Vinny thought, I shan't bother going to work at all.

A car came up fast behind her with its headlights full on and began to overtake just as another car appeared round a bend, coming towards them. Vinny instinctively braked hard, but the mini, instead of slowing down, slid sideways on a patch of ice and the engine stalled. There were a few seconds during which Vinny felt completely paralysed. Then her heart began beating much too fast and she gasped in fear. She'd missed both the other cars by a hair's breadth, and they were already moving away in opposite directions, unscathed. She looked wildly round but mercifully there were no more vehicles on the road. She had time to restart the engine and manoeuvre the mini across the end of someone's drive, and off the road.

She sat there for several minutes until her heart had slowed down and her hands had stopped trembling, and she felt in control again. It's getting dark already, she thought, and Hembrow Hill could be a sheet of ice. There's no way I'm going to risk it now. I'll have to go back to The Prospect.

She felt dog-tired, and her little finger was hurting. She drove at a snail's pace along the increasingly narrow roads, praying she wouldn't meet another vehicle. A gust of wind caught the side of the car and made it rock. She could feel the strength of it on the steering. She held on, grim faced.

At last, there were the lights of The Prospect ahead of her. She steered the mini into its own snow ruts in the lay-by and slumped with her head on the steering wheel. She'd made it.

Later that night as she went up to bed in the spare room and began to draw the curtains, Vinny looked out of the window. It was still windy and clear. A big moon had arisen, illuminating the gleaming white fields. She stared at it, watching the clouds race across its face. This is all such nonsense, she told herself. I'm with Jonathan, but I'm not (he didn't even notice my bandaged finger.). And I'm not with Pamela, but everyone thinks I should be. Thank goodness I've made my decision. Christmas can't be over too soon.

13

Later, on the night of the twentieth and the morning of the twenty-first of December, the weather worsened appreciably. It began to snow again, whipped up by north-easterly gales into a blizzard, piling into new ten foot drifts across the roads, and freezing as the temperature fell as low as five degrees below. The force of the wind felled trees, walls and even some chimneys, and electricity supplies failed over a wide area of Somerset. Local radio and television put out severe weather warnings, advising people not to attempt to travel unless their journeys were absolutely necessary. But an extra high spring tide was forecast for that afternoon, so men from the Environment Agency were obliged to struggle out in pairs to reach the sea walls and close the coastal gates.

At Amber Junction, George was awake early, making sure the emergency generator was running properly, producing light and enough heat in the building to keep any condensation off his precious engines. Every half hour he shouldered his way through the snow to check the river water level outside, to be reassured that there was no need for pumping at present.

All was quiet for now. But when this lot do melt, he thought to himself, us'll be busy. Best make sure I gets a good night's sleep tonight.

★   ★   ★

Vinny woke several times in the night feeling cold under Pamela's inadequate supply of spare bedding. She ended up putting the small floor rug on top of the bed as well, to keep her own warmth in. She had to do it by touch because the lights wouldn't work. In the morning she tried her bedside lamp again and, discovering that the power-cut was still on, she stayed in bed longer than usual, waiting for it to get light.

Dawn came slowly, turning the sky from black to white, but without any great increase in visibility, as Vinny discovered when she finally got up and drew back the curtains. She pulled on all her clothes very quickly and watched the fat flakes whirling past the window. Good heavens! she thought, *We haven't had proper snow like this for years!*

Then she realised, with a sinking feeling, that in a mostly electric house there would be no hot tea to energise her, no warm water for washing, and not much heat of any kind, as they had burnt most of the firewood two days ago. She went into the bathroom and discovered that her toothbrush was frozen. She touched the window. There was ice even on the inside! We can't stay here, she thought. We'll freeze to death.

She thought longingly of Pamela's oil-fired Aga which had no electrical connections and would still be on, warming the kitchen, providing tea or coffee, hot croissants . . . 'Hell!' she said aloud, 'we can't even have toast!'

It was clear that they would not be able to go anywhere as long as the blizzard lasted. Vinny wrapped a blanket round herself, went down-stairs and looked out of the kitchen window. She couldn't even see the Kingspill Drain for the falling snow. She drew back the curtains in the sitting room and found there were great walls of it pressed against the windows. She shivered with cold.

'What's for breakfast?' Jonathan said, at the door.

'Bread and marmalade?' Vinny suggested. 'Damn! I could murder a bowl of hot porridge! Aren't you cold?' He was wearing only his usual shirt and pullover with a pair of cotton trousers.

'No.' he seemed to be able to tolerate extremes of cold and discomfort. At breakfast he washed his marmalade sandwich down with a glass of icy water, and appeared none the worse for it.

Vinny wondered how long it would be before they could escape. She thought of Pamela and how she would say, 'Serves you right! You should have come home the night before last.' And she thought that now she could bear Pamela's rage, even her most blatant superiority gladly, if only for some warmth . . .

'You can only murder something that's alive,' Jonathan pointed out.

'It's a figure of speech,' she said. 'I should have thought you could have learned most of them by now. You've got such a good memory.'

'I don't want to clutter up my brain with rubbish,' he said.

Vinny felt irritated with him but was determined not to show it. 'My brain is stuffed with all kinds of very useful rubbish, like this rhyme that my Great Aunt used to like. It goes like this:

Little Willie from his mirror,
Licked the mercury right off,
Thinking in his childish error,
It would cure the whooping cough.
At his funeral his mother,
Brightly said to Mrs Brown:
''Twas a chilly day for Willie.
When the mercury went down!'

'Mirrors aren't made of mercury,' Jonathan objected.

'Well, they were years ago, when it was written.'

'But, did you know,' he said, suddenly enthusiastic, 'that a fall of one inch of mercury on the barometer — approximately 33.7 millibars — can raise sea level by a foot?'

'Why?'

'Less pressure bearing down on the surface. And that's on top of the tidal effect of course,' he said. 'Did you also know that the Bristol Channel has the second highest tidal range in the world — second only to the Bay of Fundy in Canada?'

'No, I didn't.'

'It's much higher on the Welsh side,' Jonathan went on, unaware of the expression on her face. 'A seventy foot tide was recorded there once! On the Somerset side it's usually quite a bit less, but in the lowest part of the moors an exceptional tide can still be twenty feet or more above the level of the land,' He looked triumphant.

'Really?' Vinny said. 'Look, we'd better decide

312

what we're going to do. There's clearly no point in me trying to get to the library, but I do think we should go up to Hembrow as soon as it's at all possible, and preferably before we both expire from hypothermia. My fingers are already going white. Look!'

Jonathan glanced at them. 'Do they hurt?'

'No, they're numb.'

'That's OK then. I've got to work.'

'You can't,' Vinny pointed out. 'No electricity; no computer.'

'I can still read my manuscript. Where's the copy I lent you?'

'In my desk at the library with the back-up discs. Don't you have another one?'

'No,' he said glumly. 'I'm waiting to get it back from an agent.'

'Well,' Vinny said. 'We may be stuck here for hours, so I'm going back to bed to try to keep warm. I suggest you do the same.'

She lay in bed wearing all her clothes with the bedding, the rug and her coat on top of her, and gradually, very slowly her body did warm up. But what to do with her brain? There were no books to read, no radio, and her thoughts tended to go round and round interminably without coming to any sensible conclusions. Lying in bed in the daytime when you weren't ill was stupefyingly boring. Vinny remembered her grandmother's reproving refrain: 'When we were young, we made our own amusement.'

Perhaps she could say some poetry aloud? She began confidently with the ones that her mother used to recite to her. She managed the whole of

Ozymandias and most of *Oh Wild West Wind*. She attempted *Beautiful must be the mountains whence ye come*, but got stuck and was reduced to *Twas brillig and the slithy toves*, and finally to *The rabbit has a charming face, its private life is a disgrace* . . .

It was still snowing hard, building up in inverted arcs at the corners of each window pane like fake Christmas decoration. Vinny could feel all her digits now and everything was warm except the tip of her nose. Her breath steamed out white in the freezing air of the room. How did people manage, before central heating? Sooner or later, she thought, I'll have to go for a pee, but not yet. She wondered where Jonathan was. Perhaps I should have sat with him on the sofa, she thought. In situations like this, aren't you supposed to huddle together for warmth?

Jonathan came up the stairs and into her room. 'What have you been doing?' she asked him.

'Thinking.'

'But you must be so cold. Come over here. Let me feel your hands.' He hesitated. 'Come on,' Vinny insisted. She took them both in her own. 'They're frozen! Don't you feel it at all?' Jonathan shrugged. 'Look,' she said, 'It's bad for you to get so cold. You'd better get in here with me and let me warm you up.'

'Oh,' Jonathan said. 'All right then, but first I've got to fetch something.'

'What?'

'It's a surprise.' He went to his room but came back without carrying anything.

'You can keep all your clothes on, but take your boots off, won't you?' Vinny advised.

★　★　★

Jonathan patted his pocket in some anticipation and then climbed in and lay down with his back to Vinny in the confined space of the single bed.

'Aarrgh!' she exclaimed, 'you really are arctic!' She put her arm over him and he flinched without meaning to.

'Pretend you're benighted on a mountain top,' Vinny said in his ear, 'and I'm a Saint Bernard dog who's rescuing you.'

The idea of being cuddled by a big dog made him laugh, and he began to relax.

'D'you know this one?' Vinny said. '*The more it snows (tiddely-pom), the more it goes (tiddely-pom), the more it goes (tiddely-pom) on snowing. And nobody knows (tiddely-pom), how cold my toes (tiddely-pom), how cold my toes (tiddely-pom) are growing.* And before you ask, tiddely-pom means nothing at all. It's Pooh Bear's special outdoor song from *The House at Pooh Corner*. Most people love it because it reminds them of their childhood.'

'I didn't like being a child,' Jonathan said.

'Why?'

'Because I had a pair of red trousers and they wouldn't let me wear them every day.' There was a silence. Then he said, 'But I liked going to the sea. I used to stand by it for hours, watching every wave come in.'

'Did you have any friends?' Vinny asked.

315

'No. No one else was interested in water.'

'But now you've written a book on it,' she said, 'will you go on to study something else?'

'Yes, I think I will.' He was pleased. He turned over. Her face was very close to his. Her hair tickled his ear.

She smiled at him. 'Warmer now?'

'Yes.' She smelt nice, but he couldn't look into her eyes. It was too difficult, too disturbing. He closed his. It did feel good to be warm.

'My arm's going to sleep,' Vinny said, moving awkwardly. 'If I could just put it . . . there. That's better. This bed is far too narrow!'

Jonathan felt her slide it under his neck, but he kept his eyes shut. He expected at any minute to feel panic stricken by her nearness, but nothing happened. Instead, he felt comfortable.

'So, what's it to be?'

'What?'

'The subject you're going to study next.'

'Astronomy.' He surprised himself by his answer, but on reflection it was a good one.

'Great idea,' Vinny said. 'There's so much scope.'

Jonathan experienced a strange feeling, which came over him all of a sudden. He thought it might be affection. At the same time he began to feel an erection swelling in the constricted space of his underpants. He shifted his position to give it room. Is this proper intimacy? He wondered. Other questions also occurred to him. Are we going to have sexual intercourse? Should I ask her first before I begin? How do I start? He had no idea of the correct procedure for making the first move.

His erection was full size by now, and demanding urgent attention. Jonathan shuffled nearer to Vinny and pressed himself experimentally against her. He opened his mouth to speak, but she pre-empted him.

'Sorry,' she said, pulling her arm rather roughly from beneath him and jumping out of bed. 'Got to go to the loo.'

★ ★ ★

Vinny sat on the lavatory and wondered what she should do. Jonathan's condition was obvious. She felt inclined to acquiesce, but it wasn't that straightforward. I'm not on the pill, she thought. I haven't made love for so long . . . What if it all goes wrong and is horribly embarrassing? I couldn't bear to lose him as a friend. She went back into the bedroom with the intention of speaking kindly to him, but still saying no.

She found him lying under the covers on his back with one fist in the air. 'I've got a present for you,' he said, waving his arm, which was bare. She noticed that all his clothes were now in a heap on the floor.

'Really?'

'Yes. I was in a shop, like you said. And I saw these and I thought, Vinny might want some, so I bought a packet.'

She went nearer, expecting sweets. Jonathan opened his hand and held it out to reveal . . . half a dozen condoms in silver wraps.

'I've put one on ready,' he said. 'Kelly showed me how.'

Vinny bent down and put her hand very gently over his mouth. 'Ssshh!' she said. 'Let's not ever mention her name again, yes? This is just between you and me.' And she began to unbutton her clothes.

★   ★   ★

At one thirty in the afternoon there was a sudden change in the direction of the weather. The wind veered rapidly south-westwards as a deep depression moved in from the warmer Atlantic. Temperatures shot up, and the falling snow changed to sleet and then to rain. The rising tide, the low pressure and the high winds combined together into a ferocious storm, which moved swiftly landwards, battering the coastline all along the English side of the Bristol Channel. Then at ten past two, just as the tide reached its height, the winds went round further until they were a full westerly, hurling the sea against the Somerset coast and producing a tidal surge of unprecedented proportions.

In twenty miles of coastline there were five breaches in the sea defences. The height of the waves overtopped the clay bank to the north of the Kingspill clyse and began to erode away its back face, causing it to collapse along a half-mile stretch and allow a major inundation. The sea poured in for nearly an hour, spreading widely over the levels as far to the east as the M5 embankment, and flooding over a hundred houses in the village of West Zoyle. It came not as a dramatic wall of water, but inexorably from the bottom up, flowing fast and rising like a running bath. Behind the tide-locked clyse, where its banks were as flat as the surrounding flooded farmland, the Kingspill Drain began to fill up as well; the salt water flowing the wrong way along it, inland towards Amber Junction.

All available inflatable boats were commandeered as police and firemen began the task of rescuing people from the floods. The Environment Agency flood patrols were recalled from their normal duties and set on sandbagging. And all this time the rain beat down and the gales continued.

Eventually the tide turned and began to recede. The water stopped coming in. In the seven hour breathing space that followed, the Mendip quarries worked flat out producing and moving huge boulders to the foreshore to dissipate the energy of the next high tide. Tons of quick-setting concrete were also used, in the hope that it would set hard enough to plug the gaps in the sea wall and hold back the renewed onslaught of the waves.

By now the thaw had begun in earnest, and the ever-increasing meltwater from the surrounding hills had started its journey, trickling downhill towards the peatlands. At Amber Junction the generator was powering the electric pump which had come on automatically as the water level rose behind it. George was also aware of the rising Kingspill at the front of the building. He kept an anxious eye on the monitors and prepared the two big diesel engines for twenty-four-hour pumping. A second man was sent to join him — struggling through the clogged roads — one of the Environment Agency's work-force who were already stretched to capacity by the tidal event. And all the while the snow went on melting.

★   ★   ★

Earlier on at The Prospect, Vinny and Jonathan were lying in bed together, warm and drowsy. Vinny's arm rested across his stomach, over the sexy line of dark hair, which ran from his bush to his belly button. There was still so much of him to explore. She longed for it to be summer, so that they could make love anywhere, unfettered by the cold.

I should buy us a waterbed. Vinny smiled at the thought. She drew back and looked at him. His curly hair was spread out on the pillow and his eyes were shut, but he wasn't asleep. She knew better than to break the spell by asking him what he was thinking, although she did want to know.

'Jonathan?'

'Mmm?'

'This is lovely.'

'Yes.' He opened his eyes. 'Did I do it right?'

'Yes, it was good.' Vinny smiled at him. 'But since we're not very experienced together, perhaps we should get in some regular practice?'

'What, again?' He got up on one elbow and looked down at her. His chest was almost hairless, and his pale body tapered elegantly to the narrow hips, which had fitted so perfectly between her thighs. She thought of the cheeks of his bottom, which were small and firm. Two handfuls.

'Yes,' she said. 'Again.'

★　★　★

Once the snow turned to rain, the thaw was magically rapid. The Kingspill Drain came into view again, filling up with flat brown water. The top of the mini and very soon most of the car was revealed, and the two tracks along the middle of the road widened, revealing stretches of tarmac. By three o'clock the wind had eased off a little and Vinny decided that they should try to leave. If they waited much longer it would be dark and might freeze again.

'We'd better get going,' she said to Jonathan. 'Can you get your things?'

'I'll stay here,' he said.

'I think you ought to come,' Vinny said as patiently as she could. 'There'll be proper hot meals at Hembrow. I need you to help me anyway. The mini will probably need pushing and I can't do it by myself.'

'Well . . .'

'I'm sure they'll sort the electricity out soon, and then I'll bring you straight back here.'

'Oh, all right, then.'

They managed to get the car out of the lay-by and point it in the right direction. Then, already wet and buffeted by the wind, Vinny drove slowly through deep slushy puddles hemmed in by dripping ice walls, praying they wouldn't meet anyone and be obliged to risk an uncleared passing place. They came upon an ancient pollarded willow, which had been split in two by the gale and lay where it had fallen. Vinny squeezed the mini past it, driving over its topmost branches and scattered twigs, hoping that there would be no others barring their way.

Finally they reached a larger road that had been salted and gritted. Most of the snow on the carriageway had turned to water and the going became more straightforward. Vinny's shoulders relaxed a little.

'You're going the wrong way,' Jonathan said.

'Yes, I know. I'm sticking to the main roads. It's the long way round, but safer.'

'Oh.' Then he said, 'Talking about the wrong way reminds me, Kelly said I — '

'Please, Jonathan,' Vinny begged. 'Don't talk about her to me. I can't bear to think of the two of you together. I just want it to be you and me and nobody else. It's very important to me.'

'Are you jealous?' He turned to look at her.

'Yes, I probably am. I'm only human.' She took her eyes off the road for a brief moment. 'And whatever you do, *don't* tell Pamela we've been to bed together.'

'Or had sex?'

'*Especially* that. Do you promise me you won't?'

'OK.'

There was a silence. Vinny, still basking in the warm afterglow, felt so open to him, so vulnerable. The thing she wanted to avoid at all costs was Jonathan saying something crushing or insensitive, or even matter-of-fact about what had just happened. She wanted to hold onto her present feelings and protect them, at least for now. She tried to think of something neutral to talk about.

'I suppose all this rain and melting snow will soon run off into the sea?' she finally said.

'Not all that soon,' Jonathan said. 'These moors are very well adapted for holding water.'

'What d'you mean? Tell me very simply in layman's terms.'

He sat up straighter and began eagerly. 'Well, the underlying geology is in the form of a basin which is bounded by hills on three sides. Then on the seaward side there's a wide coastal belt of clay.'

Vinny glanced at him out of the corner of her eye from time to time, as he was speaking, but mostly concentrated on the road ahead. In the places where the drifts had been, there were still bumpy patches of hard-packed snow which were melting only slowly.

'This coastal belt,' Jonathan went on, 'is about seven miles wide and is properly called the Levels. It was built up over thousands of years from particles of clay brought down by the rivers and deposited, on contact with the salt seawater, eventually forming a barrier which restricted the flow of the five rivers to the sea. So then of course the moors behind it got wetter and developed into marsh and peat bog.' He smiled.

'I thought the 'Somerset Levels' and the 'moors' were the same thing?'

'Strictly speaking they're not, no.'

323

'But today's rivers aren't cut off from the sea?'

'No, they've eroded their way through. But they're sluggish, because they have very small gradients. In fact, over some stretches the bed of the river Shrew is actually level, so there's not much natural drainage by gravitation.'

'So, you mean the floods tend to hang about?'

'Exactly, which is why pumped drainage is essential,' he agreed.

'And that only happens at low tide?'

'Well that's true for the Shrew, but the Kingspill is mostly big enough to hold all the accumulated water that's pumped into it during high tide, so tide-lock isn't usually a problem there.'

'I've lived in this area for ten years,' Vinny said. 'And I had no idea about any of this.' She was beginning to comprehend that what motivated Jonathan was his need to understand the workings of the physical world about him. In these days of climate change it might soon be something you couldn't take for granted, and then people like him would come into their own. Vinny felt a new respect for him; a kind of pride.

They were approaching the slope up to Hembrow. It was streaming with water and the grass was showing green again in the snowy fields on either side. The Mini heater had been on full blast, but it was a feeble effort and she was still chilled to the bone by the time they arrived. Vinny was upset to see that a large bough had been torn off Pamela's chestnut tree and was now lying jaggedly over her herbaceous border.

There was no sign of Gordon's BMW. He must have gone home. Vinny was grateful for that, but getting more apprehensive by the moment. She opened the front door and led the way into the kitchen, where she leant against the rail of the Aga and held her hands above its wonderful, reliable, *solid* heat.

'Oh, so you're here at last, and Jonathan too?' Pamela said, coming in from the sitting room with the baby in her arms. 'And about time! To what do we owe the honour of your return?'

'I came back as quickly as I could,' Vinny said defensively, turning towards her and rubbing her hands. 'I did phone you last night to explain. It's been totally impossible out there, in case you hadn't noticed. We nearly froze to death at The Prospect!'

'Oh I *see*.' Pamela turned to the baby. 'We quite understand, don't we, Chloë? It's just cupboard love.'

14

In response to the thaw and the rising water, George began the complicated process of starting up two of his great diesel engines. He lifted the big green covers and opened the red cages, oiling repeatedly, operating a vertical wheel to move the pistons to the firing position, replacing the covers, turning on the cooling water, sucking the airlocks out of the pumps, watching the gauges, and finally running to the far end to open each pump's internal door just as the engine started up, to ensure that the pumped water flowed in the right direction. Then both engines in turn gave a whirr and a thump before settling down into a steady rhythm: *Whoof putt! Whoof putt! WHOOF PUTT!*

Each was pumping seventy one thousand gallons of water a minute; powerful enough to tame any flood, given time. George worked steadily, alert to the heartbeat of his engines, making rounds with his oil can, changing the cooling water filters every fifteen minutes as they clogged up with duckweed and peat, and using a mop to wipe up the resulting water that poured out.

In spite of the cold, he had opened all the windows and the tall doors at the end of the building, but oily fumes still rose into the air all around him. More men would be sent to take over his other duties whilst the twenty-four-hour pumping was on. It was just him, his mate and his engines against the powerful forces of nature. The fate of thousands of acres of farmland was in his hands. He was a happy man.

Soon after eight pm at the end of his twelve-and-a-quarter hour shift when he was due to hand over to his relief, Jim Tucker, the water from the hills was reaching the moors and coming up fast behind the pumping station. But the tide was low, the clyse was open and the Kingspill was discharging its burden powerfully towards the safety of the sea. All was as it should be. Even the rain had stopped. George emerged from the building, took in a lungful of good fresh air and prepared for a well-earned night's rest.

* * *

At Hembrow they were listening to the news. Pamela had found her old transistor and some batteries, so they were able to get both the local and national radio stations, and catch up with the stories of the past two days. Vinny was feeling very fortunate not to have been caught up in the sea flood, and to have made it back to safety before any possible meltwater flood could cause problems. She and Pamela and Jonathan sat in the warm kitchen by candlelight, with Chloë snugly in bed upstairs, and listened.

They heard that people had been trapped in their cars for over twelve hours, rescued by the Fire Brigade and taken to hospital with hypothermia. A man Pamela knew had appeared from a drift like a living snowman.

'A little cooling-down will do him no harm, if you can believe his wife,' she said.

The coastal flood had despoiled the ground floors of over a hundred homes, but by great good fortune no one had been drowned. Elderly people and young children were rescued in rubber boats pulled by men in waders. Vinny was frustrated by the lack of television, but the pictures inside her head were vivid enough. By evening the reports were even more optimistic. The breaches in the sea defences had been adequately repaired and would hold back the next tide. The extent of the flooding had not been nearly as bad as that of the last disaster in nineteen eighty-one, and was now contained. The authorities were to be congratulated on coping quickly and efficiently with this latest Act of God.

'In 1607 and 1811 floods reached all the way to Glastonbury and most of Sedgemoor was under water,' the newsreader was saying cheerfully. 'And in the great flood of 1872, almost seventy thousand acres were affected.'

'I'm sure that's very comforting for the poor people who, at this very moment, are wringing out their carpets and sweeping the mud back over their thresholds,' Vinny said.

Pamela blew out a spent candle, licking forefinger and thumb and nipping the hot wick to prevent it from smoking. 'Well thank goodness The Prospect is safe,' she said, and stuck a new candle into the liquid wax.

'It's bound to be,' Jonathan said. 'The pumping station area doesn't flood. It's the moors that regularly flood every winter, which are likely to be particularly affected by the thaw. The ones below here, for example.'

'So, when are you going back?' Pamela asked him, rather rudely it seemed to Vinny.

'As soon as the electricity is restored.'

'Well I hope they look sharp about it,' Pamela said. 'Do you realise, in four days it will be Christmas!'

★   ★   ★

Overnight the freshwater from the thaw accumulated throughout the whole area. All the pumping stations were at full stretch, doing their best to expel it. At the next high tide the repaired sea walls held good, but the Kingspill was dangerously full. In Otterbridge the Environment Agency's Duty Engineer issued Flood Watch warnings and kept an eye on incoming reports as the night progressed.

As the Amber Junction pumps pushed more and more water up into the tide-locked Kingspill, it began to over-top at its far end, flooding West Zoyle all over again. The authorities were swamped with urgent calls from the village demanding that the pumps be turned off, until the clyse could open again and let it all out.

It was a difficult decision. Normal policy did not allow floods to be exported from one inland area to another, but if the pumping were to cease there was now a very real risk that Amber

Junction itself would be inundated from behind. The Duty Engineer ordered it to continue. By first light when the second relief operator, Steve Sweetman, took over from Jim Tucker, it was raining again but it was also low tide. Another crisis had passed.

Steve was a young, less experienced man, especially with regard to the big diesels, but he had the confidence of an old hand. Despite this he was obliged to put up with George — who wasn't due back on shift until later that day — popping in from time to time like an over-anxious mother, to check up on the welfare of his darlings.

★   ★   ★

At seven thirty am, before it got light, power was restored to Hembrow, and Jonathan began campaigning to return to The Prospect. Every time the baby cried, he put his fingers in his ears and looked pained. Pamela got so fed up with him that she finally accepted that he must return at once, and that Bertie was the obvious vehicle in which to take him.

'You'll have to mind Chloë,' she told Vinny. 'I'll be as quick as poss.'

'No, I'll take him on my way to work,' Vinny said.

'You can't go to work! Haven't you heard? They're saying the roads are likely to be flooded at any moment, especially now it's raining again. You could be swept away in the mini. No, it's still very dodgy down there.'

'But — ' Vinny looked to Jonathan for moral support.

'A car will float in eighteen inches of running water,' he said.

'Right, that's it then,' Pamela said. 'You've watched me often enough with Chloë. It'll be good practice for you. Come on, Jonathan.'

Pamela and Jonathan set off in the 4 by 4. From the top of the hill and through the rain, they could see the normal winter floods spread out below them. As they got down to the moor they found the ditches and rhynes full to the top, and water flowing briskly over parts of the road, but nothing that couldn't easily be forded by Bertie.

'Piece of cake!' Pamela said to Jonathan in triumph.

'No thanks,' he said. 'I've just had breakfast.'

'*What?* Oh, never mind.' She raised her eyes to heaven.

When they arrived at The Prospect, all looked reassuringly normal to Pamela. The Kingspill Drain wasn't even full to the top, although it had been, judging from the tidelines on its banks. Nothing looked remotely dangerous. Even the postman had managed to get through, judging by the thick brown envelope on the mat inside the front door. She tried the switch in the hall. There was still no light.

Damn! She thought. I've driven all this way down here to get rid of Jonathan, and now I'll have to take him all the way back again! But now I'm here . . . Pamela decided to move some of the furniture upstairs, just in case. After all, you never knew . . .

'Will you give me a hand?' she called to him from the sitting room. 'Jonathan?' There was no reply. She found him still standing in the hall. He was looking upset. In one hand was a letter, in the other, the envelope.

'Is there a problem?' she asked him.

'They don't want my book,' he said. 'They say it isn't suitable for their list.'

'Oh,' Pamela said, going over and taking it from him. 'So this is a rejection slip. I've always wondered what they look like.' Then she saw his expression and felt a little sorry for him. 'Bad luck,' she said, 'but don't worry. All the best writers get some of these before their books are accepted. You just have to be persistent. Now, will you give me a hand upstairs with this armchair?'

'What d'you mean?'

'Will you help me carry it?' It was like speaking to a half-wit!

'What for?'

'In case the house gets flooded, of course!'

'It won't. The bank it's built on is high enough . . . '

'Just humour me anyway, will you?' Pamela snapped crossly. 'I don't want to take any chances.'

Jonathan shrugged. Between them they man-oeuvred it up the stairs and put it in the spare room where Vinny had been sleeping.

'What's all this on the floor?' Pamela asked. 'Looks like dried mud.'

'Probably fell off my boots.'

'But you don't sleep in here now, do you?'

'Not usually, no. But I do sometimes. On my own, of course.'

Pamela gave him a sharp look. She was about to question him further, but he was now standing by the window and staring down at the Kingspill. He looked utterly dejected.

'Why don't you put on waterproofs and cycle over to see George for half an hour or so, while I sort things out here?' she suggested. 'The pumps must be banging away full pelt down there. They'd be a distraction; stop you brooding about bloody publishers.'

'Can't,' Jonathan said miserably.

'Why not?'

'Because he's not my friend.'

'Oh.' Pamela registered this information. 'Yes, well I did warn you. A man like that wouldn't understand.' He went on staring at the water. 'Right then,' she said, trying to encourage him. 'Let's go down and get the rug next, shall we?'

⋆ ⋆ ⋆

At Amber Junction, Steve Sweetman was rushed off his feet and getting more and more irritated with George's supervision or, as he saw it, nannying. He knew fine what he was doing, and he didn't need to be kept tabs on every five minutes, thank you very much!

He couldn't understand what George saw in the old diesels anyway. To Steve they were just dinosaurs and long overdue for extinction. The noise they made was enough to deafen you,

333

never mind the fumes when they were started up. Unlike George he wasn't interested in hearing the engines talking to him, so he was happy to wear the regulation ear-defenders. But Christ only knew what the polluted air was doing to his lungs.

This, however, was not his main concern. It was the basic design of the place that worried him. Beneath the gangway under heavy steel chequer plates, which vibrated with the beat of the engines, a duct ran the entire length of the building with offsets to each engine. In this channel — which was also a sump — were housed in close proximity the fuel and water pipes, the electric cables, and the engines' exhaust pipes. All were coated with an accumulated oily scum, but protected from any fire hazard by two big white extinguishers, one at each end, designed to pump foam along the ducts and meet in the middle if necessary. They were said to be full of pigs' blood. *Pigs' blood?* Steve shook his head in disbelief.

He reckoned that what the station really needed was an up to the minute in-depth going over by Health and Safety. So far, all they'd come up with were pretty red cages! It was nowhere near enough. The sooner the whole place was upgraded and less knackering to operate, the better.

George came in again, fussing like an old woman about the filters.

'I'm getting there, awright?' Steve said. 'Keep yer hair on — what there is of it!'

'*You*,' George began furiously, 'are a lazy

334

good-for-nothing waste of *space!* It's time you got off your fat backside and pulled your weight around these parts. You got no feel for the job, and that's a fact.'

Steve smarted from the unfairness of this; coming down on him like a ton of bricks for no fucking reason! He waited until George had buggered off again, before smoking an illicit cigarette just to spite him. Then he changed another filter and went to get himself a cup of coffee from the vending machine in the office. He stood at the open side door briefly, drinking it, breathing in some proper air and watching the rain. If this flood continued into next week, he'd be on night shift, and that'd be even worse. Not even double-time either — mean bastards! Maybe he should tell them where they could stick their job.

He was only away a couple of minutes but when he came back he stopped in his tracks, his mouth hanging open in shock. In the middle of the gangway a mass of thick black smoke was rising from the floor to the ceiling! Steve gulped in some good air, held it, and sprinted over to operate the nearest extinguisher. Nothing. *It wasn't working!* The smoke got worse, spreading downwards from above, filling the entire building, blotting out everything. He desperately needed to breathe. He put his head down and charged through the murk, and out through the big doors, escaping with bursting lungs and streaming eyes into the kind wet air outside.

Steve shouted hoarsely to his mate, Tom, who was out at the back on weed-pulling duties. And he ran round and along the platform at the rear of the pumping station below windows disgorging more acrid smoke. The extinguishers could be operated from outside the building as well, but would the foam from the one at the other end actually reach far enough to attack the fire? Would the bloody thing even work? In a sweat of panic Steve broke the glass and pulled on the lever. No obvious change resulted. Poisonous smoke was billowing out of the back door too.

He dared not go in, for fear of being overcome by it. *What the fuck more could he do?*

Under the chequer plates the fire spread unextinguished along the length of the duct, feeding upon the oily gunge in the sump, heating up the copper fuel pipes, melting the solder in their joints and liberating quantities of hot diesel. Then there was a sound as of a giant exhalation of breath, as the oil from the two indoor day-tanks finally ignited in the heat, and the fire, fanned by the breeze from the open windows and doors, began in earnest.

★   ★   ★

George had been fed up with Steve Sweetman for some time; he was cocky and over-confident like most young men. But at that moment George had more important things to worry about. He had an uncomfortable feeling that all was not well — a vague premonition of disaster.

Although he was not on duty, he'd put on his working clothes early and was following the news as it occurred. It was clear to him that there was a lot more water in the system than usual, and now it was being added to by even more rain. The EA had issued a public Flood Warning. Then, in the southern part of Sedgemoor, the other side of a small ridge of hills, two containment walls suddenly failed.

They were the ones that had been built in the thirteenth century by the monks of Glastonbury Abbey to channel rivers away from human settlements and to impound water safely in times of flood. But now one had over-topped and the other had collapsed completely, flooding a wide area adjacent to the River Pawlett. In itself this was of no consequence to Amber Junction, but if a similar thing were to happen on his side of the watershed, in the Shrew catchment area . . .

'Best if we move a few things up to Mandy's room,' he said to Gwen over a cup of tea. 'Can't be too careful. Come on Mand. You can help an' all.'

'Oh *Dad!* I don't want my room all messed up. It's nearly Christmas.'

'You'll do as you'm told,' George said. It wasn't like him to be so short with her, but he was worried. He sat there, finishing his tea, thinking.

'Here, take these up with you,' Gwen said to Mandy, reaching out and picking up the two nearest things to her; her sewing bag and the tin of buns. Mandy took them from her and ambled sulkily towards the ladder that led into the converted roof-space, her own special den.

'Do 'ee really suppose the water'll come in?' Gwen asked George.

'No,' he said, 'but if we don't do nothin' it will, just to spite us.'

'And if us do, it won't?' They laughed together.

'*Dad?*' Mandy's voice from upstairs was shrill with alarm. 'Dad, I can see *smoke!*'

'What? *Where?*'

'The station. It's — '

George leapt to his feet and threw himself out of his front door, running flat out towards his pumps.

* * *

'Good Lord!' Pamela exclaimed, as she put down a small table in Jonathan's study, stretched her back and looked out towards Amber Junction. 'It's on fire — look!'

Jonathan joined her at the window. They both stared in astonishment. A heavy pall of black smoke hung over the pumping station, rising in spite of the rain and then flattening out as the wind took it.

Pamela scrabbled in her handbag and got out her mobile with shaking hands, pressing 999. 'There's a fire!' she said. 'It's at Amber Junction pump . . . ' But it seemed that it had already been reported. She switched her phone off. 'Let's go!' she ordered. 'They might need help.' Jonathan didn't move. 'Come *on*! What's the matter with you?' He was still staring out.

Pamela threw him a look of withering scorn, ran down the stairs and out of the house. She drove towards Amber Junction at high speed but, soon after she crossed the bridge by the big sluice, she saw George and two other men running through the wet towards her. She lowered her window.

'Get back!' George shouted. 'Tank's going to go!' There was nowhere to turn. Pamela engaged reverse gear and backed up to what she hoped was a safe distance. She stared at the burning building. She could hear the fire as a dull roar, but the usual rhythmic noise was absent. All the pumps must have stopped. Was the whole place going to blow up, like a bomb? Images of disaster flashed through her mind. She thought of Chloë.

Then, just as the three men reached her and stopped breathlessly to look back, there was a great *WHOOOSH!* The main fuel pipe to the 50,000 litre outside tank had ruptured, sending vast quantities of oil pouring down into the station and spreading out all over the floor, to burn ever more fiercely.

George leant against the front of the SUV and bowed his head for a brief moment. And when he raised it again, Pamela was unsure as to whether his cheeks were wet with rain, or with tears.

★   ★   ★

Jonathan observed the fire with fascination from the safety of his upstairs room, opening a window so that the rain-streaked panes would not obscure his view. It was as though he'd always known that this would occur. He

339

remembered watching the lightning last summer and speculating about what might happen. And now it seemed he was about to find out.

If the pumps are starved of fuel, he thought, they'll stop, maybe even go backwards. And if the electrical systems are down, they won't be able to shut the internal doors. And since the Kingspill Drain is approximately three metres above the river at the back of the station, then its entire contents will siphon back through the pumps, the wrong way.

He estimated that it should flow at about six cubic metres a second to begin with, slower than it did when it was being pumped. But then once the height difference had lessened, it would slow down . . . He reckoned it could take a week for the whole of the Kingspill to empty itself (but that was without any remedial measures being taken, of course). Then that water would meet the rainwater coming down from the hills, and there would be nowhere for it to go but sideways, over the farmland. It could be a massive flood, and he was in a perfect viewing position!

Jonathan wondered if the water would get as high as the Bristol Channel level marked on the wall plaque. He doubted it. That would only happen if the clyse became somehow jammed open, and the sea was allowed to pour in unrestricted. But with Amber Junction out of commission, the water on this catchment could hang around for a long time. He looked down at the full drain below him. He could see the direction of flow by the progress of a floating crisp packet. It was definitely going backwards!

Jonathan was so entranced by the drama outside, that it was some time before he even considered his own safety. When he did, he reckoned he'd be all right. Even if the fields and roads all around him were to go under, The Prospect was high enough on the bank to be out of harm's way. And anyway, all his important computer stuff was upstairs in this room. He couldn't abandon that. He decided to go down to the kitchen to collect some food and something to drink. He made himself a cheese sandwich, and ate it down there.

By the time he got back up the stairs again, he could see the water beginning to spread over the fields. George's house was hidden from his view by a grove of trees, but it was not much higher than Amber Junction, so it must be surrounded by now. The water was already rising over the road. He heard a distant siren, which he took to be a fire engine but then instead of coming closer, it stopped altogether. Jonathan wasn't surprised. They were too late. The rising flood would put the fire out anyway. There was no point risking the crew or the vehicle. They'd probably been recalled.

He went into his spare room and dragged the big armchair from it into his study, close up to the window. He was glad now that Pamela had insisted on bringing it upstairs. He arranged it with a packet of chocolate biscuits and a can of beer to hand. Then he sat down as though he was in a cinema, with fizzy drink and popcorn, waiting for the main feature.

Sometime later on, when the water had crept

up over almost all the land, and only trees, hedges and the two parallel banks of the drain showed above it, two worrying facts occurred to Jonathan. One: The banks of the Kingspill had been left steepsided when the artificial drain was originally dug out. Two: They regularly slumped, due to wave erosion. But here was an unprecedented situation. The water would soon be mostly *outside* the saturated banks as the drain was emptying. It didn't take an engineering degree to appreciate that this was not at all an ideal situation as far as the foundations of The Prospect were concerned.

Could he make a dash for safety on his bike? No. He might fall into a hidden rhyne by mistake or simply be overwhelmed by the rising water. If he got wet as well as cold, he could die from hypothermia. Best to stay put and wait to be rescued. He would simply sit and watch the water. That was no great hardship after all!

He went for a pee, but when he came back into his study, he found the door was difficult to shut. Its bottom edge was grinding against the floorboards. The frame must no longer be rectangular. Jonathan fancied he could hear creaking noises. Surely the house wasn't already on the move; leaning over and cracking? If the window frames become deformed as well, he thought, then the glass will shatter dangerously under the pressure.

He quickly pulled his chair away from them and into the centre of the room. He sat down on it. He looked at his hands. They were trembling. If there's a major slump, he thought, then the entire house could break up and fall into the drain! I shall either be cut to pieces by the glass, or crushed by the roof timbers . . . and then drowned.

What was that noise? Was it his imagination or was the floor no longer horizontal? In terror Jonathan drew both his feet up into the chair and wrapped his arms around his knees, crouching there with his head down and his eyes shut — deprived in an instant of all scientific curiosity — waiting for the inevitable.

★ ★ ★

After Pamela had driven off with Jonathan, Vinny was left in charge of a little pot of apricot purée, an uncooperative baby and a resentful mood. Not for much longer, she consoled herself.

'Come on Chloë, open wide. You know you love apricot!' She managed to pop a spoonful in and redirect the gobbets that squeezed out again.

When I go, she thought, it will have to be a long way away, so that I can't weaken and change my mind. I know what I'm like when Pamela wants her own way. I just get swept along in the avalanche. So, I'd better go abroad. Librarians can work anywhere. I can speak Italian and French and a little German. I'm bound to come across something suitable. As soon as Christmas and New Year are over, I'll get down to looking for a job in earnest.

But can I really abandon Pamela to cope with Chloë all on her own? And what of Jonathan? Is there any hope at all for us? Shall we ever be together? I love him, she thought, but I don't know if I could cope . . .

'Another spoonful?' she suggested to the baby, zooming it towards her through the air. 'It's coming . . . look!' But Chloë got hold of the spoon at the last moment and pushed it aside, splattering apricot mush over Vinny's face like a well-aimed custard-pie. Vinny got up abruptly and wiped it off with the dishcloth.

Radio 4 was on, and the news was almost over when Vinny was alerted by the word 'Somerset'. She went nearer to listen.

' . . . And we're just getting a report from the Somerset Levels of a serious fire in a pumping station. There is no news yet of any casualties, but the Environment Agency has issued a Severe Flood Warning. And now for the stock market . . . ' Vinny switched rapidly to local radio, and learned that Amber Junction was 'an inferno' and that the River Shrew catchment area was now liable to flood uncontrollably with disastrous effects on property and livestock.

Oh God! Vinny thought, Jonathan's down there! What if something's happened to him? I couldn't *bear* that! She put both hands over her mouth and stood there without breathing. And then there's George and his beloved pumps. She let out her breath all at once. Poor George! I do hope he and his family are all right. Finally she thought, Pamela is down there too in Bertie, and she's such a bloody awful driver . . .

She kept her eye on the baby as she went over and got out her mobile. But Pamela's phone was switched off.

'It's Vinny,' she said, leaving a message. 'Ring me!'

And now what should she do? She could phone the police or the EA but they'd be far too busy coping with the flood. They'd probably issue an emergency number later on, if she kept listening. Vinny felt desperately helpless. She was stuck here with Chloë and there was nothing whatever she could do, but wait.

'Jonathan's safe,' she said aloud. 'He is. *He is.*'

★ ★ ★

Down at the Overys' bungalow, they were waiting too. George had been through all the correct procedures at the outset; summoning the Fire Brigade, and keeping the Duty Engineer at the EA fully informed.

So now here they all were, in this chilly attic room, surrounded by Mandy's posters and teddy bears, watching through the dormer windows as the water rose outside and sneaked up the ladder below them, and the smoke continued to pile out of the stricken pumping station.

Pamela had discovered that the two young men were called Steve and Tom. They both looked exhausted as they sprawled on the pink carpet with their backs to the wall. Steve in particular was blackened and dishevelled. Then there was herself, Gwen and Mandy sitting on the bed, and George. Pamela felt so sorry for George. He was clearly bewildered. He kept alternately pacing up and down, or simply staring out.

He said, over and over again. 'Can't understand it. How'd diesel oil get started to burn like that? 'Tisn't that inflammable! I just don't get it . . . '

'Well it did,' Steve eventually pointed out. 'So that's that, innit?'

George rounded on him. 'You bin smoking again?'

'' 'Course not,' Steve lied. 'An' that wouldn't do it anyhow.'

'It might've if some fool'd spilt something down the sump,' George said. Mandy gave a little cry and buried her face in her mother's shoulder. The men ignored her.

'Well, I didn't,' Steve said, 'and nor did Tom, did 'ee?'

'No way!' Tom said.

George pursed his mouth, and began pacing again. Pamela shivered.

'Here,' Gwen offered. 'Us'll put this duvet round, shall us?' The three of them stood up to let her lift it off and arrange it round their shoulders. 'George? Boys?' They shook their heads.

'How high do you expect the water to get, George?' Pamela asked.

'God knows!' His shoulders sagged eloquently.

Pamela was worried about Bertie. She also hoped to goodness that Jonathan was right about The Prospect. She couldn't see from here, so she had no way of knowing. It infuriated her to be so powerless. She shifted about on the bed, restlessly, glancing at her fellow refugees.

Mandy was subdued. Gwen on the other hand

appeared to have brought along some occupational therapy. She had taken a tapestry frame out of a bag, and was sitting there sewing it, for heaven's sake! Pamela couldn't admire its design — kittens and roses — but she did approve of the determination with which Gwen was attacking it. Pamela wondered whether she and George owned this bungalow, or whether it belonged to the Environment Agency. She hoped for their sake that they didn't. Once the water had been got out, it might be all of six months before it could be habitable again. It was probably their own furniture, though, which was floating about below.

'I trust you're insured?' she said to Gwen.

'Oh yes,' she frowned. 'But that's hardly it, is it?' She lowered her voice so that George couldn't overhear, and murmured in Pamela's ear, 'He loves them engines more'n what he does me. *That's* the point.'

'If Amber Junction's a total loss,' Tom was saying to Steve. 'What'd it cost to rebuild? Couple of million?'

'More like four, if they has to demolish the whole thing,' Steve said. 'Shouldn't be surprised if they didn't put in six new electric pumps, smaller ones, and a big diesel generator. Could be all for the best; make life a lot easier, eh George?' George said nothing. 'Well I reckon 'tis good riddance,' Steve said. 'I'm fed up working in a fucking museum.'

'You'd be fed up working anywhere!' George shouted suddenly. 'You'm of no more value than a pig in a post-box. *Useless!*'

'Hey, come on. Wasn't my fault!' Steve protested

'Well put it this way,' George said with emphasis, 'Us wouldn't be stuck up here and Amber Junction wouldn't be a bloody bonfire if it'd been *my* shift!' He turned back to the window and stared out again.

'No, that idd'n fair,' Tom complained. ''Was the duff extinguisher what done it. If that'd worked . . . '

'Well there's no point trying to apportion blame, is there?' Pamela pointed out. 'It's happened, and that's that.'

'Dad?' Mandy said. 'They will come and get us, won't they?'

'Course they will,' he said without turning round.

'Like when?' Steve asked sarcastically.

'When they've rescued all the people first what's really in danger,' Gwen said indignantly. She snipped off a length of yellow wool. 'You consider yourself lucky. We'm all right here. Idd'n going to get this deep, stands to reason. Best thing is to be patient. Have a currant bun?' She reached for the tin behind her and offered it first to Pamela. They all took one except George.

'Oh well,' Steve said with his mouth full. 'Lucky we'm not sheep.'

'Oh no!' Mandy cried. 'What about the poor sheep? They can't swim. They'll all be drowned!' She burst into tears and hid her face in the duvet.

'If I were you,' Pamela said to Steve, 'I'd *shut up!*'

He ignored her, feeling about in his pocket and producing a packet of cigarettes and a lighter.

'An' you can put those away again,' Gwen said with surprising authority. 'You've started enough fires for one day!' She confronted him, glaring steadfastly over Mandy's bowed head.

'Oh, come on Mrs Overy. I just — '

'This is my house,' she said, 'And what I say, goes.'

Steve sulkily put his fags away again. He sat there, drumming his fingers on the carpet. Tom closed his eyes and got himself comfortable against the wall. Mandy finally stopped crying. George stood there with his back to them, taut as a fiddle string.

Pamela shifted her position on the bed once again and wondered how long she could hold out before she had to go to the loo. What loo? She supposed if the worst came to the worst, she could go as far down the ladder as possible, and then holding onto the handrail with one hand and her clothes with the other, simply pee into the flood.

George's mobile rang, making them all jump. He fished it out of the top pocket of his overalls. 'Amber Junction,' he said. 'Right. OK.' He pressed the red button and tucked it away again. 'They're sending a boat for us now.'

* * *

It was raining when Peter Wood got off the train at Bristol Temple Meads and began making enquiries about a bus to Hembrow. Poxy British weather! He thought, as he took a taxi to the bus station. He shook his head, thinking about the total cock-up everything had been lately. He should have got here a damn sight earlier, and he would have done, if the authorities had got their fingers out and tracked him down sooner. But one thing was certain. He wouldn't hang around here for long.

He was obliged to wait an hour before the right bus would leave, and then it only went as near as Cheddar. He'd have to get another taxi the rest of the way. He sat in the draughty bus station thinking about his daughter and wondering how much Chloë would have changed in the three months since he'd last seen her. A whole quarter of a year since that stupid cow, Kelly, had done a runner; chasing after yet another Englishman in her increasingly desperate pursuit of a British passport.

Peter snorted at the irony of this. He'd never forget the day when he discovered that Kelly — quite unaware of *his* agenda — had been trying the same trick on with him. By itself the situation would probably have been negotiable, but on a traumatic afternoon soon afterwards, the bloody woman suddenly accused him of infecting her with herpes, and refused point-blank to marry him. It had been the one flaw in his carefully planned strategy that he'd hoped, above all else, to keep from her. It meant there was no way, now, that he could get permanent Australian residency. The bitch!

Peter sighed. He wondered how his mother

would receive him today. He reckoned he could put up with Pamela's special brand of maternal concern for a couple of weeks — a month at tops. And by that time he'd have re-established his bond with Chloë, and they would leave together. Maybe he'd be able to get a temporary work permit for the States? He had American friends who could put them up and look after the baby while he found a job and got things sorted.

But in the meantime he would be with his mother for Christmas. It was a novel idea. It was a long time since he'd done the full festive Yuletide thing; the decorated tree, the piles of presents, mince pies . . . God, he thought, I must be going soft! Is this middle age already?

The bus journey was interminable. Peter wiped the condensation off the dirty window with his hand, peering out at nothing but a soggy December landscape punctuated by endless stops and starts at prosperous but undistinguished villages along the way. When I'm in the US, he thought, I'll get myself a motorbike again. No . . . maybe that's not such a great idea . . . I'll need a car with a baby seat. The looming spectre of parental responsibility hung over him menacingly for a moment, until he brushed it away impatiently. I can handle it, he told himself. It's well time.

When he found a taxi, the driver was chatty. 'Been away long?'

'Years, yes.'

'You won't have heard about the floods, then?'

'No.'

'Wouldn't fancy being one of them blooming officials. Can't never do nothing right, can 'em? Farmers want the land dry for their cows. They nature conversationists want it wet for the birds an' that. Government's always piggy-in-the-middle, in't it? And now they'm buggered!'

Peter smiled. 'Why's that, then?' He hadn't realised how much he missed this way of speaking; these rounded west-country vowels of his youth. He would have to be on his guard that the soft seduction of nostalgia didn't get to him, and detain him here in this comfortable backwater.

' . . . So 'em can't get the floods off now, see?' The cabby finished the story of the Amber Junction fire with enthusiasm. 'Is a good thing you'm only going as far as Hembrow. Couldn't take you on to Glastonbury today, not with the water right up over the roads down there. They'm in a right pickle, I'm telling you!' He drove his taxi up the gentle slope of the north side of Hembrow Island and then along the winding road towards the village at its heart.

'It's out on the other side, about a mile,' Peter directed him.

'Oh well, that'll be a regular ringside seat from there. Be able to give your house a new name — Water View. No, it's a nice area, that is.'

I suppose that means he'll be expecting a bigger tip, Peter thought. He hoped he had enough change. He was determined not to ask his mother for money on the first day.

He was disconcerted to find that his heart was beginning to beat faster, the nearer they got to Pamela's house, as the familiarity of his surroundings triggered off dormant memories. He began to remember, with the same feelings of claustrophobia and frustration, all the reasons why he'd had to get away in the first place. I'm not going to enjoy this, he thought. If it wasn't for Chloë, I'd never have come back.

Time seemed to have speeded up too, the way it did in dreams. Here they were, turning in at the drive. It was all so familiar and yet so small ... There was a branch down from the old chestnut tree. The front door had been painted a different colour. It was opening. *What the hell was he going to say?* But it was not his mother after all.

'Oh,' he said, trying to keep the relief out of his voice. 'Hi Vinny! It's been a long time.'

★　★　★

Down on the Levels below, the little group of refugees sat around the rubber walls of the inflatable Zodiac patrol boat, which had been sent by the Agency's Fisheries department to rescue them. Pamela gripped the rope handles firmly as the outboard motor bounced them over the floods, and up the Kingspill Drain towards The Prospect. Her eyes watered in the keen wind, and rain seeped in round her collar sending damp fingers of cold creeping down her back. But her house was still there, above the water! It would be safe, dry and unspoilt. Pamela gave a great crow of delight. 'It's OK!' she cried above the noise of the engine to

Gwen, who was sitting next to her.

'That's nice,' Gwen said. She even managed a smile.

Oh dear, Pamela thought. Maybe that wasn't very tactful . . . But her attention was distracted as they got closer. A lot of the bank between The Prospect and the drain seemed to have disappeared. Pamela was sure it used not to be as close to the edge as that.

'Just one man inside, you said?' The boatman shouted at her over the heads of the Overys.

'Yes, one.' As they approached even nearer, Pamela could see that a large chunk of bank had indeed slumped into the river. It could be dodgy for Jonathan to scramble into the boat from it, if it was that unstable. Then she noticed a crack in the brickwork, which had opened up from under the eaves on the east wall and ran down diagonally in a series of steps to the corner of the window on the ground floor. Oh no! She thought. What if the whole house collapses on top of us, just as we get there?

The boatman was clearly of the same mind. 'Better make it quick!' he shouted, cutting the engine to idle. Steve, holding the mooring rope, managed to jump from the front of the boat and up the bank without causing a further slump. He pulled on the rope, holding the boat in place as they all yelled for Jonathan to come out. They expected him to run round straight away from the front door, and climb aboard. But there was no sign of him.

'Jonathan!' Pamela shouted. 'Where the hell are you? *Come out!*'

Jonathan was still in his perch in the illusory safety of the armchair. He was thinking, Maybe this is how I shall die? But perhaps there would be time to do a few experiments before expiring. This was one aspect of water he hadn't investigated to date, and which hadn't occurred to him before. He had always looked *at* water, never been *in* it, apart from baths. It was a gap in his knowledge. It meant his book was incomplete. It was now essential that he survive, so that he could rectify this oversight. Astronomy would have to be postponed.

He suddenly became aware of the sound of an outboard motor and then shouts from outside. He heard Pamela's voice raised in anger. He got up, stiffly, and walked cautiously over to the window where he could look down on the Kingspill. The floor creaked at every step, making him nervous. He had just time to open the window and see that there was a boat full of people below him, before two things happened in quick succession.

Firstly there was a loud bang from the ceiling as though something structural had snapped. And then Pamela shouted again, *'Jonathan! Come down! For heaven's sake, jump to it!'*

Panic-stricken, he reacted blindly to the authority of the command. He leaped at the window, flinging it wide and climbed, crouching onto the sill. Then he closed his eyes and launched himself outwards. He was vaguely conscious of a lot more shouting in the seconds before he hit the ground and fell into the water.

The cold struck him like a hammer-blow to the heart, and closed in around him. He couldn't tell which way was up. The water filled his nose, his ears, his open mouth . . . suffocating him.

His last coherent thought was, *But I can't swim!*

15

Pamela had stared at the prospect in frustration and disgust. What could Jonathan be doing? This was no time for vagueness or indecision. Then she'd caught sight of his face at the window. Why in God's name was he still upstairs?

There was a sudden alarming noise from the house — a bang followed by creaking, rending sounds. She yelled at him again. Then, unexpectedly the bedroom window was thrown wide open and Jonathan's body was hurtling down from it! There were shouts of alarm.

'Look out!'

'What the fuck?'

'Jesus!'

He's going to hit us and sink the boat! Pamela thought, before Jonathan landed, very awkwardly on the very edge of the bank. This caused more of it to collapse, toppling him headfirst into the Kingspill and under the surface with an almighty splash.

Steve leaped forward to try to grab him before he fell in, but only succeeded in dropping the rope, before nearly tumbling in as well. And now the waves from Jonathan's immersion were pushing the boat out towards the middle of the drain. It drifted, and as it did so the trailing rope fouled the propeller. The engine cut out. Tom and the boatman between them struggled to free it and recover steerage. And now Jonathan had reappeared above the surface, but face down in the thick brown water, just wallowing there and making no move to save himself.

Pamela had always assumed that she would be cool in a crisis, but there was no lifebelt to throw, no boathook to fish him out with. They were drifting further and further away from him. His lungs would be filling with water. He was drowning before their very eyes! And all the time some fool was shouting, 'Help! *Help! Hel* — ' Pamela realised it was her own voice.

There was another splash. Gwen shouted 'No!'

Someone — *Mandy?* — was swimming towards Jonathan. She was moving fast with short powerful strokes. As Pamela watched in relief, and shame, Mandy grabbed him by the head and turned him over, swimming on her back, kicking strongly with her legs and towing him towards the Zodiac. Hands reached out and hauled them up over the fat rubber sides. Jonathan was first, a dead weight and already blue with cold. Mandy was next, shivering, pouring with water, exhausted.

They'd got the engine going again and, as George straddled Jonathan on the floor of the boat, working through the stages of resuscitation, they collected Steve from the bank and set off at speed for the safety of dry land. The boatman steered with one hand and called with the other on his radio for an ambulance to stand by. Gwen took off her own coat and held it around Mandy, cradling her in her arms.

Everyone else was intent upon Jonathan. He gasped and began to cough, Water ran out of his mouth.

'He's breathing,' George reported, 'An' his heart's beating.' He turned him over into the recovery position and supported him there, trying to keep him warm.

'Aaah!' Pamela shouted, 'He's alive! Thank God for that.'

'No thanks to you!' Steve shouted back.

'What d'you mean? It was *you* that dropped the rope!'

Steve stuck to his point. 'Telling him to jump like that. Madness!'

'I most certainly did *not!*'

'Funny thing that, when *we all heard you!*'

'I didn't mean it *literally*,' Pamela defended herself vigorously.

'I was urging him to hurry up; get a bloody move on! Not my fault if he doesn't understand plain English. *It's a figure of speech.* Everybody knows that!'

Mandy, secure in her mother's embrace, turned her head so that she was facing Pamela. Her teeth chattered with cold.

'Everyone 'cept Jonathan,' she said.

★ ★ ★

Pamela alighted from the car and thanked the volunteer driver very much for bringing her home. It was pitch dark and nearly six o'clock. Vinny had put the porch light on to welcome her back. Pamela suddenly felt exhausted, too tired to find her keys. She rang the bell instead.

The front door flew open. 'Pamela!' Vinny cried, and burst into tears. 'I thought you were

359

the police with bad news.'

Pamela was gratified. 'No, no,' she murmured, stepping forward to wrap Vinny in a hug. 'I'm fine.' Something delicious was cooking. She could smell it.

'But,' Vinny said, 'Where's Jonathan?'

'In hospital.'

'What?' Vinny looked horrified. 'But, is he all right? What happened? Is he badly hurt?'

'He'll be fine. Don't panic. It's a long story and I'm starving. I'll tell you over supper.' She made as if to go in, but Vinny detained her.

'I've got something to tell you too,' she said. There was a movement in the hall behind her, and a man came forward carrying Chloë.

'Good God!' Pamela felt dizzy. 'Peter! Is that really you?' She rushed towards him and gave him an awkward hug, squashing the baby who complained loudly. It was almost as though he was carrying her like a shield! She took hold of his shoulders and gazed at him.

'You've had your hair cut,' she exclaimed. 'It looks so much better!'

'Hello Ma,' he said. 'How are you?'

'I'm fine,' she said, 'now, but you wouldn't believe what I've been through today!' She took in everything about her son as he stood there, holding his own child. He looked older, but less arrogant, as though he had lost more chances than he'd won. He's an adult, not a jack-the-lad any longer, she thought, and felt a rush of affection for him. Perhaps now they could be friends at last?

'It's wonderful to see you,' she said, squeezing

360

his arm. 'It's the best thing that could have happened. But why didn't you tell us you were coming? We haven't had time to make any preparations.'

'I did try,' he said. 'Your mobile was switched off.'

'Oh.' Pamela turned to Vinny, who was blotting her eyes with a tissue. 'So, what are we having to eat, Vin? Something special?'

Vinny glanced towards Peter. 'Fatted calf,' she said. 'What else?'

'Ah,' Peter said. 'Slight problem there.'

'What?' demanded Pamela.

'I'm a vegetarian.'

'Since when?'

'Since years.'

Pamela sighed theatrically. 'Typical!' she said.

★ ★ ★

Over supper Peter watched his mother with resigned amusement. She hadn't altered one bit. She never would. But now after such a long separation, he could view her dispassionately. He would never be able truly to relax in her company. He always had to be on his guard.

He ate with enthusiasm the excellent omelette Vinny had cooked for him, and complimented her on it. Now here's someone who really has changed, he thought, smiling at her across the table. She seems tougher and definitely more determined; a lot less like the sweet little poodle-of-all-work that I remember. He was glad for her. It was about time.

361

'So then the stupid boy let go of the rope!' Pamela exclaimed. She was in the middle of regaling them with the drama of the day. 'I knew as soon as I saw him that he was a troublemaker. I shouldn't be at all surprised to hear he'd started the fire on purpose! Anyway . . . where was I? Oh yes . . . so there was poor dear Jonathan like a sack of potatoes in the water, and we had no means to get to him, no power at all!'

Here we go, Peter thought. Here comes the *But with one bound I saved him single-handed*, bit. 'So, what did you do?' he supplied helpfully.

'What could any of us do?' Pamela threw her hands wide. 'We were helpless.' She sat forward and put her elbows on the table. 'D'you know, I've only just realised something.'

'What?' Vinny asked.

'Why it is that young soldiers are the most intrepid. It's because they have no concept of the danger they're putting themselves in. They think they're immortal.'

'What's that got to do with anything?'

'Well, I'm coming to that. Give me a chance. It was Mandy, you see,' Pamela paused for effect, 'who is all of *thirteen*, who dived in and got him.'

Oh dear, Peter thought. So someone else was the heroine of the hour? There had to be a very good explanation for that!

'And then we all pulled him into the boat, which was nearly impossible because he wasn't helping himself — or us — at all, and he was so heavy you wouldn't believe!'

'But he is all right?' Vinny asked anxiously:

'Oh yes. We got him breathing again. They're just warming him up overnight in hospital, making sure his lungs are OK. We'll probably be able to bring him back tomorrow.'

'Oh?' Peter said. 'Does he live here, then?'

'Oh God!' Pamela exclaimed. 'I haven't told you the worst bit, have I?' Vinny raised anxious eyes from her plate and stared at her with dread. 'It's The Prospect,' Pamela said. 'My lovely little house. The flood has undermined it. It's falling down! And after all the *money* I've spent on it!'

★ ★ ★

Vinny's one idea was to get to the hospital as early as she possibly could to make sure that Jonathan really was all right.

'But it's Thursday,' Pamela protested at breakfast, 'the twenty-third! I've simply got to do some Christmas shopping, especially now that Peter's here. And I've no vehicle to go in. I must have the mini, Vin, there's no two ways about it.'

'Sorry,' Vinny said. 'I have to go to work. Why don't you ring your garage and borrow your favourite car again?' Then she left, just like that. She caught sight of Pamela's astonished face through the kitchen window, as she went.

'Lavinia, One: Pamela, Nil!' she said to herself as she drove away. 'I expect poor Peter will get it in the neck all morning now.'

She drove to Otterbridge via the motorway and parked finally at the hospital, by dint of speeding to a newly vacated space, and beating a Volvo bullyboy by inches. Hey! She thought.

Assertiveness works!

On her way up to Jonathan's ward, however, her fears returned. What if he were to be much worse than Pamela had said? What if he'd developed pneumonia in the night? She walked along the anonymous corridors feeling increasingly anxious. But when she arrived at his ward, she found a media circus in full swing.

A crowd of people and a television crew surrounded Jonathan's bed. It was clearly a heroic rescue piece for the local news. Looking at him from a distance, he seemed to be all right apart from a nasty cough. He was sitting up in bed with Mandy and George on either side of him, each with an arm round his shoulders as they faced the camera. Vinny could tell from his body language that he was manfully putting up with this. Just. The Overys were coming to the end of their story.

'It was my dad who saved him,' Mandy was saying. ''Cos he knows first-aid, see?'

'And then?' the presenter encouraged her. 'I believe you had to be taken by tractor and trailer to a causeway, before you could get to the ambulance?'

'Yes.' Mandy's bottom lip wobbled. 'And there was heaps of animals there, all getting away from the water. Hares and mice and squirrels and a fox . . . And some were getting squashed by the cars that was rescuing the people . . . Just when they reckoned they was safe . . . ' A tear ran down her cheek.

'Mandy and George Overy, and Jonathan — uh — Crankshaw,' the presenter said, glancing

364

at his notes to prompt himself as he wrapped the piece up. 'Thank you very much.'

Vinny waited until they had all dispersed, acknowledging George and Mandy briefly as they left, before going over to see Jonathan. He was lying back on his pillows with his eyes shut. He looked pale but reassuringly normal.

'Hello?' Vinny sat down on the bed and took one of his hands in hers.

His eyes snapped open. 'Vinny!'

'Are you all right? I was so worried . . . '

'Will you take me home? I can't stand it here. It's so noisy.' His voice was husky.

'I'll see. I will if it's allowed. But first of all, tell me how you are. Are your lungs OK?'

'Sore throat,' he said, 'and a cough, but the doctors say that's to be expected.'

'Anything else?'

'I hurt my ankle when I jumped out of the window, but it's sprained, not broken. I've got a crutch.' He gestured towards it.

'So you can walk?'

'Oh yes. It's an odd thing, Vinny.'

'What is?'

'Drowning wasn't nearly as bad as I thought it would be.'

'Oh, Jonathan . . . ' She leaned forward and kissed his cheek. 'Thank God you didn't.'

'So, can we go?'

'I'll ask the Sister,' Vinny said. She had to wait at the desk for a good ten minutes before she was able to get an answer.

'Dr Jarvis says Jonathan really ought to stay in another twenty-four hours,' Sister said, 'but we are very busy and short of beds, so he says he can leave at four o'clock — but only if he really feels up to it.'

Vinny relayed this to Jonathan. 'I must go to work now,' she said, 'but I'll be back at four, OK?'

★   ★   ★

Vinny left work soon after lunch by arrangement with the other library staff. Since it was an emergency, they were more than usually co-operative. She went first to the big department store, where she bought a pair of brown combat trousers in Jonathan's size, some underpants, buff socks, two brownish shirts and a coffee-coloured sweater. The only things she couldn't manage were shoes. She didn't know his size. Vinny then went back to the hospital to get Jonathan.

'Now, you're sure you feel well enough to travel?'

'I do!' he said.

'And you do realise that it won't be all that quiet at Hembrow, don't you? Remember we've got the baby, and now Peter has turned up as well. And The Prospect won't be safe to go back to, so you won't be able to escape. It's up to you.'

'I'll stay in the top room,' he said, 'and after Christmas I'll go with you to the library every day.' He had it all worked out.

'All right then. I've got you some new clothes,' Vinny said. 'I hope they will be suitable.'

'Are they *brown?*'

'Yes, of course they are.'

Jonathan got awkwardly out of bed and began to pull the curtains around him, so that he could get dressed. Vinny waited outside.

'No shoes?' he called.

'No. You'll have to wear your own damp ones, I'm afraid. But I've brought you Peter's coat, just to go home in.'

Jonathan drew the curtains. He was fully dressed. 'Peter's . . . ?'

'Pamela's son. Chloë's father. I just told you.'

'Yes, I know.' He was thinking about it, standing on one foot and holding onto the curtains. Then he said, 'Is he going to take the baby away with him? That would be a lot better.'

In the car, on their way home, his words kept repeating themselves in Vinny's head: '*Is he going to take the baby away with him?*' She thought about them with a guilty delight. With Chloë safely out of the country with her father, she would be able to leave with a clear conscience.

'I'm so glad to be away from that horrible place,' Jonathan said.

Vinny glanced sideways at him. He was smiling. She smiled as well.

* ★ ★ ★

Christmas was like any other day for George Overy. He sat in a small caravan on site and waited for things to improve. At the height of the flood, seven feet of standing water had accumulated inside Amber Junction and put the fire well and truly out. Oil had mixed with the water and leaked into the rivers, causing widespread pollution. They had finally managed to close the inner doors of the pumps to prevent the Kingspill from siphoning back any more. Then they'd turned their minds to dealing with the flood.

At first they used a huge Dutch pump, imported especially from Holland where such exigencies were unhappily more common. And with it they transferred water up into the Kingspill where it could get away at low tide. Then, once the water had gone down enough to reveal the roads, they closed the one by the pumping station and brought in four electric submersible pumps, a generator to drive them, and a caravan. And here it was that George and his colleagues watched over them in shifts, pumping the water across the road in large pipes, all day and all night.

George didn't mind being on duty over the festive season. He had never felt less like celebrating anyway. He went about his duties mechanically, with stoicism. As the water receded he investigated both his own house and the pumping station. In the bungalow he found mud and slime, ruined furniture and the grotesque carcass of a sheep, from which he recoiled in disgust.

In the station there was more mud and slime. Some of the chequer plates had buckled in the intense heat of the fire and there was blistered paint, broken window glass and blackening soot everywhere. But the building itself seemed mostly all right. There was nothing combustible in its structure and the walls, the metal girders, the high ceiling and the roof were still there, apparently unscathed. More importantly, George was sure that the pumps themselves were basically sound; their massive components still intact. Of course they would need to be completely stripped down and rebuilt, but he was sure it must be possible. Would the authorities be willing to spend the money on it? Or would they sell them all off for scrap, and install modern electric ones instead? He pushed this thought away.

He would try to think positively. All phone calls to Amber Junction had been diverted to headquarters, so at least he wasn't constantly getting an earful from the Internal Drainage Boards' farmers and landowners or the bird boys either; all of whom were uncharacteristically united in complaining that the water levels were still too high.

Mind you, George thought, someone did ought to be held accountable for the fire . . . Maybe no one was to blame? He didn't really want to know. What was done couldn't be undone. He was sat there in this poxy caravan, eating one of Gwen's mince pies. Some Christmas! He gulped down some tea from his thermos. He would rather be here surrounded by water and sky doing something useful, however cold, than cooped up in the agency's dark little flat in Otterbridge, which it now seemed he and his family would be stuck with for Christ knows how long.

And there were compensations. He'd been commended for his actions on the day of the fire. He'd even been on television! His mates had stuck up a page of the local paper on the caravan wall. He read it again, although he already knew it by heart. Below the bit about the helicopters from RNAS Yeovilton rescuing people stranded by the rising water, the headline said: *MANDY — HEROINE OF THE FLOOD. Amanda Overy, 13, risked her life to save a man from drowning* . . . What better daughter could a man have? Then his eye caught a small fuzzy photograph right at the bottom of the page, which he hadn't noticed before. The caption beneath it read: *A badger snapped here by our reporter, swimming through the floods below Hembrow with a wild duck held fast in its jaws.* Well, I'll be damned! George thought. Whatever next?

★ ★ ★

The run up to Christmas had left Pamela irritable and run down. Suddenly there were two extra men to cater for, and she still hadn't been able to get down to the moor to rescue Bertie or salvage her precious things from The Prospect. Instead she was stuck at Hembrow and expected to wait hand and foot upon Jonathan up two flights of stairs; the Jonathan whom she now regarded with undisguised contempt.

'If he'd only come with me to offer George help, when we first saw the fire,' she muttered to herself, 'then he wouldn't be in the state he's in

370

now! But no, he was too cowardly to risk it. *Pathetic!*'

By Christmas Day Pamela's mood was not much better. They were all sitting in the kitchen at breakfast, whilst she fed a reluctant Chloë.

'Scrambled eggy?' she cooed to her in a high voice suffused with fake enthusiasm. 'Chloë loves her eggy peggy, doesn't she?'

'If you talk to her in that tone of voice,' Peter said, 'she'll never trust you.'

'There's no need to take that attitude with me!' Pamela said. 'But while we're on the subject of trust, why didn't you mention that Kelly was pregnant when you wrote me that last letter?'

'I probably reckoned that one shock at a time was quite enough to be going on with,' Peter said.

'So you would have got around to telling me that I had a grand-daughter eventually?'

'Look, I didn't know the feckless bitch was going to dump Chloë on you, did I?' Peter was beginning to get ratty.

'You didn't?'

'Of course I bloody didn't! I'd never have allowed it.'

'Well thank you for that vote of confidence!' Pamela said.

'Oh *Ma!* Don't twist my words.'

'So, why did Kelly leave her with me?'

'How the hell should I know? Maybe a new boyfriend told her to?'

'Oh I see! So you think there's another man involved. I might have known.' Pamela looked grimly satisfied. 'Now then,' she said, 'what's the plan for today?'

'Well, I thought — ' Vinny began, but was interrupted at once.

'Of course, we'll save the presents until after lunch as usual,' Pamela went on. 'And I expect Vinny will need some peace and quiet in the kitchen this morning, so we'd better make ourselves scarce. I'm told that it is possible to drive on the roads across the moor, now, so I propose that the rest of us take the mini and pop down to The Prospect for an hour or so, to see what can be salvaged. And with a bit of luck I'll be able to drive Bertie home and Peter can bring the mini.'

'Actually, Chloë and I are staying here,' Peter announced. 'It's far too cold outside for babies — and for me too, for that matter. I'll give Vinny a hand with the lunch.'

'Well, that would be a first!' Pamela said. 'Right then, since everyone spurns my offer of fresh air and exercise, I'll go on my own.'

'*I'm* going with you,' Jonathan said. 'I need to get my computer out before the house falls down.'

'Oh, I doubt you'll be able to do that,' Pamela said. 'It will be far too dangerous to go upstairs. And while I think of it, isn't it about time you paid me some rent?'

'Can't,' Jonathan said. 'No money.'

'I see,' Pamela said crisply. 'Then you'd better write me an IOU against the proceeds from the sale of your book. *If* it ever sells, that is.'

'What's an eye — ' Jonathan began, but

Pamela was already in the hall putting on her coat. Peter and Vinny watched him trail out after her, leaving the front door hanging open.

'What's eating her?' Peter asked, going to close it. Then he lifted Chloë from her high chair and walked round the kitchen, jiggling her up and down to her evident delight.

'I've no idea,' Vinny said, 'apart from a strong impression that she can't bear to be in the same room as me, or poor Jonathan.'

'Have you two had a fight?'

'No, but — '

'You're not getting along so well?'

Vinny sighed. 'No,' she admitted.

Peter smiled sympathetically. 'I'm not surprised,' he said. 'Quite frankly I'm amazed you've stuck it out for so long!'

* * *

Most of the roads across the moor had indeed emerged from the flood, but the journey down to The Prospect was a depressing one. The land was covered in silt and detritus and the broken branches of trees. Pamela and Jonathan saw three chairs and a table upended in one field, and two dead pigs floating, bloated, in a rhyne. At the turn off onto the minor road they passed a red sign: ROAD CLOSED — 1 MILE, and when they reached The Prospect they discovered that someone had been there before them.

At first sight, Pamela was relieved that the house was still standing, albeit at a strange angle, but when they ventured cautiously inside they found that the front door had been forced open, and nearly everything had gone.

'Oh my God!' Pamela gasped, standing in the hall and holding onto the stairs for support. 'It's been *looted!*'

The thieves had stripped the kitchen of everything but the sink. The cooker, all the units, fridge-freezer, microwave, washing machine, table, chairs — all had been taken. The sitting room was equally bare.

'My bike's gone!' Jonathan cried, scrambling up the stairs on hands and knees to check on his room. The house groaned, and a large area of plaster detached itself from the ceiling and landed in a cloud of dust just in front of Pamela.

'For Christ's sake be more careful,' she shouted after him. 'You'll have the whole bloody lot down.' Jonathan was strangely quiet, apart from his now habitual cough. 'What's it like?' she called. Far too dangerous to go up there herself.

He appeared at the top of the stairs and came slowly down them on his bottom, holding a pair of shorts in one hand and wiping his eyes on them. 'Empty,' he said. 'My computer's gone.' He looked vacant.

'What, they've stolen everything?'

'Except these.' He held up the shorts.

'Oh well,' Pamela said, 'I suppose this is what we pay insurance for. You can get an even more state-of-the-art one now.'

'It's got my book in it,' Jonathan said. He had gone very pale. He was still sitting on the bottom step.

'Surely you took some back-up copies?'

'Aaahh.' He relaxed, and a smile crept over his face. 'Vinny's got some,' he said.

'She *would!*' Pamela said. 'She's too perfect for words.'

'Yes,' he said, without a hint of irony. 'She is, isn't she?'

A nasty suspicion flared up in Pamela's mind. 'Jonathan,' she said without preamble, 'Have you and Vinny been to bed together?'

He looked at her for a moment, then away again. 'It's a secret,' he said.

They *have!* Pamela thought. How *could* she?

'Are we going back to Hembrow, then?' Jonathan asked.

'What? Oh . . . no. I've got to go and see if Bertie's OK first.'

'Bertie who?'

'My black SUV. You know very well!' Pamela snapped.

They drove down towards Amber Junction and parked in front of a second and final ROAD CLOSED notice, but there was no sign of another vehicle. They both got out. Pamela began to search frantically, looking down by the sluice in case it had been washed bodily into the river, but without success. When she looked round for Jonathan she saw that he was further along the road in front of the pumping station, hobbling on his crutch towards a man who was sitting on the steps of a small caravan. She began to walk that way too. It was obvious now why the road had been closed. It was criss-crossed with pipes, all disgorging into the drain. She recognised the man at the caravan.

Poor George! she thought, a skilled engineer reduced to being a watchman. And today of all days! Pamela wished there were something she could do to help; some action more appropriate than simply reciting seasonal greetings.

'I hope you've thanked George for saving your life?' she called to Jonathan above the noise of the generators.

'Thank you, George,' he said.

'That's all right,' George said. 'You OK now?'

'Someone's stolen my computer and my bike,' he said forlornly.

'Oh dear,' George said. 'That in't much of a Christmas present, is it?' He turned to Pamela. 'And there was me thinking you'd bin and cleared out everything from up there, an' your big black four by four an' all.'

'What d'you mean?' she asked.

'Saw your van loading up yesterday, didn't I? Very wise, I thought. Who knows how long that house be going to keep on standing?'

'You saw a *van*?' Pamela asked. 'What colour was it? Did you see the men? What about the registration number?'

George looked confused. 'Well, it were some sort of truck rental, blue, I think . . . But why are you asking me? Didn't you — ?'

'No,' Pamela said shortly.

'Oh dear,' George said again. 'Oh dear, oh dear. I wish I'd 'a known.' He shook his head. 'They looked like they had a right to be there. I never thought . . . Can't trust nobody nowadays, can 'ee?'

'Can't be helped,' Pamela said. 'Not your

fault.' She took several deep breaths, and tried to remind herself that what had happened to her was as nothing, compared with the ruin of his livelihood. 'How's Mandy?'

'Oh, fine.' George frowned. 'Well I'm saying that, but then again I can't always make her out.'

'In what way?'

'Dunno. 'Tis like she've got something on her mind. Moody, like.'

'Teenagers!' Pamela said understandingly.

'It's no good getting any other computer,' Jonathan said suddenly. 'I need to have my own one back. Only it will do.'

George and Pamela exchanged meaningful glances behind his back. Pamela tapped her forehead and smiled wryly. George gave a little shake of his head in response. He and I understand one another, Pamela thought, and I admire him. He's a good hardworking honest man and he's having a really rough time. I shall survive; the insurance will be small reparation, but I wonder if there is anything I can do for him?

★ ★ ★

Christmas lunch was edgy, Vinny thought. She and Peter had been getting on famously until Pamela came back; he'd been a great help in the kitchen and with looking after Chloë. But Pamela's news of the looting had been a dampener of spirits, and Jonathan was unusually pale and silent. Vinny felt so sorry for him.

Pamela carved the bird as usual. Peter helped

377

himself to several slices of nut-roast instead, much to her disgust. Vinny passed round the roast potatoes and parsnips.

'Bread sauce?' Peter asked Jonathan, who had a large portion of turkey and stuffing on his plate.

'Yes.'

'Yes, *please*,' Peter corrected him cheerfully.

'What?' Jonathan was busy helping himself to sprouts, and didn't look up. Vinny caught Peter's eye and shook her head slightly. Peter made a self-deprecatory face with downturned mouth, and changed the subject smoothly. 'Will you rebuild the house on the moor?' he asked his mother.

'Certainly not,' she said. 'I've had enough of building work and builders to last me a lifetime. I suppose you could say that those looters have done me a favour. I mean, what good would all that furniture have been to me, with no house to put it in? I'll just have to make sure I get the maximum insurance payout. That'll be some small recompense, I suppose, but I doubt very much if I shall get any compensation at all for my loss of future earnings from renting The Prospect out. No, there's no doubt about it; it's been an unmitigated disaster. All that work and effort, and for what?' She shook her head sadly from side to side. No one said anything.

When they had finished their first course, Vinny brought in the Christmas pudding alight with brandy, to murmurs of appreciation.

'I'll just have fresh fruit,' Pamela said virtuously. 'That's really far too heavy for me.'

She looked meaningfully at Vinny.

Vinny smiled brightly and cut a large wedge. 'Peter?'

'Yes please!'

'But surely you can't eat that, can you?' Pamela said.

'Why not?'

'Because it's made with suet. *Animal* fat!' She looked triumphant.

'Rubbish!' Peter retorted, taking the bowl from Vinny and adding a good dollop of brandy butter.

'Oh I see,' Pamela said. 'It's not so much a fundamental conviction then, more of a trendy affectation?'

'Ma?' Peter said tightly. 'Just back off, will you?'

'It's vegetarian suet,' Vinny put in quickly. 'Jonathan? Pudding?'

'Yes!' He took it eagerly and added large amounts of double cream.

Vinny cut another slice for herself, without looking at Pamela. She added brandy butter and cream as well. It was utterly delicious. I'll probably get the most violent indigestion, she thought to herself. The atmosphere in this room is enough to curdle the strongest stomach.

Jonathan had already finished his, and was looking round for seconds. He drained his wineglass for the third time, in one gulp, and banged it down jovially on the table, smiling round at all of them.

'Happy Christmas!' he said.

★ ★ ★

379

The present giving wasn't a great success either, Peter thought. There was no way he was going to be able to take all those big bulky toys to the States with him and Chloë. He hoped his mother wouldn't be too upset when it came to leaving them behind.

The best gift in his opinion was the one that Vinny gave to Jonathan. He couldn't make Jonathan out at all, but he had gathered that he was an engineer especially concerned with water. So Vinny's embroidered quotation from St Francis in a little blue frame, was apt and charming and had the added advantage of being easily portable. It read:

Praised be my lord for our sister water,
Who is very serviceable unto us,
And humble and precious and clean.

'What's it for?' Jonathan asked on opening it.

'It's to hang on your wall,' Vinny said.

'But I haven't got a wall, and I don't believe in God.'

'Never mind,' Vinny said. 'I'll keep it for myself then.' She looked resigned, rather than hurt, but Peter felt indignant on her behalf.

'That's not very gracious!' he complained to Jonathan.

'It's all right, Peter,' Vinny said warningly. 'Really.'

Later on, over the washing up, she said to him, 'It's my own fault for giving Jonathan something I particularly liked myself. I might have known that it would mean nothing to him.' And then she explained the situation to Peter.

'Oh, now I understand,' he said. 'It makes

perfect sense. Ma's always had a horror of anyone who's even a little bit odd, mentally. I wouldn't like to be in his shoes!'

★ ★ ★

Pamela went to bed at ten o'clock that night, pleading exhaustion. 'It's probably post-traumatic shock,' she said.

'I don't think I've got that yet,' Jonathan said, as he struggled up to his room at ten thirty as usual.

'But he'll probably have developed it by tomorrow, eh?' Peter grinned at Vinny as soon as Jonathan was out of earshot. They were sitting cosily by the fire and drinking coffee.

'Oh no,' she said. 'He's not a hypochondriac. He's just egocentric, and that's because it's the only point of view he's got.'

'You're fond of him, aren't you?'

'Yes,' Vinny said. 'For all the good it does me.'

'Vinny?'

'Yes?'

'There's something I need to tell you. I'm leaving in a week or so, and taking Chloë with me.'

'Really?' She felt her heart quicken.

'Sure thing. She's my daughter and I want to bring her up normally.'

'Away from undue influence?' Vinny smiled.

'Couldn't have put it better myself!'

'Pamela will be distraught,' Vinny said.

'For a while, yes. That's why I'm telling you now, so you'll be prepared. But she'll soon find

381

another victim who needs her.'

That's cruel, Vinny thought, even if it is true. 'But you will keep in touch with her, won't you?' She was surprised to find she cared. 'You will let her know how Chloë's getting on?'

'Course I will! I'm not totally heartless.'

'And maybe she'd be able to go to Australia and see you sometimes?'

'She'd have a wasted journey.'

'Why?'

'Because we're going to the States.'

'But I thought you loved Australia?'

'Oh I do. There's nowhere I'd rather live.'

'But?'

'But I can't get a work permit, and now I've got Chloë I can't take the risks I used to. She needs proper security. Of course if Kelly and I had actually been married, I'd have got residency, no bother.'

Oh I *see!* Vinny thought, with a flash of insight. That would explain everything. 'Was it your idea to have a baby?' she asked.

'Yep. But Kelly changed her mind once she was pregnant. She even threatened to have an abortion, but I managed to talk her round. I reckoned she'd feel different once Chloë was born.'

'But she didn't?'

'No. She never seemed to bond with her at all. Said she couldn't be bothered! What kind of woman says that about her own child?'

Vinny made a face. 'I suppose we can't all be earth mothers,' she said. 'But, won't you have the same problems in America as well?'

'Maybe, but I've got friends there. I've applied for a visitor's visa to begin with, and you never know what'll turn up. I plan to become a naturalised US citizen eventually.' He looked pleased with himself.

There was a silence whilst Vinny took all this in.

'So, when are you going to tell Pamela all this?'

'Probably the night before we leave.'

'But can't you see, that puts me in a very difficult position?'

'How so? You and Ma aren't close these days, are you? In fact I've been getting the distinct impression that you're thinking of quitting too.'

'Well . . . ' She was unable to deny this.

'But I would be grateful if you could hang on for a month or two after Chloë and I have gone,' Peter said earnestly. 'To pick up the pieces. I mean, if you bugger off at the same time as us, it would be a bit hard on the old girl, wouldn't it?'

16

It was now January, the month when Vinny had planned to make final preparations for her escape. But Peter's imminent departure with Chloë had scuppered things, at least for now. Why is it, Vinny thought, that everyone seems to feel able to dump on me?

More pressingly, it was also time for Jonathan to return to his job. Vinny had hoped by now that it would have become more obvious what she should do for the best. She'd had daydreams about going to Africa with him and finding herself some employment out there. But the dreams had been constantly interrupted by doubts and practicalities and she realised she had to make a choice; she might be obliged to get herself a proper job somewhere else, without him.

She longed to have uninterrupted time with Jonathan, to discuss it properly, but Pamela was always there and her very presence in the kitchen below had an inhibiting effect on Vinny anywhere in the house, even in the attic.

Once the snow had thawed completely and the roads were clear again, Pamela began to organise weekend outings in the mini. Peter sat in the back, with Chloë in a car seat borrowed from Gordon. Vinny was in the passenger seat in the front. Pamela of course had to drive. Jonathan was never invited. Vinny was only persuaded to go once. She found herself packing the buggy, a bag of nappies, wipes, bottles, and food to cater for Chloë's every need into an annoyingly inadequate space.

'I do wish this boot wasn't so *small*,' she complained. 'At times like this we could really do with a VW Polo, or better still a Golf.'

'Well I'm sorry you feel like that,' Pamela retorted huffily. 'Next time I go to the trouble of buying you a car, I'll think twice!'

'Oh no . . . ' Vinny said at once. 'I didn't mean . . . ' If I wasn't just about to leave, I'd buy my own bloody car! I should have done so years ago. But she didn't say that.

As they drove off, she was thinking, no one could live anything even approaching a normal life, if they always had to be as unconditionally, eternally *grateful* as me. I'm right to go. She thought back regretfully to their first years together when Pamela had been so carelessly generous, so full of affection and largesse.

I accepted presents because she said it gave her joy to give them to me, Vinny remembered. And I took them, of course I did. Who wouldn't?

'You take me for granted,' Pamela accused her now. 'I expected better of you.'

'Well maybe if you expected less, you'd be pleasantly surprised more!' Vinny retorted.

'Surprised, yes, but hardly pleasantly.' Pamela shook her head slowly in apparent sorrow and disillusionment.

God save us! Vinny thought, irritated beyond endurance. What in hell am I supposed to have done now? She caught Peter's eye in the rear view mirror. He made a sardonic face. Next time, Vinny thought, I shall stay at home with Jonathan which is where I wanted to be anyway.

Jonathan's ankle was mending fast. He had discarded his crutch and was able to walk up and down the stairs more easily. In spite of this he mostly stayed in his room at the top of the house, working on his book, apart from occasional visits to the library with Vinny.

The following weekend when the rest of the household had gone off in the mini, Vinny climbed the stairs and tapped on his door. 'Jonathan?'

'Yes?'

'Can I come in?' He was sitting by the window and writing on an A4 pad, but he looked up with a smile. 'I thought we might spend some time together,' Vinny said.

'To do what?'

Vinny took a breath. 'Go to bed?'

'Oh,' he said. 'Well I'm a little busy at the moment.'

Vinny was hurt. 'I thought you said your book was finished?'

'No,' Jonathan said. 'I'm rewriting it.'

'What are you talking about? Why?'

'Because I've realised there's a lot more I don't know about water; things I hadn't covered in the book. I need to do more research.'

'Oh Jonathan,' Vinny shook her head. 'So, are you going to stay on, to do it in Somerset? And where will you live? Not here, surely?'

'No, I'm going back to work as soon as possible,' he said. 'It's much too noisy here, and anyway I can't afford to take any more time out. I'll finish the book one day. It's fine.' He looked quite happy with the idea. 'Now then, I'd better get on.'

The phrase, 'But what about us?' hovered in Vinny's mind, and died. To respond to it, it was essential for him to have a mental concept of 'us' in the first place. 'I don't want you to go,' she said. 'I shall miss you terribly.'

'Well, come with me, then.'

'I'd need a job,' she said, 'an income. I can't imagine there's much demand for librarians where you're going.' Vinny frowned. 'Come to that, where *are* you going? You always just say Africa, but which actual country?'

'That's because I've worked in lots of places in Africa,' he explained. 'In Zambia, in Kenya, and in Zimbabwe as well as Botswana, which is where I'm going back to this time.'

'And jobs for librarians?'

'I don't know.'

'I'm sure there must be — in the big cities,' Vinny said, 'but you won't be living in a city, will you?'

'No.'

'You'll be out in rural areas, living in mud huts?'

'Yes.'

'So I wouldn't be much use?'

'Probably not.'

Vinny managed a smile. She went over and sat down next to him. She took his hand and held it in her own two. 'So what are we going to do then?' she asked.

'I suppose you could always marry me,' he suggested.

'Do you want me to?'

'Well, it would be a practical solution. They might even give me a rise in salary as a married man.'

Vinny stared at him. He looked entirely at ease, completely unemotional. He might just as well have said, '*I suppose you could always pass me a biscuit*'.

'I'll . . . think about it,' she said.

'If you want an engagement ring,' he said, 'it would be best if you went to the shop and bought it yourself. Then I'd pay you back, if it weren't too expensive. I don't know anything about such things.'

'I'll see.' Vinny got up. 'I'd better leave you to get on.'

She went downstairs and poured herself a slug of Pamela's whisky. Then she sat at the kitchen table and drank it down, neat.

It's no good, she thought. I have to face it. I just couldn't bear to live the rest of my life without even one crumb of emotional support; with someone who has no empathy and no imagination, even though it isn't his fault. It would kill all my joy. My spirit would simply wither away . . .

Vinny got a tissue from her pocket and held it against her closed eyelids, soaking up the tears as they oozed out.

★   ★   ★

The next day was Sunday. Pamela put a dab of *L'Air du Temps* behind each ear and drove off alone in the mini to have lunch with Gordon and escape, at least for a few hours, from all her domestic and family burdens. She hoped her defection would gee Vinny up a bit too. She needs to be jolted out of her complacency, Pamela thought crossly, leaning on the horn to blast an innocent bystanding dog out of her road. Instead of the authoritative *BHAAAHB!* she was accustomed to, this one went *Peeep!* She snatched her hand away.

'Pamela!' Gordon said, embracing her warmly at his door and ushering her inside. 'How lovely to see you. Do come in.' He showed her into his drawing room and she sank into the welcoming bosom of a plush white leather sofa. 'What will you drink?' he asked. 'G and t?'

'That would be lovely,' Pamela agreed. She looked about her as he mixed their drinks. His three cats were there, very much at home. Two were asleep together on an armchair, and the third stretched out in a kind of cradle hanging from a radiator. Photographs of Gordon's dead wife still adorned the grand piano, plus one of himself at Westminster with his party leader, and several of his children's graduations and weddings. Amongst them, Pamela recognised one daughter who was a graphic designer. There were also pictures of babies in silver frames and, in the corner of the room, an untidy box full of garish toys. Gordon had attained the coveted status of grandparent before her. But now, she thought with satisfaction, so have I! She took the glass of gin gratefully and settled back, luxuriating in the comfort of her surroundings.

'So tell me . . . ' Gordon said, leaning forward and regarding her with concern. ' . . . About the fire and its aftermath. It must have been a dreadful ordeal.'

'Indeed it was,' Pamela said, so she told him all about it. He was a very attentive listener and she was gratified. The conversation eventually came round to life at Hembrow.

'What's happening about your strange lodger fellow?' Gordon asked. 'Where's he going to live, now The Prospect is a wreck?'

'Jonathan? God knows! It's time he went back to his job in Africa, but he never tells me anything and he's run out of money. D'you know, I had the phone bill yesterday and found a great list of hugely expensive calls to America! He does all this without so much as a by-your-leave too — takes me totally for granted.'

'Dreadful,' Gordon said. 'I'd never do that.' Pamela raised both eyebrows, but said nothing. Gordon went a deeper shade of pink. 'I hear Peter is back,' he said. 'How is he?'

'Oh much the same.' Pamela made a resigned face. 'I don't suppose he'll ever change.'

'Is he home for long?'

'I've no idea. He never says, and one can hardly greet him on the doorstep by saying 'Oh, hello! When are you leaving?' can one?'

'My step-grandmother used to say exactly that!' Gordon said, and they both laughed.

Over the meal, cooked by Gordon's housekeeper and left with instructions for heating up,

Gordon talked about his grandchildren, giving Pamela licence to boast about Chloë.

'And Peter is very attached to her, I expect?' Gordon asked.

'Oh yes,' Pamela agreed, 'but I think a lot of it is novelty value. I mean — and I wouldn't say this to just anybody, you understand — Peter's not known for his tenacity of purpose, is he? A dear boy, but unreliable.' She shook her head. 'It's a sad thing to have to admit about one's own son.'

'So you think he'll be off on his travels again soon?'

'I fear so, yes. When I had that letter from him a while ago, about getting married, d'you remember? I did hope then that it would be the making of him; settle him down, you know.'

'Yes, I do know,' Gordon said. 'It did wonders for my eldest.' He took a sip of wine, and replenished their glasses.

'Excellent casserole,' Pamela said.

'Yes,' Gordon agreed. 'Nearly up to Vinny's standard.'

'Don't talk to me about *Vinny*!' Pamela said.

'Oh dear.' Gordon paused with his wineglass half way to his mouth. 'Something wrong there?'

Pamela sighed. 'I wish I knew,' she said.

Gordon took a good gulp and put the glass down. He leant forward and put his hand over hers across the table. 'You're not going your separate ways, are you?' he asked, his voice full of concern.

'Not yet,' she said, 'but who knows?'

'But that would be very sad,' Gordon exclaimed. 'You've lived together for so long!'

'Ten years of friendship, yes,' Pamela agreed, consciously stressing the penultimate word.

'But, surely you can't let that happen?'

'Oh I wouldn't,' Pamela said, 'if it were up to me.'

'You mean, it's all Vinny's idea?'

'I really can't discuss it,' Pamela said. She looked down at her hands and clasped them together. 'You must understand that I believe in absolute loyalty. Even if she doesn't.'

'Oh my dear,' Gordon said. 'I am sorry. Here, have some more wine?' He poured it out.

Pamela, satisfied with his response, changed the subject. 'So, what d'you think the Environment Agency will do about Amber Junction?' she asked him. 'Will they reinstate it, or will they just give up and let the whole area revert to marsh and wasteland? I believe that's known as a 'controlled retreat'.'

'Well I do actually know quite a bit about this,' Gordon admitted. 'One of the chaps I play golf with is fairly senior in the Agency, and he says it will be enormously costly whatever they decide to do. The big flood in 1981 caused 12.7 million pounds worth of damage, you know, and this one with the additional problem of Amber Junction will be much *much* worse.'

'So what will happen?'

'Can't tell you, I'm afraid. It's all very much under wraps. Unlikely that they'd let it revert to nature though. The compensation costs payable to the farmers and the odd householder would be prohibitive, no question of that.'

'But if they build a new pumping station, what will happen to the old pumps? George told me they were built in the 1930s. And that boy, Steve, said it was like working in a museum. He's right! They're treasures of industrial archaeology. It would be sheer vandalism if they were to be scrapped.'

Gordon shook his head. 'All comes down to money, in the end.'

'What about the Lottery?' Pamela suggested. 'They've got millions of pounds.'

'That's as maybe,' he said, 'but it takes a dedicated person to wheedle it out of them.'

'*I'm* dedicated,' Pamela said. And a wonderful new idea occurred to her.

★ ★ ★

Pamela at last knew the details of Chloë's birth. Peter told her that she had been born in July, on the sixteenth at half past eight in the evening in Adelaide, South Australia.

'It would have been helpful if I'd been told that a lot earlier!' she said.

It was now mid January, so Chloë was six months old. She had begun to sit up and shuffle about under her own steam, making little burbling noises, which sounded like speech but weren't quite.

'Just listen to that!' Pamela called excitedly to Peter. 'And look how advanced she is for her age!'

Vinny watched Pamela getting more and more attached to her grand-daughter, and worried about the inevitable day when Peter would take Chloë away. Many times she'd been on the verge of warning Pamela beforehand. But then, knowing that it was Peter's absolute right to take his daughter abroad, if he so chose, she realised that it would simply cause a tremendous amount of argument and fury, which in the end would solve nothing. She was angry with Peter for putting her in this invidious situation; angry and resentful too.

Early next morning Chloë had inched her way on her bottom across the kitchen floor and over to the saucepan cupboard, where she was now happily engaged in banging a milk pan against the table leg.

'Breakfast time my angel!' Pamela called to her, going across and lifting her, 'Weeee!' into the air and down into her high chair.

Jonathan was still upstairs in his room. Vinny was at the table, spreading toast. She glanced at Peter who had just come in, and thought he looked rather tense. The reason was soon apparent. 'Er . . . Ma,' he began. 'I've got something to say.'

'When haven't you?' teased Pamela. 'Daddy's always got something to say, hasn't he Chloë? Open wide!' And she deftly inserted a spoonful of mashed banana.

'Seriously,' Peter said. Vinny bent her head and applied some marmalade.

'Go on then!' Pamela said.

'We're leaving in two days time.'

'*We?*' Pamela said.

'Chloë and I. We're — '

'Chloë's not going anywhere,' Pamela interrupted. 'And that's final!'

'Look, Ma — '

'No, you look! Kelly entrusted her to my care, and that's where she's staying. You couldn't possibly look after her. You've got no job, no prospects and no experience. I never heard such rubbish!'

'Nevertheless,' Peter said with commendable calm, 'we *are* going. She's my child. I have her birth certificate to prove it, and you have no power to stop me from taking her wherever I wish. We'll talk about this properly later.' He lifted Chloë out of her chair and as he did so, she gurgled and distinctly said, 'Mamama.'

'That's her first word!' Pamela exclaimed, and burst into tears.

As Peter carried his daughter away into the sitting room, Pamela looked wildly to Vinny for support. 'She said Mama! She wants to stay with me!'

'I don't think it means — '

'And he *can't* take her. I'd miss her learning to crawl, her first steps, her first proper sentence, her first day at school, everything!' Pamela began to cry with loud gasping sobs. 'It's so unfair . . . after all I've done . . . Chloë loves me . . . She won't manage without me. I won't let it happen.' She sank down in despair until her forehead was resting on the table.

Vinny felt torn between pity and a strong urge to tiptoe away. She hesitated. After a moment, Pamela sat up and held out her arms.

'You'll help me, won't you, Vin? You won't fail me?'

Vinny went over, pulled her gently to her feet and enveloped her in a hug. Pamela's coarse hair irritated her cheek. Her hands were gripping Vinny's shoulders much too tightly.

Pamela seemed unaware of her discomfort and soon disengaged herself. She blew her nose, pushed her hair into place and went over to the telephone.

'Gordon will know what to do,' she said. 'He trained as a lawyer. We're not going to let this beat us, eh Vinny?'

★   ★   ★

Breakfast the next day was unusually silent. Vinny was acutely conscious of the noise Bran Flakes made when chewed. It was like trying to eat Pringles in church. Pamela sat tight-lipped at the head of the table, eating half a piece of toast without marmalade, drinking little sips of orange juice, and watching as Peter fed Chloë. Her every movement was a reproach.

A bran flake stuck in Vinny's throat and she coughed loudly, her eyes streaming with the effort. Pamela made no attempt to pat her on the back. Vinny spluttered, and then breathed again, with difficulty.

'All right?' Peter asked her.

'Yes,' she croaked.

'Right,' Pamela said, getting up. 'I'm off.'

'Where are you going?' Peter enquired cheerfully.

'To see my solicitor.' Pamela picked up her handbag from the dresser and walked out.

'Phew!' Peter said, relaxing into a grin. 'Was that an atmosphere and a half, or what? So, what are your plans for today, then?'

'I've got the morning off,' Vinny said shortly. She got to her feet and went upstairs to her room.

Once there, she found an A4 pad and a pencil, drew a line down the centre of the first page and began to write lists. She headed the two columns, *Take* and *Store*.

After an hour or so, she became aware that Peter was calling to her from the front hall. '*VINNY?*'

She went to the top of the stairs. 'What?'

'We're just off.' He was standing there with the baby in his arms. Both were dressed in their outdoor clothes. Two large suitcases, Chloë's folded buggy and a carrier bag of toys filled the stairwell.

'What d'you mean, you're just off?'

'Taxi's here. Apologise to Ma for me, will you, but this is the only way to do it. A lot less upsetting in the long run.'

Vinny rushed headlong down the stairs and grabbed him by the arm. 'But you're due to leave *tomorrow!*' she protested. 'You haven't said goodbye. You can't just disappear without a word!'

'Believe me,' Peter said, 'it's better this way.'

She let go of him. 'Better for whom?'

'Good old Vinny,' He smiled at her very sweetly. 'Grammatically correct to the bitter end!' He bent to kiss her cheek. 'Thanks for everything,' he said. 'Look after Ma, OK? And don't neglect your own best interests either.' He opened the front door and called to the taxi driver, who came over to help carry the luggage. Vinny was speechless. Peter got into the back seat of the cab with Chloë on his lap, and pulled down the window. 'Oh, and could you tell Ma I've nicked a little cash?' he said. 'Just so she doesn't panic and think she's been burgled! Amazing isn't it, that she's been stashing it in exactly the same place, all these years!'

Then he closed the window and took Chloë's hand to wobble it in a parody of a farewell wave. The taxi revved up and they drove off.

Oh Christ! Vinny thought. And there was me, thinking it couldn't possibly get any worse.

★ ★ ★

Pamela came home from her meeting with Mr Booty of Gamble, Sly and Booty feeling thoroughly pissed off. The fact that he was a charming and helpful solicitor did nothing at all to soften the blow of the disheartening advice he had been obliged to give her. It seemed that grandparents had no rights at all.

The house was abnormally quiet. She went into the kitchen and dumped her bag on the dresser. Then she went to the bottom of the stairs and shouted 'Vinny?' She must be in; her car was parked outside.

Vinny appeared from her room and came slowly downstairs. She looked like a beaten dog.

'What's the matter? Where's Chloë and Peter?'

'I'm so sorry . . . ' she began. 'I'm afraid . . . '

398

Pamela felt a stab of alarm. 'Spit it out then!'

'They're probably at the airport by now,' Vinny said. 'And before you ask, I've no idea which one. Peter didn't say.'

'They've *gone?*' Pamela was flooded with rage. 'And you *let* them go?'

'I couldn't stop them. The taxi came . . . I'm really sorry . . . '

'You could've lain down across the fucking gateway!' Pamela shouted, 'snatched the keys, nobbled the bloody driver, anything! But oh no, you had to let them go!' She stared at Vinny with unblinking fury.

'I didn't know they were going today. It took me totally by surprise. Honestly.'

'I think you *did* know. You're *glad* Peter's taken Chloë away. Go on, admit it!' Pamela challenged.

'No!' Vinny said, and covered her mouth with her knuckles.

'I am right, aren't I? You should have told me. It's the very least you could have done.'

'I didn't know, and even if I had, what good would it — ' Vinny tried. 'I mean, you have no power to stop . . . '

'*I have a right to say goodbye to my own grand-daughter!*' Pamela shouted. 'Or hadn't that thought entered your stupid selfish head?'

'Oh go to *hell!*' Vinny finally spat. 'You're right. I am glad she's gone. You would have *ruined her life!*' Then she turned and rushed clumsily upstairs again, banging shut the door of her room.

Pamela was too angry to feel anything but

rage. Rage against Peter for his selfishness and deceit, and rage against Vinny for her spineless betrayal. She went back into the kitchen to make herself a cup of coffee, forcing herself to think sensibly. There was no point in rushing off after them. She didn't know the airport, the terminal or even which part of Australia they were going to.

She could do without Peter — she'd had a lot of practice in that — but Chloë? Her heart fluttered, and she had to take deep breaths to calm it. I'm not going to wallow in emotion and crack up, she told herself. I've got more backbone than that. She stood up very straight, pushed the hair back off her forehead and slid the kettle across onto the hotplate to boil.

★   ★   ★

George Overy was just leaving for his shift when Mandy waylaid him.

'Dad?' she said. 'What if it was proved that someone spilt stuff into the sump and caused the fire?'

'What, you mean a solvent, something inflammable?'

'Yeah.'

'Well I don't think that's very likely,' George said. 'And to be honest, even if someone had, that wouldn't a' been the whole story. Amber Junction weren't designed for safety an' that's a fact.'

'So if anyone had done it, they wouldn't be to blame?'

'Why?' George smiled at his daughter. 'You bin throwing petrol about the place, have 'ee?'

''Course not!' Mandy blushed.

George patted her on the head. 'Don't you go fretting on about it,' he said. 'What's done's done.'

'Thanks Dad!' She looked happier than he'd seen her in a long while.

'Right then,' he said. 'Best be off.'

He drove out of Otterbridge and turned off onto the road towards Amber Junction, noticing the deteriorating state of The Prospect as he passed it. He saw that a part of the east wall had now actually collapsed. The roof had sagged and tiles had fallen off. It was a ruin. They'd have to pull it down, for certain.

'Not much of a prospect now, is it?' he said to himself. 'Pity, that.'

He wondered what his own prospects might be. The future looked bleak. Depression crept in and took a hold of him. Working with electric pumps wouldn't be the same. The job he had loved was effectively finished.

He arrived at the caravan and relieved Jim Tucker. The flood had all been drained off now and the process of clearing up was well underway. But they were still having to pump water over the road, and as yet no decision had been made on the future of the pumping station.

'Bout time they pulled their bloody fingers out! George thought.

Before he left at the end of his shift, he planned to pop in and see how his bungalow was coming on. It was still not dried out properly. All its walls needed re-plastering, plus new floors, new doors . . . It would be a long time before he and the family could return. He sighed.

His mobile phone rang, and he hitched it out of the top pocket of his green overalls. 'Amber Junction.'

'George? Is that you?' It was a woman's voice.

'George Overy, yes?'

'It's Pamela here.'

'Pamela?' Who?

'Pamela Wood. The owner of The Prospect. You *know*.'

'Oh . . . yes. How did you get this number?'

'I rang the Environment Agency, told them I'm a friend of yours, said it was urgent.' She sounded pleased with herself.

Can't rightly call her a *friend*, he thought. 'What can I do for you?'

'It's more what *I* can do for *you*,' Pamela said. 'I've been so concerned about the disaster down there. It keeps coming to mind and bothering me, so I've decided to actually *do* something about it.'

'Oh yes?'

'Yes. I'm going to start a campaign to save the old diesel pumps in Amber Junction. I plan to make the whole place into a working museum and fund it with several million quid from the lottery. I shall fundraise locally as well, of course. What d'you say?'

'Well . . . ' George began. 'I'd certainly like to see the pumps working again, but I'm not sure . . . '

'Oh don't worry,' Pamela said, 'I'm not

expecting you to do any actual campaigning. I realise that you're quite busy enough as it is. But I do need information to feed to the press, to get the public interested. I'm very experienced in this sort of work actually, and I do understand the full implications of what I'm proposing. So, maybe I could come down and pick your brains from time to time?'

'Well, I don't see . . . '

'There could be a job in it for you,' Pamela put in swiftly, 'in the end. We'll need a good man in charge to run the pumps on a regular basis, and to maintain them of course. And who better than you?'

'As I was about to say,' George said stolidly, 'I don't see why not.'

'Excellent!' Pamela enthused. 'Now we'll need a good logo that will be instantly recognisable. The daughter of a friend of mine is a graphic designer, so I'll get her onto it at once. What do you think we should call it? Save Our Pumping Station? Well, maybe not. SOPS doesn't convey quite the right message, does it? Anyway George, plenty of time for all that. The main thing is that you're in favour of the general idea. I couldn't be more delighted! Speak again soon. 'Bye!'

'Cheerio.' George took the phone away from his ear and pressed the off button deliberately, shaking his head slowly from side to side. Then he spoke one word aloud. 'Barking!' he said.

★ ★ ★

'Jonathan?' Vinny said. They were up in his attic room and she'd just brought him a cup of coffee and a biscuit.

'Yes?' He glanced up from his writing and then looked down again.

'I'm sorry, but I can't marry you.'

'Oh.' He looked at her properly now. He seemed a little put out. 'Why is that?'

'Because you can't love me, and I so much need to be loved.' She perched on the edge of his table and smiled at him as best she could. 'Will you forgive me?'

'What for?'

'For getting involved with you, and then letting you down.'

'Letting me down?'

'Disappointing you.'

'You haven't done that, Vinny. You're the best person in Somerset.'

Vinny gave a little laugh and wiped her eyes. 'So, will you keep in touch with me? I shall always want to stay friends and know how you are, and what you're doing. Do you have email in Africa?'

'Oh yes, in some places.' He tore off a sheet of paper and wrote on it. 'This is my email address.'

'And can I write to you by post, if you're out of email contact?'

'You can send letters care of Waterway, yes.' He wrote down that address too. Already, Vinny thought, they were into practicalities. She felt justified in her decision, but wretched for having failed him.

'I've fetched the computer discs of your book

from my desk in the library,' she said, 'and your manuscript too. I've kept copies of the discs for myself. I hope that's OK?'

'Will you still try to sell it?'

'When it's ready, if you want me to.'

'Yes. I'll send you the rest of it as I write it,' Jonathan said. 'Keep the manuscript. It's too heavy to carry.'

He looked businesslike and, yes, cheerful too. He was clearly looking forward to getting back to his normal life again.

He'll be all right. The thought made Vinny feel calmer. 'When are you thinking of leaving?' she asked him.

'On the thirty-first.'

'But . . . that's only a week away! There won't be time to get your jabs.'

'Jabs?'

'Injections — immunisations against disease. And you'll need anti-malarial drugs too.'

'I've done all that already.'

'When?'

'One time when you took me to the library.'

'You never said.'

'Well, you didn't ask.'

Vinny frowned. 'And what about the air fare? Don't you need a visa and suchlike?'

'The Waterway head office in London have arranged it all. I telephoned them, and they're sending me my return ticket and my passport.'

'But, why have they got them?'

Jonathan looked suddenly shamefaced. 'My father insisted that I leave important documents with my employers for safe keeping,' he said. 'He

405

says I'm no good at looking after them.'

Vinny snorted derisively, but then a point occurred to her. 'In fact, it's just as well, under the circumstances,' she said. 'If he hadn't, they would have been lost in the flood or stolen, like everything else.'

Jonathan's face relaxed into a wide smile. 'I hadn't thought of that,' he said. 'So, will you take me to the airport? It's an overnight flight.'

'Yes,' Vinny said. 'Of course I will.' She got up, and went slowly downstairs.

'What's up with you?' Pamela asked.

'Jonathan's leaving a week today.'

'Oh well, it's about time. It was never going to work out, Vinny. You must have known that.'

'*What do you know about anything?*' Vinny shouted.

'I know that I've lost Chloë, my darling grand-daughter; my own flesh and blood. And you — what are you about to lose? Some boy who's not right in the head, who you slept with because you felt *sorry* for him! I don't think the two are remotely comparable, do you?'

Vinny lifted a hand to slap Pamela's face.

'Go on then,' Pamela taunted her. 'Hit me!'

Vinny turned and ran blindly upstairs again, to her room.

★ ★ ★

Vinny drove the mini up the M5 and east along the M4 towards Heathrow. It had been mild and sunny all day and the roads were clear of ice. Vinny didn't like motorway driving in the dark, but this would be a relatively easy journey, except for the last bit. She was nervous of getting lost in the maze of Heathrow. She wondered if she would ever see Jonathan again.

'When d'you think you'll next be back in England?' she asked him.

'No idea. Maybe never.'

'Oh.' Vinny took a breath. 'Do think this visit has changed you at all?' she asked, hoping for some validation of their time together.

'Oh yes,' Jonathan said.

'In what way?'

'Well, I used to think you could never have too much water. And now I know that you can.'

'I see,' Vinny said.

They arrived at the terminal with less difficulty than she had feared, and Jonathan checked in. He only had hand luggage. Then they sat down to wait. 'D'you fancy anything to eat?' Vinny asked.

'No, there'll be food on the plane.'

'Well I'm going to get a sandwich anyway.' She sat next to him, munching it. 'Have you a seat by the window?'

'Yes.'

'So you'll be able to look out at the stars and think about studying astronomy?'

'No, I haven't finished with water yet.' There was a silence.

Jonathan has never asked any questions about my life or about me, Vinny suddenly thought. And he doesn't now, even though it's his last chance to do so. There was a time when I found his lack of curiosity restful, but now it just seems

407

uncaring. I *am* doing the right thing. 'You must be pleased to be going back again,' she asked him, knowing that she was probably laying herself open to further chagrin, but needing to say something.

'Oh *yes!*' His face brightened. 'I'm really looking forward to getting on with my work.'

'I've always imagined that it must be simpler in some ways, being a foreigner?'

'I like it, yes.'

I can see why, Vinny thought. It seems a paradox, but for Jonathan communication would actually be easier, because less would be expected of him. But when *I* work abroad, she thought, I shall find it much harder, for exactly the same reason — because I actually want to be able to talk to other people in some depth.

'I'm going to get a job abroad too,' she told him.

'That's good,' he said.

'I'm a bit worried though that friends will think I've done the wrong thing in abandoning Pamela.' There's no point in telling him this, she thought. He won't understand.

'That doesn't matter,' he said.

'Why not? It does to me!'

'Well, I never know what other people are thinking, so I don't worry about it.'

'You mean, if you don't know about something, it doesn't exist?'

'Absolutely.'

Vinny laughed. 'Thank you. I shall try to hold onto that thought.'

The gate number for his flight came up on the

overhead screen, and he stood up to go. Vinny went with him as far as the barrier.

'Give me a farewell hug,' she said.

He put both arms around her and held her for a moment.

'I shall miss you so much,' she said.

'Thank you for being my friend.' He stood away and picked up his bag, slinging the strap over his shoulder. 'Goodbye Vinny.'

''Bye,' she said. 'Have a good flight. I hope all goes well with the job.'

'I hope so too,' he said. Then he turned and walked away.

Tears welled up in her eyes and fell down her cheeks. She made no move to wipe them away, but simply stood there watching him go, ready to raise a hand in valediction if he should look back. But he didn't. He showed his passport and his boarding card and went through into the departure lounge, disappearing from her view.

Vinny sank down onto a seat, got a tissue from her pocket and wept into it, with both hands over her face. Then eventually she got her composure back and stood up, preparing to leave.

'It's always so hard when they go, isn't it?' A kindly woman on the next bench said to her sympathetically. 'My daughter left home eighteen months ago, and I'm still not properly over it.'

17

Twice a month the library association issued a vacancies supplement to its members. Vinny waited with impatience for each one and scanned its pages anxiously for suitable jobs a long way from Somerset. She found a number of possibilities, but in March there was the ideal one. She nevertheless filled in a succession of application forms and waited with impatience for the replies.

Pamela meantime was pulling out all the stops for her new project. Vinny kept as low a profile as possible, recognising the signs, which she always thought of as Pamela 'going hyper'. In her experience, whenever Pamela was seriously thwarted or upset she channelled her febrile energy into some manic activity or another. Vinny hoped that Gordon and George would each be man enough to withstand the blitz.

At least it took the heat off her for a while, for which she was grateful. She continued with the surreptitious business of applying for jobs and sending out her CV. She had told Pamela early on about Peter taking the money, and had surprised herself at her own reaction to Pamela's response.

'Are you sure Peter said that to you?' she had demanded. 'You didn't just run short and help yourself, by any chance?'

'*Of course not!*'

'Well, naturally I used to trust you implicitly, Vin. But these days . . . '

Vinny didn't bother to reply. She was almost pleased to be attacked. Pamela was playing into her hands; strengthening her resolve to leave and giving her absolute justification for going. Pamela had in fact been dishing out the cold-shoulder treatment for some time now, in an attempt to bring her to heel. This suited Vinny well. She had discovered the happy truth that if you don't care, you can't be blackmailed.

Pamela tried another tack. 'Why don't you resign from the library?' she asked her one morning, 'and join me in the pumping station campaign? You know you hate your job. You could be in charge of slogan writing: *Don't throw us sops — support SOPS!* Only better than that, of course.'

'I don't think so,' Vinny said.

'Oh Vinny!' Pamela said irritably. 'Do get a life!'

Vinny smiled. 'Don't worry. I intend to.'

As the days went by, she made sure she got to the post first as it plopped through the letterbox onto the mat. Then she could read in private the various letters, which began: *Dear Miss Henderson, Thank you for your application. I regret . . .*

But on one occasion Pamela beat her to it. 'Why are the British Council writing to you?' she asked, reading the franking on the envelope.

'No idea,' Vinny said.

'What do they do anyway?'

'I think they're some sort of cultural relations

411

thing,' Vinny said, deliberately vague. 'They promote the English language abroad, that sort of idea.'

'Well they're onto a loser with you, then,' Pamela said. 'I can count on the fingers of one hand the number of times you've been overseas!'

'True,' Vinny said. She carefully slid the letter to the bottom of her heap and left it unopened. Pamela was busy with her own mail — a keenly awaited form, and the rules for applying for a lottery grant. She scanned it at speed and looked up triumphantly.

'This looks very promising,' she said. 'If we can raise enough money ourselves, I think we're in with a fighting chance here!'

We? Vinny thought. Later, in her bedroom, she opened her own letter. It was an invitation to attend for an interview in London for the job she most wanted.

When the day arrived, Vinny was on tenterhooks about escaping without Pamela knowing where she was going.

'Are you not having any breakfast?' Pamela asked her.

'No, I'm not very hungry.' Vinny sipped her orange juice nervously.

'I'm off to collect my brand new four by four this morning,' Pamela announced. 'I've ordered a red one this time. Much more cheerful, don't you think?'

'Much,' Vinny said. 'What are you going to call it?'

'Harriet. Hattie for short.'

Vinny began to giggle.

'You coming with me? It's your half day, isn't it?'

'Sorry,' Vinny said, sobering up. 'I'm afraid I can't.'

'We could lunch at that expensive French place?'

'No, not today. Sorry.'

'Oh well, it's your loss!' And she left in a huff.

Vinny went upstairs and put on a smart navy blue suit with a bright silk scarf at the neck. She slid her feet into newly polished shoes, picked up her best shoulder bag, checked that she had all the relevant bits of paper with her, and left the house with a sick feeling in the pit of her stomach. Then she drove to Castle Cary station to catch the London train.

Later on, she could not remember the course of the interview in any great detail. The people were businesslike but not fierce. They tried to put her at her ease. They asked good predictable questions. Vinny struggled to conceal her anxiety and her nervous inclination to answer them truthfully but frivolously.

'And why do you want this job, Miss Henderson?'

'To escape from my friend-from-hell!'

But she managed to control herself and answer sensibly. It was a long and detailed interview. They gave her an oral and written test in Italian, which she found tough. She sweated over them. She really wanted this job.

At the end, she was obliged to wait in a room with the other candidates. They were all younger than her and looked far more out-going and

413

confident. She didn't stand a chance.

She made herself think positively. I'm very experienced. I speak the language. I have no dependants, no house to sell and therefore no relocation expenses. And they did seem to like me . . .

The door opened and everyone looked up hopefully. 'Miss Henderson, would you come in please?' Then they offered her the job!

She was to give her month's notice to the library and take a fortnight's holiday before starting. Vinny came back on the train, the personification of the Cheshire Cat.

The euphoria wore off suddenly as she arrived home and saw the shiny red four by four taking up most of their joint parking space. She would have to tell Pamela at once, and get it over with. She went into the kitchen. Pamela was eating a boiled egg and looking aggrieved.

'Where on earth have you *been?*' she demanded. 'I couldn't find anything for supper.'

'I've been to London for a job interview,' Vinny said, crossing her fingers behind her back.

Pamela's head jerked up. She looked at her shrewdly. 'Have you indeed?' she said. 'What on earth for? You know you hate London.'

'It isn't in London,' Vinny said.

'So where is it then? And when are they going to let you know?' She made a mocking face. 'Don't call us, we'll call you.'

'I wouldn't sneer, If I were you,' Vinny said, emboldened by success. 'It might make you feel foolish sooner than you think. The job is in the

414

British Council Library in Rome. They've offered it to me. I've accepted, and I start in six weeks time. OK?'

★   ★   ★

Pamela had never seriously considered how she might feel if Vinny went away. It had once been unthinkable, but now it seemed inescapable. It struck through her like a cold terror. How would she manage without her? Pamela had never before had the time to be ill, but all of a sudden her boundless energy deserted her. She felt as though all her batteries had run down at once. She couldn't concentrate on anything or face the simplest problem. The pumping station project loomed, large and impossible. Pamela took to her bed to escape it.

She lay there listlessly. Mozart made her weep uncontrollably. She couldn't even face her Daily Telegraph. Bills remained unpaid, and phone calls unreturned. The only thing she kept close beside her was a little photograph album with 'Grandma's Boasting Book' on the cover.

She was in mourning, leafing dejectedly through her favourite pictures of Chloë again and again, when Vinny came in.

'Tea or coffee?' she asked.

'Tea,' Pamela said. ' . . . No, coffee . . . Oh I don't know.' The decision was too difficult. She burst into tears.

'Come on Pamela,' Vinny said, not unkindly. 'This isn't like you at all.' She came and sat on the bed, patting Pamela's arm awkwardly.

'Don't tell me to pull myself together,' Pamela wept.

'Of course not. You're depressed. You need help.'

'No doctors!' Pamela moaned.

'But why not?'

'I don't want Polly to see me like this.'

'But she'd understand! And more to the point, she'd probably be able to help you.'

'What can she do? Everyone's left me: Peter, and Chloë, and now *you!*' Pamela was overwhelmed by hopelessness. She felt utterly worthless. 'I wish I was dead!' She lay awake all that night, but slept through much of the next morning and awoke to find Polly standing by her bed and looking down at her with concern.

'I was just passing, on my way back from the surgery,' she said, 'so I thought I'd pop in. How are you? Vinny's very worried about you.'

'No she isn't,' Pamela said, breaking down again. 'She's going to leave.' She turned her face to the pillow so that Polly shouldn't see her tears.

'No, you must have got that wrong,' Polly said gently. 'I'm sure Vinny wouldn't be so cruel, not with you in this state. Now, I know this isn't the answer to your problems, but it will help in the short term.' Pamela turned over, to see her taking out a pad and beginning to scribble on it.

'I'm not taking any pills.'

'Why not?'

'Because I never do!'

'Just because you've never needed to before, doesn't mean you shouldn't now,' Polly said

416

firmly. 'They'll stop you feeling so desperate; let the old Pamela shine through again.'

'I hate the old Pamela, and so does everybody else.' Her eyes brimmed over again.

Polly handed her a tissue from the box beside the bed. 'Come on, blow your nose,' she said. Pamela sat up, like an obedient child and did so. 'That's better,' Polly said.

There was a tap at the door, and Vinny came in. 'This has just come,' she said, holding out a postcard. It's good news.' Pamela just shook her head. 'I'll read it to you, then. It's from Peter and it says: *Chloë and I have fallen on our feet here. We're staying in a small apartment in Manhattan* (he's written out the full address at the top) *while the owner is away, working abroad. We've got a good childcare network and I'm going all out to get myself a job. Sorry we left the way we did. I'll make it up to you, I promise. Thanks for Xmas. Chloë sends lots of kisses to her Grandma. Love, Peter.*

'There you are!' Polly exclaimed. 'So you haven't lost them after all.'

'Absolutely!' Vinny said. 'And he's put his phone number at the bottom, look! So you'll be able to talk to him and Chloë regularly.'

★　★　★

As the anti-depressants took the edge off her despair, Pamela gradually began to feel more herself again. Vinny administered the pills faithfully, and looked after her with a devotion that Pamela couldn't help but appreciate. She

417

was almost seduced into thinking that Vinny really did care for her after all, but then realised the wounding truth. Vinny only wanted her to be well, so that she could *leave* her!

But this understanding did not cause a recurrence of the depression, as Pamela had feared. It actually gave her back her fight; her determination. Over the next month she did her utmost to win Vinny back, but she couldn't seem to get through to her any more. The sensitive, considerate, *obliging* Vinny appeared to have gone for good. Pamela was at a loss as to how she should proceed. Appeals to Vinny's better nature seemed unlikely to penetrate this hurtful new egocentricity. She tried pathos.

'After all I've been through, you can't leave me, Vin?'

'I'm sorry you feel that way,' Vinny said. Pamela only just restrained herself from hitting her.

'You're only happy when I'm miserable,' she said in a little voice.

'That is an utter travesty of the truth, and you know it!' Vinny lost her cool completely. 'It was always *you* who enjoyed being in charge when *I* was unhappy!'

Pamela experienced a tiny spring of hope. Over the following days, she reverted to her normal modus operandi. She tried to undermine her. 'You'll be really lonely without me,' she said.

'You may be right,' Vinny replied.

'You could always write to them and say you've changed your mind about the job,' she suggested.

'Don't be daft,' Vinny said.

'Seriously though, is your spoken Italian really up to the mark?'

'The British Council obviously think so.'

Pamela was getting desperate. 'I might sell this house. So don't expect me still to be here when you come crawling back.'

'Fine,' Vinny said.

'You'll be sorry, and then it will be too late!'

'I appreciate your concern.' Vinny was now entirely self-possessed again, like a fucking robot!

Christ! Pamela thought. I've never known her so stubborn! She tried concern. 'Look, Vin, you're confused. You don't know what you want. Let me help you, as I've always done. Eh? What do you say?'

'Sorry,' Vinny said. 'I don't want to discuss this any further.'

★ ★ ★

For Vinny the last six weeks were a nightmare. She felt sorry for Pamela, but just as concerned about her own future. She was terrified that this depressive illness might be permanent, and that it would engulf her in an intolerable burden of care. Polly stoked this fear. She came round regularly after work to check on her patient's progress.

'This isn't a professional visit,' she would say. 'I'm just here as a friend.' Then, after she'd had a long chat with Pamela, she would take Vinny to one side and lecture her. There was no other word to describe her behaviour.

Vinny bore it stoically, but managed not to promise her anything. She felt disapproved-of and suffered horribly from this most under-mining form of social control. She had no one to confide in. All their friends had taken Pamela's side. Vinny began to weaken. Maybe she would not be able to leave after all? Should she perhaps write to the British Council and give up the job? It would be so much easier *not* to go . . .

Once Pamela had more or less recovered she began to nag. She wheedled. She got angry. She was sarcastic. She recruited Gordon and Arthur to plead for her, and Ron and Sue to attack Vinny verbally. And then she began to break things accidentally on purpose, beginning with Vinny's treasured bone-china mug, and her favourite little Denby casserole.

Vinny hung on. A fine thread of obstinacy held her on course, but never in her life had she been obliged to control her feelings so tightly, so completely. She was full of emotion, which threatened all the time to leak out and betray her. She knew that if Pamela got a hint of it, she would lay siege to her determination and break it down. Vinny was determined to win. She began to act 'As if', as if she were a terrifically important and confident person who was trying to get rid of a toxic hanger-on. And surprisingly, it did help.

Cheryl and her other colleagues in the library said they would miss her a lot. They presented her with a glossy book on Rome inscribed with all their names. Vinny put most of her other books into storage, along with what little furniture and household effects she owned. She got herself a new passport and filled in more endless forms. And all the while she shopped conscientiously to feed Pamela and herself, and cooked supper every evening. She felt like an automaton.

Then, finally, the day dawned when she would be able at last to leave. And instead of relief, she was gripped by terror at the thought of her journey and a new life in a foreign country. All her innate fears of the unknown came crowding in on her at once.

Pamela seemed to sense it. She got up from the breakfast table, where Vinny was unable to eat a thing, and came round to stand behind her chair. She massaged the taut shoulders, and stroked her hair.

'Dear Vin,' she said. 'It's not too late to change your mind. You haven't burnt all your boats. The mini is still here!'

It was a fatal miscalculation. The gentle joke jarred warningly deep in Vinny. It gave her the determination to get to her feet, push Pamela away and hold her at arm's length, looking steadily into her eyes.

'Of course the mini is still here,' she said. 'And this is where it's staying. Because, as you never tire of telling me, you *paid* for it!' She felt a huge sense of relief. This had been the last hurdle. She was now free to go.

★ ★ ★

421

Vinny sat in the departure lounge at the airport, drinking coffee and thinking, I've done it! After all this time, I've finally escaped. She sipped her coffee. The last time she'd been here was when she saw Jonathan off. I couldn't have got this far without him, she thought. He loosened Pamela's hold on me. I'll always be grateful to him for that.

And what of Pamela — the Pamela who had known all her secrets and her vulnerabilities, and had discovered early on that Vinny was compliant, apologetic even, in the face of anger? It was clear that Vinny had provided her with the perfect subject for emotional blackmail. It was my own fault, she thought. I was weak. Not any more.

All those years, she thought, I did my best but in the end I couldn't be the person Pamela wanted me to be. And now I'm convinced that no one should feel totally responsible for someone else's happiness. It can never work.

She thought again of Jonathan, and his obsession with water. This is *my* watershed, she realised. She examined the small circular pink scar on the tip of her little finger. And if I should ever feel guilty about Pamela in future, she decided, I'll cure myself by looking at this.

After what seemed a long wait, the flight was called and Vinny went through the gate with her fellow passengers. On the plane there was a man in the aisle seat, who stood up to let her into the one by the window. Vinny struggled to lift her hand luggage into the locker.

'Allow me,' the man said, taking it from her

and putting it in. The luggage label hung out, and he was about to push it inside when he stopped and looked at it more closely. 'British Council?' he said, sitting down next to her. 'Are you a linguist?'

'A librarian,' Vinny said.

'And going to Rome.'

'Yes.' He had thick grey hair and kind, dark eyes. She supposed he must be in his mid fifties. She felt inclined to confide in him. 'It's my first job abroad,' she said. 'I'm a little apprehensive.'

'I'm sure there's no need to be,' he said. 'I too have worked abroad, but now I'm going home.'

'You're Italian?'

'Yes indeed.'

'Your English is perfect.'

'My wife was English,' he said. 'She died just over a year ago.'

'Oh,' Vinny said. 'I'm so sorry.'

He gave her a bleak half-smile. 'Life has to go on.'

The stewardess was demonstrating the oxygen masks and the life jacket routine. Vinny watched obediently. The plane taxied to the runway and stopped. Vinny gripped the arm supports and held on tightly as it began to move again. The engines roared. The airport buildings zipped by, and then disappeared below. They were airborne. Vinny sat back in her seat with a sigh and closed her eyes. When she opened them again, the man next to her was reading a book.

Lunch arrived, and he put the book to one side. Its title was *Straw Dogs — Thoughts on Humans and Other Animals* by John Gray. Vinny recognised it at once. She'd found it fascinating, alarming, and entirely engrossing. She looked at him with more interest this time.

'Good book,' she said.

'You've read it?'

'Yes. It's very unsettling, but brilliant too, don't you think?'

'Yes indeed it is.' He smiled at her properly now. 'Is philosophy a particular interest of yours?'

Vinny blushed. 'No. I just like to have my fixed ideas challenged, now and then.'

'Very admirable,' he said. 'I wish my students were more like you.'

'You're a university lecturer — a professor?'

'I am, yes. My name is Alfredo Orvieto.' He put out his hand for her to shake.

'How d'you do,' Vinny said. 'I'm Lavinia Henderson, Vinny for short.'

'Lavinia? A new name to me,' he said. 'We must talk about books some more, but first the plastic food. Shall we drown it in red wine?'

Vinny laughed. 'Yes,' she said, 'let's do that.'

EPILOGUE

Vinny had been working in Rome for two years, and was happier than she'd ever been. She wrote regularly to Jonathan and looked forward to his eventual replies. Pamela wrote to her too, but her letters always contained reproachful or triumphal barbs. It was as though she tried her best to write cheerfully but was unable to prevent herself from inserting a sting in the tail. At first these annoyed Vinny, but gradually even they lost their power and she came to regard them with a wry amusement. It was safe now to think fondly of Pamela. She was good to me, Vinny thought. She rescued me when I needed it, and cared for me, and made me laugh — in the early days. I'm glad I knew her.

Everything's lovely here, Pamela had written, the summer after she'd left. *The herbaceous border is the best it's ever been. You'd love it. I'm fine now too, but Gordon is still angry with you and Polly (in particular) hasn't forgiven you. I had an unexpected visitor the other day — none other than Kelly, would you believe! She brought me back Jonathan's mobile phone as a peace offering. She says she's broken up with the latest boyfriend and is desperate to see Chloë again. I refused to divulge Peter's address, of course, but she did seem genuinely* concerned and, more importantly, <u>penitent</u>. So I relented and gave her his phone number. I believe I gave her more than she deserved.

She's not the only one!

★   ★   ★

There was the postcard in September from New York:

Having a wonderful time here. Peter is marrying a beautiful American girl called Gail. She has a little boy of Chloë's age and is also having Peter's baby, so I shall soon be a triple grandmother!!! There is no doubt — children are life's greatest blessing.

★   ★   ★

And the one from India in May:

This is a fascinating place. I'm here with Gordon tracking down spare parts (circa 1930s) for the pumping station's diesel engines, from far flung corners of the old empire! Gordon is finally eating curry with the best of them and is a marvellously undemanding companion.

Poor bloody Gordon! Vinny thought. Serve him right.

★   ★   ★

The letter in June did irritate her, but only briefly. Pamela had enclosed with it a photocopy of another; an official letter from Ron Foster. It read:

Dear Pamela,
Re: Scholastica Henrietta Rodney-Stoke of Elm Lea Nursing home, deceased
This firm is acting in the administration of the estate of the above named who died on the 25th January inst. We enclose a copy of the grant of probate, and of the will of 13th September 1982 and codicil dated 3rd January inst. As you will see, you are the principal Residuary Beneficiary referred to in the codicil. Accordingly a cheque for £110,009 in your favour is enclosed.

Ron had scribbled under his signature, *Nice to see that your devotion to the elderly has been so suitably rewarded. Sue sends love. R.*

Pamela had ringed the amount of money in red ink and peppered it with exclamation marks.

Typical! Vinny snorted. 'Unto everyone that hath shall be given'. But then she reminded herself of her own good fortune. I have something infinitely more precious, she thought. And anyway, I certainly wouldn't want to be Pamela!

★ ★ ★

Part of a letter in August said:
Gordon's self-published autobiography came out this week. I think the poor man was rather hoping for some interest from the media (which he didn't get). I'm afraid he's

427

yesterday's man, but I wouldn't dream of saying so, of course. Still, at least he is published, which is more than poor Jonathan ever will be! Saw Mandy Overy (remember her?) the other day in Otterbridge. She was draped all over some youth in an open top car with so-called music blaring out. Some people's emotional attachments are easily transferable, it appears.

* * *

In December Pamela sent her a glossy pamphlet entitled:
AMBER JUNCTION — THE MUSEUM OF THE SOMERSET LEVELS
This is the prototype publicity handout, she wrote. The Environment Agency have at last decided to build a brand new all-electric pumping station, on land they already own next to the present A.J. (They're proposing to call it A.J. South or something equally imaginative!) Our beautiful stripped-down/rebuilt pumps will be used in parallel with it as backup during floods, as well as for our own demonstration purposes. George is to be our technical advisor and part-time operator. He really has been splendid! Only one minor problem — between the bird people and the Internal Drainage Boards, who are at loggerheads as usual. This time it's over the space allocated to the IDBs in the museum!
This is a wonderfully satisfying project, Vinny.

You should have had the vision to stay and do it with me.

★ ★ ★

In February Vinny came across something of particular interest in a publisher's catalogue. There was to be a new series of *Boffin's Guides* — mini technical encyclopaedias, each devoted to a single important or topical subject. The blurb said: *All the information you could ever want — Scientific data, statistics, history, future projections, and even the odd WOW! Factor. All in a pocket-sized volume.* The first was to be on Climate Change. Maybe, Vinny thought, a subsequent one could be on water? She wrote a long email to Jonathan, and crossed her fingers.

★ ★ ★

In another letter in late May, Pamela wrote:
I've been thinking that it's high time I had a holiday. I've worn myself out over this pumping station business, and now that it's all going along so well, I really think I deserve a break. So Gordon and I are planning to come over and 'DO' Italy this summer. I thought perhaps all three of us could tour about and stay in out of the way hotels, and live on pasta and wine ... wonderful prospect! Pity spaghetti is so fattening, but I'm sure it's fine — eaten in moderation. Do you have a car we could use? I'll pay for the petrol and our food, of course. I can almost feel the sun and smell

the olive groves! Write soon, so we can make PLANS!

Vinny, eyes closed and a smile curling up the corners of her mouth, was sitting on a shady terrace in the heat of the day with a bottle of red wine and two full glasses beside her. Also on the table, unused, lay a writing pad and a pen.

She was thinking, Pamela was right. I wasn't in love with Jonathan. It was pity. Maybe that's what I felt for Nathaniel too, all those years ago. One thing I know for certain now — I shall never confuse the two emotions again.

After a while she opened her eyes and forced herself to write:

Dear Pamela, thanks for your letter which was forwarded here (note change of address above). I'm afraid a tour of Italy is out of the question, as we shall be in Botswana then, visiting Jonathan. However if you and Gordon care to call in to see us in September, then we'd be very happy to give you lunch.

She put the pen down and raised her glass to her companion, as he came out from the house to join her. 'Here's to us!'

He picked up his glass and clinked it against hers.

'Cin cin, Lavinia carissima,' Alfredo said.

We do hope that you have enjoyed reading this large print book.

Did you know that all of our titles are available for purchase?

We publish a wide range of high quality large print books including:
Romances, Mysteries, Classics
General Fiction
Non Fiction and Westerns

Special interest titles available in large print are:
The Little Oxford Dictionary
Music Book
Song Book
Hymn Book
Service Book

Also available from us courtesy of Oxford University Press:
Young Readers' Dictionary
(large print edition)
Young Readers' Thesaurus
(large print edition)

For further information or a free brochure, please contact us at:
Ulverscroft Large Print Books Ltd.,
The Green, Bradgate Road, Anstey,
Leicester, LE7 7FU, England.
Tel: (00 44) 0116 236 4325
Fax: (00 44) 0116 234 0205

Other titles published by
The House of Ulverscroft:

A SCENT OF BLUEBELLS

Meg Henderson

They called her Auld Nally — a moneylender in one of Glasgow's roughest areas, Inchcraig. Once, though, she'd been Alice McInally from Belfast, beautiful and beloved by her childhood sweetheart. But his family was Catholic and hers Protestant, and opposition to their marriage plans meant they must leave Ireland and their well-to-do families. However, their dream for their future founders in war-torn Glasgow, and Alice struggles to make ends meet. To protect the children in her care, she relies on the man Inchcraig knows as 'him', and lives among people far from her background; people she admires and doesn't want to leave. Every day, though, she must live with a lie that could destroy everything — unless she can find the exact time to put it right . . .